T0182527

# THE WIND THAT SWEEPS THE STARS

## ALSO BY GREG KEYES

# ·THE·
# WIND
# ·THAT·
# SWEEPS
# ·THE·
# STARS

# GREG KEYES

**TITAN** BOOKS

## THE WIND THAT SWEEPS THE STARS

Print edition ISBN: 9781789095500
E-book edition ISBN: 9781789095517

Published by Titan Books
A division of Titan Publishing Group Ltd
144 Southwark Street, London SE1 0UP

First edition: August 2024
1 3 5 7 9 10 8 6 4 2

A CIP catalogue record for this title is available from the British Library.

Printed and bound by CPI Group (UK) Ltd, Croydon, CR0 4YY

For Rosemary,
Or Rose by any other name.

## CHAPTER ONE

# DZHESQ THE NEEDLE

DZHESQ, MASTER of the Blue Needle Tower, murdered a slave and read the portents in the dimming of her eyes. He traced signs of pulverized bone around the corpse, burned the resin of a plant from another world, and called upon his *xual* to aid him. The xual answered, and the scent of wildflowers filled the room. Demons of pestilence and despair drifted out of the smoke from the burning pitch. Dzhesq the Needle set them on a north-blowing wind. Afterwards, he washed his hands and groomed himself, admiring his beautiful, tapered face and dark eyes in a mirror before descending from his tower to visit the Princess Yash of Zeltah.

"I'm afraid I have some bad news," Dzhesq told Princess Yash.

She had been standing near the window when he arrived, staring into the distance, probably pining for her barbarous homeland. Now her dull black eyes were fixed on him where he stood in the doorway to her chambers. She had changed out of her colorful and elaborate wedding dress and now wore a tan *silukur* robe. The garment hung from her broad, bony shoulders, emphasizing the deficits of her wiry, unlovely figure. She looked like a starved, mangy dog that had been shoved into expensive cloth.

"I'm so happy for you," she said.

"I'm sorry," Dzhesq said, unsure what she meant. "You're happy for me?"

She nodded and made a grimace that was probably meant to be a smile. Her eyes were too far apart, and her mouth was so wide she reminded him of a frog.

"People say they hate to bring bad news," she said. "But almost everyone rushes to do it, don't they? To be the first to tell it. To see the reaction—the frown, the sadness, the fear. The tears. When you bring bad news, you can see all of that. You can be the one to make that happen. But there's no guilt—you can't be blamed, can you? It's not *you* making them cry, it's the news. You're providing a service. They'll be grateful to you. Maybe they'll even be a little sad for you that you're the one that must tell them." The ends of her mouth turned further up, so that even on her unfortunate face there was now no mistaking the attempted smile. "So, I'm happy for you, that you have bad news to tell me. I hope you enjoy it. Does it concern my husband? I was expecting him by now."

Self-awareness was important, Dzhesq knew, so he paused to reflect that he had never wanted to hit anyone so much in his life. No, not hit her. He wanted to unsheathe the demon-bone knife at his belt and stab it through her windpipe, end her crude attempt to speak his language. And her insolence. She was making fun of him. No one did that. No one spoke to him like that. Not for many years, and for good reason.

Least of all an ugly little barbarian.

It was all made worse, of course, by the fact that at present he couldn't hit her or stab her. The Emperor wanted her alive. But when the day came that she was of no further use to the Empire, things would be different. That thought soothed him. It got him through the moment.

"No," he replied, evenly. "Your husband is not yet done with his purifications. He will soon be ready for you. You need not worry on that account."

"I'm not worried in the slightest," she said.

It was the *way* she said it that got his attention. As if she was asserting herself.

"I take it that this marriage was not of your choosing?" he asked.

"I would not have chosen it, no," she said.

"You thought you could do better than Prince Chej? Or marry for love, perhaps, rather than for reasons of state?"

"I didn't say any of that," the girl replied. "You asked a question. I gave you an honest answer. I don't want to be married to Chej. I don't want to be here, in this place."

"But you agreed to the match, did you not? Your family said you did. You said so at the wedding. You seem to value honesty. Were you being dishonest, then?"

She cocked one eyebrow and took a step away from the window toward him.

"I'm sorry," she said. "We were not introduced. Who are you?"

"I am Lord Dzhesq nXar Hsa, Master of the Blue Needle Tower. By custom you may address me as Master Needle or Master Dzhesq the Needle."

"Oh," she said. "One of the tower masters, yes? A, um, *dj'ende*? I don't know your word."

He knew the word *dj'ende*. In her language it meant "evil spirit."

"You don't know your own words," Dzhesq retorted. "Much less mine. In your language I would be called a *duyenen*. In mine, the title is *zuen*. A holy man."

"You practice sorcery," she said, wriggling her fingers at him. "You send plagues and demons to destroy your enemies, yes?"

"Among other things," he agreed.

She shrugged. "Then we agree on what you are. The word we use does not really matter, does it?" She smiled again and nodded, as if they were friends sharing a little joke. "But," she went on, "now that we are introduced, I am pleased to answer your question. Of course I agreed to marry Chej. Our kingdom is small. Yours is large. If our countries had not been joined by marriage, you would have joined them with your army. So here I am."

Dzhesq nodded. He was starting to feel better now.

"So, you are a dutiful woman," he said. "That is good."

She shrugged. "You said you had bad news?"

"Yes," he said. "I'm afraid there has been a change in your accommodations. You must accompany me to the Blue Needle Tower. Rooms have been made ready for you there."

"That isn't news, bad or good," Yash said. "It makes no difference to me where I stay. But you will have to show me. This place is altogether confusing."

"A bit grander than your little pile of rocks back home?" he asked, stepping aside and ushering her toward the door.

"Yes!" she said. "It's very big, with so many rooms. And so many towers! It looks like a mountain covered in yellow pines from a distance. And every tower has a master, like you, yes? I imagine you must be the grandest master of them all."

"I am highly ranked," he said. In fact, of the nine tower masters, he was reckoned third in power and prestige. "The Emperor is most highly ranked, of course."

"Oh yes, of course," she said. "I meant after him."

Let her believe what she wanted. What the awful, despicable creature thought was less to him than what a red ant could carry.

They wound their way through the twisting corridors of the fortress. The barbarian princess prattled the whole way, asking questions about everything she saw. "What's through there? How does this curved roof stay up by itself? Is that carving a toad or a bug of some kind?" When they reached the polished stone floor of the lowest court of the Blue Needle Tower, her eyes widened comically.

"So many warriors!" she said.

Dzhesq glanced at the twelve guards in their lacquered leather cuirasses watching them enter the tower.

"Sentries," he replied. "To keep you safe."

"Safe?" she said.

He nodded.

Once they began up the spiral staircase, Princess Yash became mercifully less verbose, saying only, "It's awfully tall," and, "Are we going to the very top?"

He answered yes to both questions.

When they reached the uppermost floor and stepped into the chamber there, she nodded.

"Cozy," she said. "I like it."

It consisted of only three rooms and was less than half the size of the suite she'd had downstairs.

"More like what you're used to," he said.

"Yes, of course," she replied. She went to the window. "The view is fantastic, too. I can see the Tsewe Zeł Mountains."

"Yes, we're quite high here."

"Why the change in rooms?" she wondered.

"That's the bad news," he said. "You see? I did not hasten to tell it to you, as you predicted. The bad news is that a short time after your wedding concluded, the Emperor ordered the invasion of your kingdom. You are now a valuable hostage, and we cannot run the risk of some sort of misguided rescue attempt. You will be quite safe here, and in a matter of days, when the war is over, you will no doubt be allowed to take up residence in your husband's quarters."

He paused to enjoy her look of perplexed horror even though it wasn't exactly what he had been imagining. If he didn't know better, he might think she didn't look shocked at all. Maybe more… relieved?

"Let me be sure I understand," the princess said. "The terms of my marriage included the provision that the Empire would *not* make war on my country?"

"Yes."

"But your emperor has nevertheless sent an invading army there."

"Also yes."

"Well," she said, nodding. She looked around the room, then went over to the padded mattress on the floor. She knelt and picked up a small soapstone incense bowl, turning it in her hands.

"You will be my keeper, Master Dzhesq the Needle?" she asked. "That is why you brought me to your tower?"

"If you want to look at it that way," he said.

She nodded again and started to set the little fist-sized bowl down. Then she moved. Very quickly.

The stone bowl hit him in the throat before he realized what had happened. He stumbled back, clutching at his windpipe as she ran toward him. He couldn't breathe, his scalp was tingling with alarm, and he didn't understand what was going on. He put his hands out toward her and tried to command her to stop, but he couldn't get the words out.

She drove her small fist into him, just below his breastbone. It felt like it was made of granite; all the air went out of him, and he fell back, black spots filling his vision. The next thing he knew she was behind him, her arm wrapped around his neck.

*She's attacking me*, he realized. But that was ridiculous. He was twice her size. He could beat her to death with one hand. But more than that, he was a tower master, with all the power that entailed.

With no voice, he couldn't call his xual—it was too far way. But there was help nearer, so he didn't have to speak the word aloud, only to concentrate on it, form it in his head. Even though at this moment that was harder than it should be, especially for someone of his power.

*Neheshhish*, he finally managed.

Then the *chuaxhi* sewn inside of Dzhesq's skin burst forth from the tattooed line on his sternum, looking at first like a stream of white smoke but quickly forming into a bent, lizard-like figure armored in alabaster scales standing half again as tall as a man.

He was relieved, but he still couldn't breathe. Everything went dark.

But then the light returned; his ears were ringing, and his lungs were filled again. Now he could smell the burnt-air scent of the chuaxhi. It was across the room, slashing at Princess Yash with talons as long and sharp as knives. Dzhesq knew he was going to get in

15

trouble for this—the chuaxhi was going to shred the ugly little girl, and the Emperor wanted her alive. But there was nothing he could do now. This was her fault, as anyone could see.

As he watched, Yash ducked and dodged the chuaxhi's attack and slammed her hand into its belly; white smoke sprayed out. How was that possible? The chuaxhi had skin harder than quartz. What could—

Then he saw. She had a knife, *his* knife, whetted from a sliver of demon bone from the White Brilliant.

He realized the chuaxhi was leaking smoke from at least five holes in its armored hide.

He pushed himself to standing as Yash cut one of his protector's feet off. As the chuaxhi fell back, Dzhesq tackled Yash from behind, intent on knocking her to the stone floor, but she pivoted and twisted so they fell side by side. Her small frame was hideously strong, as if knotted together from sinew. She grabbed his wrist, bent it painfully and banged it against the floor. He heard one or both of the bones in it snap, the pain traveling like lightning up his arm. Then she was up and away from him again, returning her attention to the chuaxhi.

Dzhesq fought back to his feet, clutching his broken wrist with his good hand. He ran. At first he wasn't sure where he was going —just *away*—but then he knew. His summoning room, where his power was greatest, where his xual waited to protect him. Once there, she would face the full measure of his might, and none of this would matter. No one would know.

He reached the stairs and began stumbling down. His breath wheezed in through his swollen throat. He tried to scream for help, but still no sound came out. But he was almost to the next landing.

Looking back, he didn't see her. She was still fighting the chuaxhi. Maybe it had killed her, even. But he wasn't taking that chance. He took another step, and another. He could see the door to his rooms.

Something hit him in the small of the back, hard. He fell forward on the stairs, trying to catch himself with his broken hand before his face crushed against the stone. He was fine, he thought. This was stupid. This was not happening to him.

He realized he had tumbled the rest of the way down the stairs and was on the landing. The door to his room was just to his left. Trying to rise again, he saw Yash was in front of him now, her eyes as cold and sharp as obsidian chips.

"Stop it," he managed to say, in a hoarse voice just above a whisper. "You are nothing. No one. I am Dzhesq nXar Hsa."

"I have some bad news for you," she said.

## CHAPTER TWO

# YASH

### TSAYE (IN ANCIENT TIMES)

WE DON'T *know how the world that contains all other worlds began. That is a mystery it holds to itself. But we know there are many worlds. Some are far away from the one we call home. Some are as near as the outside of your skin is to the blood in your veins. Our people traveled through many worlds before they reached this one, where we made our true home. During that journey we changed, many times.*

### DII JIN (NOW, TODAY, THE PRESENT)

YASH WITHDREW the knife from the base of Dzhesq the Needle's skull and sat on the stairs for a moment to catch her breath. She touched the sorcerer's neck to feel whether his blood was moving. It wasn't.

The dead sorcerer lay on a landing five or six strides wide, beyond which the stairs continued down, curving along the outside wall of the tower. All was made of polished dark-blue granite with streaks and patches of white, like clouds swirled in an evening sky.

Her gaze came to where a pool of Master Needle's blood was still spreading.

She had killed many things in her life. Animals. Monsters. But this was the first human being she had slain. Or did a sorcerer count as a human being? Yes. This was a new thing for her.

She hadn't known what she would feel at this moment. She still didn't, and it didn't matter. The tower master was her first. More enemies might already be on their way.

She closed her eyes and listened. To her relief, the stairwell was quiet. But for how long? There was no telling. She couldn't take the body back to her room; there was no place to hide it. If she shoved it out the window, someone might see it falling or hear it land. But there were other rooms.

She rose, took hold of the corpse by the hair and began dragging it across the blue stone.

She had noticed the door on the way up. Most of the doorways she had seen inside of the tower were simply open, but this one was closed by a slab of dark wood. It hung on metal pins fitted into the stone wall. A loop of copper halfway up suggested it pulled open.

She took hold of the handle and yanked.

It was *heavy*, so she had to release Needle's hair and brace one foot against the wall to start it opening. But when it had cracked about the span of her arm, someone began pushing it from the other side. She jerked her feet up and clung to the copper as the door swung wider.

She couldn't see who it was, but they made a grunting sound. Whoever it was could surely see Needle's corpse lying on the landing. She pulled the knife out and dropped quietly to the floor.

Then someone stepped out and toward the dead sorcerer.

He was big, taller than any human, but he looked more like a man than the thing that had come out of Needle's chest. But he wasn't. His skin was roughly pebbled and grey. His long hair was coarse, each strand of it as thick as her little finger. He wasn't wearing any clothes.

She leapt toward his unprotected back, but the being spun around far faster than she had imagined he could and caught her right arm with his huge hand. She thrust the blade at him with her left, but his other hand clamped on her wrist. She swung up, twisted, and kicked him in the chest with both feet. That surprised him and broke the hold on her right arm. He growled and hurled her through the door. She skidded across polished stone and then rolled back to her feet. He bent and picked up a heavy wooden club bristling with flint spikes from where it lay on the floor. He took a step toward her. But he paused, his eyes cutting back to the landing.

"Wait," the giant said. "You killed him."

"Yes," she replied.

"Good. But why?"

"Does it matter?"

"No," the giant replied. "But I'm pleased. I did not like him."

"I didn't like him, either," Yash said. "Maybe you and I don't have to fight."

"Maybe," the giant said. "Who are you?"

"I am Yash," she said. "I—"

But then he jumped toward her. She saw it coming; he had been inching forward as they spoke. He was big and fast and very strong. She had been lucky to get away from him when he caught her before. She couldn't let that happen again; he probably wouldn't make the same mistake twice.

He whipped the club toward her head. She dodged, barely, then she ducked under his arm and stabbed him in the armpit. To her surprise, she felt resistance; whatever he was, he had bone there, where a normal person did not. The blade went in anyway and came right back out. She skittered past his ribs, hoping to get to his back, but he managed to turn with her, swinging a backhand at her head. She quickly ducked beneath the blow again and sliced open his inner thigh. Blue-white blood sprayed out; she smelled wildflowers.

He stumbled and then lurched at her.

She weaved through the large, cluttered room. He crashed after her. She ran under a table, toward an open window beyond. Something whooshed by her head and shattered against the wall near the opening. She turned around in time to see him flip the table toward her. She jumped into the window frame and teetered there on the sill, which was only barely wider than her footspan, fighting to keep her footing as the table slammed into the wall, briefly blocking the window before falling back into the room. She dove back inside, barely evading the next wicked swing of his club, and sprinted back toward the door with him panting at her back. Getting slower. The pale blood was everywhere now.

"You're waiting for me to bleed to death," he growled.

"You didn't give me much choice," she said.

"I don't *have* any choice," he said. "Even dead, his command on me remains. I must kill you."

"I'm sorry for that."

He charged but was a lot slower this time. She feigned backing up but then stepped quickly to the side and lunged to meet him, making him badly misjudge his swing. She shoved the knife through the ribs where his heart should be. The blade lodged there, and rather than sticking with it—easily within the grasp of his monstrous arms—she let go and spun around, ready for his next attack.

His back was still to her. Wheezing, he sank slowly to his knees and toppled forward.

She watched for a few heartbeats to make certain he wasn't trying to fool her. Then, giving the giant's body a wide berth, she went back to the door, dragged Dzhesq's body inside, and closed it behind her.

The giant still hadn't moved, and the huge pool of blood he now lay in was convincing evidence that he wouldn't. Still wary, she examined the room a little more closely. It was almost round, which meant it probably took up this entire floor of the tower. There were two large tables and dozens of smaller ones, racks of shelves filled with scrolls, pots, urns, and cauldrons, three of which had been toppled and broken during their fight, spilling ochre, green, and dark purple powders on the floor. The giant had thrown one of the big tables at her, and it lay upended near the window. On the table that was still upright, bits of bone, metal, shell, and stones of various colors and sizes had been sorted into piles, but she couldn't discern what categories they had been grouped into. Near the window a pedestal supported a large incense bowl, this one blue-green and carved from precious *dedłiji* stone.

A large wooden case contained an assortment of tools—knives with blades of bronze, bone, and obsidian; hammers with heads of progressively larger sizes, the largest a little bigger than her closed fist; and an axe with a coppery-looking blade. A large cabinet contained clothing, none of which would fit her.

When she ventured to the side of the room farthest from the entrance, she discovered a corpse; the clutter had prevented her from seeing it earlier.

There, beneath another window, the floor had been traced with strange symbols. Some looked like writing, others appeared to be stylized animals. They formed a double-armed spiral. It looked to her like four of the symbols indicated the cardinal directions.

A woman lay in the middle of the markings. She was probably around thirty, dressed in a dark yellow shift. Her hands and feet had been bound with rawhide strips, and her mouth and nose were covered with what Yash at first took for some kind of paste. Her dead gaze was fixed somewhere between the floor and the ceiling. Her skin had a blueish tinge.

She had been smothered to death slowly. Whatever Needle had put in her mouth and nose had hardened into a rubbery substance while she was still trying to breathe.

It was one of her own people, a woman of Zełtah. Yash didn't know her name, but by the arrangement of piercings in her ears she guessed her to be a white-spruce woman, probably from Tsecheen.

She wished there was something she could do for her, but there wasn't. Whatever the sorcerer had done to her, the woman's soul was either consumed or long gone. Her body was just that: a corpse. Her people didn't bother much about those.

"He is dead," she whispered, in case something remained that could hear her. "If that can be of comfort."

It was all she could do, and she had to move on. But a pitch-knot of anger had formed inside of her, a splinter, but one that could become a white-hot fire, given the chance.

*I don't need you*, she told the pitch-knot. *I will do this without you.* She took a long, slow breath, and the splinter flowed out of her. She took one more to be sure.

Now certain the giant was dead, she rolled him over. It wasn't easy, but it was the only way to get the knife back. Then she pried the giant's own weapon from his fingers and crushed Needle's chest with it, placing a dagger from the case in the sorcerer's hand and returning the giant's club to him, folding his thick dead fingers around the handle. Now it looked like the two had killed each other. How long that would fool anyone—if it fooled anyone at all—she did not know. But from now until she was finished, every pulse of the heart counted. If the deception gave her a dozen or thousands, it was still worth the effort.

But as valuable as time was, there was something more to do before she left.

She knelt by the dead giant and touched two fingers to his blood. Then she closed her eyes and tried to clear her mind.

Shame, bondage, and misery met her touch, surging from the corpse up through her fingers and quickly spreading throughout her body. She felt ill. She struggled not to vomit. She clenched her teeth as tears started in her eyes.

"*I am sorry, my foe*," she whispered.

*I am sorry.*
*But we were fated to fight*
*And one to die*
*I am sorry, my foe*
*I am sorry I do not know your name*
*Or the place that gave you life*

*And meaning.*
*Who are your kin?*
*Where is your place?*
*I want to know.*

Slowly, the darkness beneath her eyelids brightened, as if a dense fog was dispersing. She began to make something out. The smell of flowers grew stronger until she saw them in a mountain prairie: a field of yellow, white, crimson, and violet surrounded by the pale trunks and green spring leaves of aspens.

"*I see you now, my former foe,*" she sang softly.

*T'chehswatah*
*In the fields of flowers*
*Among the Aspens*
*In winter wears a white mantle*
*Waiting for the spring*
*It is spring for you now*
*Go there, my brother*
*Go there, my sister*
*Be among them once more.*

Her vision grew clearer. All of the trees and flowers bent in the same direction as a wind came up. Then all was still.

*Thank you*, the wind whispered.

"You are welcome," she replied. Then she stood and went to the window. She looked off toward the mountains.

"*Shechu,*" she murmured.

*One has gone now, my grandmother*
*One has returned home*
*One of the naheeyiye*
*To T'chehswatah*
*Perhaps they left*
*A way in*
*A way in here*
*Into Dj'eendetah, Among the Monsters*
*Into Qen Dj'eende, The Abode of Monsters*
*I could use some help*
*Shechu*
*My grandmother.*

She waited, but no answer came. And she could wait no longer, not in this room.

She hurried back up the stairs to her new quarters and stripped off the robe, now soaked in blue-white blood. A quick search of the suite turned up a low table with a pile of clothes on it that seemed meant for her. She found another robe, this one dark blue. She shoved the bloody one under her bed and looked over the rest of the room. The chuaxhi was now gone without a trace, evaporated back into steam, returned to its alien realm. To her eye, nothing looked out of place.

The adjacent room had a washbasin and some cloth; she wiped her face and arms until they looked pretty clean, squeezed the blue tinted water from the rag out the window, threw the rag back by the basin, then donned the robe.

Then she went back to the window and leaned out.

She could see half of the fortress, and beyond that, part of Honaq city: thousands of houses built on the hills around the river. She had seen it upon arriving and thought it both amazing and repellant. Far too many people crowded into one place for her taste, too much smoke from too many fires. Even so, Honaq had a certain beauty. Toward the center, where the fortress she now occupied stood, it was orderly, a place designed by clever people who liked straight lines and perfectly round circles. But as it spread, it became more like a living place, more accountable to the contours of the river and landscape than to human imagination. The yellow and brown swaths of stone and mud-brick buildings were striated with vivid green gardens and flood-marsh, expanding at the city edges to join the verdant fields filling the rest of the valley. Boats like colorful water-beetles cut ripples in the surface of the river and tree-lined canals. She was sure that, given time, she could find more beauty in Honaq.

Right now, however, the city was not her concern. The fortress was.

The fortress was surrounded by two circular walls, the innermost of which had eight towers along its circumference, with a ninth, larger tower in the very center of the structure. From this window of the Blue Needle Tower she could see four others.

The closest was the color of pine pollen: possibly the Yellow Bone Tower. It had a window facing her about two lengths of her body lower and another farther down. Just at the edge of the distance she could jump.

She heard something behind her and turned.

A big man—tall, wide-shouldered, with a rounded, soft face and substantial nose—stood in the doorway.

Chej, her husband.

## CHAPTER THREE

# CHEJ

PRINCE CHEJ met the woman who was soon to be his bride in a fortress on a mountain ridge in the barbarian kingdom of Zełtah, north and west of Honaq city, and seven days' travel beyond the boundaries of the Empire. They were introduced in a courtyard beneath the shade of a cottonwood tree and seated on stone benches facing one another, surrounded by their respective entourages. The meeting was awkward, made more so by the need for translators, and he did not leave the meeting with warm feelings about his upcoming wedding.

Not that he had expected to. His fondest hope had been never to marry at all, and as his age had trickled through his twenties and into his early thirties, that had begun to seem possible. He was not, after all, an important prince. That was not his opinion, but a plain fact, and one that had been made clear to him since birth. He had been mostly ignored by the court, but at a certain point he had stopped feeling sorry for himself and begun to realize that it could be a blessing. The essence of neglect was that no one was watching you. And if no one was watching you? Well, that was at least similar to freedom.

Now, suddenly, people were paying attention to him again, and he didn't like it.

The meeting with his bride-to-be was over, and the whole thing a blurry, rapidly fading memory. His advisors met with her advisors, his family with hers, and he managed to slip off with his bodyguards and return to his encampment on the high ground just below the fortress. He dug a bottle of blackberry wine from his things and took it out to the edge of the bluff where his escort had built him a fire. The wood burned with a scent of juniper, almost like incense. He sat, drinking, looking down at the many dozens of campfires below. The barbarians were planning some sort of ceremony to see their princess off. He was told that they had come from all over the mountains and high plains, and now their tents were spread out beneath the fortress and their fires were like a night sky fallen to earth.

He had traveled before. A brief stint in the army had taken him to some of the downstream kingdoms, but, on reflection, those were all very like Honaq, at least compared to this place. The "fortress" was rudimentary, a structure carved from the living rock of the ridge, built up here and there with closely fitted stones. From a distance, it looked almost like it was just part of the cliffs. There was a town of sorts situated at the bottom of the ridge, a collection of round huts of various sizes, and some fields arranged near the spring that flowed out there. But most of the people of Zełtah, he had gathered, didn't live in towns or cities, but were scattered over the landscape with their herds. He had found that land forbidding, at first—harsh and arid, with none of the lush vegetation of his valley home. But in the days coming here, he had come to appreciate the spare red cliffs and the distant mountains that bordered every horizon and the huge sky above it all. Each sunrise and sunset was spectacular beyond his ability to describe them. It was as if the sky invented new colors each day.

She arrived at his fire without him knowing it, although his men had noticed and dragged a log over for her. She sat down on it and nodded at him. At first he didn't recognize her. Back in the courtyard, she had seemed tiny, almost like a child. Standing facing each other, her head had only come up to his chest. Out here, in the night, she seemed larger, even though he knew she couldn't be.

"Princess," he said. He tried to remember the four or five words of her language he had learned on the trip here.

"Daxudzhue," she said.

"Oh, you know how to say hello in my language," he said. He knew that shouldn't be embarrassing. It was expected. But he felt at a disadvantage.

"Ah, huchun," he attempted, in hers.

"Hee'echuun," she corrected. But she looked pleased. "Nice of you to try," she said.

"You—you speak my language?" he asked.

"Yes," she said. "Of course. You in the Empire are my cousins, are you not? Or so they say. And an important fact in our lives. In my life now. How could I live in a place where I couldn't understand anyone?"

"Yes," he said. "I can see that. Of course, I can see that. But earlier, at our meeting…"

"It was best to let the interpreters talk," she said. "It was all so formal. But I thought now we should really meet."

She seemed earnest and younger than the twenty-seven winters her family claimed she had.

"Do you want some wine?" he asked.

"No, thank you."

He nodded, trying to think of what to say. He studied her for a moment.

"So, we are to be married," he ventured, after a moment.

She smiled. "I see you aren't all that happy about it, either," she said.

It was so unexpected he choked on his wine. She laughed as he wheezed it out of his nose.

"What's wrong?" she asked.

"You were honest," he said. "I wasn't expecting that."

"That's too bad," she said. "Everyone deserves honesty. I hope I haven't offended you."

"Do you?"

"Of course. We have to live with each other, don't we? Make children together?"

He wagged a finger at her. "You're trying to make the best of this," he said. "How dare you."

She smiled. Her face was nearly round, and her smile was *huge*. Her eyes flickered like stars in the flame.

"I will be in a place unknown to me," she said. "I need at least one friend, don't I? It might as well be my husband."

"I think I can manage that," he said. He took another drink. The wine was starting to warm him up inside, loosen him. "Look," he said. "We needn't take any of this too seriously. We can put on appearances, and all of that. But I want you to understand, I don't expect anything from you that you aren't willing to do."

"You mean like sexing?" she said.

"Having sex," he corrected. "But yes, that, among other things."

She shrugged. "That's nice of you. And I fear you might crush me if we did that."

He froze for a moment, remembering someone else who had said exactly that.

She must have noticed.

"I'm sorry," she said. "I didn't mean to upset you. It was a joke. You're a large man, but there's nothing wrong with that. I know there are ways to do sex without me getting hurt. If we must make babies."

He examined her face, trying to see if she was still joking.

"Do you want babies?" he finally asked.

"Not anytime soon," she said. "Maybe not ever."

"We agree on that," he said.

She nodded. "But your family? What will they think?"

"Believe me, whether I have heirs is of no real importance to anyone."

"How can that be?" she asked. "The marriage is an alliance, isn't it? Between the Empire and Zeltah?"

He nodded. "Yes. But it's complicated. I guess. To be honest, I'm not sure why they chose me to marry you."

She nodded. Then she looked out at the campfires below. "My people," she said, pointing with her lips. "Some traveled twenty days to be here."

"I heard about that," he said. "Your people do you proud."

"And I will return the favor." She seemed to hesitate over something then reached her hand out toward him. At first he thought he was meant to take it in his, but then she opened her fist and he saw something in her palm. A small red-orange stone, like a shard of sunset.

"What is this?" he asked.

"The stone is called *tsedukuu*," she replied. "Ants bring them up from beneath the ground. They are thought to be lucky. This one is for your ear."

"Oh," he said. Now he saw the stone was set in a silver claw and had a small hook attached.

"I noticed you had some already," she said, extending her lips to point.

He smiled and reached up to take out one of the four earrings in his right ear. He took the ring from her palm and put it in the now-empty piercing.

"Thank you," he said. "It pleases me. But I have nothing for you."

"Be a good husband," she said. "Remember the things you said. It will be a fine present."

"I won't forget," he said.

A breeze came across the desert. He closed his eyes to savor it.

"There are words, if you want to say them," she said.

"Words?"

"Yes," she replied. "I say *neyeesheshuh*. This means I'm asking you if you will accept my bride-gift."

He smiled. It was all so quaint, but he was touched, and despite himself, flattered.

"Very well," he said. "And I say the same thing?"

"Not exactly. You say *hee'echuun*."

"That sounds like the way you said 'hello.'"

"Same word," she said. "It can also mean yes."

"Hee'echuun," he said, trying to get it right this time.

"That's good!" she said. She beamed at him. "And now you say *sheyeeneshuh*."

"Sheh-yaaaay-neh-shuh," he managed, after several tries.

"Good enough!" she said. "This may work out, Chej. I am hopeful."


## DII JIN (THE PRESENT)

EIGHT DAYS later, the conversation came back to haunt Chej like a hungry spirit when he was pulled from the purification rituals meant to prepare him for his wedding bed and rushed into the lesser council chamber, where he met with Zu the Bright, Master of the Bright Cloud Tower. Some people called him the Emperor's Dog, although never to his face. Zu was an imposing man: tall, fat, old in appearance, his oiled grey-and-black hair pulled into one long braid. He wore a dark red robe over a gold-colored gown.

Zu informed him of the army now invading Zełtah. Chej thought he had misheard him at first. When he finally understood, he took a few moments before answering.

"But why?" he finally said. "I thought the marriage was to create an alliance between us and Zełtah. Why did the Emperor change his mind?"

"He did not," Zu said. "The plan was always to invade once the marriage took place."

"Why go through with the marriage, then?"

"There were a number of reasons. The barbarians usually live dispersed in their mountains, but they gathered at their fortress to wish their princess well. Dzhesq and Hsij infected them with various plagues. It was simpler with them all in one spot. They are a stubborn lot, and this will make them easier to conquer. Also, the princess will make an excellent hostage. It might make their eventual decision to surrender easier."

Chej stared at Zu, horrified. "Why wasn't I informed of this in advance?"

Zu wrinkled his brow in what appeared to be genuine puzzlement. Then he barked out a single unpleasant laugh.

"Why would you have been informed? It would only have given you a chance to botch the whole plan. As it is, they suspected nothing." He shook his head. "There are those, Chej, that believe you are worthless in every way. But they overlook how amusing you can be at times. And I did find a use for you, didn't I?"

Chej wanted to be indignant. Furious. Righteous. Instead, all he could think was that he should have known. He was a head taller than Zu, but at the moment he felt like an insect cowering before a giant.

"And what now?" he finally said. "Must I tell her?"

"Dzhesq has probably done that already. He seemed to relish being the bearer of the news."

"Yes, he would, wouldn't he?" Chej said.

"You can't be disappointed," Zu said. "After all, she's hardly a beauty, is she? You needn't get her with child. Xues is cousin to these people on his mother's side. We can put him on the throne of Zełtah. And you can go back to doing… whatever it is you usually do."

"I'm her husband."

Zu rolled his eyes. "You are many things, Chej," he said. "All meaningless. Let this be another of them. You will be happier."

"As if you care about my happiness."

"You are a child, Chej. You always will be. And now I have other things to attend to."

Chej was well aware when he had been dismissed, but this time he felt he should say something. Do something.

But what? There was nothing to say or do that Zu wouldn't consider a joke.

So he left, dragging his dignity behind him, reflecting that Zu was right: he didn't have to face Yash now.

But then he thought of that night with Yash under the stars and reached to touch the earring she had given him.

She had come here in good faith, married him with the best of intentions for her people. If nothing else, he owed her a visit. It would probably not be pleasant. She would probably scream and cry and blame him for everything. But he could take that. He was used to that sort of thing.

## CHAPTER FOUR

# HSIJ THE YELLOW

CHEJ ARRIVED at the top of the Blue Needle Tower a little out of breath and still unsure what he was going to do or say when he saw Yash, puzzling at the scent of flowers permeating the upper stories. It was likely, he finally decided, that it was something Yash had brought with her, to remind her of her homeland.

When he reached the topmost rooms, he saw Yash immediately, standing at the window with her back to him. She no longer wore her wedding gown and had changed into a dark blue shift.

He was trying to think of how to announce his presence when she turned around and put her onyx gaze on him.

"Hee'echuun, shegan'," she said.

That was her language. He remembered her lesson around the campfire, but he was notoriously bad at learning such things. He had been tutored in both the Moon Language and in Thengnawa. Both tutors had quit in frustration.

"I think that first means 'hello'?" he said, after a few breaths. "Hechun?"

"Hee'echuun," she corrected. "You make those sounds longer, see? Hechun sounds more like *hechu*, which means 'egg.' But that's not bad. You have a good memory! *Shegan* means 'husband.' Or, rather, 'my husband.' Since a husband has to belong to someone."

"True," he said. He glanced around the room. There wasn't much to see, but he found he was having a hard time looking her in the eyes.

"You're uncomfortable," she said. "Because your people have waged war on mine."

"Ah—yes," he replied. Zu said she knew. But the way she was acting—maybe she was still in shock. Maybe she didn't really believe it yet. "I'm sorry," he went on. "You seem to be—ah—taking it well."

"I hoped it wouldn't happen," she said. "But I thought it might. How much do you know about it? The attack?"

"Not much," he said. He knew he shouldn't tell her anything, but she deserved to know. And he was her husband, after all, even if Zu and the rest thought of the whole thing as a farce. "They don't tell me much. Only that they wanted your people to gather together so they could send plague demons while they were all in one place. Now they've sent an army. I don't know how big. And they think you will make a good hostage."

He stopped, feeling out of breath. Like he had just half-run half-fallen down a hill. Also, he was sure he had told her more than he meant to and far more than he was supposed to.

But what did it matter?

"It's fine," she said. "I'm not angry at you, you know."

She seemed serious, but he didn't know her all that well.

"Really?" he asked. "Because I'm pretty angry about it. I didn't know this would happen. No one ever told me about this." He paused. "I'll understand if you don't believe me."

"I believe you," she said.

He studied her for a moment, still trying to see if she was telling the truth or just attempting to make him feel better. She had no obligation to do either.

"I—" he began, not sure what he was going to say. But she held up her hand.

"Wait a moment, please," she said. "I hear something."

Chej didn't hear anything, but an instant later he *saw* something. A large insect appeared on Yash's shoulder. It had a long, slender jewel-green body with two pairs of translucent wings. A metal fly. They were common near the river and skimmed the canals, but seeing one up here in the fortress was a rare occurrence. He hadn't seen it fly in.

"Where did that come from?" he asked.

"Hello, Deng'jah," Yash said, glancing at the insect. "What kept you?"

"No time for long hellos," the insect answered, in a voice that sounded almost like the strings of a wind-harp humming in a breeze, or like copper chimes or—something. Not human. "There are many guardians here. I was noticed."

"Did that bug just talk?" Chej yelped.

"Go into the next room, shegan'," Yash said. "Try to stay out of the way."

Chej had a lot of questions about the talking insect. But the light coming through the window suddenly dimmed, and something in Yash's voice made him think that he should just follow her advice and shut up.

As he crossed the threshold into the next room he turned and looked back, half hiding behind the doorway. Yash was where he had left her but had turned to face the window. She stood with her knees slightly bent, hands in front of her chest. Waiting. But for what?

Light was streaming through the window again, but once more a shadow fell across it, and this time he caught a glimpse of what was casting it: a gigantic bird, so close he could see the individual feathers and hear the *whoosh* of it passing. Chej relaxed a little.

"That's Ruzuyer," he told Yash. "He guards the fortress. He's upset, but he's too big to get in here."

"That one isn't, though," Yash said, as a blue-grey cloud drifted in through the window. While Chej watched, the cloud swirled, tightening into a whirlwind and finally solidifying into a person.

"Hsij," Chej said.

"Hello, Chej, you useless toad," Hsij said.

Hsij the Yellow, Master of the Yellow Bone Tower was ancient, but he looked no older than a boy of sixteen or seventeen years. He kept his head shaved and oiled so that it gleamed in the evening light. He wore only a short red-and-black striped skirt held on by a black cord knotted in the front. More smoke blew in from behind him and formed four of his guards, all dressed in dull yellow armor of lacquered *xewx* chiton. All of them wielded fighting hatchets and small shields made of the same stuff as their armor.

"What is amiss here?" Hsij demanded, in his smooth, musical voice. His every word sounded almost like singing. "Ruzuyer is losing his mind. About something in *here*. What is it?"

"Hsij, I've no idea," Chej said.

"I wasn't asking you," Hsij said. He took a step toward Yash. Chej noticed that the green bug was either gone or on her other shoulder, where he could not see it. She also looked more relaxed now—just standing there in a natural fashion.

Yash bowed her head in respect. "Master Hsij the Yellow, of the Yellow Bone Tower. It is an honor. But, you see, it is our wedding evening. We were hoping for privacy."

"Ugh," Hsij said, looking her up and down. "The very thought. I may vomit." He walked around Yash, staring at her in an unseemly fashion, shaking his head. Then he stopped, his nostrils widening.

He nodded, turning his head and inhaling conspicuously. "That's an interesting scent," he said. "Something familiar about it. Something of yours, princess?"

She shook her head. "I noticed it on the way up," she said. "When we passed Master Needle's door."

"I see," Hsij said. "Perhaps I should pay Master Dzhesq a visit. Maybe he knows why Ruzuyer is so agitated. Princess, come along with me. Chej, you stay here."

"I can come, too," Chej said.

"No, you can't," Hsij replied. He nodded at one of his guards. "You stay here and keep Chej company. The rest of you, come with me. Princess, lead the way."

"Of course," she said. She waved at Chej. "I shall see you soon, Husband."

He noticed this time she used the word in his language, *hesrem*, for husband.

He watched them go. The remaining guard placed himself in the doorway to the room Chej had gone into.

"Move back," he directed.

Chej did as he was told. The room was rather small, containing little more than a washbasin, a jug of water to fill it, three stools, and

41

a small table where some clothes were stacked. He took a seat on one of the stools, his legs still tired from traversing the seemingly endless flights of stairs in the Blue Needle Tower.

What could be happening? Had the metal fly really spoken? Or was he losing his mind? Maybe Yash had done something artful with her voice, like the entertainers who made puppets seem to speak? Had she been trying to amuse him?

But now he was remembering the stories about the Lords of Decay, and how they used metal flies as walking sticks. Could the insect be an evil spirit? Did that mean Yash was a sorcerer?

And what did Hsij the Yellow intend with his bride? Hsij was the most volatile of the masters. You could never tell what he was going to do. Had Hsij taken a notion to murder Yash?

If so, Chej should do something about it. Or at least try. He was, after all, a hje as well as her husband. He should have some say in the matter. Yash had done nothing to deserve how she was being treated. Nothing but being born a barbarian. And maybe he would have thought of her that way a year before. But since visiting Zeltah, he had formed a somewhat favorable impression of her people. The disdain his family showed them—and her—was unearned. And the way people kept calling Yash ugly was starting to irritate him. Her looks suited her. In fact, he had never seen anyone who looked so much like who she really was. He should tell her that. If he saw her again.

What if Hsij really did mean Yash harm? What could he do, with the guard standing there? Maybe he could talk to the man. Convince him to let him go. But he couldn't start with that, could he?

"Is it strange, traveling as smoke like that?" Chej asked the man.

"A little," the man said. "But I've served Master Yellow for ten years, so I'm used to it."

"What does it feel like?"

The guard started to answer, but then he looked away as if something else was demanding his attention.

"What's wrong?" Chej asked.

"I heard something."

"Perhaps Hsij is calling you?"

"No, not like that," the guard said. "Stay here." He walked away then came back and shrugged.

"I guess my ears are fooling me," he said.

Chej heard a weird, meaty *thump*. The guard took a step toward him and then crumpled. To his horror, Chej saw the man had a war hatchet buried in the back of his skull.

"Shit!" he swore, jumping up from his stool.

Then Yash walked into view. Her face and dress were spattered in red and she had a knife in one hand.

"I hope you weren't bored," she said. "I hurried back as soon as I could."

"What—what is happening? What did you do?"

"There were four of them," she said, brightly. "Hsij was the hardest. Did you know his skin was enchanted against weapons? Not his eyes, though."

"What?" Chej said. "Is there something down there? Did one of Dzhesq's monsters escape?"

"No," Yash said. "At least, I don't think so. Everything down there is dead. But I need your help."

He looked at the dead guard. Yash had killed him, hadn't she? With an axe.

"H—help you?"

"Yes! Let's drag this guard down to where the rest of them are. And we should try not to get too much blood on the floor. Though at this point, we may be beyond that."

Numbly, Chej stood, realizing he was going to do as she asked. It seemed like the easiest thing to do.

CHAPTER FIVE

# DENG'JAH

DA'AN' (NOT RECENTLY, BUT NOT IN ANCIENT TIMES.
THE MIDDLE PAST)

### SIXTEEN YEARS EARLIER

YASH WAS bruised, limping, half-starved, and not nearly as far ahead
of the meat-craving monster pursuing her as she wanted to be. There
had been three of them to begin with. She had managed to kill one
with her arrows and wound another badly enough by dropping a
rock on it—the biggest rock she could lift, thrown from the top of a
cliff—that it no longer followed her. But the third one was unhurt.
She was out of arrows. Her only remaining weapon was an antler
knife. Even a grown fighter would have trouble killing a *jenełch'eh*
with just a knife, and she was only eleven, with a bleeding cut in her
right leg. Things were not looking good. Her only hope was to find
Grandmother's cave before the monster caught up with her. She had
never been to Grandmother's dwelling, but she thought it might be
in the red-rock cliffs ahead; she had followed her mother's directions
as best she could. But running from the jenełch'eh was not good for
her concentration, and she might have taken a wrong turn.

A glance back showed the monster coming over the edge of Tu Seqani, the escarpment that she had just ascended, a series of slopes and cliffs that stepped down to the great flat bottom of the Tch'inelen valley. Now she was facing another series of weathered red-rock cliffs stretching left and right as far as she could see. The sky was clear and turquoise, but a breeze bent the sage and scratch-the-rock-plant, and it carried the sweet scent of distant rain on it. A brown-striped lizard raced from the shade of one scrubby nut-pine to another, the flash of its blue-patched ribs almost the same color as the sky. Somewhere an unseen mimic jay screeched in alarm, *sgee-aah*, imitating the call of a hawk, alerting everything with ears to approaching danger.

"I know," she told the jay. "But, thank you."

She pushed on into what looked like the box canyon her mother had described, sweeping her gaze around looking for a rock shelter, but saw nothing but unbroken cliffs, sage, scrubby juniper, and pine. The rock face at the back of the canyon was slightly slanted, though maybe enough to climb. If she was lucky, when she reached the top she would find another boulder to push down on her pursuer.

The slope was steeper than she thought, too steep to climb, and now she heard the harsh panting of the creature's breath, the scrape of its clawed feet on stone. She spied a nearby crack in the two cliffs, about as wide as her outstretched arms. Daylight showed from the other side, but a few steps in the fissure narrowed to the point that even her little body wouldn't fit through. But there was one way to go: up. Panting, trying to ignore the flame of pain in her leg, she wedged herself between the two rock faces, one foot and one hand on each opposing surface, and began bracing her way up.

It hurt so much, and her muscles were so tired, her breath so loud in her own ears, that she almost forgot about the monster until she looked down and saw it right below her.

It had two arms, two legs, and a head like a human being, but the resemblance ended there. It was taller than the tallest person and covered in coarse brown feathers. Its legs bent twice: deeply at the knee and then once again in the other direction halfway down its elongated shins. Its feet were lizard-like, with four long, clawed splayed-out toes. Its hands were big, with long, five-jointed fingers. The head was oblong and mostly mouth. Their jaws could come unhinged, like some snakes: a jenełch'eh could swallow prey bigger than its own head. Its eyes were huge and solid black, like plates of obsidian.

It tried to scrabble up the stone to her, making awful noises as its claws scratched at the rock. When that didn't work, it tried to replicate her feat, but its limbs weren't suited to the task.

Yash had reached a point where the crack was blocked by a fallen boulder. She couldn't see any way to get around it. The monster couldn't reach her, but she couldn't go any higher, couldn't attain the top of the cliff. The only thing supporting her were her own muscles, which were rapidly tiring. All the jenełch'eh had to do was wait.

And it knew it. After a moment it settled onto the ground, legs beneath it.

*Well*, she thought. If she waited, she wouldn't have the strength to fight it. Still braced with three limbs, she freed up one hand and pulled out her antler knife. If she could manage to sort of throw herself forward and fall on top of it, she might at least be able to wound it.

She took one long, deep breath for strength, then another. On four she would go.

She had reached three when a dense grey mist descended, blotting out the light of the sun. Something big fell past her, and the jenełch'eh shrieked. The sound cut off. Down through the fog, she saw something moving, something big. She had the impression of long, slender things moving about, like huge stalks of river reed. Many of them.

Finally her injured leg quaked and then gave way. Her other foot slipped, and for a few breaths she kept her place only with the pressure from her hands. She tried in vain to brace her feet again, but her arms failed, too, and she fell. But instead of the hard ground she was expecting, something soft and sticky caught her, wrapping itself around her.

The next thing she knew she awoke lying on a sleeping mat of woven rushes next to a little fire, bundled in a grey blanket. The air was thick with the scent of burning oak and of something acrid she didn't recognize. A blackened clay cooking pot sat near the edge of the fire.

She sat up. Her leg was throbbing, but it didn't hurt as much as it had.

"Hee'echuun, Shegaye," someone said.

"Grandmother?" she replied, looking around for the voice. She saw her then, an old woman with long, grey hair bound in two braids twisted together, clothed in a long, black skirt and bone-white top. She sat cross-legged, well beyond the fire. She was stitching something in her lap, pulling the needle and thread with deft, quick movements.

Yash gathered her scattered senses. She was in a cliff house, a wind-carved shelter in the red stone. She was not far from the ledge. She felt a breeze. In what she could see of the sky, stars were visible; the land was dark with night. The smell of rain from earlier was gone, and the air was chill. The cave roof hung over her; smoke pooled against it and then rolled up and over the lip, falling backward into the sky. The back of the rock shelter was filled with shadow. In fact, she couldn't see much but herself, the fire, and Grandmother.

She pulled back the blanket and noticed her hurt leg was wrapped up in finely woven grey cloth.

"There was a monster chasing me," she said, squinting out the cave mouth into the night.

"And now there isn't," Grandmother said. "I'm glad to see you, my child."

"I'm glad to meet you, Grandmother," she replied.

"We met before, of course," Grandmother said. "Not long after you were born. But you wouldn't remember that, I know."

"No, Shechu."

"You had a hard time coming here," Grandmother said.

"Everyone knows there are all kinds of niłyeeti monsters in these uplands," Yash replied.

"But you came anyway."

"Yes," she replied.

"I'm glad I was here to welcome you, then."

"I'm glad, too," Yash said. "I think I might be dead if you had not. Did you kill the jenełch'eh?"

Grandmother shrugged. "It won't bother us," she said. "My hospitality always includes safety from monsters. And food! I have something for you to eat if you're hungry. And cool spring water."

"I'm hungry," Yash said.

The old woman got up and vanished into the darkness. She reappeared a moment later carrying a ceramic bowl. She ladled something into it from the cooking pot with a spoon carved from horn and then handed the bowl and spoon to Yash.

Yash discovered it was grain mush with bits of meat. It was warm, filling, and delicious, spiced generously with salt leaf.

Grandmother watched her eat a few bites before speaking again.

"You've been training as a warrior," Grandmother said.

Yash nodded, her mouth too full of food to answer properly.

"The fist, the heel, the knife, the spear, the bow," Grandmother said.

"Yes, Grandmother," she managed, this time.

"You've trained at The Place of the Whirlwind, at Shooting Lightning Place, at Rocks Form a Line, at Where Knives are Born?"

"Yes, Shechu."

"You're still alive," Grandmother said, "so you must be an accomplished warrior. But you need something more. If you are to defend Zełtah and liberate the naheeyiye you need something more than weapons of flesh, stone, and wood."

"That's what I'm told, Grandmother."

The old woman nodded. "It's good," she said. She leaned forward a little. "But are you happy with these choices, Shegaye? This is a rough path you have stepped onto, covered in sharp rocks and thornbrush."

"I think I was born on this path, Shechu," she said. "I am happy when I fight. And I love all of this. The mountains, the forests, the plains, the streams and washes. The lakes in the highlands. And my people! I love my people. Shechu, I have seen the cursed dj'ende places, the places stolen from us by the Empire. I have seen what happens there and what comes from the rot that festers in them. I mourn for the Abducted, the naheeyiye. I long to restore them. The people, the land, the spirits—they all deserve someone to fight for them. To protect and restore them. I have wanted to be that person since I can remember."

"And when you kill?" Grandmother asked softly. "How is it then?"

Yash stared at the fire, unsure what to say.

"So far I have only killed different kinds of niłyeeti," she said. "Like the jenełch'eh that chased me here. Monsters. But it doesn't make me feel bad. After all, they would have killed me."

Grandmother stopped her sewing and steepled her fingers together.

"Listen to me, Yash. This is important. You are a warrior, yes? Warriors fight, and sometimes they kill. But you are a special sort of warrior. Above all, you must fight to restore and to protect. Never to destroy or kill for no reason. That is what niłyeeti do, and dj'ende. That is what the Empire does. Your war is to heal our land and our people. To return what was ripped away from us. Make everything whole. Keep everything whole. It is not to take glory in the mere act of killing. Do you understand?"

"I think I understand, Shechu," she said, although she wasn't certain she did. Wasn't killing enemies a good thing?

Grandmother could tell she was unsure. Her mouth bowed in a slight smile, but it was a smile of sadness.

"Nelch'en'," Grandmother said. "You know this word?"

Yash nodded. "It means someone who is unhappy."

"Miserable," Grandmother corrected. "Worse than unhappy. But think about that word. How would you explain it to a stranger who doesn't know our language?" Then she said something Yash didn't at first understand, before she realized Grandmother was speaking the language of the Empire and the sounds clicked together. "You know these words?"

"Yes, Grandmother," she said in the same language. "I have been learning this."

"Explain it to me in this language, then."

Yash looked back at the fire and thought the word *nelch'en'* through in her head. She sounded each part out. When she got it, she lifted her gaze back to Grandmother.

"*Ch'en'* means to be dirty or rotten," she said. "Or ugly, or bad. We mostly use it to mean 'to be angry.' I could say *qeelch'en'*, I am angry. *Qenelch'en'*, you are angry."

"That's right. Because anger is when something ugly or rotten has gotten into you. And nelch'en'?"

"And so *nelch'en'* means someone who is always angry."

"And thus miserable," Grandmother said. "Anger can be useful… for a moment. But it cannot be your nature, or you will be in a constant state of misery. It is an ugliness inside of you, growing stronger until nothing else is left. This is not just a thing we say, Shegaye. It has happened. In the past there were people who became always angry, always miserable. Full of sorrow caused by their own grievance. They did great harm, and they drove our people from world to world. We call them Nelch'en'i, The Rages. The Terrors That Follow. You must not become one of them."

"I don't want to become a monster, Grandmother."

"Good," she said. "Then I will help you."

She closed her eyes, and a long time seemed to pass. Yash finished her food and watched the fire. Finally Grandmother opened her eyes again.

Yash felt something on her left shoulder, something very light. She looked and saw a blue-green insect perched on it. It was a *natch'elqatcha'h*, big-one-who-carries-things-in-his-basket. She had seen them many times at creeks and pools. The "basket" in the name referred to its tightly bunched legs.

"This is Deng'jah," Grandmother said. "He will be your helper."

"He's a bug," Yash said.

"Be polite," Deng'jah told her.

She frowned. "Haven't I met you before?"

## DII JIN (THE PRESENT)

SIXTEEN YEARS later, Deng'jah reappeared on Yash's shoulder after scouting the tower. "The warriors are all still in the bottom room," he said. "They must not have heard anything."

"That's good," Yash said, as they descended the stairs, dragging the dead guard with them.

"It's back," Chej said. "The talking bug."

"Deng'jah, Chej doesn't need to hear us all of the time."

*"Understood,"* Deng'jah said. This time he used his *beeni'yash*, his little voice, the one only she could hear.

She answered in her own little voice.

*"And Yellow's tower?"*

*"The sorcerer you just killed? He brought some of his guards with him. I think he came straight over without telling anyone else."*

*"Sure,"* she said. *"He was proud, that one. He didn't think anything could threaten him. What about the other towers?"*

*"I haven't heard much. There is some wonder about the big bird outside, but so far no one else has been moved to investigate. Hsij the Yellow was the only one close enough to make the connection when I arrived. You were right to send me away before we reached the fortress, though. I would have been noticed for sure if I had come in the front gate with you. It's fortunate I managed to get here at all. This is a terrible place, full of awful sorcery."*

*"Agreed,"* Yash said. *"But we have time?"*

"*Some. Not much. You have killed two of the nine tower masters. They will eventually notice. And then this place will be like an ants' nest someone has kicked a hole in. Even you can't fight hundreds of warriors at once.*"

They had reached the landing where the remains of Yellow and his other guards lay. Chej made a strangled noise, and Yash realized he was vomiting. She smiled. It was sort of endearing.

She waited until she thought he was done.

"Chej," she said. "Are you well?"

"No, I'm not well," he said, wiping his mouth with the back of his sleeve. "This is horrible. What killed them?"

"I did," Yash said. "And I also killed Dzhesq the Needle. He's inside." She pointed at the closed door. "We need to drag these others in there with him, in case anyone comes up the stairs."

Chej stared at her for a moment, to the point where she began to wonder if he'd understood her.

"Did I say all of that right?" she asked. "Did it make sense? I've studied your language for a long time, but I still make mistakes."

"Yes," he said. "It all made sense. As… words. I—that's… how did you kill them?"

"They each died differently," she said. "This one I stabbed in the heart, that one I killed with an axe. I can tell you in detail while we move the bodies, if you want?" She opened the door.

"No," Chej said. "That's not what I meant. I meant, who are you that you can do things like this?"

"Yash of the Spread Across Water Clan. Princess of Zełtah. Yeqeeqani…"

"Stop," Chej said. "That last one. What does it mean?"

"Um—She Who Kills Them All. Or He Who Kills Them All. He and she are the same word in my language, so you choose."

"But you're a woman," he said.

"Sure," she said. "If that's what you see."

"What does *that* mean?"

"Chej," she said, "I don't know how much time we have. Maybe not much. You take that one." She pointed at one of the men while she grabbed Yellow by the ankles.

Chej did as he was told.

"Kills all of whom?" he asked, as they returned to the landing to pull in the remaining corpses.

"Everyone here, I guess," she said.

"In the tower?"

"In the fortress."

His mouth opened, closed, opened again. "Everyone?" he said. "All of the masters? All of the guards?"

She shrugged. "We'll see. It's just a name, after all."

"But why?"

"Are you serious?" she asked. "Your people just betrayed mine. You lied to us. Now you invade my country. That would be enough, wouldn't it? But the crimes of the Empire are far older and far deeper. You must pay for them, and what was stolen from our land must be restored."

"Wait," Chej said. "Was this always your plan? Did you marry me just so you could get inside of the fortress and murder everyone?"

"Yes," Yash said. She saw the bewilderment on his face and tried again. "Look here, if the Empire hadn't broken trust with my people and invaded my country—on the very day of my wedding, mind —my path would be different. I would still free the naheeyiye, of course, but I could have done that when the time seemed right. As it is, though, I must now do everything I can to end this threat to my people. The army is marching to my homeland, but those who sent it and control it are here. The sorcerers who visit demons and plagues on my people are here. So I must kill them."

Chej blinked. "You admit it?"

"Why shouldn't I?" she asked. "You are my husband, Chej. I won't lie to you."

He took a step back. Then another.

"You're going to kill me, aren't you? As soon as I've helped you move these bodies."

*Poor Chej*, she thought. He was a sensitive person, and good-natured, so far as she could tell. It was a shame she had to pull him down this hole with her. But she didn't have a choice.

She didn't have to worry him needlessly, either.

"No, Husband," she assured him. "I won't kill you. I need your help."

"What?"

"At the moment I don't think they—the Emperor, the tower masters, the war leaders—have any idea about what's happening. They believe I'm on my bed weeping, and Needle and Yellow are alive and well and doing foul deeds. The tower masters keep to themselves, I take it?"

"Ah—some of them. Hsij and Dzhesq—Yellow and Needle—don't come down much. It could be a while before anyone knows either of them are dead. But others are more social."

"So you see, you know things I do not," she said. "Therefore, I need your assistance. But first help me finish this."

After hiding the bodies in Needle's room, she noticed that there was an appreciable amount of blood on the floor, but the polished blue stone was not very porous, so a few minutes with a basin of water and some rags rendered it nearly clean. After that, Yash found paper and a charcoal pencil in Needle's things. She gave them to Chej.

"The tower I can see from my window. That's where Yellow came from, yes?"

"Yes," Chej said. "The Yellow Bone Tower."

"Have you ever been in it?"

"No," he said. "Not that one. Hsij the Yellow didn't like me. I was never invited there."

"Very well," she said. She pointed to the paper. "Draw the fortress," she said. "As best you can. I need to know which tower is which, who is master of each tower, and what you know about their sorceries. And any guardians you know of. And the location of guard posts. And the barracks—all those sorts of thing."

"That will take a while," he said.

"Don't take too long," she said. "The map doesn't have to be beautiful, just reasonably accurate. Stay in here to do it. I've got something else to attend to."

"How do you know I won't leave and tell the guards about all of this?" he said.

"Because I'm asking you not to," she replied.

He was frowning when she left, but it didn't worry her. She could trust him, at least for a time. She closed the door behind her and trotted back up the stairs, acutely aware that each step was a moment she couldn't get back. Then she climbed up into the window and gauged the distance to the nearest window in the Yellow Bone Tower.

"What do you think?" she asked Deng'jah.

"It's a near thing," Deng'jah said. "Jump upwards as well as out."

She nodded, looking down for the first time. All she could see was a narrow stone walkway far below. The drop was easily enough to break most of her bones.

*It's just like leaping through the Splintered Rocks*, she thought, remembering one of her favorite places as a child.

She took four deep breaths, relaxing.

"Maybe I should—" Deng'jah began, as she sprang up and forward with all of her strength.

The air was all around her, and the space beneath her heart was a feather. From the edge of her vision she saw the huge bird, Ruzuyer, high above. Already turning toward her.

The window came up; she stretched out her fingers. But as she reached, a wind blasted from the opening, pushing her the other way. Her belly went light again. The ledge of the window slipped past as she fell. She clawed at the stone surface, trying to find some purchase, something to slow her down.

And then her fingers caught. She was falling so fast that she nearly couldn't hold on, and it felt as if her arms were being pulled off, but then she was hanging: not by the sill of the window she had aimed for, but from one a story lower.

"Good catch," Deng'jah said.

Yash didn't answer. She was working too hard, pulling herself up by her fingers, then the flats of her palms. Finally she got far enough up to get an arm over. She heaved and flipped herself through the window and into the room beyond.

A room full of guards. She didn't have time to count, but she reckoned about a dozen.

For an instant, no one moved. She stared at them, and they stared at her. Most of them rested on benches around the perimeter of the room, but five of them were in the center, sitting cross-legged around a basket, playing the tossing-cane game.

"Daxudzhue," she said, hopefully.

Then everyone moved at once, either coming straight for her or scrambling for their weapons.

Deng'jah began to burr his wings and flew up. Her vision transformed and widened. She was looking down on herself, but also in each of the four directions.

Most of the guards were armed with either hatchets or short, heavy spears. The nearest man to her had a spear, and he thrust it toward her abdomen. She dodged, caught the shaft, twisted it, closed in, and punched him in the throat. He let go of the spear and now it was hers. She drove the point into her next attacker. He was fast and tried to slip to the side, but she stabbed him through his shoulder. She dropped and spun a half-circle with her leg stiffened out, sweeping a third man's feet from under him, and as he fell she turned away, pulling the hatchet she had taken from one of Yellow's men from her belt, and threw it past the next two nearest opponents at a third coming up behind them. It hit him in the face and he pitched backward.

Yash skirted left, keeping to the wall so they couldn't come at her from all sides. She slipped out Needle's knife, ducked under a spear thrust, and pierced her assailant's neck above his slat-wood armor. At the same time she kicked the guard coming on her right in the knee. She caught the stabbed man's spear as it fell and shoved the butt into her next opponent's face, feeling teeth break. Then she pushed forward and speared the man she had swept to the floor before he could return to his feet.

With half of the guards down in a few heartbeats, the others backed off, presumably to develop some sort of strategy. She threw the spear and hit another guard in the thigh before scooping up an axe from the floor and hurling that at someone else, still working her way left around the room, toward the entrance. By the time she got there, it had occurred to one of the guards that he should run for help, but he never got through the door.

A thrown hatchet hit Yash in the chest before she could dodge it, but it was a bad throw, landing handle-first so the blade didn't bite. It hurt, though, sending her stumbling back into the stairwell. One of the men—she didn't know if it was the axe thrower or someone else—hit her at the waist, like a wrestler, lifting her off her feet and smashing her into the outer wall of the staircase. She curled to absorb the impact, grabbed him by the hair, pulled his head back, and jabbed the knife through his eye.

"Dodge left," Deng'jah advised.

She did, and a spearhead shattered on the wall, right where she had just been.

She rolled away from the man who had knocked her down, aware that her ears were ringing; she smelled blood deep in her nose and tasted it in the back of her mouth.

And now she was back on her feet, charging them.

There were four left in fighting condition. One of them tried to get down the stairs, but she stopped him with a hatchet. Two came at her and died for it. The last one jumped out the window she'd come through.

She took a few deep breaths as Deng'jah's gift of vision faded and she was left with only what she saw with her own two eyes. Then, wearily, she finished the fallen. She looked down from the window and saw the jumper splayed out in the alley. She couldn't tell if he was dead or just unconscious.

"Someone is going to see him," she muttered.

"True," Deng'jah said. "You should have sent me to scout ahead."

"I didn't intend to end up in this room," she said. "I was aiming for the one above. But you're right. Check and see who or what is upstairs."

"I will," Deng'jah said. And he was gone.

He returned a few heartbeats later.

"There is someone upstairs," he said. "The one who pushed you out of the window."

"What are they?"

"I'm not sure," Deng'jah replied. "They are too changed. But someone from the Nełts'eeyi Clan, I believe."

"Let's go meet them, then."

## CHAPTER SIX

# THE NEŁTS'EEYI

## TSAYE (IN ANCIENT TIMES)

THE FIRST *world was Nyen' Tu, The Ocean World. The people of that world were people of the water and people of the wind. At that time, spirits and people and animals were the same. They had not become what they are now. But they were also all different from one another. Some lived in the winds, most lived in the waters. Some were like insects, some like fish, some like worms. They were of all sorts, those people. But none of them lived on dry land, because at first there was none. Dry land, they say, came from the north, from the Ice Horizon. Dry Land was a person both male and female, and they settled among the waters of the Ocean World. Dry Land still moves, now and then, and everything shakes. In time, Dry Land would become home to many sorts of spirit-people-animals, but at that time there was nothing but bare stone. There were no trees, no rushes, no grass. There weren't even any cacti or tumbleweeds. It was all just rock.*

*The Ocean World was surrounded on four sides by four other worlds. In the east lay the White Brilliant, and in the west stood the Silent Stagnant.*

On the north side was the Ice Horizon, and on the south the Sky World. At times the Sky World and the Ice Horizon fought, and their battleground was the Ocean World. The Ice Horizon fought with snow, glaciers, and the weapons of night. The Sky World fought with flying stars, volcanos, and lightning. Some spirit-people-animals fled into the Silent Stagnant, and there they remain, just as they were when they left the Ocean World, eternally the same. Others escaped into the White Brilliant, and there they changed. Their lives flew by. They lived and died in the blink of an eye. Their children also lived and died quickly, always changing. In times of peace, some came back to the Ocean World in their new forms. And this continued, back and forth, for many, many lifetimes. And the Ocean World changed, too. The fight between the Ice Horizon and the Sky World changed it. The back-and-forth tug of the Silent Stagnant and the White Brilliant changed it. On dry land, mountains rose up and valleys formed. Rivers flowed and forests grew. And still spirits and people and animals were all one, but they were also different. And we call all of these spirit-people-animals the Heeyets, The Ones Having Breath.

There came a time when things were worse than ever. The Ocean World was in turmoil. The skies burned and the waters boiled and the air became poison. Food was scarce, and the Heeyets were dying. But this time someone did not want to retreat to the Silent Stagnant or the White Brilliant. Someone said they should search for another world in which to live. They called this spirit-person-animal Tsenid'a'wi, The One Who Goes First, and she (or he, or it) set out to find the Heeyets a better place to live.

## DII JIN (THE PRESENT)

YASH DELAYED long enough to drag the men she had killed on the stairwell into the guardroom. There was no door to close, but she arranged the bodies so they couldn't be seen without entering. As her blood slowed and the killing disposition subsided, she wondered if she should feel bad about these men. Had they attacked her first? Yes. But if they had not, she would have killed them anyway. She was at war. She hadn't felt bad about killing Needle. He was a sorcerer, more and less than human. It had been like killing a niłyeeti. Yellow's guards, though. Did they have spouses, children, homes someplace? Favorite foods? Did they like the scent of bruised juniper or the song of the whippoorwill in the evening?

"Not anymore," Deng'jah said.

"Right," she said. She hadn't realized she had been using the little voice. "It doesn't matter. Come on."

There was no door closing the way into the room upstairs, only a curtain of beaded strings sparkling in many colors. Yash pushed them aside and entered. Like Needle's quarters, the room was round, and it looked bigger in circumference than the one in the Blue Needle Tower. But that might have been because there was almost nothing in it, not even a bench or a bed. A basin stood on a plinth in the center of the room. From where she stood, it looked like it was filled with water or some other liquid. The floor and walls were of polished red marble veined in milky white, forming patterns that reminded her of wind and lightning. The ceiling was blue-black.

"There's no one in there," Yash said.

"They are in there," Deng'jah replied. "We just can't see them yet."

Yash stepped into the room, the dagger in one hand and a hatchet in the other. She cautiously stepped around the chamber. Through the window, she saw the Blue Needle Tower, which from outside was actually grey, like the trunk of an aspen, and the window to her room, too far above to jump to. She would have to find a lower way in, but looking now, she didn't see one. She might have to modify her plans.

One thing at a time. She went to the basin. She peered into it and saw her reflection in the water there.

"Wait," Deng'jah said, as she started to turn away. "Something about this."

He flew from her shoulder and skimmed across the still surface of the water, raising little waves with the wind from his wings. The ripples spread out, and with them shadows, colors, light. They began to settle into patterns she recognized. A white-capped peak, a lower ridge, a cleft between them.

"That's Where the Snow Goes Down as Rushing Water," she murmured. "The pass that leads into Zełtah from the Empire."

As she studied the scene, it grew nearer, as if she were flying, winging down toward the pass in the mountains. Details came into focus.

She saw houses burning. The earth was littered with the dead of her people.

"So, it's already started," she said. "They must have moved their army up days before my marriage."

Her qualms about killing the guards were gone like morning dew. They served *this*, this thing, this empire murdering her people. She would kill all of them, if need be, and she wouldn't feel any guilt for it.

The water rippled again, and the image broke into fragments.

"Oh," Deng'jah said. "Here they come. Step back. Quickly."

She did, as the water in the basin sprayed up, whirled about, became fog, a whirlwind. A sudden gust blew Yash off the floor and toward the window, but she caught herself at the edge and flipped so she rolled along the wall and fell back to the floor.

"Run left, with the wind," Deng'jah advised.

Yash did that; Deng'jah was right that the wind was moving in a cyclone, and so long as she went with it she could retain some control and work her way toward the center where something was forming. As the air and mist took shape, the wind died down.

She resembled a human woman, but made of rainbow beetle-shell, with two legs but four arms: two where they ought to be, the other two sticking out of her chest and from her back. Each hand gripped a white knife. Her eyes were like a beetle's, too, hard and black. Four delicately veined brown-gold wings rose from her shoulders, fluttering erratically behind her. They looked much like Deng'jah's wings, although much larger.

"You are not welcome here," the beetle-woman said.

"I know," Yash said. "But the one you serve is dead already. I killed him. And I came here to return you to your rightful place."

"I have no memory of any other place," the beetle-woman said. "This is where I live. This is what I protect. And my master must be avenged."

"That's not true," Yash said. "None of it."

"It is what I know to be true," the beetle-woman said.

"I know," Yash replied. Then she dashed forward.

The beetle-woman spun, striking at her with each of the four knives in the same heartbeat, each attack coming from a different angle, forcing Yash to weave and dance and then retreat, unable to reach her target. The beetle-woman leapt after her, the white blades a blur. It was like fighting a whirlwind, but not the sort that dressed in dust. She was something else. The smell of water was strong, like the first kiss of gentle rain on the high desert, like a cloud teasing its intentions.

With the aid of Deng'jah's sight, Yash timed the next flurry of attacks, stepping in quickly, blocking one arm with her axe and stabbing the beetle-woman in the chest, but her plastron turned even the demon-bone splinter. Once more Yash was forced to retreat, but this time she wasn't quite fast enough; a white blade nicked her arm just below her shoulder. It felt like she had been cut with ice. Instead of continuing her retreat, however, she leapt high, over the next slashing blade, landing with one foot on the beetle-woman's shoulder, springing from it to avoid another knife-cut.

She flipped, turned, and landed behind the beetle-woman, who spun to face her. But one of her amber-colored wings drifted to the stone floor.

"I see," the beetle-woman said. Yellow smoke bled from the wound, drifted up toward the ceiling.

"You are naheeyiye," Yash said. "I honor you. We have no cause to fight."

A tear oozed from the beetle-woman's eye. "I am not," she said. "I am what they have made me. I do not remember my name."

"Yash!" Deng'jah said. "Look!"

The smell of rain arriving was stronger now. Through Deng'jah's memory Yash saw willows and rushes, a spring in the cliffs. An on-the-water-surface-it-moves-swiftly glided across a small, clear pool, its surface a mirror reflecting red cliffs and blue sky. Then Yash realized that she had been there, too. She knew the place. But it hadn't been like that. It had been empty of life and color, a dj'ende place, a place where monsters were born.

"I know you!" Yash shouted. "I've heard of you."

"You have not!" the beetle-woman screamed, and she rushed at Yash, no longer measured, but wild and quick. Yash sought an opening, but there wasn't one. She could only retreat and then run.

And she was tiring. Soon the beetle-woman would catch up to her and cut her to pieces.

Yash summoned up what breath she could.

"I trained at Whirlwind Place," she shouted. "That spring was near there. My war teacher told me the story!"

"Lies!" the beetle-woman shrieked.

"You are Going in Front of the Big Rain," she said. "You are Older Sister Who Watches the Spring in the Winding Canyon. Your mother's clan is Nełts'eeyi and your father's clan is Tu Nełchan. The dj'ende hunters took you long ago and brought you here."

A white blade cut through her dress at her belly but only lightly scratched her skin. Overbalancing in her attempt to dodge, Yash fell against the wall. There was no time to evade the next attack. The blades sliced toward her.

But the beetle-woman stopped. The blades withdrew and she went back to the center of the room, her whole body a vibrating blur.

"My names?" she said. "Those are my names, my clans, my place?"

"I believe so," Yash said, pushing herself back to her feet.

"It isn't enough," the beetle-woman said. "It's not enough."

"Don't worry," Yash said.

"Hurry," the beetle-woman said, beginning to twitch her arms again. "Be quick or die."

Yash stabbed her in one of her eyes, then through a seam in her shell where her heart might be. The beetle-woman stiffened.

"Watch out!" Deng'jah said, as two of the knives lashed out at her. Yash leapt back as the deadly blades soughed by. The beetle-woman leaned forward, as if seeking an embrace. Then she collapsed, knocking the basin from its pedestal. It cracked as it hit the floor, and the water spread in a pool. A mist suddenly covered everything. Droplets formed on Yash's skin.

Yash swayed for a moment, just breathing, savoring the smell of rain. Then she knelt by the corpse.

*Go home*
*Wandering water*
*Wayward wind*
*Going in Front of the Big Rain*
*Older Sister Who Watches the Spring in the Winding Canyon*
*Go home*
*Be in harmony*
*Go home.*

A wind wrapped around her.

*Thank you,* it said.

"One thing more," Yash said. "One favor. You can refuse, and I will not fault you. I have slain your enslaver and will not myself enslave. You sent your master and his men to the other tower in a smoke. Can you send me to where the Emperor is?"

*I cannot. He is guarded against my kind. And I cannot take you so far, not like this. I am no longer what Hsij unshaped me to be.*

"Can you take me back to the Blue Needle Tower? Would you?"

*I can,* the spirit said. *I will.*

Yash was thin, she was gone, she returned. She was back in her rooms in the Blue Needle Tower.

She let out her breath, and a plume of smoke emerged with it, spreading into the air and fading away. The spirit was gone, flying home.

*That's two*, she thought. *Even if I die now, that's two.*

But she wasn't dead, so she wasn't done.

"Deng'jah," Yash said. "Scout the tower."

She sank onto a stool for a moment, steadying her breath, letting her pain in so it could speak to her. She was bleeding from two cuts, and her chest felt like a bone had cracked, although she imagined it was just bruised.

She stripped off the ruined smock and returned to the basin. She washed both cuts. The one on her belly was hardly a scratch, but the one in her shoulder was deeper, with darker blood welling out of it. She made bandages of the old dress and tied them on the wounds. Then she washed the blood from her face, arms, and legs as best she could. She found some in her hair, sticking there in little clots, but it wasn't visible in her dark bristles unless you were looking for it. If someone was searching for blood in her hair, it was probably too late to fool them about what was going on. If she hadn't reached that point already, she would soon. Probably very soon.

Deng'jah returned.

"No one is coming up the tower," he said. "The guards are all still down there. Chej is drawing."

"Let's go see Chej, then," she said.

HER HUSBAND looked up when she came in. She felt a little smile tug on her lips and realized it was the sight of the big man hunched over his drawing like a child. For a moment she wished she could just walk away, leave him to his life. But he looked up at her, and it was just another moment wasted.

"You've changed clothes again," he said. "Did you get too much blood on them?"

"Yes, as a matter of fact," she replied. "And my last clothes got cut up a little."

He peered at her more closely. "Your shoulder is bandaged," he said. "How—who did you find to fight up there? Did they come by on the stairs? I didn't hear anything."

"I went over to the Yellow Bone Tower," she said.

His eyes widened. "You just… went over there? Can you fly?"

"I can jump," she replied.

"Jump," he said. His eyes shifted back and forth, as if he were trying to imagine it, remember how far she had to leap to reach the Yellow Bone Tower. Then he shook his head.

"I see," he said. "But why? You already killed Hsij the Yellow."

She sighed and sat on a bench where she could see what he had been drawing. "I told you I wouldn't lie to you," she said. "I went over there for two reasons. The first is that the more of my enemies I can kill before everyone in the fortress becomes aware that something is happening, the better. After that, everything will become more difficult."

"It will become impossible," he said.

"Difficult," she repeated.

Chej shook his head. "Clearly you are an effective assassin. The evidence is all around me. But I imagine you killed Needle and Yellow before they understood what they were up against. There are seven tower masters left. Once they know what you're doing, they can attack you with their sorcery without you ever seeing them.

You won't have a chance to stab them or strangle them or whatever. Aside from that, there are at least a hundred guards in the fortress, and more can be called in from the barracks."

"Can they?" Yash said. "I imagine many of your warriors have gone to war, yes?"

Chej looked thoughtful. "Maybe," he said. "At least some of the war leaders—xarim—will have gone and taken their own men. So maybe fewer than a hundred. I hadn't thought of that."

"But you *have* been thinking," she said. "I appreciate that."

"I have been thinking," he confirmed. "About a great many things. For instance, while you were gone, why couldn't I leave this tower and warn my people of your intentions to murder them all? I wanted to."

"Because you don't like anyone here very much?" she said. "Because I am your wife, and you stand with me?"

"I think it's because of this," he said, touching the earring she had given him. "I find I can't remove it."

"Well, yes," she said. "There is that, too. Although it's less the stone itself and more the promises you made me."

"In a language I did not understand."

"That's hardly my fault," she said. "I learned *your* language."

"True," he replied. "But it makes me feel foolish, thinking back on it. I thought you liked me. I thought we were going to be friends."

"We're more than friends," she said. "We're husband and wife."

He held her gaze for another moment, then sighed. "The other reason?"

"Sorry?"

"You said there were two reasons you went to the Yellow Bone Tower. The first, as I understand it, was to kill his guards so you don't have to fight them later. But there was a second reason, yes?"

"Yes," she said. "The discussion about your earring distracted me. Each of these sorcerers has a monster, you know?"

"The xual from which they draw their power," Chej said. "I know about those."

"Yes. But do you know where they came from?"

"They were demons originally, bent on our destruction. They were conquered by the tower masters and bound as servants," Chej said.

"They are spirits, stolen from Zełtah. The naheeyiye, my people call them. Without them, our land is unwell. My people are unwell. And the sickness spreads. Your sorcerers now send them against my homeland, which will cause the rot to spread even more quickly. So I am here to kill the monsters you have made from them, find their names and send them home. I went to the Yellow Bone Tower to send a naheeyiye home."

"I have never heard any of this," Chej said.

"Maybe we can talk more about this later," she said. "Maybe I can tell you some of the stories of the dj'ende hunters and what they did. But now I need you to tell me about your drawing."

He looked like he wanted to say more but instead he shrugged. He tapped on the paper.

"It isn't pretty, I know," he said. "This is where we are, the Blue Needle Tower. That's the Yellow Bone Tower next to it."

She studied the whole map.

"These eight towers form two arms," Yash said. "Curving toward this one in the center."

"Yes," he replied. "The middle is the Earth Center Tower. It's the tallest tower, and it's surrounded by this other circular wall. That's the Emperor's Keep. Inside is where his court is, his personal guard, gardens, and so on. This right spiral arm, going from left to right from the middle: Standing Pinion Tower, Bright Cloud Tower, Red Coral Tower, and Blue Needle Tower, where we are now. Starting back at Earth Center and going along the left spiral arm, right to left, there is Yellow Bone Tower, Abalone Shell Tower, Sharp Horn Tower, and Obsidian Spear. I've written them down, see? And the names of their masters: both their Hje names and their titles."

"I can't read this," Yash said.

"My drawing may not be outstanding, but my handwriting is excellent," Chej said.

"No," she replied. "I speak your language, but I don't know your writing marks."

"Oh!" Chej said.

"So you must tell me. I will remember. If I don't, Deng'jah will."

"Very well," Chej said.

She listened carefully as he named the towers again, this time including the masters of each and what he knew of their powers. When he was done, she nodded.

"And the rest of the fortress?" she asked.

"You see the spiral arm walls separate the fortress into east and west halves. The eastern part is divided into four xarim domains. Each xarim commands a qhes, a fourth of the army. Each xarim has his own compound: houses, barracks for their personal guards, courtyards, training grounds, and so on. That's also where the armory is. The west half is divided into four administrative sections that see after the needs of the fortress: food, water, sanitation, fuel. Each of those sections is governed by a xi who controls one of those resources. Around all of that is the Mountain Wall. Lesser

Hje and favored foreigners live between the Spiral Walls and Mountain Wall."

"Thank you," she told him. "This will help. And now I need you to go and spy for me."

"What do you mean?"

"Go back down into the fortress. Find out what you can about the war against my people, how many guards are in the fortress, what the masters are doing, that sort of thing."

"Can't your bug do that for you?"

"I can mostly go about them unseen," Deng'jah said. "But there are things here that might detect me. Including some of the masters. Anyway, I cannot ask questions, like you can. Not without raising suspicions, to say the least. Can you imagine? I also do not know this place, these people. I might not look in the right places. If I *could* ask questions, I might not ask the right ones."

"So you're going with me?"

"I will check in from time to time," Deng'jah said. "We will work together to help Yash."

"To help her kill my people," Chej said.

"Exactly," Deng'jah said.

Chej looked back at Yash. "Don't make me do this," he pleaded. "I don't like most of them, it's true, and most of them don't care for me. But they are my family."

"I am also your family," Yash reminded him. "I am sorry about this, Chej. I understand, and if our places were changed, I might feel the same. Except that I like my family, and they like me. And they are in the right, and yours is in the wrong. In fact, maybe *you* should think about what *you* would do if our situations were reversed."

"If I promise to do that, will you let me choose for myself?"

"No," she said. "I cannot. This is war. My people are counting on me. I will not betray their trust."

"They sent you here to die," he said.

"No, shegan'," she said. "They sent me here to win. And that is exactly what I will do."

Chej stood up and nodded. "I am at your command, Wife," he said. "Literally, apparently."

"I don't know that word, 'literally,'" she said. "But yes."

"It has to do with writing," he said, "so it makes sense you wouldn't know it. Shall I go now?"

She nodded. "Is there a place of command?" she asked. "Someplace they control the war from?"

"The xataxh," Chej said.

"I don't know that word," Yash said. "*Xa* means war, I think?"

"Yes. And *taxh* is this," Chej said, touching his chest. "The restless thing inside of the chest."

"Oh," Yash said. "I understand now. We say *tiq'*."

"Similar," Chej murmured.

"Our people are said to be related," Yash said. "Our words must be, too."

Chej cocked his head thoughtfully. Then he lifted his shoulders back. "Shall I go now?" he asked.

"Please. Hee'echuun, shegan'."

"I thought that meant 'hello' and 'yes,'" he said.

"It also means 'goodbye,'" she replied.

"Of course it does," Chej said. Then he turned, walked to the door, opened it, and went through. He closed it behind him.

"Shall I go with him?" Deng'jah asked.

"No," she said. "See if there is a viable way to the Earth Center Tower. If we strike directly at the Emperor, it may save a lot of effort. If you don't find a reasonable path to it, have a look at the Sharp Horn Tower next. Then come back here."

CHAPTER SEVEN

# XARIM RUESP

RUESP RECEIVED the dispatch from the courier. He checked it over to make certain it was authenticated and carried the signature of Shuejh, the xarim of the third army qhes. Satisfied, he countersigned and made a notation on a chart. He paused to study his handwriting. It was his name, but the script didn't look like his. He stared for a moment, disgusted, at the pen in his trembling fingers. He put it down and returned his attention to the young man who'd brought the communication.

"Thank you, you can go," he said.

"You're most welcome, Xarim Ruesp," the young man said.

*Xarim*, Ruesp thought. They still called him that. He retained his military title. Then why was he here, taking dispatches in the stale air of the room so despicably named the war-heart? Why wasn't he with the other xarim, in the keening winds of the high plains, leading a charge against the enemy?

Because he had done the unthinkable. The thing that no xarim should ever do.

He had grown old.

The war-heart was old, too. The walls had once been stained white, but they were now a dull yellow-brown, darker near the low ceiling from years of exposure to smoke. The smoke and the only light in the room came from lamps of red and black stone carved into fanciful animal shapes. They cast luminous pools around tables and desks that did not quite overlap—an archipelago of lights in a night-dark sea. It was larger than most rooms in the fortress, but it didn't feel that way. It felt claustrophobic. The inside of a tomb with the vault door still cracked open. For now.

He shuffled over to the map table and was moving the markers to indicate the new position of Shuejh's men when someone else entered the room. A big fellow. It took him a breath or two to recognize him.

"Hje Chej," he said, as he shifted the colored stones. "I admit, I was not expecting to see you here today. Isn't this your wedding day?"

"Yes," Chej said. "But as you can imagine, that is not going so very well."

Ruesp took his fingers off the markers. "The bride is upset, I take it," he said.

"That is an understatement," Chej said. His mouth stayed open as if he wanted to say more then closed as he apparently thought better of it.

Ruesp waited to make certain it was his turn to talk. "That explains why you are not with her," he eventually said. "It doesn't explain why you are *here*."

"This war was as much a surprise to me as it was to her," Chej said. "I suppose I want to understand what's happening."

"Then you should go to where the fighting is," Ruesp told him. "That is the only way to understand a war."

"Well. Failing that, I assumed the war-heart was the place to come."

"War-heart," Ruesp muttered. "A pointless room for pointless tasks."

Chej looked surprised. "Why do you say that?"

For the first time, Ruesp really focused his attention on Chej. Even with the man standing there, in Ruesp's mind Chej was seventeen years old. But he was, what, thirty-three or -four now? He had rather liked the young Chej. He had been a bright boy with a flexible mind. What was he now?

"Do you remember when your father made you a part of my personal guard?" he asked. "Had a uniform tailored for you and everything. How you went to war with me in Chenpatte?"

"Yes, of course."

"Did you think you were really a soldier?"

"I guess I did at the time. Sort of."

"Did you fight in any engagements?"

"No."

"No. Like me, and the rest of my men, you didn't do anything. We camped far from the fighting, guarding a pass through which no army would ever come. The whole thing was a fraud."

"Of course," Chej said. "I see that now. Xues was also there, and Ruixhp, and Chuang. All young princes. That way our fathers could say we fought for the Empire, although none of us ever had to actually fight."

"For me, this room is like that," Ruesp said. "Do you know what really happens here?"

"You receive all of the information on the war and add it together," Chej said.

"That is true, as far as it goes," Ruesp said. "When they choose, the tower masters send me word of what they have seen in their divinatory pools and vapors, what their xual report from afar. If I'm very lucky, they tell me what sort of sorcery they have inflicted—or attempted to inflict—on the enemy. And I get dispatches from the xarim whose men are actually fighting. From that I make maps and write reports that in turn the Emperor and the other tower masters can review to help inform them of what their next actions ought to be."

"That all sounds… important," Chej said. "How can you fight a war without a clear vision of its progress?"

"How, indeed," Ruesp said. "And how wonderful if clear vision was what this room produced. But the tower masters don't like being around one another, do they? They rely on this room to inform each other on what they have seen and what they are doing. Each has their own sources of intelligence, and they only share what they care to, and almost never with each other directly. And each only does what he sees fit. The Emperor can command them, but he rarely does so. The dispatches from the field are similar; some of the xarim are more fixed on their own reputations than on strategy, so they often exaggerate their gains and minimize their losses. No source of information that enters this room is entirely reliable. But we pretend that it is."

"You don't seem to be pretending much of anything," Chej said.

"That's because I'm talking to you," Ruesp replied.

"Ah," Chej said. "Because I don't matter."

Ruesp shrugged. "You shouldn't take that as an insult. You see what I think of the people who *do* 'matter.'"

"I guess?" Chej said.

Ruesp clapped him on the shoulder. "I have walked my tongue to Fsa and back. Tell me why you're here."

"Well—given all you've just said—I want to know what you at least believe is happening up there in the highlands."

Ruesp shrugged and motioned at the map.

"As you may have surmised, this was all planned months ago. Your journey to meet your bride-to-be was used as cover to move advance troops into position along the mountains at the border. As of this morning, our army has entered Zełtah through this pass. They haven't yet met a real force to oppose them. Instead, small bands of Zełtah warriors are harassing our army. Trying to slow them down. In return, imperial forces have destroyed several villages and occupied two fortifications. Dzhesq inflicted plagues on them. Hsij brought an unseasonable snowstorm in the mountains to delay whatever reinforcements might be coming from Zełtah's allies in Heełtes and Jełinge. Sha drove their forces on the plains to shelter with a massive sandstorm. The other tower masters are busy now with their own sorcery, but I don't know what they're doing and I won't until they've done it, if then." He sighed and sat down. "Does that answer your question?"

"Are we winning?" Chej asked.

"At the moment? Who can say? It's only just started. If the Emperor wants to win, we will win. It is only a matter of how many soldiers he is willing to spend in the effort, and how long it will take. And of course, how many of the enemy he is willing to kill."

"And how many is he willing to kill?" Chej asked. "Why do we even want Zełtah in the Empire?"

"Zełtah has many useful minerals," Ruesp said. "But more importantly, it is a border and a check against the growth of the

Vhaleg Hegemony in the northwest. If Zełtah makes common cause with the Vhaleg, we could have their garrisons looking down on us in a few years. The *people* of Zełtah, on the other hand, are less than useful to the Empire. There aren't that many of them, and they're too proud and stubborn to make good subjects. It's the land we want, Chej. I believe to get that, the Emperor is willing to kill every last one of those barbarians. He can then move loyal subjects onto those lands. With proper irrigation, much of it could produce crops to feed our cities, and much more of it could furnish pasture. He could build roads and fortify the passes in the mountains without having to negotiate or get consent from anyone."

"All of them," Chej said. "He would kill all of them. Very well. Thank you."

"There's no point in telling your bride any of this, you understand," Ruesp said. "I wouldn't expect her to sympathize with the Emperor's point of view."

"Zu said that Xues might take the throne of Zełtah," Chej said. "That suggests the goal is not to eradicate them."

"If they surrender," Ruesp replied. "It would be easier that way. Over time we can break up their clans and scatter them across the Empire, as we have in other conquered lands. But I don't imagine that will happen. As I said, these people are stubborn."

"Did you know this would happen?" Chej asked. "This war?"

"I suspected it. A marriage alliance seemed implausible to me. It might have paid off… eventually. When your children were born, or their children. And if succession worked in Zełtah as it does here, which it doesn't. Really, it would eventually have led to war anyway, with the pretext being that one of your offspring had claim to the throne of Zełtah. This is quicker."

"Pretext? Why does the Emperor need an excuse?"

"That all comes back to the Vhaleg Hegemony," Ruesp said. "And the unaligned kingdoms in the north. If they see us annexing territories without any good reason to do so, they might fear they are next. They might ally with Vhaleg against us."

"What reason have we given, then?" Chej said. "What is the pretext now?"

"I believe the story is that the bride rejected you in the bedchamber," Ruesp told him. "It is a flimsy pretense, and even our strongest allies know that, but it is all they need to remain loyal to us. And all the unaligned kingdoms need to continue courting us." He grinned slightly. "Especially if it's true. There are sorcerous methods of determining if you have consummated the marriage. They'll prove you haven't, won't they?"

"Well, I—" Chej darkened. "I mean I didn't try and press the matter. Not given the circumstances."

"Of course," Ruesp said. "You always were a thoughtful boy. I don't fault you for that, as some do. And I know you aren't attracted to her."

Chej's eyes widened, and Ruesp read anger on his face. "You, too?" Chej snapped. "She may be a barbarian, and we may be at war with her people, but I am rapidly tiring of this implication that my wife is unattractive. There's nothing wrong with her!"

"That's not what I meant," Ruesp said softly. "I meant your attractions do not tend toward women."

Chej's face darkened further, and he looked away.

*I shouldn't have said that*, Ruesp realized. The thing about old age was that you both lost and gained perspective. From where he stood at seventy-two winters, he could almost see the Midnight Road. There were so many things he didn't care about anymore because he was so close to escaping the need to care about anything. If he died today, how much life would he have lost? Very little. Not enough to worry about.

But Chej had many years left to live, and he doubtless cared about those years a great deal.

Ruesp waved his hand. "Forget I said that," he went on. "I am in a mood today. I spoke from the wrong end of my tongue."

But Chej shook his head. "No," he said, very quietly. "You're right. I just... I didn't know you knew."

That should be the end of the conversation, Ruesp knew. He should change the subject.

"Everyone knows, Chej," he said, instead. "At least, many people do."

"Then..." Chej frowned, clearly trying to work it out.

"Why haven't you been purified?"

Chej nodded.

"Because you're not just anyone," Ruesp said. "You are Hje and a prince. Maybe not an important prince, but a prince nonetheless." He paused, then plunged on. "And also because—"

"They had a use for me," Chej said. "*This* use. An unconsummated marriage that they can tout if anyone questions this war." He paced away and back. "I *can* consummate it, you know."

"Yes," Ruesp said. "I don't doubt that you could. It won't stop the war, though, if that's what you want. They will think of some other excuse to assuage the unaligned kingdoms."

"What?" Chej said. "Stop the war? No, that's not what I want. I—I was just thinking out loud. The Emperor has declared war, and I am his subject. I don't oppose him. In fact, I came down here to offer my help."

"Help?" Ruesp said. "Why?"

"I'm not a warrior. I'm not a sorcerer. I'm of no use to the army. But I might be able to help you. I can read, and I'm good at numbers. Remember when I used to help you take inventory of the arms? I may not have done any fighting, but I did learn a few things when I was in your qhes."

Ruesp pursed his lips. "I remember," he said. "You were just a boy then. Eager to help."

"Have I changed that much?"

"I thought you had," Ruesp said. "But I see that I may have been wrong. If you really want to help, I won't tell you no."

"That's wonderful," Chej said, bobbing his head. "What shall I do?"

"Tally the supply numbers in these dispatches. Compare that to the master list of supplies issued and to the requests for more. Calculate what is *actually* required, and then check our armory and storehouses to see what we can fulfill and when."

"I can do that," Chej said.

"You understood everything I said?"

"Surprisingly, yes," Chej replied. "I'll begin now."

Ruesp nodded and watched him start through the pile of dispatches.

*What are you really up to, Chej?* he wondered. Chej was the last person he had expected to take anything seriously enough to form some sort of plot. And yet here he was, conniving his way into the war-heart for reasons Ruesp couldn't begin to guess at. It was interesting, bordering on exciting. He hadn't felt either thing in a long time.

CHAPTER EIGHT

# HANA

## TSAYE (IN ANCIENT TIMES)

TSENID'A'WI BUILT *something like a boat with a frame of bone, and she traveled on the river that flows between the worlds. She made friends with some of the spirit-people-fish in that river, and they led her on. She came to a canyon with high walls and fierce rapids where a monster-fish— it-is-armored-in-bone—waited to eat her, but she slipped through the rocks where it lay in ambush. It followed and almost caught her, but she changed herself into something quick and escaped. After that, in the course of her journeys she changed herself many times. This is how she survived. Because of that, we sometimes call her (or him, or them) Nelehi, The One Who Becomes Repeatedly. As a title, it is not unique to her. It is an appellation we all strive toward.*

★ ★ ★

DISLIKING THE company of corpses, Yash returned to her rooms to await Deng'jah and plan her next move. Halfway there she thought she heard something and stopped to listen, and after a few moments realized it was footsteps, getting closer.

A fine time to be without Deng'jah. She continued to listen for the sound of Needle's door opening. But the footfalls continued to draw nearer. Someone was coming to see her—or possibly Chej.

Moving as quietly as she could, she finished the ascent to her room. She rumpled the bed covering and then sat on it, keeping the knife behind her, hidden under a fold of cloth where she could easily reach it. The room was darker now but suffused with the red-orange glow of sunset filtering in through her west-facing window.

Soon, a woman of middle years appeared at the top of the stairs. Her black-and-grey hair was bundled up and mostly hidden underneath a grey cotton wrap. She wore a shift of the same material and carried an ornate wooden tray with several covered bowls and one bottle on it. Her face was marked by half a lifetime of expressions, and from the way the lines on it lay, it had not often been used to express joy. But, as Yash very well knew, looks could be deceiving.

"Hello," Yash said.

"Princess," the woman replied. Her voice was surprisingly high, girlish, although there was weight there, too. "I've brought some food for you and the prince, if the time is appropriate."

"I'm hungry," Yash said. "So it is appropriate, I think." She studied the woman for any sign that she was suspicious. Had she noticed anything passing Needle's room? Was she headed there next? If so, she might have to kill her, or at least take her captive. Killing an unarmed servant didn't suit her, but if that was what was required, she would have to find the resolve.

But not yet.

"And the prince?" the woman asked.

"He has gone down the stairs on some business of his own," Yash replied. "But I do not mind eating alone. May I ask your name?"

"My name is Hana," the woman said.

"Hana, my name is Yash, of the Spread Across Water Clan. Are you the cook as well as the bringer of food?" she asked.

"I am Tower Master Needle's servant," she replied. "I do a number of jobs for him. Cooking for his guests and serving them are among my assigned tasks."

"I am certain I will enjoy this meal," she said. "Does Master Needle also eat at this hour?"

"No," the woman said. "He eats… whenever he wants. He comes to the kitchen when he is hungry."

"Really?" Yash said. "May I also do that? To spare you the trip up?"

"Yes. But the food will be better if I know in advance when you are coming. Master Needle does not care about that, but I thought you should know. Also, if you tell me your preferred time of dining, I can prepare the food at that time."

"I understand," Yash said. "This is all new to me, so I thank you for explaining. If I want to find you, where should I look?"

"The kitchens are on the fifth level of the tower."

"I wonder, I have not smelled smoke from the cookfire."

"We do not have a cookfire, princess. We have a stove. It is situated on a covered balcony and well vented, so there is no danger of smoke or fire in the tower."

Yash didn't miss the slight condescension in her voice, but that was to her advantage. The less these people thought of her, the more she would be able to accomplish before they caught on.

"How astonishing!" Yash said. "You may put the tray on the floor, there by the door."

"It's getting dark," Hana said. "Should I light a lamp for you?"

"I'm enjoying the sunset right now," Yash said. "I can light the lamps on my own."

"You know how to use the spark-striker?"

"Yes," Yash said. "We have spark-strikers in Zeltah."

"Very well," the woman said. "When shall I return for the plates?"

"Morning?" Yash asked. "When my husband returns, I don't wish us to be disturbed."

"Of course," Hana said. "Night be kind to you."

"And you," Yash said.

She watched Hana exit and vanish down the stairs.

She felt a slight puff of air touch her cheek as Deng'jah reappeared.

"There you are," she said.

"Here I am," Deng'jah replied. "What sort of mess are you in now?"

"Follow that woman, please," she said.

"Of course." Deng'jah vanished. Yash took the knife in hand and padded down the stairs. Hana passed Needle's rooms and kept going.

By her count, the tower had eight floors. When Hana said the kitchen was on the fifth, Yash didn't know if she was counting up from the ground or down from the top. On her way up, she had seen the openings to various rooms but hadn't been able to tell much about them. She thought they were mostly empty. Certainly there were no guards higher than the ground floor, or Deng'jah would have said so.

She stopped when Deng'jah reappeared on her shoulder.

"She's gone into a room on the next floor," he said. "There's a kitchen there and a storehouse. Three other servants. Your friend has just uncorked a bottle of wine and has begun to drink. She is drinking a lot, quickly."

"Good," Yash said.

"One of the others is asleep. The third is just a child. If you wait a bit, you can probably kill them all with very little effort and without raising any alarm."

"Maybe," Yash said, starting back up the stairs. "But why waste my time on servants when I can strike at greater targets? What did you discover about the Earth Center Tower?"

"There's no straightforward way from here to there," he said. "You would have to go down into the fortress and back up, or climb the wall around it, where I sense many eldritch sentinels."

"And the Sharp Horn Tower?"

"That's easier. You could go west across the rooftop. It has windows near the level of the roof."

"I see," Yash said. "Let me think about this. Go ahead. The woman brought me some food, and I'm hungry. Can you tell if it's poisoned?"

"Yes. It isn't."

"Thanks, Deng'jah."

THE BIG bowl contained *deel* meat stewed with sharp and sour spices and garnished with little spherical dumplings. The two smaller plates contained fried grass-ear mushrooms and some sliced yellow and orange fruit she didn't recognize. The stew was too spicy, and the fruits were too sweet and had a weird aftertaste. The mushrooms, though, she liked a lot. She ate as much as she dared; she couldn't become completely full, or it would make it harder to fight. The carafe contained wine of some sort, which she did not drink. There was potable water in the room, and she needed her senses about her.

"What's in the Sharp Horn Tower?" she asked Deng'jah as she finished eating.

"I don't know," he said. "It has many eyes watching out for it. I couldn't find a way in without being noticed. And there's that bird. It's calmed down a bit, but it is still watchful."

"Well, I will find out, won't I?"

"We're going now?"

"There's really no time to waste, is there?" She rose and looked out the window, focusing her attention not on the city or the fortress, but on the far away: the direction of her homeland.

The western horizon was limned by a dim yellow glow, and a few high clouds burned with red-gold light, but higher in the heavens, the stars had begun to reveal themselves. A wind fluttered and died, but it carried a familiar smell. She studied the distance more closely. To the north, she saw faint flashes and a darkness that suggested heavy clouds. She could see some of the stars of the Tail flickering more than usual.

"The wind is sweeping the stars," she murmured. "A storm in the mountains. But I think it's moving this way."

"You may be right," Deng'jah said. "Although it would be strange this time of year. It's too far away for me to tell."

"Any storm in the mountains is strange this time of year," she said.

"Should I go see?" Deng'jah asked.

"No," she replied.

The sky brightened then. At first she thought it was a flying star, but it lasted much longer than any she had seen before, leaving a long, sparkling trail behind it.

Then she saw another, following almost exactly the same path.

"What is that?" she wondered. She looked in the direction the first two had come from and saw a third coming from out of sight. As she followed its course and watched the light dwindle to a tiny point but never burn out, she felt a gall form in her.

"Those are going to Zeltah," she murmured. "It's coming from someplace on the other side of this tower."

She took the stairs two at a time going down, paused to make certain no one was there, then ducked back into Dzhesq the Needle's sorcery room and went straight to the eastern window. Facing away from the sunset, there was little light at all. Even the rising constellations were dimmed by the smokey haze from hundreds of cookfires. She looked down and saw the balcony Hana had spoken of.

She noticed the next flash from the verge of her eye, but the streak of its trajectory was enough to determine its origin. As she suspected, it came from one of the towers.

"Deng'jah, you saw Chej's drawings," she said. "Which tower is that?"

"The Bright Cloud Tower," he said.

"Master Zu the Bright, correct?"

"If Chej is to be believed."

"Second only to the Emperor himself."

"Again," Deng'jah said.

"Let's kill him, then."

"Yes," Deng'jah replied. "Let's do that. I feel time may be turning against us soon."

CHAPTER NINE

# ZU THE BRIGHT

YASH RUSHED farther down the stairs, past Hana's rooms to the fourth level where she remembered seeing another doorway. There she slowed, took a breath, and went in quietly, not certain what to expect.

*"Deng'jah?"* she asked in her little voice.

*"No one in here,"* Deng'jah said.

The room was a storehouse, packed with boxes, urns, sacks. She took a moment to look for anything that might be useful—weapons, say—but it all seemed to be either food or fuel.

But there was, as she hoped, a window. It was narrow, but not so narrow she couldn't squeeze through. From here she had a much better view of the Bright Cloud Tower and the eastern half of the fortress.

At the northern range of her vision she could make out of the Earth Center Tower and the wall surrounding it. It was closer than the Bright Cloud Tower, and she now saw what a difficult ascent that would be, although she had some thoughts about how to accomplish it. In none of her plans, however, did she manage to enter without sounding an alarm, not given what Chej and Deng'jah had told her of it. Anyway, it was the Bright Cloud Tower currently raining fiery destruction on her homeland. That had to be stopped immediately, and she might manage it without starting a general call-to-arms against her.

She had to cross the fortress rooftops. Getting there in daylight unseen would have probably been a hopeless cause. But now, in this dimming grey-gold light, she could probably do it. She had to try; there was no time to wait for the full embrace of night.

She leapt from the window, sailing out over the alley separating the tower from the rooftop jutting up below. She landed with almost no sound and rolled to absorb the impact and returned to standing. It was a little like running in the cliffs at night, she thought. The roof was not one flat plane: rather, it was a jumble of smaller roofs at different levels, some made of brick, some of tile, some of slate, some of plaster over lathed wooden beams. She thought that maybe once the fortress had been many smaller buildings that eventually grew so crowded they were now all stuck together with few gaps between them. It was rapidly very nearly as dark as the cliffs at night, too. Lamps and lanterns lit windows in the towers, and scattered courtyards were wells of faint light, but most of the fortress was under her feet, and whatever fires shone there were not in sight. The few that were visible were obvious and easily avoided. She saw a handful of sentries in the distance, but they were all facing outward, watching for enemies approaching the fortress from outside.

Ahead of her one of the courtyards opened up like a canyon. She skirted around it and caught a few muffled lines of conversation as smelled smoke and grilling meat. In her homeland, most people slept when the sun went down or soon after. Would they do the same here? Probably.

If Chej's map was accurate, she was presently crossing over the xarim quarters. The Bright Cloud Tower loomed closer, northeast of her. To her right, south, the Red Coral Tower stretched starward. In the north, she could make out the Standing Pinion Tower and the Obsidian Spear clustered together like the Blue Needle and Yellow Bone towers: close enough for her to jump between. She wondered why. The other four towers on the spiral arms were more evenly spaced. It might be important. She would ask Chej when she saw him again.

In the north, something blotted out the stars. Yash ducked into the deeper shadow of a wall.

"The bird," Deng'jah said. "It's looking for me. And maybe you now. Maybe we should deal with it first."

"If we kill the bird now, everyone will know," Yash said. "Better if I kill it later."

"You have a point there," Deng'jah said. "But if we're going to be running around on these rooftops…"

"The bird is one of the naheeyiye," Yash said. "I cannot liberate it without killing this flesh the tower masters have imprisoned it in. But if I knew its name—"

"I don't know them all," Deng'jah said. "But that one is easy. That has to be Tch'etsagh."

"You could have told me that earlier," Yash said.

"It didn't come up."

Yash glanced back up. Fighting the bird right now would attract unwanted attention and probably rouse the whole fortress.

She had to deal with Zu the Bright first. The bird would come later. But there was something else she could do now that she knew its name.

"Quiet," Yash told Deng'jah. She closed her eyes, feeling the rhythm of her pulse, listening, trying to hear the distant thunder of the bird's heart.

*"Help me, Deng'jah,"* she little-voiced.

*"You told me to be quiet."*

*"I still want you quiet."*

For a moment there was nothing, but then, on her shoulder where Deng'jah sat, she felt the faint *tiq tiq* of the bird's pulse.

*"That's it,"* she murmured. Then she sang, timing her words between her heartbeat and the bird's.

*Tch'etsagh*
*Inside there*
*In the monster they have dressed you in*
*Listen*
*I am the mouse too small to see*
*I am the wind with no fragrance*
*I am the tall grass that only moves with the wind*
*I am nothing at all*
*Less than that even*
*Why notice me?*
*I am not even here.*

She finished her song. The bird was out of sight now. Had it worked?

Only one way to find out. She stood from the shadow and

continued toward the Bright Cloud Tower. Deng'jah went off ahead. The bird continued to circle above.

Two more of the flying stars had come from the tower since she started toward it, but now they seemed to have stopped. They were coming not from the highest window, but from maybe three floors down, still far higher than the roof she was on. She would have to enter through a lower opening and ascend. She studied the few lighted windows, searching for movement to indicate inhabitants, but didn't see anything.

Deng'jah appeared on her shoulder.

"The bird is resting," he said. "Your song appears to have worked. And the Bright Cloud Tower seems empty. Other than whoever is sending the flying stars."

"How can that be? Did you go in?"

"I looked, but I didn't enter. It stinks of sorcery, and there may be alarms I can't see from outside. I can go in alone, but if I'm noticed, Bright will be ready for you. If we go in together, he also may notice us, but we'll also already be inside. It's up to you."

"We'll go in together," Yash said.

By that time, they were at the base of the tower. As with the Blue Needle Tower, there was a gap between the wall of the xarim compounds and the tower, and a window facing southwest that she thought she could jump to. It was dark inside, but, as she gauged the distance, the opening suddenly flashed with a blinding white light, as if lightning had struck within. Except the light was brighter and whiter than lightning.

"What was that?" she asked.

"Something sharp and quick," Deng'jah said. "Something that doesn't belong here. I don't like the feel of it."

"Interesting," she said. Then she jumped.

This time, nothing interfered with her trajectory, and she landed feet-first on the stone ledge of the window, folding into a crouch, catching the walls of the opening to steady herself.

She waited a few breaths for her vision to adjust to the deeper darkness of the room. "Deng'jah," she said. "I need more light to see by."

The insect didn't answer, but he began to glow with a soft, yellow-green light, enough for her night-familiar eyes to find the way.

Then the smell entered her, like the sharp air after a lightning strike, like coal heated to burning in a fire.

"What's here?" she whispered.

"Nothing," Deng'jah said. "Nothing alive, anyway."

As she turned through the entranceway, she saw what he meant.

The floor was littered with bones, mostly of small animals, but a few very large ones. They were piled around four tall crystalline stones that stood floor-to-ceiling. The pillars formed the corners of a square, with a tall person's arm's length between them. The bones were thickest just around it, some of them still articulated into skeletons. There were many different sorts of animal: some with sharp teeth, some with dull, flat, grass-chewing teeth, some with beaks. But none of them looked familiar. As she got closer, she saw some of the remains weren't bones at all, but more like the outside shells of insects. On the top of a pile lay one skeleton that glowed a very faint orange color, fading as she watched. It was the size of a small dog, but it had a long carapace, like a turtle that had been stretched thin.

"Deng'jah, what is this?" she asked.

"It's a crack," he said. "A crack in this world that leads to the White Brilliant."

"And these animals came through it?"

"Yes," Deng'jah said. "So it appears."

"And why are they all dead?"

"Because they cannot live here," Deng'jah said. "In the White Brilliant, everything burns more intensely than here."

"Don't speak in riddles, Deng'jah. Be plain. I have some experience with the White Brilliant."

"You've been at the edges of it," Deng'jah said, "where it meets other worlds. This opening goes to somewhere near the navel of that world. Living things there move faster. They don't live as long. The fire that gives them life burns hotter than in our world. But so does the air, the water, the earth itself. Everything is brighter, hotter, more alive. When they pass into our cooler world they—I think they just burn up."

"And if I go through there?"

"I don't know what would happen to a human being. The White Brilliant is a big place, like a house with many rooms. Some of those rooms are tolerable to your kind and our world tolerable to them, at least for a time. Others—like this one—may be too extreme. You might burn up, or age ten years in a heartbeat, or change into something unrecognizable. I couldn't say without entering. In your room—in the Blue Needle Tower—you fought something? I smelled something there."

"Needle had a chuaxhi sewn into his skin."

"Yes. Often sorcerers choose chuaxhi from the dimmer reaches of the White Brilliant because they can survive in our air without catching fire. But these bones we see? Those creatures were different."

"This is some sort of trap, then? For creatures from the White Brilliant?"

"It appears to be."

"For what purpose?"

"Ask your knife," Deng'jah said.

Suddenly Yash saw the skeletons with new eyes.

"Demon bone," she said. "To make weapons. And armor."

"Yes, of course. Where did you think those things came from?"

"Dead demons," she said. "But I suppose I imagined something more… like a warrior or a hunter, seeking out the demons as foes or prey—you know, defeating them in combat. Not… this."

"You don't understand the Hje, then," Deng'jah said.

"I'm starting to," Yash replied.

Skirting the bones, Yash made her way to the stairs and started up as Deng'jah flew on ahead.

The next floor was a garden of sorts, full of potted plants. Or at least, that's what she thought they were, for most of them were… weird. The tallest had thin, light-green stalks that went almost to the ceiling, where the stem divided into four or five thinner, shorter shoots that ended in little spheres. They had no leaves. Others resembled clumps of reeds in colors varying from red to deep brown, and still others were cone-shaped, white and grey, and reminded her of large mushrooms without caps.

She didn't go in, instead continuing upward.

The next room was the one she was looking for. Four arched windows provided a spectacular view of the fortress, the valley, and the mountains beyond. The floor was polished blue stone, which she was astonished to realize was purest dedłiji. She had never imagined so much of the precious material in one place. But as she tracked her gaze around, she saw that the walls were mosaics of precious minerals: red coral, agate, rose quartz, polished obsidian, jade, bits of copper, silver, and gold. The patterns were abstract but formed around dozens of holes in the wall, each about the size of her head and all filled with darkness.

"Deng'jah?" she asked.

There was no answer. But his light was gone.

Her scalp was tingling. She took a step back.

Light flashed all around her, incredibly bright, and for an instant she couldn't see. She backed up until she was against the wall, holding her knife in front of her. Another flash, and this time she felt something pressing her down, as if stones had been heaped on her. She couldn't breathe. She struggled harder then relaxed, hoping whatever it was would think she had passed out.

The next thing she knew, she was in the same room but upside down, turning slowly. She was tied, hands and feet, and suspended by rope from the ceiling. And she was naked.

A few arm's lengths away, a man stood watching her. He was a big fellow in red robes with a long, oiled braid. She recognized him from the wedding.

Tower Master Zu the Bright.

Master Bright approached her, hands behind his back. He tilted his head.

"Can you understand me?" he asked.

"Yes," Yash said.

"Then tell me—who are you?"

At first, Yash didn't understand. Bright had seen her already, several times. Then, glancing up at the length of her exposed body, she understood his confusion.

"My name is Tchiił," she said.

## CHAPTER TEN

# HSHENG

HSHENG SAT at a table in a darkened courtyard she did not recognize. The table was very long, seating dozens of people; oil lamps provided the only light. The cloying sweet scent of moonflowers hung in the air; she could see the blossoms and the snaking vines that bore them climbing up the stone walls enclosing the yard. All sorts of food had been placed on the table. Always hungry, Hsheng reached for it but then she saw the meat had maggots in it, the bread was full of bugs, the wine choked with dead moths. No one else seemed to notice; they ate and drank, they laughed. She didn't know any of them; they were strangers, which was unusual. But after a moment, she realized she was wrong. The man at the head of the table was the Emperor in one of his disguises. He was dressed as a very old man in purple robes and looked like he was asleep.

Thunder boomed, loud and near enough to rattle the bowls on the table. Still no one seemed to take notice. Hsheng looked around.

The sky was devoid of light. The flower-clad walls had no doors or windows. Thunder sounded again and again.

"I've never had food like this," the woman next to her said. She had the face of a beetle and was tearing apart bug-infested scrolls of bread as thin as paper.

"I hear the food is from the West," Hsheng told her. "From Zeltah."

"Aren't we at war with them?" a lizard-headed man asked, picking the maggots from a haunch of venison and flicking them up, one by one, on his long, forked tongue.

"That's why we're eating their food," Hsheng replied.

"That's a brilliant observation," the beetle-faced woman said. "But why aren't you eating?"

"I don't eat food like this," she said.

The thunder sounded again.

"Hear that?" the Emperor said. He looked awake now, and much younger, but his eyes were empty, like bits of polished white shell. "Listen to that, everyone."

"I hear it now," the lizard-headed man said. "I always heard it. From the very beginning."

"No, you didn't," Hsheng said.

"I heard it, too," the beetle-faced woman said. "But what does it mean? No one knows."

"You're all lying," Hsheng told her. "But I know what it means. It means I have to go."

THE ONE thing Hsheng liked less than sleep was being awakened from it. Sleep was a state that was difficult for her to achieve, but, more than that, she found that as she got older it grew harder and harder for her to come easily to complete wakefulness. The fog and illogic of dream, annoying even in its proper place, was doubly a nuisance in that it clung to her in the waking world. It was the muddiness of mind sleep left behind that she despised.

But the same impairment, of course, was her gift and her purpose. Her dreams had meaning, and that they stayed with her helped her sort out what they signified. However unpleasant she found it, it was one of the things the Emperor valued her for. She lay still for another few moments, enjoying the scent of something cooking nearby. Then she rose from her bed, bathed by way of a rag and a basin of water, and slipped on a robe of black cotton. She descended from her small apartment to the courtyard it overlooked, where four children were playing with a feather-trailing-ball and two of her sisters were readying the evening meal. The eldest, Dzhi, looked up as Hsheng came down.

"Sister," she said. "Did you have a good rest?"

Dzhi had a single streak of silver in her black hair, which was tied back with a bright yellow strip of cloth. The years had sculpted pleasant lines in her face, which showed best when she smiled, which was often.

Hsheng nodded and pretended to swat at her four-year-old niece Qek as she went flying by. "I need to sleep outside of the tower sometimes," she said.

"Because the dreams are different," Dzhi said.

"Because I love my sisters and never see enough of their children," she replied. But Dzhi was right; in the Earth Center Tower, her father the Emperor and Nalzhu, his xual–guardian, were such overwhelming presences they tended to cloud her dreams with their own.

"I don't see how you can sleep in the day," her sister said. "Not with these little creatures running about."

"They don't bother me at all," Hsheng said. "And I've been sleeping by day most of my life."

"The nights must be quiet in the tower," Dzhi said. She sounded a little wistful.

Hsheng nodded noncommittally. Usually the nights in the tower were quiet. Often enough, however, there was a certain amount of screaming and wailing that had to be ignored. Hsheng anticipated she would soon be enduring a season of such racket, as the captives from the war with Zełtah arrived and her father picked his new brides from among them. But she didn't want to dispute Dzhi's fantasy of what life in the tower must be like. Dzhi, after a long day running a household and caring for children, must also cater to the needs and desires of her husband. Dzhi didn't like her husband very much, and Hsheng didn't blame her or envy her in the slightest.

In the tower her father, the Emperor, was the only man. He did not trust other men near him, and he did not generally like men or care for their company. There were sixty women in the tower. Fifty-nine of them were her father's wives. The sixtieth was her.

"Will you eat with us?" Dzhi asked.

Hsheng glanced at the pot of stew simmering on the hearth. Her stomach felt flat and empty.

"I would like that," Hsheng said. "But I'm afraid I have to hurry to see Father."

Dzhi took her in her arms. "We don't see you enough, sister," she said. "Come again soon."

All of the daughters with male children lived in the Emperor's Keep, a walled area surrounding the Earth Center Tower—that included wives and daughters. The men married to the daughters were also allowed, but the Emperor's adult sons lived elsewhere. There weren't many of those. Her father didn't like male offspring.

There were also plenty of male guards in the Keep. Most were at or near the entrances to the Keep, either at posts or in their barracks. But there were always four in the outer yard of the tower, and they watched her arrive. She recognized the xi of the guard among them, a burly man named Ruj. His face tightened a little as she approached. When he reached for her, she stepped back.

"You recognize me, don't you?" she said.

"You are Hsheng, daughter of the Emperor," Ruj replied. "But you must be searched, like anyone else."

"You're sure of that?"

"Very sure," Ruj said.

"If you know who I am, you know I speak for the Emperor. You know I am his instrument."

"Inside of the tower, maybe," Ruj said. "Among the women in the tower you are first. But not out here. Out here, I'm the one who speaks for the Emperor. I'm the one who interprets his will. And you certainly cannot command me to do anything, and most especially not to shirk my duty."

For a moment she did not respond as she struggled to keep her fury contained. Then she bowed her head slightly and lifted her arms.

Ruj began searching her. "Hsheng likes to test us," he said to his companions. "She wants to be certain the laws are always observed. If I had failed to search her, she would have reported us to her father. Isn't that true, lady?"

She cocked an eye at Ruj. "We all must take out duties seriously. And we all must know the roles we play."

Ruj kept his hands respectful. Then he nodded. "You may enter the tower, lady," he said.

She passed through the stone arch and climbed the stairs until she reached her father's chambers where she found him on a bench, his head in his hands. He was naked except for a long strip of white cotton cloth wrapped around his lower stomach, legs, and groin.

He had the body of a young man, long-limbed and soft in appearance. He had no wrinkles; his muscles had almost no definition. He moved as if the joints of his arms and legs were only pretending to be normal. Sometimes she expected them to bend in the wrong direction, even though in her many years with him she had never seen that happen. His eyes were changeable, sometimes quick and alert like a falcon's. Other times they were more like coral beads or holes drilled into a hollow tree. Just now they seemed human, and old, and tired.

The chamber itself was vaulted, windowless, with flowers painted in gold and silver on the curved ceiling. The bench her father sat on was at one of the narrow ends of a rectangular pool. The water glowed from the light of the golden fish that swam in it, fish that were said to have been brought from the Moon World. In fact, the entire chamber—the Earth Center Tower itself—was rumored to have descended from the Moon World in a single piece and settled right here. The fortress and the Empire had grown outward from it. She thought it was possible; she also believed it could be a lie. It could even be something that the elder Hje really believed but that wasn't true. Her father knew, of course. Of all of the Hje, only he remembered the Moon World. Of all of those living, only he had been born there. He was old. Very old.

And for Hsheng, that was becoming a problem. There were

tales of true immortals, but she did not believe them. Everything and everyone grew old, and eventually everything either died or transformed into something so different the result was indistinguishable from death. Her father still looked young, but his mind… his mind was old.

"Father," she said. "Emperor."

"I'm here," he replied. "Is it you, Nalzhu?"

"No," she replied. "It's Hsheng, your daughter. I am here in the room with you."

His gaze wandered around the room, seemingly at random, but when it found her, it came to rest.

"I've been dreaming," he said. "I have trouble sometimes. Knowing when the dream is over."

"I understand the feeling, Father," she replied.

"Yes, of course you do. You are my daughter."

"You mentioned Nalzhu," she said. "Is he speaking again? Have you heard from him?"

"I thought his power was fading," her father said. "In the old days, he spoke often. Sometimes he was hard to control. He was willful. But in recent years, he has been silent. He… it seemed like every passing year made him less. As if he was fading away."

"You've told me this before," she replied.

"It was supposed to be a secret," he said.

"From the other tower masters," she said.

"Exactly," her father said. "You must tell no one. But you must make the tower masters believe that one of them will soon succeed me, do you understand? Some will seek alliance with me. Others will plot against me, and each other. It will keep them occupied. Keep them from noticing."

"I have done that, Father," she replied. "Remember? We already spoke of this."

"And we must invade Zeltah. Find another xual for the tower, one more powerful than the others."

"The war began this morning," she said. "Try to remember. You gave the order yourself."

He frowned, then nodded. "Oh, yes," he said. "I do remember. And all of this—*but* all of this, it all—"

His gaze sharpened, and she suddenly sensed intelligence behind it. A mind fully present, his eyes glassy, a viper contemplating prey.

"Something has changed," he said. "Nalzhu spoke to me. He tells me he is growing stronger once more."

"Does he?" she said. "Is it true, do you think?"

He nodded. "Yes. It is almost as in the old days. He is pushing again. He wants more."

"More what?"

"I don't know. Neither does he. Something is changing, but we do not know what. From this tower, we cannot see. Something prevents us. But you are different, daughter. You were born of this world. Find out, daughter. Discover what is happening, why Nalzhu is suddenly in my skull again. He has filled up the tower and rages against it. I feel power as I have not in many years. This is good. But why? We must know and make certain it continues."

"Of course. But—you mentioned this just now, but you've spoken of it before—once, didn't you have trouble… containing Nalzhu? Didn't he once overpower you?"

"Long ago," her father said. "But I know better now. I know better. As my bones grow brittle and my mind weakens, as the line between light and shadow dims, as power leaks from a thousand tiny holes…" He smiled. "I know better now."

She put her hand on his and wondered if he had really answered her. Or if he had heard the question she had asked. It seemed like he was talking about something else.

But she knew better than to press it. And her father was right. His power was here, and to leave it at his age was dangerous. But it also limited him.

That was what she was for. The Emperor had many children, but she alone attended him in this way.

"I exist to serve you, Father," she said. "But you could make my job easier."

"Yes?"

"You could give me command over the guard. Or at least give me a title equal to the xi. It makes it difficult if I must play at subservience to them."

"In this tower, your only superior is me," her father said.

"Yes. But the moment I step outside of this tower—"

"The reason you are subservient to none but me—in the *tower* —is because I am the only man here," he snapped. "But it is a fact that you are a woman, and as such you must be submissive to any male Hje. This is not a flexible rule. It is the core of our covenant as a people. You can pass on my commands to men, but you can never command them yourself. You know this. Your wishes are irrelevant. That it might make your life and my life easier is irrelevant."

She put her head down. It had been a long time since he had spoken so forcefully and with such conviction. She had believed he had begun to waver, and in that she had seen—what? A possibility. A different life than the one prescribed for her. But he was right, wasn't he? The universe was made a certain way and no other. She was lucky that he had chosen to have only women in the tower. It gave her power she would not have otherwise had. But it had also created illusions she must now overcome.

"I will do as you say, Father," she replied.

"Do that," he said. "I will rest. Wake me when I am needed."

CHAPTER ELEVEN

# XUEHEHS THE OBSIDIAN

AT FIRST, Chej could do little more than stare at the numerals in front of him, distracted as he was by thoughts of the things Yash had done. Part of him was still having a hard time accepting it all. It occurred to him that he hadn't actually *seen* her kill anyone. Maybe she hadn't done it herself. She had the metal fly demon; perhaps she had another bigger, more dangerous one, like those the tower masters controlled. Some monster he just hadn't yet seen. Certainly she was a sorcerer, capable of compelling him to help her. He knew that even before she confirmed it.

Could he tell anyone about Yash and her plan? Could he tell Ruesp? Probably not, or she would have never sent him down here. Even thinking about it made him feel ill. And even if he did manage to say something, no one would take him seriously. He was, at best, an object of ridicule. He was used to that. But considering what Ruesp had just let slip, he now understood that he might face a fate far worse than being the victim of derision.

He had been careful, or thought he had. He thought no one knew of his secret shame. But according to Ruesp, it was common knowledge. This seemed bizarre, as he had been unaware of it himself for many long years, or at least unwilling to admit it to himself. The consequences of being like he was were terrible to contemplate. Death or purification were the usual punishments, with exile occasionally thrown in to keep one guessing. And purification was only marginally better than death from what he understood of it. He had heard it rumored that sexual deviance was sometimes overlooked among the Hje themselves, so long as the person so afflicted took care to never act out their desires or behave inappropriately in public.

It seemed that the rumors were true. He had been careful to preserve appearances and so had been 'tolerated.' But knowing that did not offer him any comfort. His mind revisited his conversation with Zu, and many other conversations he'd had with the other Hje, and with each remembrance he became more and more convinced that Ruesp was right. He was a fool, living in a house built of his own stupidity. Yesterday, he had been unaware of the danger he was in—had been in—for years. He now felt that somewhere an unseen bowman had an arrow pointed at him and that it had been pointed at him for a very long time. It would take very little on his part to give the archer cause to shoot that arrow.

Consumed by these worries, he at first pretended to do the figures more than actually *do* them. But by the time he got through the first sheet, his concentration improved as his mind fled from the terror of his predicament.

Chej had forgotten how much he really enjoyed working with numbers. It gave him a sense of control, of consistency. If the numbers didn't come out right, it was never anything wrong with them—it was either the person providing the numbers or figuring them who was wrong. If a manifest claimed a hundred and seventy-eight bows had been sent with the army, but the armory account was of five hundred bows total and only a hundred remaining, that could only mean a mistake had been made. A massive one. Or it might not be a mistake at all; the numbers might have been misreported on purpose.

He brought this to the attention of Ruesp.

"It's like I told you," the old man said. "You have to check it against the actual inventory."

"I will," Chej said. "But let me first have a look at the spears and shields as well. No need to make more than one trip to the armory."

"When you go you'll need this," Ruesp said. He pushed a scroll toward him. Chej opened it and saw that Ruesp had designated him by name as his personal agent. He put his own signature on it where Ruesp indicated, feeling… something. Pride? Or shame that the old man trusted him? How could such disparate emotions be confused? Once again he reached to try and remove the earring Yash had given him, but when his fingers touched it he wasn't able to complete the motion.

So much for that.

Chej went back to his numbers. Couriers came and went, some tired and ragged—runners from the battle—some from the towers. He managed to get the gist of what most of them were reporting. So far there was no news or alarm over a bunch of murders in the Blue Needle and Yellow Bone towers. Or wherever Yash was now.

What was he even doing? He shouldn't be helping her. Maybe the spell she had put on him obliged him not to work against her, but did it really require he actively render her aid?

He already had, hadn't he? Of course, when she was present, fear for his life was certainly part of what motivated him. But here, now, couldn't he just do nothing?

Doing nothing should be easy. He had done a great deal of nothing in his life. He was an expert in that field. But now there was a spark in him, a little fire he had never felt before. Like part of him honestly *wanted* to help her. It was certainly the spell, but it felt so real; knowing where the impulse came from didn't help.

He was only half-done with the shield count when Xuehehs, Master of the Obsidian Spear, entered the war-heart.

To Chej, Xuehehs the Obsidian had always looked weirdly fragile. He was one of the few people Chej knew who was taller than him, but the zuen's arms and legs might have been reeds knotted onto a longer reed of the same circumference. His features were fine, and rather lovely, but not entirely human-looking. His eyes were very large and luminous, his cheekbones absurdly high, and his chin was as pointed as an awl. His voice, on the other hand, had a sort of drawl to it and a faint accent that was either affected or a holdover from an earlier era. He started speaking to Xarim Ruesp immediately, without noticing Chej was there at all.

"Have you heard from Hsij?" he demanded.

"Hsij sent me a report a little after midday," Ruesp answered.

"It is now sundown," Xuehehs said.

"I am aware of that, Tower Master," the xarim replied. "As you must know, when one of you exerts himself, there is often a period of recovery needed."

"And how did Hsij exert himself?" Xuehehs demanded.

"See for yourself," Ruesp said, indicating the map. "He created a snowstorm in the mountains, from here to around here. It is meant to delay reinforcements to Zełtah."

"Is it?" Xuehehs said. "If that were the case, I should think the storm would stay in the mountains and fill the passes with snow. But my reconnaissance says there is a storm moving down from those mountains. Directly toward us. At the speed of a hawk on the wing."

"Indeed?" Ruesp asked.

"Indeed. I was formulating an attack of my own for nightfall, but this quite spoils it. Now I shall have to think of something else. Hsij has much to answer for."

Ruesp was frowning, studying the map. "Why would he move the storm in that direction?" he wondered. "That will sweep across our own troops and, yes, pass through this very valley."

"Ask him!" Xuehehs snapped. "I have better things to do—no, *vastly* more important things to do."

Chej watched the exchange nervously. If someone went to talk to Hsij, they would find him missing. And they would find a roomful of his guards dead, if Yash was to be believed. And if Yash was found out, what would happen to him?

As if that even mattered. The curse she had put on him ensured he had to act on her behalf anyway.

"I can carry a message to Hsij," he said.

Xuehehs turned his head. He looked startled.

"Chej," he said. "I didn't see you there. What could you possibly be doing in the war-heart?"

"He's helping me, as a matter of fact," Ruesp said.

"Oh," the tower master said. "That seems strange, Chej. But perhaps not so much, hey? I'm sure your wedding day is not what you hoped it would be."

"My bride is not in a romantic mood," Chej said.

"It should hardly matter," Xuehehs said. "She is your wife now, not some blushing flower. You don't need her consent."

"I would prefer it," Chej said. "Our marriage is just beginning, after all."

"Yes," the tower master said. "That really *is* my point. You must establish the law early on, especially with an outland barbarian who no doubt has wrong-headed views of such matters. But I suppose you have your—ah—own feelings about things. But look, push that over here, out of the way. See this instead. Do you know how convenient this is? The Emperor only just now gave me a message to deliver to Dzhesq. You and your bride are guests in his tower, aren't you?"

"We are," Chej said.

"Wonderful. Then I need not bother myself with the trip. Dzhesq is insufferable even on the best of days." He reached into his robes and pulled out a small letter with the Emperor's seal on it and handed it toward Chej.

Chej hesitated. If Xuehehs went into Dzhesq's tower, wouldn't Yash kill him? That would probably be what she wanted: a third tower master out of the way.

"Are you sure?" he said. "If the Emperor wanted *you* to deliver it, perhaps you should."

"Oh, nonsense," Xuehehs said. "It will be fine. The Emperor just wanted it delivered, and I happened to be there. I trust you, Chej. Just be very careful not to break the seal. The Emperor was very explicit that only Dzhesq should read this. Even I haven't the slightest idea what it says."

"But I am needed here," Chej said.

"Didn't you just volunteer to go to Hsij's tower?" Xuehehs said, his face darkening and eyebrows beginning to lower. "Then Blue Needle Tower is practically in the same place. I've already made it plain that I have important things to do."

"Very well," Chej said. He couldn't think of any way to refuse. He took the letter and slipped it into a pocket in his robe.

"And bring that idiot Hsij to account," Xuehehs said. "Tell him not to spoil any of my plans in future."

"I shall," Chej said.

Xuehehs spun on his heel and walked off. His peculiar gait was somehow ungainly and elegant at the same time.

"Hsij doesn't like you, as I recall," Ruesp said, when Xuehehs was gone.

"No, he doesn't. But if you send me, he will have to receive me."

"Yes. But as you know, he may abuse you anyway."

"This seems important enough to risk that possibility," Chej replied.

Ruesp nodded. "I like this Chej," he said. "Far better than the fellow I've seen skulking about the palace for the past many years. Very well. Go see Hsij and find out what his intentions are. Ask especially about the storm. Tell him the question came from me and that I will not take it well if you are injured. Then you can deliver Dzhesq his note and return here, with my thanks."

"It is my pleasure, xarim," Chej said. "I'll also make my trip to the armory while I'm out."

★ ★ ★

CHEJ DID go to Hsij's tower, even though there was no one there to speak to. He needed witnesses to say he had gone there. There weren't many: Yash had been right and more than half the warriors in the fortress were either in Zeltah already or marching there, and most everyone else was asleep or gone to their homes in the city. But he did say hello to some guards in the hallway before entering the Yellow Bone Tower. He climbed the stairs and soon saw more of Yash's handiwork. A dozen guards, killed by one woman with a knife and a talking insect on her shoulder. His wife.

He vomited again and then retreated down the stairs where he found an empty room and sat by a window to clear his head. He felt in his pocket for the letter to Dzhesq and pulled it out.

He remembered Xuehehs's warning, but of course Dzhesq was no longer in any condition to receive the letter, so, after struggling over it for a few moments, he decided to risk the Emperor's wrath and see what it had to say.

Tower Master Dzhesq the Needle,

Certain ambassadors from the Unaligned Kingdoms remain unconvinced, and reports are that the groom has been seen coming and going from the bride's rooms, contrary to expectations. Whether consummation has occurred is unknown, but it has created an appearance. The bride must be protected, of course, even after the untimely murder of the groom. Who could have imagined her reaction would be so violent? She is such a little thing, seemingly harmless.

Make it plausible. A kitchen knife, perhaps. You are inventive. Once all the evidence is in place, send word to the master of the Obsidian Spear.

The Emperor's mark followed.

It was all so absurd, he wanted to laugh. They meant to murder him and make it look like Yash had done it. Make it plausible, the letter said. Maybe a kitchen knife.

If only they knew how very plausible it was. That Yash could easily beat him to death with her fists.

He took a few deep breaths, and a few more, trying to think. He had not adjusted to the reality that his aberrant nature was widely known. Now he was holding the mandate for his execution. It was hard to get hold of. Hard to breathe.

How quickly did they expect Dzhesq to do the job? By the end of the night, certainly, and probably immediately. That didn't give him much time to—to what? Escape? He didn't know. What could he do, with everyone he knew turned against him?

Several more guards saw him leave Hsij's tower. He forced a smile at them and nodded. Then he went directly to the armory, as he had said he would. He showed the attendants there his license from Ruesp and then quickly began hunting through the inventory.

Through the weapons.

Maybe he *could* do something. It wasn't much, certainly not a plan; but it was an idea.

He found a bow, some arrows, and a xarim's long knife. He wrapped and tied them in packing cloth.

The guards looked a little curiously at his packages when he left, but they didn't ask any questions. The sentries in Dzhesq's tower were a little more pressing, but he told them he had some things for the sorcerer, and, given that he had a warrant from Ruesp, they let it go at that.

Yash wasn't in her rooms, nor was she in what Chej had begun to think of as the Chamber of Corpses.

He paused a moment, trying to sort out his options, but now that he had time to think some more, he found he was starting to have an even harder time breathing.

*They are going to kill me*, he thought. His own family. The Emperor himself had ordered it. Chej had thought that he knew what he was doing. Sort of. He would get Yash more weapons, and she would do what she had promised. She would kill all of the tower masters and the Emperor, and whoever else crossed her path. With them all dead, maybe he would be safe.

Now he was starting to realize that he had probably lost his mind. The shock of reading the order for his own murder had been too much, and he had verged into madness.

And now, to find that Yash wasn't even here…

Where was she? Surely storming another of the towers with her talking insect.

He sat down on the steps and put his head in his hands, steadying himself to take deep, slow breaths.

Ruesp would be wondering where he was right now. He might send someone else to Hsij's tower, or to this one. His thoughts were jumbled, and he was all but certain that he was doomed, but the longer he could put off his fate, the better. The more time for *something* to happen.

So he had to act as if nothing was wrong. He had to go back and report to Ruesp that Hsij was fine and that he had delivered the letter to Dzhesq. After that, who knew? But at least he would be doing something.

He left the weapons in Dzhesq's rooms. If someone else found them, they might not immediately connect them with his demure bride. Then he went back downstairs to the war-heart.

CHAPTER TWELVE

# TCHIIŁ

TSAYE (IN ANCIENT TIMES)

SEEKING A *new home, Tsenid'a'wi at last came to Nyen'łtchiki, The Red World. The Red World was mostly desert. It was hot and dry and inhospitable. But there was life. There was a great river, and rains came every year to replenish the waters. Tsenid'a'wi thought it would be a hard, but a better place than the Ocean World. There were many spirit-people-animals already there, of many clans. Some were like the animals we know today: some were like insects, some resembled fish. Many looked a lot like frogs. In fact, the Red World was also called Nyen'ch'ahł, The Frog World, because so many of its inhabitants resembled the frogs we have today. Still others were more like lizards. Some were very large, some small. Some had learned to walk on two legs, as humans and birds walk today, although there were no humans or birds. Tsenid'a'wi saw this and wondered if walking on two legs might be useful. He kept that thought for later.*

*Tsenid'a'wi went back and told his people about Nyen'łtchiki, The Red World, and many of them agreed that it sounded like a better place. But* many of the Heeyets would not go. They preferred the Ocean World, even with all its problems. Even with the risk of death, they preferred their home. And so they stayed.

But the others decided to go with Tsenid'a'wi to the Red World. But first they had to go to Qeemelehk'e, The Place Where They Changed and prepare to live on land. When they had changed into land creatures they went to the Red World, the Frog World, and made their homes for many generations. They met the spirit-people-animals who lived there. Some they became friendly with, some they became relatives to, some they became enemies of. Everyone kept changing, but still spirits and people and animals were the same. And like the Ocean World, the Red World was bounded by the Silent Stagnant and the White Brilliant, and so it changed, too.

## DA'AN' (THE MIDDLE PAST)

### TWENTY YEARS EARLIER

THE SOUND of thunder ran down the canyon, an invisible drummer the size of the sky. Wind came with it, mostly gentle, but gusting playfully now and then, stirring up the red, yellow, and brown leaves, ruffling Tchiił's hair like a grandmother's hand.

"It's raining on Spruce Everywhere Mountain," Q'esh said.

Q'esh was Tchiił's cousin, and his friend. They were of the same age. They had spent the day wandering up Tsełtchik Tch'i'a'i Gorge, playing in the creek, catching water-diver beetles and letting them go. They had made a magnificent dwelling inside of the compact limbs of a nut-pine and cracked its hard kernels between stones to get at the sweet white meat within. And they had wandered far from the tents their elders had pitched on the ridge downstream. When they started out, the sky had been blue, without the faintest mist to screen the sun. Now cloud-people were gathering in the northeast.

"Yes," Tchiił said. "I think it must be. But it isn't raining here."

"No," Q'esh said. "It isn't. But my uncle said to come back if it started to rain."

"It's not raining."

"He said if it rained *anywhere*," Q'esh said.

"It's a long way back," Tchiił said.

Q'esh nodded. Thunder muttered again, and more wind came, smelling wet. The willows nodded as if growing sleepy. A flight of mimic jays went by, all in a line. Reluctantly, the two boys started back down that canyon, toward the encampment, walking along the edge of the creek.

As they traveled, it seemed to Tchiił that the stream was talking to them, or perhaps singing. It began as a whisper, but with each step it grew louder, its message more urgent.

"It's getting deeper," Q'esh said.

His cousin was right. The stream was quickly becoming a river.

No, not a river. A flood. In the dreaming part of his mind, he could see it now: the rain falling on the plateau above, running off the sunbaked soil, finding its way downhill, filling all the dry stream beds.

All flowing here.

"We have to climb," Tchiił said.

The creek was twice the size it had been, climbing out of its bed and spreading into the oaks and sycamores, willows and cottonwoods and nut-pine along its banks. The tops of the long-shaggy reeds that grew at the edge of the water were almost covered already. The boys reached the slope of dirt and crumbled rock and scrabbled their way up it, pulling themselves along by the trunks of the trees. Below them, the sound of running water became a hushed roar.

The slope came up against the layered walls of red-and-yellow stone, and there they could ascend no higher, for the cliff was too steep and without sufficient handholds. Q'esh and Tchiił stumbled along, hoping to find a better surface for climbing. The water kept rising toward them. Thunder sounded again, this time very near, and the sky grew darker. Huge drops of rain began spattering against the leaves, and their feet began to slip.

"We're in trouble," Q'esh said.

"Yes," Tchiił agreed. Maybe they shouldn't have strayed so far. But it had been a nice day...

He closed his eyes as the rain began pounding them in earnest. It was cold, surprisingly so.

*Help us*, he asked.

But the stream was in no mood to help. He was excited, exuberant, running as fast as he could after long seasons of crawling. And the sky—the sky and its people did not care about the little things below them.

They pushed on as the sandy soil turned to slippery muck and began dragging them toward the flood of churning brown water. Tchiił saw a whole tree go by, roots and all.

A figure appeared in the rain ahead of them, walking in the same direction they were.

"Hey!" he said.

He saw it was a girl, maybe a little younger than they were. She gestured for them to keep up.

Not knowing anything else to do, they followed, and pretty soon she led them into a crack in the cliffs hidden by nut-pine that they probably wouldn't have seen in the downpour. Water was rushing down it, but the girl knew where the hand- and footholds were, and by following her they were able to climb up until at last they reached a pocket in the cliff, a little rock shelter that shed the rain.

Once they were in she turned around, and for the first time they could see her face.

It looked as if she was wearing a mask made of white sycamore bark, with two little holes for eyes and a slightly larger one for her mouth. Then Tchiił understood it wasn't a mask at all.

The girl was a naheeyiye. Someone had heard his plea after all.

"Older sister," he said. "Thank you."

"You are welcome," she said. "You are welcome, Yeqeeqani."

"That isn't my name," Tchiił said. But even as the words escaped his mouth, he knew it was, or would be.

The girl's mask-face showed no expression, but she inclined her head toward him.

"Remember us," she said. "And remember those who were taken."

"I will," Tchiił said.

"It is good," the spirit said. Then she turned and vanished into the rain.

He felt tired. He and Q'esh curled up together and were soon asleep.

When they awoke, the sun was shining. Everything outside smelled wet.

"You've changed again," Q'esh said. "You are T'ade now."

T'ade nodded. So she had.

"I never know when it will happen," she said. "They say when I was a baby, every time I fell asleep I woke different. Sometimes with the parts of a boy, sometimes with those of a girl, sometimes both. Now it doesn't happen as often."

"I wish I could change," Q'esh said.

"Mother says everyone does," T'ade replied. "And no one does."

"But everyone can *see* your change," Q'esh replied.

"Does that matter?" T'ade asked.

Q'esh shrugged. "Do you think one day you will be just a boy or just a girl? Just Tchiił or just T'ade?"

T'ade considered that for a few moments then shook her head. "I will always be both, whether I change like this or not."

"Then why do you have two names?"

T'ade thought about that as she poked her head out of the shelter and gazed up at the sky. It had been grey, but the cloud-people had moved on and now it was blue again. Tonight it would be black. But it was always the sky.

"That spirit called me one more name," she said. "Yeqeeqani."

"I heard her," Q'esh said. "Everyone has been saying that about you."

"I know," T'ade said. "But it's one name too many. You're right, Q'esh. No more boy names and girl names. No more T'ade and Tchiił. And I'm not Yeqeeqani, either—not yet, at least."

"So what can I call you?"

"Cousin."

"I have other cousins," Q'esh pointed out.

"Then call me what my father and my uncle always do," she replied. "Call me Yash."

"And what about those other names?"

"They'll always be there, if I need them."

★ ★ ★

"TCHIIŁ?" TOWER Master Bright said, as if the name tasted bad in his mouth. "Isn't that just the word for 'boy,' in your barbaric language?"

"It's what they call me," Yash said. It wasn't *exactly* a lie.

Bright put two fingers to the dimple between his nose and top lip, with his thumb on his chin.

"I know you people dislike revealing your real names," he said after a moment. "That is fine, for now. It's something I can pronounce, anyway. Do you care to tell me why you're here, Tchiił?"

"No."

Master Bright sighed. "I refuse to let this become tedious," he said. "You came to the fortress either to rescue Princess Yash or to murder tower masters, or both. And when you arrived, what did you see? The light of my bright-star arrows, speeding toward your homeland. You accurately guessed I was the most dangerous and immediate threat to your people, so you came here to kill me. Does any of that sound correct?"

Yash didn't say anything, but she strained at her bindings. They were strong.

*"Deng'jah?"*

But no answer came.

"I admit, I am impressed," Bright continued. "I still don't understand how you approached the fortress without being detected. More remarkably, you *almost* entered it unnoticed. But Ruzuyer— that's the large bird you might have seen overhead—perceived *something* out of the ordinary, which occasioned me to make a closer inspection. When I couldn't find you—which is strange, in

131

and of itself—I thought I might lure you to me by attacking your homeland in the most visible way possible."

"How did you know I was from Zełtah?"

"An educated guess. But correct, I gather."

Yash closed her eyes. "You are wise," she said. "The flying stars. What do they do?"

"It would be difficult to explain the agency to you," Bright said. "But imagine a ball of light, small where it strikes, but expanding: the size of a man, then a house, then a village, and everything in its illumination as if struck by lightning. It's really quite terrifying, but most effective where there are a lot of people at once. Towns, encampments, warriors massed for an assault. The farther the arrow flies, the larger the explosion. I can show you later, if our talk does not go well."

"You want something from me," Yash said.

"Yes," Bright said. "I want you to tell me everything about why you are here, what sorcery you used to fool our wards and sentinels, and whether there are more of you."

"Really?" Yash said. "That's all you want?"

"I'm asking nicely at the moment," Bright said. "But I expect I'll have to torture you. That will be nice, as I haven't tortured anyone in a long time. I have some new techniques I've been wanting to try. So, please, be as stubborn as you like."

Yash smiled. "As you say, I came to rescue Princess Yash. I told you my everyday name, but I am also called Yeqeeqani, the killer, the hero of my people. I came alone—there are no more like me. To enter your citadel, I disguised myself as a wind, a trick I learned from Nełts'eeyi Cheen, The Black Wind of the North. You are also correct about what brought me here—I was searching for our princess when I saw your flying-star arrows and decided to stop them."

Bright blinked. "You are forthcoming," he said.

"You have bested me," Yash said. "I am at your mercy, and now you know my secrets. What next?"

"I… well…" Bright said.

"I imagine you've already reported my presence to your emperor, and to the other tower masters."

Bright's gaze dipped slightly.

"Or maybe you haven't," Yash went on. "Maybe you were waiting to extract my secrets before presenting me to your emperor."

"Yes," Bright said. "That's it exactly." But the tower master stood there, frowning slightly. The silence washed downstream for a time.

"Unless you want something else from me," Yash ventured. "Something you don't want to bother the Emperor with."

Bright's frown deepened. "I do have another question," he said. He pulled something from his belt and held it up. The knife Yash had taken from Master Dzhesq the Needle.

"Where did you get this?"

"Um," Yash said. "That is a… um, knife, sacred to my people. Miłhushi, we name it. It is the weapon of the Yeqeeqani, given to us by the Yachaa, The Sun, in ancient times—"

"It is a knife made of demon bone, of Hje manufacture," Bright interrupted. "Where did you get it?"

Yash sighed and closed her eyes. "I found it," she said.

"I'm only going to ask you this once more," Bright said. "Where did you get this?"

Yash hung there for a moment, silent. Then she sighed. "If I say, my princess will die. I can tell you anything, but not that. Torture me if you must."

Bright snarled, turned, and strode forcefully out of the room.

When he was gone, Yash worked at her bonds some more, but they were too tight. She pulled herself up by her belly muscles, thinking she might chew through the rope holding her feet, but the fibers it was woven of were too tough. So she rested, conserving her strength.

Presently she heard footsteps, and then Bright came back into the room. He stood for a moment with his hands behind his back.

"You know by now that you are helpless before my power," Bright said. "Even if you were free of those bonds, you would have no hope of harming me. The same power that struck you down before would incapacitate you again, just as quickly, just as surely. Or simply kill you, if I desire."

"I believe that," Yash said. "The tower masters are mighty. This is known."

"And yet you meant to kill me. Don't deny it."

"I won't," Yash said. "I did mean to kill you."

"And someone *sent* you to kill me. Not your people. Someone here. Dzhesq. Master Needle."

Yash flinched then hesitated. "I know no one by that name," she finally said.

"Ha!" Bright said. "I knew it. I can see you are lying. Did you really think you could conceal the truth from me? I knew the moment you arrived that you must have had help from a tower master. The rustic little spirits of your country have no power here. Your princess is in the Blue Needle Tower. That tower belongs to Dzhesq. He caught you trying to rescue her, and then he sent you to kill me. He must have promised you he would release her if you did so."

Bright paced toward the south window. "It was a good plan. If you killed me, no one would suspect Dzhesq was behind it. If you failed and I killed you, still no one would be the wiser, and he would have lost nothing. He must have promised you that if you did as he asked, he would release the princess."

"I have never been in the Blue Needle Tower," Yash said. "But why would this—Needle, is it?—want to murder you, one of his own? A tower master like himself?"

"You do not understand our politics and doubtless have no interest—and perhaps not the capacity—to do so. Here it is, then. Dzhesq and I have our… differences. He has long plotted against me. This is not the first time he has conspired to do me harm. I never thought he would go so far as to kill me, but now we stand in front of it, don't we?"

"Please," Yash said. "I only care about my princess and my people. I only do what I must."

"Is that so, my would-be assassin? Do you confess that my reasoning is sound?"

Yash put on a doleful expression and then nodded. "I see I cannot deceive you," she said. "It is all as you say. Except that Master Needle himself arranged for me to enter the fortress."

"Of course," Bright said. "Dzhesq, for all of his faults, is as clever as he is devious."

"My princess knows nothing of this," Yash said. "Please do not punish her for my mistakes."

Bright regarded her for a moment. "Well, *Boy*," he said. "Here is what we shall do. Or rather, what you *must* do. Return to Master Needle. Tell him you have killed me. That will distract him and might earn his trust, at least for a few moments. Use those moments to kill him and return here with his head. Do this, and I will cease visiting destruction on your people."

"And my princess?"

"With Dzhesq dead, you may be able to rescue her. I will not hinder you, but I cannot be seen to help you, either. Your only other choice it to perish—here, now—with no hope of success whatsoever."

"If I attempt this, how can I kill a tower master?"

"Dzhesq plans to kill you, of course, so you will be unable to tell the Emperor of the bargain he made with you. But he will want to know if you succeeded in killing me. You will have a moment. Act quickly. He keeps a chuaxhi in his skin. Perhaps you have met it? Do not give him time to release it. He also keeps a creature of some power in his apartment, but, if he allows you in, it will not harm you."

Yash nodded with as much seeming reluctance as she could muster.

"I will do as you say, Tower Master Bright."

Bright nodded. "Of course you will," he said. He made a motion with his hand, not directed at Yash.

As she followed his gesture, she saw a creature emerge from one of the holes in the wall.

It was black, mostly head, the size of a toddler, with insect-thin legs and little feathery wings. It stared at her hands, and a dazzling beam of light shot from each of its eyes. She felt a flash of heat, and the ropes fell smoking from her wrists. She let her arms down so they were touching the floor as the creature repeated the trick with the bonds on her feet. She broke her fall with her hands and rolled up to standing. She went to the where her clothes were folded and started to put them on.

"I didn't ask," Bright said. "Why were you wearing a woman's shift?"

"It is what Master Needle gave me to wear," Yash replied. "He said I would not be noticed.'

"Some private joke of his perhaps," Bright mused. "Or perhaps he wanted you to appear more harmless than you already do. For a hero of your people, you are remarkably small and scrawny. You're hardly more imposing than your princess. But again, perhaps that is the point, yes?"

Yash nodded. "Master Needle believed that a larger, more imposing warrior would attract more attention," she said. "It does not seem to have mattered."

"No," Bright agreed. "He should have known better than to plot against me. I have always been his superior. Now, go the way you came."

"That will be difficult," Yash said. "I jumped out of his window and crossed the roof. I do not think I can jump far enough to reach his window *from* the roof. I may have to go through the fortress."

"Very well," Bright said. "It is no concern of mine how you reach him."

"But you said the clothing was wrong. And he had guards at the base of his tower."

"If you are wearing something different than you were when you left him, he will be suspicious. It will put him on guard."

"I understand that much," Yash said. "I will keep the woman's garment and change back into it when I enter his tower. But until then, perhaps I need clothing that will not attract attention."

"I see," Bright said. "Very well. Wait here."

While he was gone, Yash examined the room, this time from an upright perspective. The creatures in the holes must have been what rendered her unconscious. But what were they? She reached back through her memories, trying to remember some story that would explain them. But as with Needle's giant and Yellow's beetle-woman, they were too changed for her to identify. There was something a little familiar about them, but she could not quite fit the stones together to make a wall.

Perhaps Deng'jah would know. Or perhaps he had been destroyed.

Bright eventually returned with a bundle of garments.

"This is the uniform of a tower courier," he said. "Couriers are young men who take messages between the tower masters and other important people. It should allow you to move about without attracting attention. But do not test that. Go as quickly and directly to Dzhesq's tower as possible."

"Are there guards below?"

"Yes. Tell them you arrived here yesterday at midday and have been helping me with a task. None of them were on duty then."

Yash nodded and donned the outfit, which consisted of a skirt and top that wrapped around and tied at the waist. She wondered what set it apart from the clothes women were supposed to wear. The shift had been a single garment, but her wedding dress had been two, much like this.

She listened as Bright explained how to reach the Blue Needle Tower through the halls of the fortress. When she was sure she understood, she left, descending the stairs of Bright's tower.

The guards were alert by the time she reached the bottom floor. They stared at her suspiciously, but when she told them as Bright had instructed, they let her pass without comment.

When she was in the fortress, alone in a corridor, she felt the air stir on her shoulder.

"There you are," she said.

"I couldn't follow you into Bright's chambers," Deng'jah said. "The things he has in there would have discovered me."

"Do you know what they are?"

"Not for certain. But I have some ideas."

"Good. We'll talk about that later. Right now, find Chej for me."

## CHAPTER THIRTEEN

# PLOTS

ONCE CHEJ realized that his murder was imminent, it was hard not to think about it. It was frightening, of course. He didn't want to die. Maybe when he was old, when his body and senses were failing, the Midnight Road would be more attractive, or at least less terrifying. Maybe. But for now he preferred his heart beating. He had a small life, as such things were judged. Everyone who had ever been important to him was either dead or far and forever out of reach. But he liked himself well enough, and that was reason enough to go on living, wasn't it?

Maybe not. But it was what he had—*all* he had. And he didn't want to lose it.

But along with the fear, there were also other feelings that were becoming increasingly difficult to ignore. One was a sense of relief; yes, Yash's sorcery was forcing him to betray his family, and part of him still felt bad about that. The fact that his own people were planning his demise, however, helped that sit more easily. The other, related feeling was a growing sense of outrage. It had prompted him to carry weapons up the Blue Needle Tower for Yash. That impulse had come from him, not from any witchery she might have cast on him. The more he thought about it, the surer he was of that fact. If he had any chance of survival, it probably lay with his wife. Maybe she really could kill everyone. Or at least everyone who wanted to kill *him*.

That didn't stop him from trying to come up with another plan, though. Currently, he was pondering the logistics of simply leaving the fortress and going elsewhere. He wasn't sure where, exactly. Someplace outside of the Empire, surely, or else he would eventually be dragged back for execution. But where? North were barbarian kingdoms and then the Vhaleg Empire, where he would likely be taken prisoner or killed. West were more barbarians. South were the Nanj Kingdoms, vassals of the Hje. There could be no safety for him there. East was the great desert, and beyond that the fabled lands of Xiqa and Fsa, although what he knew about those distant kingdoms was probably mostly baby stories. He was beginning to regret not paying more attention during his geography tutorials.

Had someone just said his name? He looked up from his numbers. A person had entered the war-heart and was talking to Ruesp. A courier, one he didn't recognize. That wasn't unusual. More than half of the couriers were from the Nanj provinces. Wealthy vassals sent their sons to the fortress to ingratiate themselves to the Emperor. They came and went.

"Tower Master Zu?" Ruesp was saying. "Did he send a report?"

"Not written," the courier said. He had a low, scratchy voice and spoke with a thick accent Chej did not recognize. "He said to tell you."

"I see," Ruesp said. "Where are you from? Your accent is awful."

"Huiy, in the South, xarim," the courier replied.

"Chej!" Ruesp barked. "Take this courier's statement from Master Zu the Bright, will you? I have enough to do."

Chej squinted. The courier looked familiar. His broad, rounded face, the set of his mouth. Chej beckoned him over.

"I'll take your report," Chej said. "What is Tower Master Zu up to?"

"Do you really want to know, shegan'?" the boy said, very softly.

At first Chej thought the courier was making fun of him. He had changed his accent, for one thing; it had been broad, almost a parody of the Southern way of speaking. Now it was the same as Yash's. And the boy looked like Yash: startlingly so. He was a little taller, but just as compact. His face was not exactly the same, but they could certainly be brother and sister. Or cousins. Had Zełtah sent someone to rescue Yash?

What was happening?

Ruesp was back across the room, examining his maps.

"Who are you?" Chej demanded, his voice pitched low.

"Don't you know your own wife, shegan'?" Accent aside, he didn't sound like Yash. His voice had an unmistakably lower pitch and timbre. Chej continued to stare at the courier. Was he going mad? Was this just Yash, but in different clothing and using some weird sorcery to alter her voice?

No. More likely Zu was making fun of him. He'd used some enchantment to make someone look like Yash, but male. A male wife for the deviant Chej. Hilarious. Another little cruelty before they murdered him.

"This isn't funny," he finally said. "Who are you and what do you want?"

"I am Yash," the courier said. "I know I look a little different now. I do this. I change sometimes. We had a conversation in your camp, back in Zeltah. I gave you the earring, remember? The stone that the ants bring us from beneath the earth?"

Had he told anyone about that conversation? No. But maybe one of his guards had been listening. But the story he was telling himself was now getting too complicated, wasn't it? A guard would have to have reported an otherwise unnoteworthy conversation to Zu, almost word for word. Then Zu would have had to find a man that looked like Yash and had her same accent, taught him what to say, and then trusted he would do it. All for a cruel joke?

Zu didn't care enough about him to go through all that trouble. "Yash?"

"Yes, I've been trying to tell you. I change."

"Change?" he said. "What do you mean, change?"

"Well, at the moment I have a penis, for instance."

Chej saw a flash of color. For a moment, the blue-green insect was perched on the courier's shoulder. Then it was gone again.

"That's…" Chej looked again. "It *is* you."

"Yes."

"This is impossible. Not to mention an abomination." The very thought was revolting. Wasn't it? In all of the stories he'd heard growing up, the wickedest villains had been women who disguised themselves as men and men who disguised themselves as women. And yet, looking at this… male… Yash, he now saw the same eyes. The same person.

And yes, a killer, which suggested the stories might contain some truth. But somehow, it wasn't as upsetting as it should have been.

"Abomination?" she—no, he—said. "That is unkind, Husband."

"You're a sorcerer, too," Chej said. "I should have known. It explains how you were able to kill Dzhesq and Hsij."

"I killed both of them with a knife," Yash-not-Yash said. "I may need a little bit more than that to kill Bright. Are you able to listen to me now?"

"I—" He glanced back at Ruesp, who was now talking to another courier, this one with the markings of one having come from the battlefield. "Yes."

He listened as Yash explained her—his?—trip to Zu's tower and what happened there.

"Bright thinks Needle sent me to kill him, and so he sent me back to kill Needle. How much rivalry between these sorcerers is there? Do you think any of the other tower masters would turn on one another?"

"I am not a political creature," Chej said. "I do not think about such things."

"Well, try."

Chej stared down at his account sheets. "The tower masters are all in competition," he said. "Any one of them could be the next emperor, and they all know that. So it is well known that they plot against one another. Politically. It never comes to… assassination. A least not in a long time."

"But it has happened?"

Chej nodded. "Yes. In past generations. When the Empire was younger. Some attempts were even made on the Emperor himself, although they were all unsuccessful. It is now frowned upon."

"Yes, Bright clearly doesn't want to be seen as responsible for Needle's murder. Are there factions? If Bright is to become Emperor, what other tower masters must die?"

"Let me think about that." He looked up. "But look, if you can... change your form... why not become Needle, or Yellow? Or imitate one of their guards? Why imitate a courier that looks like... this?"

"I can only be different versions of *me*," Yash said. "I can be as you saw me before. I can be like this. Sometimes I am both. But I can't be someone else, and I can't do it whenever I please. It just happens."

Chej stared at Yash. "Just happens," he repeated. "How did this happen to you? Was it *done* to you?"

"What do you mean?" Yash said. "I've always been like this."

"Are all of your people like you? Able to change sexes?"

"Some. Most, maybe. But not all in the same way. Everyone is different."

"No," Chej said. "Not here. Here, almost everyone is the same. And if we're not the same..." He stopped and took a breath.

"If you're not the same, what?"

"Never mind," he said. "It's just—we aren't different. This—changing. Is this why you are the—whatever it is you said you were? The One Who Kills Them All?"

"Yeqeeqani."

"Yes, that."

"Of course not," she said. It looked like she was trying not to laugh. "That has nothing to do with how and why I change. That is another thing entirely. I chose to become Yeqeeqani. It was my wish. I had to study and train. It is a choice I continue to make."

Ruesp was done talking to the other courier. Chej saw him glance in their direction, register that they were still conversing, and then turn back to his work. Chej was torn; he wanted to know more. To know everything about this... magic. But it couldn't be now.

"Ruesp will become suspicious soon, if he hasn't already," he told Yash. "And I need to tell you something, too."

He told Yash about the message the Emperor had sent Dzhesq: the order to kill him and fabricate evidence that she had done the deed. When he was done, Yash studied him with those flinty eyes.

*I'm married to a man*, he thought. The world had turned upside down, and now it was going to crush him.

"I'm sorry," his 'wife' said. "That's awful. I can't imagine how I would feel."

"Just wait. When they find out what you've been up to, they'll make plans to kill you, too. In fact, that's probably planned already, even when they thought you a harmless little girl. The penalty for murdering a hje is execution."

"Oh, yes," Yash said. "Of course they plan to kill me, no matter what. But they aren't my family, are they?"

"No," Chej said, remembering what she'd said earlier about her family liking her. "You have a point there. Even though…"

She didn't say anything. She waited to see if he would come back to it.

"My mother and father were my family," he finally said. "But they're dead. The rest of these people…" He shrugged.

"Tell me what you want to do," Yash said. "When I sent you down here to spy, I didn't think you were in much danger. You can stay with me. It will be dangerous, but at least I can keep an eye on you. Or do you think you are safer here?"

"I'm more visible," Chej told her. "If they come to kill me here, at least someone will see it happen. I don't think anyone will lift a hand to prevent it, but…"

"You could go to Needle's tower and pretend to be dead."

"I could. But once the Emperor believes I am dead, he will wonder why Needle hasn't informed him of it. He will send someone, and they will find all of the bodies. And me."

"It could be a long time before that happens," Yash said.

"I don't understand," Chej said. "Why do you care if I'm in danger?"

"Because you're my husband," Yash said. "When you accepted my bride-gift, I took on an obligation to you. I may have had motives you didn't know about, but my oath is not lightly given. Ever."

He examined her expression. She—he—looked serious. Chej didn't know what to think. To him, it seemed ludicrous that she could be telling the truth. But it would have made sense to his father, who also took oaths seriously, and to his mother, who had never shirked a responsibility in her life.

They both seemed so distant now, so alien to his life these past ten years. His life in the fortress.

Chej sighed and clasped his hands together.

"What?" Yash asked.

"I feel useful here," Chej admitted. "Hiding, I would only worry about my fate. Here, I feel like I'm doing something."

"You are," Yash said. "You're helping my enemies with their war."

Chej shook his head. "I'm helping you, as you must know. Go back into the Needle's tower. You'll see. And I can do more. I just have to think about how."

Yash looked at him skeptically for a moment and then shrugged. "Very well," she said. "But if you suspect your life is in immediate danger, go to Needle's tower and stay there. I will send Deng'jah to check on your whereabouts from time to time."

Chej nodded. "Your earlier question," he said. "I believe that Needle and Yellow were allies, along with Sha of the Sharp Horn

Tower, Xuehehs of the Obsidian Spear, and Qaxh of the Red Coral Tower. Horn, Obsidian, and Coral. They are all friends of the Emperor. And all of them have opposed Bright in the past." He dropped his eyes. "I could be wrong," he admitted. "As I told you, I am not good at politics. But you asked me to think about it. That is what I know."

Yash smiled. "It is an excellent place to start, Husband. Thank you."

"What are you going to do?"

"I have some ideas," Yash said. "And if you do want to help, I think I know a way."

"What is it?"

"First, tell me this. Bright has some creatures living in his tower. Small things, with big eyes. Do you know anything about them?"

"Just rumors," Chej said. "Some say they can kill with their eyes or turn intruders to stone. That they are his children by a demon, or that they are former lovers he has transformed with his sorcery. That he feeds them human babies or his own entrails."

"His own entrails?"

"I suppose he grows them back somehow?" Chej said. He realized he was smiling. "It always seemed ridiculous, but if you can be both my wife and my husband, maybe anything is possible."

"That's the way to see things," Yash said. "Do you remember anything else about those creatures?"

"No," he said. "Sorry."

"Alright," Yash said. "Here's how you can help me."

Yash explained and then left. Chej pretended to turn his attention back to the ledgers, thinking how best to approach Ruesp. But mere moments later he looked up and found the xarim standing an arm's length away.

"That was a lengthy conversation," Ruesp said.

For an instant, Chej felt panic coming on. What did Ruesp suspect? Worse, what did he *know*? He couldn't trust anyone anymore.

But then again, Ruesp had known some things about him for years, hadn't he?

His fear faded, and an odd calm settled over him.

"A long conversation, and a strange one," he said. "It wasn't a report on what Zu has seen or done. Zu wants to know what some of the other tower masters have been doing. In detail."

"That's not so very odd," Ruesp said.

"Maybe not," Chej said. "But I got the impression... maybe I misunderstood."

"What impression?" Ruesp demanded. "Don't play beetle-and-sand with me. Say what you're thinking."

"I felt as if the courier was accusing some of the tower masters of... well, plotting?"

"Plotting what?"

"I'm not sure," Chej said. "I don't understand a lot about these sorts of things. But that was my impression."

"Which tower masters was he asking about?"

"Umm—Dzhesq, Hsij, Sha, Qaxh, Xuehehs."

"Interesting," Ruesp said. "And stupid. And irresponsible."

"What do you mean?"

"Never mind," Ruesp said. "What did you tell the courier?"

"I didn't know what to tell him. Just what you told me: that Hsij conjured a storm and Dzhesq sent disease. Our records say nothing about the others."

"That's a good point," Ruesp said. "You've just seen Hsij, Dzhesq, and Xuehehs. Maybe you should drop in on Sha and Qaxh. Take their reports. Are you on good terms with them? You were once apprenticed to Sha, were you not?"

"I was apprenticed to his apprentice," Chej corrected. "I am not on bad terms with either of them, that I know of."

"Then go see them. Ask what they've been up to. Don't press. Then come back here and report."

"Your words are my path, xarim," Chej said.

"A simple 'yes' will suffice," Ruesp said. "I am tired to death of that kind of nonsense."

"Yes, xarim," Chej corrected. "Should I go this minute?"

"Wait," Ruesp said. "I forgot to ask. When you went to see Hsij, what did he say about his storm? The one Xuehehs says is now coming our way?"

Chej had thought about that one.

"He said not to worry about it," he told Ruesp. "It will turn back before it reaches the valley."

Ruesp nodded. "I thought something like that."

"I'll go see Sha now," Chej said.

"Wait," the xarim said. "Let me write you a warrant."

## CHAPTER FOURTEEN

# THE GREY WORLD

## TSAYE (IN ANCIENT TIMES)

EVENTUALLY NYEN'ŁTCHIKI, *The Red World also became difficult, and not just because the weather changed. Some of the people became unruly. They did not behave well. Some of them became filled with ugliness and fury. They became Nelch'en'i, The Rages. They became monsters and preyed upon the others. Once again, the spirit-people-animals sought a new home. Once more The One Who Goes First embarked on the river in their boat framed of bone. The river took him through the Silent Stagnant, and he was almost lost there, among the bones and stone. But he passed through. He came to an icy place with no sunlight, where two glaciers tried to grind him up between them, but he changed into a cold-water fish and swam beneath them as they crushed one another. After leaving there he changed into a four-footed animal with long, warm fur and traveled overland until he discovered another world, Nyen' łwai, The Grey World. He returned to the Heeyets and told them the news, and they decided to follow him to the Grey World. When they went there, some of the spirit-people-animals from* the Red World went with them. But this time, some of the Rages disguised themselves and came along, too. We call these the Terrors That Follow.

The Grey World was a wetter place than the Red World, although not so wet as the Ocean World. It was covered in dense forest and grassy plains. It had its own spirit-people-animals. Many of these were like the animals we know now: some resembled bears, wolves, and lions. Others were much like antelope, elk, bison, eagles, hawks, and mimic jays. Some did not want the newcomers, but others welcomed them. Some became friends, some became relatives, some became enemies. And all the time, all of them were changing. But because of the Rages, the Terrors That Follow, the Heeyets did not stay in the Grey World for long. They moved on. And on, one world after the next, seeking harmony. But the Rages also came to each world, and in each world other monsters joined them. Despite their efforts, the Rages traveled with them in disguise or simply followed them. So that by the time they reached Nyen' Dl'ee Shaa, The Moon World, there were many Terrors That Follow among them, from many worlds.

## DII JIN (THE PRESENT)

DESPITE HAVING the courier's outfit, Yash returned to the Blue Needle Tower by way of the rooftops. The inside of the fortress was more crowded than she had thought it would be at night. Some were guards, some were dressed like her, couriers. She wasn't used to people she didn't know, and it made her uncomfortable, partly because she knew she might have to slay them. Most didn't notice her, but one young man in an orange skirt and black top caught her eye and smiled at her. She found herself picturing him curled on the ground, bleeding to death, his expression one of pure confusion, wondering why someone he didn't know had killed him.

She had already seen that look today, many times.

She tried to run the image away. She also had practical reasons for returning to the roof. She didn't want to take a chance of passing through Needle's guards on the first floor. Because she had changed to an outward male appearance, Chej hadn't recognized her right away, but one of Needle's guards might. Even if they didn't, if she pretended to carry a message up into the tower, they would expect her to come back down soon. She could do that, but if they asked to see what she was carrying, there would be trouble. The Blue Needle Tower was still a place where she felt at least somewhat secure, so why kick sand on that?

Everything seemed to be just as she'd left it, so she went right to work, returning to the sorcerer's tools and selecting the largest axe. She then decapitated the dead tower master with four blows from the weapon. Then she did the same to Yellow.

"You're taking the heads back to Bright?" Deng'jah said. "That's not a good idea."

"No," Yash agreed. "It's not. I'm making another visit first. Scout out the path to the Red Coral Tower. Then come back here."

The insect fluttered off, fading into mist as he did so.

Yash was looking for a sack to put the head in when she noticed a cloth bundle that hadn't been there before.

Chej had said something about leaving her something, hadn't he?

"Well, my husband," she said, after unwrapping it. "Well done."

Chej had brought her a bow. It was a sturdy weapon, constructed of sinew and *duwe* horn laminated on a cottonwood core. It was short, deeply recurved, made for mounted fighting, but those same qualities made it ideal for use in close spaces—and for a person like her who wasn't very tall. She strung it and tested the pull. It was a little less than what she was used to, but it would certainly do. Chej had also brought two packets of arrows, all birch, fletched with turkey feathers and tipped with points of demon bone. She counted thirty in total.

There was something else in the cloth. She pulled it out.

It was a knife, but longer than her forearm. It was slightly curved, with one very sharp edge and a wicked point. It was also fashioned from what she guessed was bone from the White Brilliant. It felt hard, but it was quite light and beautifully balanced. She knew of longblades like this; they were usually carried by xarim for personal protection and for dueling, often in combination with a shorter knife or small shield. She had even handled one before, training at Whirlwind Place. The weapon had been captured during an earlier fight with the Empire. Her people didn't normally use such blades, because a knife that size made of flint or copper or even sky iron would be impractical, and her people didn't usually make anything out of demon bone because they didn't have much of it. Functionally, though, it was a lot like a *sheyimiłqu'*, a flat club with an edge of obsidian shards. She made a few passes and performed a few feats with it, getting comfortable with it in her hand.

Chej had done well. Very well. Better than she could have ever hoped for.

For an instant, she had an image of Chej. Like the young man in the corridor, he was dying on the floor. But he didn't look confused. He looked sad and like he had expected it.

She heard a gasp and looked up to find a guard in the doorway, staring at her. At least two more stood behind him on the landing.

"Put that weapon down," the guard said. He had a pair of bladed fighting sticks in hand.

153

"I'm... I just found them this way," Yash said. "I had a message for Tower Master Needle." She heard the fading sounds of footfalls on the stairs. Another guard, running downward.

"I recognize you," the guard said. "Needle brought you up here earlier. The princess."

"No," she said, taking a few steps toward him. "I'm a courier. The Emperor sent me."

"Put that down," the guard repeated. "What happened here?"

She took another few steps.

"Please," she said. "I don't know. They were dead when I got here."

"Stay where you are," he cautioned, raising his weapons. They resembled very short spears with proportionally long two-edged heads. Heavy leather gloves protected his hands, and lacquered leather armor shielded his body.

She started walking toward him, quickly. She hoped to confuse him, but he seemed to immediately understand what was happening. He let her come into range, and then he feinted a thrust, followed by an oblique cut toward her right wrist.

She flipped her hand out of the way and slapped her knuckles against the flat of his blade, deflecting it as she speared the long knife toward him. He blocked the thrust with his right-hand stick and lashed at her shoulder, and when she withdrew that, followed through toward her knee. She twisted aside and then darted back, driving above the failed attack and stabbing him in the left eye. The bone blade cut through the back of his skull as if it were a gourd, and it came out easily, so that she could hack the head off the next warrior's javelin as it flashed through the air. The headless shaft tumbled and struck her thigh. It stung, but she pulled the dying first man out of the way so she could reach the spearman.

She loved the new blade. It gave her a lot of reach; it cut through their armor like it wasn't there. It was almost like a part of her hand.

It didn't take her long to finish the other two on the landing, but she knew she would never catch the one speeding down the stairs, so instead of chasing him she went back for the bow, glad she'd strung it already. She grabbed one of the sheafs of arrows and hurried downward, taking two and three stairs at a time.

She was almost to the third floor from the bottom before the first of the guards came around the curve of the stairwell. Her first arrow missed, striking the wall, causing the man to look up. Her second shaft hit him in his open mouth and sent him tumbling backward, out of sight. Two more pushed past him. She shot the first in the torso, which slowed him down but probably wasn't fatal. Her next arrow slipped past the second warrior, who gained another five stairs before she shot him in the neck. She retreated upward, slowly, as they kept coming. Predictably they became more cautious, showing themselves and then ducking back into cover. She wondered absently if any of the guards in the fortress carried bows themselves; she hadn't seen any so far. Were there any archers from the army still in the fortress? That could be a problem eventually. Or maybe sooner. There had been a dozen guards when she first entered Needle's tower. She counted five dead at this point and another three in no shape for fighting. How long before they sent outside of the tower for help? Maybe they already had.

She loosed two more arrows, and when the guards ducked away, she drew the longblade and leapt down the stairs.

The first man never saw her coming. The second hurled his spear at her, but it was a wild, panicked throw. She cut them both in passing, fairly certain both blows were fatal but not willing to stay around and see because the remaining two were running.

She jumped after them, landing with both feet on the shoulders of one and slamming him into the stone steps. The other had a longer head start, and he was fast. He made it all the way to the ground floor and was headed for the door into the hallway when he realized he was about to get stabbed in the back. So he turned, cutting at her with both of his blade-sticks.

It was a surprise. She barely managed to check and pivot to the side; she felt the wind from one of the blades on her cheek. It put her off-balance, and he caught her with the backswing, which was fortunately the blunt haft of the blade-stick, but it struck her on the back of the head, filling her skull with flashing light as she tumbled away. He shrieked and came after her. Everything felt like it was spinning.

Spinning, like at Whirlwind Place. Except that now the whirlwind was in her head.

She dropped flat and rolled, felt his feet catch on her, tripping him and sending him tumbling past her. She rolled to her feet, the spots in her vision still there but clearing. He struggled up, facing her. She put her back toward the door to the hall.

"This was a good fight," she said. "Thank you."

When it was over, she stood there, panting, waiting for her head to clear completely, and to see if anyone was about to come through the door. After a moment, though, she realized it was still bolted from the inside. That suggested that no one had gone for reinforcements. If they had, there wasn't much she could do about it, anyway.

She felt something wet on her cheek and wiped at it. She'd thought it would be blood, but it wasn't.

She was crying.

Why?

She closed her eyes, imagining a high place, a single hawk in a blue sky. She had to keep focused, now more than ever. She had things to do.

A few of the guards on the stair were still alive. From questioning them she gathered that their relief wasn't due until around dawn, still more than half the night away.

As she was retrieving the arrows that weren't broken, Deng'jah returned.

"You've been busy while I was gone," he said.

"Yes," she said. "So tell me what you found."

"The way to the Red Coral Tower is clear. There isn't anything guarding the outside of it that I can make out."

"And inside?"

"Master Qaxh the Coral is there. I'm not sure what else."

Yash nodded.

"We've got company," Deng'jah said.

"Where?"

"Coming down the stairs."

Yash drew the longblade. Behind her, one of the guards groaned.

At the bend of the stair above her, someone came into view. Hana, Needle's servant. When she saw Yash, she stopped. Her eyes flicked to the dead and injured men, then back to Yash.

"Are you going to kill me, too?" she asked. She looked unsteady, and her eyes were glassy. Yash remembered that Deng'jah had last seen her drinking wine.

"I don't know," Yash said. "I wish you had stayed asleep."

"There was a lot of noise," Hana explained.

"Yes," Yash replied. "Sorry about that."

"You look like her," Hana said. "The princess. Are you her brother?"

"Something like that," Yash said.

"Have you come for her? I can show you where she is." She glanced up for an instant.

"Are there more guards up there?" Yash asked.

"Guards?" Hana said. "No. Not human ones. But there is Master Needle. And his giant. And demons, I think."

Yash nodded. "You heard me fighting?"

"Yes."

"Why didn't you go upstairs to rouse Needle? Surely you did not think you would fight me yourself."

"I don't know," Hana said. She looked down at her feet. "I don't know. Did you—" She stopped, then wandered her gaze past Yash again.

"Are they all dead? All twelve of them?"

"A few are still alive," Yash said. "I was just about to finish them off."

"Why?"

"They are my enemies. If I leave them alive, I will have to fight them again."

"Will any of them be able to fight again today?"

Yash shrugged, recalling each of their injuries. "No."

"How long do you plan on staying in the fortress? If you defeat Master Needle and rescue your princess, won't you just leave? I can help you with that. Umm. If you don't kill me. And these men will not fight you again, even if you spare them."

"What if Needle kills me?"

Hana opened her hands and shrugged. "He'll probably kill me, too. And any of the guards who survive. For failing him."

Yash sighed. "Hana, I wish… I'm sorry."

For a moment, it didn't register. Then she blinked. "How do you know my name?" she asked. But then she understood that, too.

"Oh," she said. "You're *her*. The princess. You—look different. I don't understand."

"I'm her," Yash agreed. "And Master Needle is already dead."

"That seems so unlikely," Hana said. "But, if that's so, what are you? A demon of some kind?"

"No. I am the person my people sent to fight for them. To restore our land. And to break the power of this place."

"And to kill everyone here. Including me."

Yash studied the older woman's face. She looked frightened, confused, and resigned.

Hana was easily as dangerous as any guard. If she went downstairs, into the fortress, she would tell everyone what had happened. Every remaining tower master would be alerted, every guard would come for her. She didn't have that many arrows.

"Yes," Yash said. "Yes. But I can make it quick. You won't feel it."

Hana spun around and ran. But she only went up three steps. Then she turned back, paused, and slowly began to descend again. She nodded, as if in answer to a question. She came closer and knelt on the stone of the landing.

Yash looked down at her for a moment, readying the longblade. Then she began to recite.

*I am sorry, my enemy*
*It has come to this*
*But I scatter petals before you*
*Guide you on your path*
*Listen*

*There is a way to avoid the pitfalls*
*The errors on the trail*
*A way to the Dancing Houses*
*So you won't get lost*
*Let me guide you there*
*With a single swift blow…*

She focused on the longblade, so Hana was just a blur. This was the time.

## CHAPTER FIFTEEN

# THE NAHEEYIYE

### DA'AN' (THE MIDDLE PAST)

### TWENTY-TWO YEARS EARLIER

"WHAT ARE thinking about, sheyashi?" Yash's mother's brother asked. "Your face is all pinched up."

"I was thinking about the sandstorm, Shede'e," Yash replied. She glanced to their left, where the ridge they had been climbing all morning sloped down, crinkling into slot canyons and melding into the broad, scrubby, red plain they had been crossing the day before. Beyond that the distant purple tiers of the mesa called They Stepped Down Four Times formed the horizon. Above it all the slender, sharp-winged silhouette of a sparrowhawk drifted nearly motionless in the sky, kiting on the wind.

The two-humped *yene'ghane* her uncle was leading—an old bull named Spitter—snorted, as if the subject bored him. Shede'e patted the beast's brown flank and then ran his hand between the beast's long neck and forward hump.

"Spitter doesn't like carrying all of that stuff," Yash said, waving at the bags and boxes strapped all over the poor beast.

"Do you want to carry them yourself?" Shede'e asked. "Besides, he knows we're grateful, and when we reach the high pastures, he'll be able to graze on the sweet grass and rushes up there for days and days, drink from streams that were snow a month ago. It's the deal we made with his kind in tsaye, the ancient times. Do you remember that story?"

"That really long story about the bargains we made with all of the animals?"

"Yes."

"I remember now," she said. "But was that real, or just a story?"

"That's an interesting question," Shede'e said. "And maybe it's the question that's most important, not the answer."

"Can't you ever just say 'yes' or 'no'?" Yash complained.

"I can," he replied. "When it's that kind of question. But take back a few steps. You said you were thinking about the sandstorm. What were you thinking?"

"I couldn't see anything," Yash said. "The sand got in my eyes. And it hurt. It felt like my skin was being scrubbed off." Yash paused and looked at Shede'e, but he didn't say anything. He was waiting for her to finish. "Anyway," she said. "It made me think about how most of the time the air is… just air. It's just there. You can't see it. You don't even notice it. And when the wind blows, it's usually weak, it can barely move a feather. It can't do much. But then sometimes, like in that sandstorm, it gets really strong."

Shede'e kept holding his words. When, after a while, he understood she was done, he started talking again.

"It's good you think about things like that," he said. "About how the things we don't always notice are important, about how harmless things can become dangerous under the right conditions."

She looked at Shede'e suspiciously. Was that what she had been thinking about, really, or had he just guided her there? Now she couldn't tell.

The path turned a bit steeper, and Spitter didn't like it. He balked a little, and Shede'e had to coax him to continue. Yash watched how he did it, how he kept his voice low and soothing. He didn't shout. And after a little bit, Spitter calmed down and started walking again.

She saw her mother, far ahead, glancing back at them. Shede'e saw, too, and waved. Everyone else was ahead of them, but Yash didn't care. She liked it in the back, with Shede'e. He was funny and patient. He was old, too, almost twenty, and it seemed like he knew everything.

"Why are we going to the high pastures?" she asked.

"Do you really not know? We've been preparing for this trip for half a month. I can't believe you haven't already asked someone about it."

"Mom said something-or-other," Yash said. "I wasn't paying attention."

"We're going to the high country so we remember who we are," he said. "So you will learn more about who *you* are."

Yash nodded. "Yes," she said. "That's exactly what mother said. But I don't understand it."

"Do you need me to explain, or would you rather think about it for a while?"

"I've been thinking about it," she admitted. "We *know* who we are. We live in the Mountain Stone Mansion. We rule all of Zeltah."

"Is that true?" he asked. "What are we called? What is your mother called?"

"Queen," Yash said.

"That is an empire word. That is what the Empire calls your mother. What do *we* call her?"

"Tsenid'a'wi," she said.

"Did you never think about what that means?" Shede'e asked.

Yash said the word to herself again. She shook her head.

"Say it slowly," he said. "It's a real word, not just some sounds that means 'queen.'"

He was right, she realized. She just hadn't thought about it that way before.

"First-she-travels," Yash said, slowly. "She Travels Ahead."

"Yes," Shede'e said. "It's an old word. The name of one of the spirit-people-animals we are descended from. But it can also mean *they* travel ahead. So it means all of us. All of our clan. We go first. And so when it is time for war, we lead the way. When something needs to be done, we go first. When the summer comes, and it is time for the people to move to the highland pastures..." He trailed off, to let her finish.

"We go there first," she said. "So that's what it means to know who we are?"

"Yes," he said. "But there is more than that. There was a time when there was no Mountain Stone Mansion. When there was no ruler, no queen or king. When all of the people did the same things, followed the same cycles of the seasons and the land. And so do we still, even though our clan has other duties now. Any person of our nation who does not know all of it—the mountains, the plains, the valleys—is not what a full person should be. You were born in the Mountain Stone Mansion, yes. But you must know how to hunt antelope and snare rabbits, how to tend crops and herd duwe and yene'ghane, how to know when the rains are coming, what the clouds are telling us, the language of the stars. We are this land, Yash, the Land Among the Mountains. We are related to it. We are descended from it; we are younger brothers and sisters of it. When anything in Zełtah is hurt, we're all hurt."

Yash thought about that for minute.

"I guess I knew all of that already," she said. "But I hadn't really thought about it."

"It's like the air," Shede'e said. "It's invisible to you until it stirs up sand."

She looked back down at the distant valley, the little grey-green track of Tch'inelen creek, the Tu Seqani escarpment beyond.

"Is it hurt?" she asked.

"What?"

"You said if the land is hurt, all of us are. Is the land hurt?"

Shede'e was silent for a while.

"Yes," he finally said.


THE WALK to get there was long and hard, but Yash loved the high pastures. Mountains held up the entire rim of the sky: dark, mysterious peaks covered in yellow pine and rock oak, their highest summits brushed with white even in early summer. Streams wound through bright fields of green grasses and wildflowers, feeding rush-bordered mountain lakes. The birds were almost all different from those around the Mountain Stone Mansion, and their songs were exquisite, especially in the evening and at night. She liked the old houses, the *yiht*. They were tiny, compared to what she was used to, just one room each, with foundations and low walls of stone. On top of that, logs had been split, fitted together, and chinked with clay. The roofs were made of bark and wooden shingles. Most of them needed repair when they arrived, but by the fourth day they were tight and cozy, and they were able to put their tents away for the trip back. Yash spent some days wandering with Spitter and the other livestock. Shede'e and some of her cousins were usually not far away, keeping an eye out for wolves and lions and stranger, more dangerous things. At night it was cold, and she stayed near her mother's fire, listening to the stories. Winter was really the time for important stories: the ones about the beginnings of things, about the Sky People like Thunder, the Sun, and the Winds, the ancestors, the foundations of the world and the travels of her people before they found their home here, among the mountains. Summer was the time for silly stories that really weren't true, like the one about how Tselełgayshi the Skunk killed a niłyeeti by farting at him, or how Yeshashi the Coyote tricked some girls by pretending to be a baby.

But as the summer stretched on, she kept thinking about what Shede'e had said about the land being hurt. Finally, one evening, she asked him about it again.

"Let me talk to your mother first," was all he said.

But the next morning he woke her before red rose in the east. He had five other people with him, all cousins of hers. All of them were fixed for traveling.

"We're going," he said.

"Where?"

"To see what you asked about."

It was cool but not quite cold as they started walking. The stars were fading in the east, but the western skies were still dark, and in the north she saw the stars of the Tail, hardly flickering in the calm, dry air, which foretold a clear day. When light spilled over the mountains behind them, it came in a rush, filling the long mountain lake they were following with golden light. She brushed her hands across the tops of the rushes and sang a song about them. In the distance, a forest of pine and oak closed the valley but beckoned them on. A trout leapt from the water, poised for an instant in the air, snatching a fly. It was all good, all beautiful. She felt filled up by it all.

They traveled mostly uphill for the first day, up to a high pass in the mountains, where the north sides of the trees and rocks still had a little snow in their shadows. They saw eagles, and one lion, slipping through the trees in the distance. One evening, she noticed an aspen-spirit watching her from the shadows. He looked like a boy, but he was grey and had leaves for hair, and his face was like a bark mask with two long slits for his eyes.

After the pass they started back down, a steep, switch-back trail that took them farther from home than she had ever been. The forest was thick here, thicker than she had ever seen before, and sometimes the air even felt wet. It was so steep, at times it was better to run than walk; it hurt the knees and legs, and it was fun, although Shede'e warned her more than once not to break her neck. Midday, they stopped at Cliff Where She Cascades Down to drink the melting snow from farther up. The water was wonderfully cold and tasted of the earth. She enjoyed standing under the vertical stream for a little while until she was thoroughly wet, for she was hot from walking.

They were making camp when an owl called in the distance. Shede'e, poking at the fire, stood up. All of the others stopped what they were doing, too.

"What?" Yash asked.

"The owl," Shede'e said. "He is disturbed by something." He took his bow off his shoulder and an arrow from his quiver. Miłtcheeh—her cousin, daughter of her mother's sister—pulled her fighting club from her belt, a wicked-looking piece of curved oak that ended in a ball with a sharp spike of sharpened horn sticking out of it.

"I see it," Miłtcheeh said.

A moment later, Yash saw it, too, emerging from the shadows of the trees. It looked something like a bear, except its forelimbs were almost twice as long as its hind limbs, and it didn't have ears that she could see. Its fur was coarse and spare, showing patches of pebbled skin beneath. Its teeth were bearlike, with four much longer and sharper than the others.

The hairs on her neck and arms pricked up.

"What is it?" she whispered.

"That's a niłyeeti monster," Shede'e replied. "The kind we call Tsashtlehhi."

Everyone had weapons in their hands now. Everyone but her, because she didn't have one. She glanced around and found a branch with a knot on one end someone had broken for the fire. It didn't feel like much, but it was better than having nothing in her hand.

The monster moved fast, charging suddenly toward Cha' who was nearest. Shede'e shot it; the arrow stuck in the niłyeeti's neck. Cha' had a bow, too; he waited until it was close, shot it in the head, and tried desperately to get out of the way. He almost didn't, but as his arrow glanced off the monster's skull, Miłtcheeh leapt between him and the Tsashtlehhi and hit it with her spike-mace. It spun, fast, its mouth gaping, and clamped down on Miłtcheeh's arm.

Yash yelled, charged the niłyeeti, and slapped it with her stick. It was weird, almost like she was watching someone else do it.

"Leave her alone!" she hollered.

"Get Yash!" Miłtcheeh yelled, as the beast worried her like a dog would a stick. Someone grabbed Yash from behind as Miłtcheeh managed to plant her feet and swing her weapon again. This time the spikes in it sank into the monster's skull and the club stayed there like a weird hat. It jerked its neck and flung Miłtcheeh away. She hit the ground and rolled, her arm sheathed in blood.

Yash screamed and thrashed, dimly understanding that Shede'e was the one holding her and wondering why. She kept struggling to get to the niłyeeti as it writhed on the ground, attempting to dislodge the spiked club from its head. Cha' stepped close and shot it in one of its eyes, and then the others closed in. In a few moments, the beast wasn't moving anymore.

Miłtcheeh's eyes were closed, and there was more blood than ever.

Yash was finally able to shake off Shede'e's grasp on her. She went to the injured woman and knelt by her, stroking her hair. "Is my cousin dead?" she asked.

"No," Shede'e replied. "Our cousin is made of hard stuff. She'll live through this. Cha' will take care of her wounds. Come."

He led her over to the dead monster.

Yash stared at the thing. Even in death it looked dangerous.

"Are you going to sing for it?" she asked.

"No," he said. "What was there, what was in this flesh: we do not encourage it."

"What *was* there?" she asked.

He folded down to a cross-legged position and gestured for her to sit as well.

"We believe that in the worlds the niłyeeti come from, they have souls," he said, as she settled on a log. "But coming here, to our world, they lose them. So their flesh looks for a new soul, any soul. But the only souls they can have—the only ones available to them —are dj'ende. Do you know what that is?"

"It's the bad soul," she said. "The one that makes evil ghosts and sorcerers."

Shede'e nodded. "That's mostly right. Dj'ende are the part of a person or an animal that stays around after death. Everything that wasn't right about that person, everything out of balance. The worst of them. And there isn't a song that can do anything about that, not after they die. Sometimes you can make them leave, where they are to go someplace else, but that's about it. Even as ghosts they can do harm: cause sickness, drive the living to madness, that sort of thing. But if they get into one of these niłyeeti bodies, they can do much more damage." He took her hand. "Come on," he said. "We shouldn't stay here for long."

"The dj'ende is still here, isn't it? Looking for a new body."

"Yes," he said.

Although it was getting dark, they traveled until the brightest stars were visible before making camp. By that time Miłtcheeh was awake again. Yash went over and sat by her. She saw her cousin was sweating even though the air had a deep chill in it.

"Shede'e says you're going to live," she said.

"I think he's right," her cousin said. "But it hurts."

"They say your blow killed it," Yash told her. "It just took a little while to know it was dead."

"That's the way niłyeeti are," Miłtcheeh said. She reached for Yash and patted her head. "You were very brave," she said. "You have a warrior in you."

"I didn't want it to hurt you," Yash said.

Miłtcheeh nodded. "A protector," she said. "A shield. Even better. I'm tired. Will you stay here and protect me while I sleep?"

"I will," Yash said.

Off in the darkness, a whippoorwill called and, in the far distance, another answered. *Hush'ełdii. Hush'ełdii.*

* * *

THE NEXT morning, Yash woke to discover she had changed. The day before, she'd had the outer appearance of a girl; now she had both girl and boy parts. She helped break camp and pack up for the day's walk.

Shede'e decided Miłtcheeh was in no shape to travel, so they left her with Cha' and one other and continued on. There were only four of them now, but Shede'e said they didn't have all that far to go.

As the sun was setting the next day, they came to the edge of a long, wide valley.

"There," Shede'e said.

For a few heartbeats, everything looked fine to her, just a nice lake surrounded by meadows and trees. But after a few moments, something didn't seem right about it.

Understanding came like summer rain. A few drops at first, but then more, faster, stronger.

The sun still rested on the edge of a mountain, washing the western sky in red, orange, and gold. The lake was calm and flat, and had no color at all. It wasn't reflecting anything from the sky. And once Yash saw that, she saw the rest of it wasn't right, either. It was as if the grass and trees were just *pretending* to be those things. And when she stared at them, really studied them, they weren't at all what they seemed. The stand of aspens was more like grey-white bones sticking up out of the ground. The grass was slowly crawling, as if made of worms. The pines blurred together where they touched, and some of their trunks didn't really seem to reach the ground. Then, in an eyeblink everything would look normal again. In the next they were strange once again, only different: the aspens like scratches on granite, the reeds like a field of flint knives. And each leaf on the oaks had an eye of some kind staring out of it: human, hawk, snake, frog, fish…

Yash became sick, and she vomited until her chest ached.

"What is it?" she asked, when she could.

"It was a place once," Shede'e said. "Listen."

"I don't hear anything," she said.

"Because there's nothing to hear," he said. "This used to be a place. It had names. Hush'ełdiik'e. Ch'eh'mikunik'e'. Wesdzik'e'. This time of night, this time of year, you would see fireflies rising against the forest, and hear the whippoorwills greet the night and owls call for each other in the darkness. Now it's this."

"Why? What happened?"

"Hunters came from the Empire, years ago. They took the soul of this place. Places have souls, too, you see. And places have dj'ende. What you see is the dj'ende of a place, and it attracts others. These broken places are where the nilyeeti find their way into our world, and it's where they get their wicked souls." He put his hand on her shoulder.

"I brought you here because it was the nearest. But there are other places like this. Many of them. Places where the hunters of the Empire came and left *this* behind."

"But why?" Yash asked. "Why do they do this?"

"Because they can," Shede'e said. "They unshape those they steal. They dress them in strange flesh, and they make their sorcery from them. They were naheeyiye before they were stolen. Spirits of our land. Without them, our land is not whole, and neither are we."

She stared at the place that was no longer a place. At first, she'd felt grief, sadness. But now she was feeling something else.

Anger.

"Can't we do anything about it?" she asked.

"One day," Shede'e said. "One day, one of our people will go to the fortress at the heart of the Empire, and they will kill the sorcerers and liberate the lost ones, the stolen naheeyiye."

"Is that a prophecy?" Yash asked.

"No," Shede'e said. "It is a plan."

"Who will do it?" Yash asked.

"We don't know that yet," Shede'e said.

Yash looked across the silent, still, colorless lake.

"I do," she said. "It's going to be me."

## DII JIN (THE PRESENT)

YASH HELD the knife, looking down at Hana. The moment stretched. Her unfinished song hung in the air, deprived of weight and usefulness. The slightest breeze could carry it away.

"You know," she finally said, in her native tongue, "maybe I don't have to kill *everyone* in the fortress." She lowered her blade.

*"This is interesting,"* Deng'jah said in his little voice. *"And probably a mistake."*

*"I don't care,"* Yash said. *"I came here believing I was the avalanche, the lightning strike, the sky falling. But I'm not. I'm a protector. A shield. The One Who Walks Around the People and Watches Over Them. I will kill all the tower masters. I will find all of our stolen ones and set them free. I will cripple the Empire and its ability to make war. But Hana—how is she my enemy? Or the young girl who works with her? Or even these guards?"*

*"The guards? Are you serious? Their job is to kill you."*

*"I understand that,"* Yash said. *"And when I must, I will not flinch from severing their souls from flesh. But Hana is right. If these injured ones*

present a threat to me, it will be on some distant day I may never see. How much longer before what I've done in this tower is discovered, no matter what I do?"

"Every breath fills lungs," Deng'jah said. "The more breaths you take before the whole fortress comes for you, the better. My sense is you don't have much longer, and my senses are good."

"Let them come," Yash said. "Anyway, we're done here. No matter what happens, we're not coming back to the Blue Needle Tower."

She noticed Hana still had her head down. Of course. She couldn't hear them, and even if she could, she wouldn't understand Zełtah Meqenets.

"Stand up," Yash said.

The woman did so. Her face was streaked with tears.

"I am grateful," she said.

"Grateful is for strangers who give you food," Yash said. "Not for the person who set fire to your house and then put it out. But if you care to do me a favor, do not tell anyone who I am. Say it was a monster, a demon of some sort. Tell them you saw me for an instant through a crack in the door, and no more."

"Yes," Hana said. "A monster. I can say that."

"And if you wish to tend to those wounded men, I will not kill them."

"I will do what I can for them," Hana said.

"It's good," Yash said. Then she started up the stairs to get the two heads and the rest of the arrows.

CHAPTER SIXTEEN

# QAXH THE CORAL

QAXH STOOD at the window, dreaming the colors his eyes could not see. That no human eye could see. He wandered his otherworldly vision across the far distance, searching through the tints and shades, envisioning how he wanted them to be. How they needed to be.

And when he was done, he returned to the world-as-we-see-it, to his room of white, grey, and black. He went to his desk, folded down onto the low stool, and began to mix his paints. He measured out ashes of juniper, alder, pine, sage, saltbush, powdered pumice, chalk, shell, burnt ivory and wolf bone, pulverized teeth and bones from the White Brilliant, white clay and black coal from the Silent Stagnant. He mixed these pigments with oils common and mundane. Then he took in hand his rabbit-hair brush, his duck-feather brush, his flat brushes and pens of reed, quill, and bone. He remembered the colors of the Dream of the World, but he translated them into shades of grey as he painted those memories. And he changed them a very little, because he could not alter them much, for the Dream of the World has incredible momentum. Even one as powerful as he could only do a little. But that little would seem very large to the people of Zełtah. In the highlands, a fresh stream would become salty. In another spring, frogs and fish would die and putrefy in an instant. In a mountain pool, oil from deep in the earth would seep up and shimmer on the surface.

He was half-done with the painting when his Thing made a noise.

"What is it?" he asked his Thing.

"Someone is here," the Thing said. "Shall I kill it?"

"Let me see it first," Qaxh replied. "It may be that the Emperor sent it."

"It arrived through a window," his Thing said. "The Emperor usually does not send servants in that way."

"That is suspicious," Qaxh agreed. "Still, there is no call to be hasty."

"Ruzuyer is agitated," the Thing said. "Someone has entered the fortress from without. This may be that person."

"Now I *must* see it," Qaxh said. "My curiosity is aroused."

"As you command," the Thing said. The door to the chamber began to open, and someone stepped inside, a stranger, but dressed in the clothing of a fortress courier, carrying a bag. He was angular, thin, broad-shouldered. He was round-faced, dark, with large eyes. He didn't look much like a hje or even a thinblood. He looked very much like a highland barbarian, albeit a somewhat scrawny one.

"I do not like to be interrupted," Qaxh said to the newcomer. "I hope you bring an important message."

"I know you tower masters are a busy bunch," the stranger said. "I wouldn't bother you if I didn't think you would be *very* interested in what I have to say." He untied the bag and lifted something out.

It was, Qaxh saw, a human head. Hsij's head. Both eyes were gone, so it was difficult to tell for sure, but the expression on the tower master's face appeared to be one of surprise. Indeed, he must have been, since Hsij had held forth many times on the subject of death and how he did not intend to ever die. Whatever research he had done toward that end seemed to have been wasted.

"Thing," Qaxh said. "If this person takes another step toward me, or threatens me in any way, slay him."

"I don't know who you're talking to," the stranger said. "But you can tell them I've come to chat, not to die. Or kill."

"Name yourself," Qaxh demanded.

"My name is Tchił," the stranger said. "You know this head, I presume." He knelt slowly and placed the head on the floor. Qaxh studied it for a moment longer. He had rather liked Hsij. They had been brothers, after all, although that was certainly no guarantee of friendship. But he had enjoyed Hsij's company as much as anyone's, and more than most. And he had been formidable. Qaxh looked back at the stranger. He must have hidden talents, this one, if he had murdered Hsij. It would not do to underestimate him.

"I know him," Qaxh said. "Or knew him, I suppose. Did you kill him?"

"No," Tchił said. "I found him growing on a head tree."

Qaxh suppressed a smile. Who was this person? He didn't seem frightened of Qaxh at all. But that followed, if he had already killed a tower master. Still, it wouldn't do to look weak.

"You have entertained me," Qaxh said. "I am not often entertained. I'll give you another chance to answer my question."

"If you want the boring, obvious answer," Tchił said. "Why yes, I suppose I did kill him."

"Interesting. Why?"

"Because someone told me to," Tchiił replied.

Qaxh leaned back on his stool, regarding the stranger. "Someone, eh?" It wasn't impossible. It wasn't even improbable. But it was... disappointing. And it would explain how an outland barbarian had managed to slay a tower master. He'd had help.

"Yes," the stranger said. "The same person asked me to kill Tower Master Needle, which I also did."

Was that true? Qaxh wondered. Has this person really killed two tower masters? And yet there was no alarm in the fortress, no uproar.

"And now I suppose you've come to murder me, as well?" he ventured.

The stranger shook his head. "Not at all. I think you are too reasonable to die. Listen—I was promised something if I killed Master Needle. I did as I was told, but I was not rewarded as our agreement stipulated. Instead, I was then told to kill Yellow and two other tower masters. At that point I began to believe I was being duped. You see why, don't you? You would surely have felt the same way, because you are a smart, reasonable person who thinks things through. I saw that about you immediately. We have that in common, Tower Master Coral. So, instead of going to kill Yellow, I decided to talk to him instead. But—maybe you know this, I imagine you do—Yellow was *not* a reasonable person. He didn't believe me, so I was forced to kill him to survive, and then his beetle-monster as well. You were next on my list of assassinations. Once again, I've decided to try talking instead of fighting. I'm far more interested in getting what I came for than killing anyone. And I really have no interest in local disputes and grievances."

Qaxh traced his gaze over the unfamiliar face as he listened to the words flow out in an awful but intelligible accent. He was seized with a sudden desire to dream the man's face, to know the colors there. But there was some risk in that. Fortunately, the Thing could watch out for him.

"Sit down there," he said, indicating a stool on the other side of the room. "Wait for a moment, if you really want to talk to me."

Tchiił nodded and took a seat.

"Do not stir from that spot until I say you can. If you do, my Thing will boil your blood and shatter your bones."

"I understand," Tchiił said. "What is your Thing? I'm very curious about that."

"I absolutely believe you are," Qaxh said. "Hold still, and please be quiet."

Qaxh took a long, slow breath. Then he closed his eyes. He exhaled, and the dream began to settle on him, first like drifting snow, and then all at once, an avalanche.

And there was color. So much of it, so bright and clean and clear it was hard to understand it. He thought he had dreamed every color possible. But dreaming the stranger, he saw more than ever before.

When he was done, and returned to the room, it hurt almost physically to open his eyes and gaze on light and shadow again. Dull, so dull.

"Are you well?" the stranger asked. "You sounded as if you were in pain."

Qaxh shook his hand. He steadied his breath. Then he began mixing more paint.

"It was pain," Qaxh said. "And ecstasy."

"What did you do?"

Qaxh forced a smile. He mixed blackened nut-pine with powdered bile and rendered human fat. "My mother," he said. "She gave me a gift when I was very young. Or gifts, I should say. She plucked out my human eyes and replaced them with these." He pointed to his face with his mixing stylus. "When I use them as you use your eyes, I see no color. None at all. It's all ash of various tones. But when I turn them inward, when I look on the Dream of the World, I see... beauty. When you look at the sky, how many shades of blue and green do you see? Four? Ten? Some tell me they see as many as six or seven. I see hundreds, many hundreds. All distinct, like words, and like words, each one means something different. A thousand kinds of red in a sandstone cliff; a single yellow flower, to me, speaks meaning in forty-eight different shades. I see the stuff that makes up the Dream of the World, and thus the world itself. And you—you are, I must say, quite beautiful and absolutely abominable. You are all of the colors of male and female, both and neither. Of animal and human, spirit and flesh, and all that boils between them. May I ask what you are, exactly?"

"I am just a person," Tchiił said. "Just me, come here to run some errands."

Qaxh selected a brush and began to paint in quick, bold strokes.

"You came from Zełtah, did you not? Did you come to retrieve your princess? Is that what Zu—Bright, I imagine you call him—promised you, if you killed Needle?"

"I think you're trying to trick me," Tchiił said. "I didn't mention anyone named Zu or Bright."

"You didn't have to," Qaxh replied, changing to a smaller brush made of arctic fox tail. "Bright wants be Emperor. I support the true emperor. So did Yellow and Needle. And Horn. Did he also command you to murder Horn? Was he the fourth on your list of murders to do?"

"You're asking a lot of questions," Tchiił said. "But I would like to be on firmer footing before I answer them."

"What is it you want?"

"As you said. To find the Princess Yash and take her home."

"I don't have her," Qaxh said.

"No," Tchiił said. "I believe that. That is why I have come to you."

"You think that Bright has her," Qaxh said. Zu had probably told Tchiił that. From what Qaxh had been given to understand, Dzhesq had the barbarian princess in his tower. But Tchiił obviously didn't know that. If he did, why wouldn't he have already taken her and escaped?

"Yes," Tchiił said. "He all but said it."

"So you admit it was Bright who tasked you to these killings?"

The barbarian paused, his eyes cutting side to side as he thought about it. "Yes?" he said at last.

"Then why come to me? Kill Bright and take your princess. It would be easier than killing me, I promise you."

"He has… helpers," Tchiił said. "Nasty little things, with witch-eyes. I'm sure you know what I'm talking about. I know a few tricks, but none of them helped me against those things."

"Ah. The xualudeh. They are formidable."

"Hwa-loo-deh," the barbarian repeated, poorly. He smiled. "I didn't know what they were called. Not that that helps me at all, but it's fun to know. What are you painting?"

"You," Qaxh said. "I've never seen anyone like you before. I must have a record. But don't let that distract you. You have a plan?"

"Well, I do want to kill Bright," Tchiił admitted.

"Or want me to kill him for you?" Qaxh said.

"I would not object to that."

"Or, perhaps I should bring this to the attention of the Emperor, and present you and Yellow's head as evidence of Bright's plot."

"You might do that," Tchiił said. "But that could force Master Bright to attack the Emperor and those that support him, yes? And two of the Emperor's allies are already dead. How many more would support Master Bright?"

Qaxh had already been thinking about that, and he knew the answer, or part of it. Zuah of the Abalone Shell Tower would probably side with Zu. So would Yir of the Standing Pinion Tower. A day ago, the Emperor's faction consisted of the Emperor and five tower masters—Dzhesq, Hsij, Sha, Xuehehs, and himself—for a total of six, opposed by three tower masters: Zu, Zuah, and Yir. If Tchiił was to be believed, and Dzhesq was also dead, the count was now four to three. The odds were still in the Emperor's favor, numerically anyway. But the margin was very thin, especially when you considered the unpredictable nature of a war of sorcery.

He paused in mid-stroke, staring at what he was painting. It was beginning to take shape. He glanced toward the other side of the room, at another painting he had begun years ago but never finished. He had begun to think he would never finish it. But now—now, it seemed, things had changed. He might have the colors he needed now.

He began to feel something he had almost forgotten. Something wonderful. Something above all of this plotting and deception. Something real.

The barbarian was staring at him, awaiting his answer.

"In theory, no tower master is allowed to work sorcery against another," Qaxh said. "That is why Bright is using you as his tool. In reality—well, it has happened before. The results were devastating, and I will not be the first to break that rule."

"I don't blame you," Tchiił said. "I certainly wouldn't want a tower master mad at me. May I see my portrait?"

Qaxh rose and walked across the room, away from the intruder. Then he gestured at the painting. Tchiił stood up and went to examine the portrait. He looked at it for a while, cocking his head this way and that.

"It really is beautiful," he said, after a moment. "I've never seen myself like that before. But I like it. You really are gifted, Tower Master Coral. Thank you for letting me look at it."

"Beautiful," Qaxh said. "And abominable. Our law says that such a thing as you cannot exist."

"Which is more powerful?" Tchiił asked. "Your law or the Dream of the World?"

"At the moment?" Qaxh asked. "Or eventually?"

"Oh," Tchiił said. "I think I understand. That's… well." He straightened up. "What's that painting over there?" he asked. "The one you keep looking at?"

"An old project," Qaxh said. "Nearly forgotten. But I believe—I believe you have given me new ideas about it."

"I'm glad I could be of help," Tchiił said. "I wonder if you would consider returning the favor?"

Qaxh closed his eyes for a moment, shutting out the awful grey of the world. Weighing the question. Thinking of his painting. Then he went to his shelves and selected a ceramic jar, its lid tied on with sinew.

"This is salt," he told Tchiił. "But it is not just any sort of salt. It is from the deepest dry ocean in the Silent Stagnant. It is very good salt, stronger and purer than any you will find in this insipid world. Take care with it. Don't get any in your eyes. If you do, I promise you will regret it."

He put the jar of salt on the floor and walked away. After a moment, Tchiił picked it up.

"Thank you for the gift of salt," the barbarian said. "I will treasure it."

Qaxh motioned toward the door. "I will say farewell now," he said. "It was most interesting meeting you. But I have no desire to meet you again, yes? I have my painting of you. It is more than enough. So do not come back here."

Tchiił backed away, turned away, and left.

Qaxh walked over to the old painting. He considered it for a long moment. Then he went back to his shelves and took down the most ancient thing he had. It was in a small jar, covered in the fine white dust that preserved it. He fished it out: a single flower blossom, bone-colored, dry and brittle. Cradling it gently in his cupped hand, he placed it in his mortar, took up his pestle, and very carefully began grinding it into powder. The scent of it was delicate but freighted with memories of a place he had never been.

CHAPTER SEVENTEEN

# THE NEW BARGAIN

YASH TOOK the jar of salt and left Coral's tower, returning to the shadows where she had hidden her weapons and Needle's head. A chill was in the air, and through the stink of fire and sewage and other smells her nose did not understand, a little breeze intruded with the scent of juniper and pine on it. She looked up, tracing her eyes over the stars. In the east, an orange moon was rising into a clear sky. But in the north and west, the stars wavered. The distant shadow of an approaching storm.

"Deng'jah?" she whispered.

"I'm here," the insect said, appearing on her shoulder. "That was an evil place. I could not enter it. I'm glad you returned. Did you kill Master Coral?"

"No," she replied. "That's for later." She laughed softly.

"What is it?" Deng'jah asked.

"You called it an evil place. Yet of the tower masters I've met so far... Coral is not the worst. I almost liked him."

"He may actually be the worst," Deng'jah said. "Certainly the danger I sense there is the greatest so far."

"Maybe," Yash said. "But still, he has redeeming qualities."

"First mercy to the woman and the soldiers, and now you like one of your most dangerous adversaries?" Deng'jah asked. "Do you need me to remind you of your purpose? It is one of my tasks."

"Oh, calm yourself," Yash said. "I will kill Master Coral when the time comes. But I do not need to hate him to do it."

"It helps," Deng'jah said.

"Does it?" Yash asked. "I doubt that. And I know why I'm here. That's all that's necessary. Come on."

"You aren't taking your weapons?"

"To see Bright? They didn't help much last time, did they? No, it would only make matters more difficult."


THIS TIME Yash entered Bright's tower by the front entrance. The guards searched her person for weapons, as she had known they would, but when they reached for the bag, Yash pulled it close.

"This is for Master Bright, and Master Bright alone," she said. "I came down earlier, you remember."

"Yes, I remember," said an older guard whose eyebrows were half silver. "But you didn't have that with you."

"I'm supposed to bring it up and show no one. Go ask him, if you doubt me."

The older guard waved at a younger one, who ran up the stairs like an antelope. As she waited, Yash smiled.

"You're new to the fortress?" the older man ventured.

"I have not been here long," she replied.

"I'm Thesh Deh, the xi of this bunch. How are you called?"

"Tchiił."

"Where from?"

"Tugan," she lied. Tugan was in the Empire, albeit at the very western edge. She had been there and spoke some of the language.

"Oh," he said. "That far? Have you ever seen the ocean?"

"Once, when I was younger," Yash said. It wasn't a lie. She really had been to the ocean, not far from Tugan. It was one of her favorite memories. She had chased the waves, battled them with driftwood clubs, eaten oysters raw from their shells. She had ridden in a sea canoe, watched dolphins play. She had seen whales.

"How much younger could you have been?" Deh asked. But he was smiling. "I've never seen it. But I've been downstream, at Irthoq, where the rivers converge. I've seen the lake."

Yash nodded. "I'll bet it was beautiful. I would like to see that one day."

"Count yourself lucky to still be here in the fortress," Deh said. "We could be fighting the barbarians in the highlands. That's nasty business, I can tell you now."

"You've been there?" she asked, looking at Deh with new eyes.

"I fought in the Yechi Valley," he said. "We lost hundreds of soldiers, for what? Red rocks and sand, and the barbarians took it back three years later anyway. I don't see what the Emperor wants up there. Better to let them have it, I would think. But the Emperor knows more than I do."

Yash knew the battle. She had been eleven. Four of her cousins had died there. Shede'e, her mother's brother, had died there.

"That sounds bad," she said. "I don't know anything about it."

"It wasn't a famous battle," he said. "Almost no one has heard of it. But I lost friends there."

Everyone Yash knew had heard of it. Everyone she knew had lost family there. But she didn't say anything. She just smiled.

"You're right," she said. "We're lucky to be here, where we're safe."

Deh's expression grew more serious. "Yes," he said. "Safe. But don't—that is to say, be careful around the tower masters. You've been up there, and obviously you're well. But, where you're from, I'm sure your family is important, or you wouldn't be a courier. You'd be one of us. But even a courier…" His voice dropped down to a whisper. "Be careful, that's all. Don't offend them. Don't imagine you are their equal. Do what they say, and don't complain. Don't look at them too much, especially Master Bright." He glanced at the bag. "And if one of them gives you something to give to another…" He looked meaningfully at the sack she was holding. "Be sure it's something they… ah… want."

"I wasn't supposed to look," Yash said. "I don't know what's in it."

"Then you had better not," Deh said. "But, good luck. Ah, there's Dar back."

The younger guard reappeared at the bottom of the stairs.

"He says to bring the bag up and not to search it," Dar said.

"Well," Deh the xi said. "Go on up. But remember what we talked about."

ZU MET the barbarian in the Jeweled Room again, surrounded by his xualudeh. The guard's announcement of Tchiił's arrival had given him a little time to overcome his astonishment and to have a small table placed in the center of the room. And to think more carefully about consequences and possibilities.

What it came down to: he had not really expected the barbarian to succeed. In fact, he had begun to worry that the failed attempt on Dzhesq's life would draw attention to him. What if the barbarian implicated him in an attempt to save himself? He could dismiss the claim, but it might yet leave a cloud over him. The Emperor could decide that even a slight possibility that Tchiił was telling the truth constituted an unacceptable risk.

It seemed he needn't have worried—about that, anyway. But for the moment, all he saw was a barbarian and a sack.

"Is that what I think it is?" Zu asked.

Tchiił reached into the bag and withdrew a head.

"Place it on the table," Zu said.

Tchiił did as directed and then stepped back. Zu approached the severed head, walking completely around it as he examined it. At first, he had his doubts. It looked so unreal. Was it even a head? The eyes looked like dull gems, the flesh like wax. There was blood, and the neck was severed unevenly…

His feelings came at him in a rush. It *was* Dzhesq. A hje, like him. He remembered those same eyes, full of life as they sat through their first communing, the scent of resin and smoke, the full moon above, the wailing song of the Imprecators. Later, bathing and playing in the river, splashing one another. Most of the other tower masters were far older or younger than he. Dzhesq had been his age.

A long time ago, they had been friends. A very long time ago.

He smelled salt and realized he was weeping.

"Dzhesq." Zu sighed. "You fool." He stroked the dead sorcerer's hair. He looked up at the barbarian. "This is his fault," he said. "He should have known better than to cross wits with me. Still, I am saddened that it has come to this."

"I've done as you asked," Tchiił said.

Zu nodded. "I see that," he said.

"I expect you will now do as you promised."

"Do you?" Zu asked. "I see that you do. And yet it is not that simple. When you were last here, I was uncertain whether you could do it. Kill a tower master. After all, you failed to kill me. But now that you have, it presents me with a small problem. With Dzhesq dead, the Emperor will become concerned. There is a balance of power in this fortress, and without Dzhesq, it shifts somewhat. The Emperor may act to correct that shift."

"I will never tell anyone of our agreement," Tchiił said. "Even if I am caught, the Emperor will believe I killed Master Needle for my own reasons."

"Even if he believes that, the Emperor will not like losing an ally. He will replace Dzhesq with someone he can trust, or he may eliminate one of my supporters. Or most likely, both."

"As you said," the barbarian replied. "I do not understand your politics."

"I know," Zu said. "It is one of my faults that I assume others are my intellectual equals. I apologize. I shouldn't have tried to explain. I should have skipped the hunt and gone right to the kill. Now that Dzhesq is dead, I need you to kill four other tower masters. Hsij of the Yellow Bone Tower, Sha of the Sharp Horn Tower, Xuehehs of the Obsidian Spear, and Qaxh of the Red Coral Tower."

Tchiił blinked. "That wasn't our agreement," he said.

"No. It wasn't. My apologies. But we must have a new agreement."

The barbarian looked away, his eyes picking around the room. Perhaps remembering his last time here.

"Very well," Tchiił said. "Clearly you are in command here. I will do as you say. I will kill the tower masters you name."

"I thought we could come to an understanding," Zu said.

"And I will kill all of the others, as well," the barbarian continued. "Starting with you."

For a moment, Zu thought Tchiił was joking. He was smiling after all. But the threat hung there for too long. Then Tchiił took a step toward Zu.

"Xualudeh, defend me," he shouted.

Instantly the creatures emerged from their holes in the wall, eyes already blazing.

## CHAPTER EIGHTEEN

# SHA THE SHARP HORN

### DA'AN' (THE MIDDLE PAST)

### SEVENTEEN YEARS EARLIER

CHEJ WAS just three days past his sixteenth birthday when his father invited him to drink sweet pine tea. They had it in the little courtyard of their house, with its cracked pavers of ochre stone and single gnarled old willow tree. His father, a soft-face man with a streak of silver in his black hair, smiled uncertainly as he sipped tea, found it too hot, and put the cup back down on the small square table. Behind him, a hummingbird flitted from flower to flower of the crimson butterfly vines that smothered the eastern wall.

"Is everything alright?" Chej asked.

"All is well," his father replied. "Better than that, actually. I heard from the fortress. About you. Tomorrow, you're to go there, to the Sharp Horn Tower." He paused and tried the tea again. "You're expected."

"Expected?" he asked.

"By Tower Master Sha the Horn."

A tower master? That was unexpected, bordering on bizarre. No one at the fortress had shown the slightest interest in him. Besides, he was already serving in the army.

"Why?" Chej asked.

His father tried another sip of the tea then pushed his hand through his greying hair.

"First," his father said, "I want you to remember that you are Hje. You have some of the same ancestors as the Emperor and the tower masters. In the gaze of Heaven, you look the same as them. Bright. Beautiful. Noble."

He met Chej's gaze to see that he understood. He did; it wasn't the first time he'd heard some version of this speech. And he knew the rest of it: that whatever the eyes of Heaven might see—despite their linked bloodlines—the great lords of the Hje did not look upon Chej as one of them, exactly. That partly had to do with Chej's mother, who was not Hje. She was from the noble line of another kingdom. The marriage had been a good one and helped bring peace between the two peoples, but it meant Chej's blood was… diluted. But even his father, while of pure blood, was a few degrees removed from the tower masters because he was so much younger than they. The Emperor was of the first generation of Hje to live and rule in this valley; Chej's father was of the seventh generation. That meant, however pure his blood, he was farther from Heaven than the great ones. It was, his father often said, how things were, and they should be no less grateful and proud of their heritage. They were, after all, still far better than the subject peoples of the Empire and the inhabitants of the other kingdoms. Chej always knew his father included his mother in that last, but his father never actually said that. It was just always *there*.

So he nodded at his father's words as he usually did.

His father nodded back. "And you have more to be proud of than just your bloodline," the older man went on. "You have shown yourself to be good at numbers and letters. Xarim Ruesp spoke well of your service abroad."

"Xarim Ruesp is kind," Chej said.

"And his recommendation carries much weight," his father said. "Because of it, you are offered a rare opportunity. You have been put forth as an apprentice to Tower Master Sha."

"Apprentice?"

"Well, apprentice to *his* apprentice, actually," his father said. "But what it means is that you shall go to the Sharp Horn Tower and study sorcery."

"What do you mean, study sorcery?" Chej asked. "The tower masters are granted their powers and knowledge by Heaven."

"That's true," his father said. "But think of it this way. You trained to be a warrior, didn't you?"

"Yes."

"Only a trained warrior receives weapons and armor. A warrior ready for battle. Yes? Without training, a man could put on armor and hold a mace, but he would not be a real warrior."

"I guess so," Chej replied.

"So, perhaps Heaven has given you sorcery you would never know about until you trained to use it."

"I have sorcery?" Chej said.

"I don't know," his father said. "I only know that the Emperor has asked for you to go and learn from Sha the Horn. Or from Sha's apprentice. And I know it is a great honor."

"I—can't I continue in the army? I think it suits me."

"I know that," his father said. "And I have been proud of your service there. But this isn't my choice to make. Or yours. But think, you will be near. Your mother and I will see more of you if you're in the fortress than stationed in some faraway place."

He must have seen something in Chej's face. "I know that was selfish of me to say," his father admitted. "Your mother and I, we were so old when we finally received the gift of your birth. We had come to believe we would never have children at all. But you are a young man, and I know you dream of travel and destiny, and all of that. This isn't my doing. We aren't *trying* to keep you here, your mother and I. But I cannot say it won't please us to have you close by. Nevertheless, I can try to intercede. Xarim Ruesp might be convinced to ask for you back. But consider—to have a chance to be a tower master…"

"Of course," Chej said. "Of course, if nothing else I can try. If the Emperor thinks I should, of course I will try. Tomorrow?"

"You're expected in the morning," his father said.

Chej looked at the shadow of the willow. It was no later than noon.

"I will be ready," he said. "But now, I would like to take a walk, if I may?"

"You may," his father said. "When you return, we'll have some fruit and a cold drink with your mother to celebrate, and tonight a fine meal. It may be some time before we see you again."

"I understand," Chej said.


THE HIGH walls of the fortress were surrounded by the second, lower wall of the Terrace, where Chej's parents lived, along with most of the Hje. Below that, the great dirty beast that was Honaq city sprawled across the river valley. From the gate, the city looked like a watery maze, built as it was on the low, sandy ridges between old oxbow meanders of the river and the more recently raised ground along the canals built to channel the river's annual flooding. Low ground was mostly in cotton, grain, and beans. Rectangular stone and mud-brick houses joined together to form serpentine compounds that covered the higher ground. Four broad, raised avenues bisected the city at the cardinal directions, but that was the only sign of symmetry beyond the fortress; the lesser streets and avenues twisted along the natural hills. Honaq was loud and smelly and crowded. Smoke curled up from each complex of houses. They were only allowed one communal oven each, but that still produced fumes sufficient to cover the city in a clingy fog on windless days.

He followed the East Road toward the river, where the houses got smaller and transitioned from mud-brick to wooden longhouses raised on stilts, to the Island, a bastion of stony ground that rose up in a bend of the river where the imperial war barges were docked and the Outer Barracks were housed.

There he searched through narrow lanes of the Barracks until he found his friend Ajenx, and together they walked down along the Shorn Moon Canal as Chej explained his news. Chej cast frequent glances at his friend, trying to gauge his reaction.

"What do you think?" he asked when he was done.

Ajenx was normally talkative and highly opinionated, but today he seemed reluctant to answer. He stopped and skipped a pebble across the canal, startling an egret wading on the other side into sudden flight.

"What?" Chej asked.

Ajenx looked around before answering, as if afraid someone might be close enough to hear them.

"Is this wise?" he asked. "Is it safe? Will *you* be safe?"

"What do you mean?"

"What do I mean? Chej. You know sometimes… I've heard that sometimes people who serve in the towers aren't—ah—safe. They—I had a cousin that was assigned to the guard in a tower. One day he never came home, and there was never any explanation. There are many other stories like that. You know this."

"Those are just tales to frighten children."

"Maybe if you're Hje," Ajenx said. "Maybe for you, it's different. But for us—who grew up down here—those stories are not just for children."

Ajenx and Chej were the same age, but they hadn't met until the two of them served under Xarim Ruesp. Ajenx had grown up in the large, crowded houses of the Back Hills, where few had more than a trace of Hje blood. Most of the inhabitants there were descended from the peoples who had lived in the valley before the Hje arrived, or from more recent immigrants from other parts of the Empire.

"I'm not better than you," Chej said.

"Oh, I'm clear on that, old soldier," Ajenx said, for a moment more his old self. "But it's not what you and I know that matters." He shrugged. "I just hope you're safe. I want you to be well."

"I don't want to go," Chej said. "I'd rather stay in the army."

"Why is that?" Ajenx asked.

"Well…" Chej began. He faltered. "Is something wrong?" he asked. "You seem different."

"Yes," Ajenx said. He started walking again. "It *was* different. When we were in the South, with the army. It was more like we… really were the same. But we aren't, you know. We never will be. And maybe—maybe we should stop pretending we are."

"Ajenx," Chej said, softly. "Don't. Please don't."

"What happened between us," Ajenx said. "I'm not sorry about it. It was—it was perfect. It's like a gemstone I keep in my pocket. Very deep in my pocket. You will never be far from my thoughts, Chej. But even if you stayed in the army—you know. You know, don't you?" Chej realized Ajenx had tears on his face. "I want to live, Chej," he said. "I want to grow old."

"Do you think anyone knows?" Chej asked, in alarm.

"No," Ajenx said. "If they did, they would have already purified you, and I..." He didn't finish. He didn't have to. Customs were far less forgiving for those who weren't Hje.

They walked a few more paces. Chej's throat tightened, making it difficult to talk. "If we were both in the army, stationed very far away..."

"There is no place that far away," Ajenx said.

They crossed a footbridge over a canal stocked with blue bluntheads. The fish swam lazily, untroubled by their passage. Metal flies skimmed above the surface on spider-silk wings.

"So it's just as well, then," Chej said. "That I go to the Sharp Horn Tower. It's for the best."

Ajenx nodded. "Yes. Only don't get eaten by a monster, please. It would be horrifying. For me. I might even have a nightmare."

"Well, at least it would be a dream about me," Chej said.

"There it is, just the sort of thing I would expect you to say," Ajenx replied, shaking his head. "Let's talk about something more cheerful."

"I hear they have a plague in Lobuthup," Chej said. "Vomiting, diarrhea, bleeding from the ears."

"Oh, tell me more," Ajenx said. They spent another few hours together, but the real conversation was over, and they never returned to it. And, after a pleasant evening with his parents, Chej spent a mostly sleepless night, rose, bid his father and mother farewell, and went to the Sharp Horn Tower.

## DII JIN (THE PRESENT)

CHEJ FELT the Beast as soon as he entered the Sharp Horn Tower. The stones themselves shivered with his presence; the musky stench of him filled the air. He hadn't exactly forgotten what it was like being around the monster, but he had put it out of his mind. He had nearly pissed himself the first time he actually saw the Beast. Sha had laughed, and so had his apprentice Dzhen, although he could see in Dzhen's eyes that he also feared the xual.

Dzhen was long gone; Chej had never been clear on what happened to him. But Sha's latest apprentice, Ruez, a young man with a round, open face, met him at the entrance and escorted him up.

"You were once apprenticed to my master?" Ruez asked him as they climbed the ramp that twisted along the outer wall of the tower.

"Years ago," Chej said. "Or, rather, I was apprenticed to Dzhen, who was apprenticed to Sha."

"Oh, yes," Ruez said. "Dzhen. Umm. But what happened to you?"

"Nothing," Chej said. "It's just that I had no aptitude at all for any of this. I never really understood why I was here, or what I was supposed to be doing."

"Well," Ruez said. "It is, in fact, a challenge."

"I'm sure you're doing better than I did," Chej said. "I didn't mean to imply—"

"No," Ruez said. "Of course not."

"To be honest, I spent a lot of my time hiding from the Beast."

Ruez nodded. Chej thought he looked unhappy, but there was no way to be certain. Meanwhile, the sound of breathing grew louder and louder. There had been a time when the sound had been as familiar as his own heartbeat, albeit not a time he cherished in memory.

The Sharp Horn Tower was broader than all of the other towers, with the exception of the Earth Center Tower itself. This was so the ramp could be wide enough for the Beast to wander from floor to floor if it pleased. The Beast could take many forms, but it was always *big*.

"If I may ask," Chej ventured. "Where—"

"It's in the Alabaster Chamber today," Ruez said. "We'll be passing it momentarily."

The Alabaster Chamber was on the fourth floor; the sound of the monster's huge lungs was loudest there. He couldn't see it, because the huge portal to the room, usually open, was closed today. Sha did that on some occasions, mostly when the Beast was in a particularly irritable mood. The panting gradually got softer as they approached Sha's chamber three levels higher.

Sha was busy dissecting something on a big wooden table as they walked in. It might have been a wolf. Another six tables held the remains of as many animals: Chej was able to identify a rabbit, a tortoise, and a marmot. He noticed a sleek grey creature that looked like it had once been a large fish, although its organs resembled those of a fur-bearing animal more than fish guts. Had it come from the ocean? He remembered Sha particularly valued creatures from the ocean. He remembered once someone had delivered what was purported to be a young whale, although that looked like a fish, too. Sha had been enraptured with it and had spent many days taking it apart. So long, in fact, that the entire tower had been filled with the stench of it rotting: the only odor that Chej had ever known to overpower the reek of the Beast.

Sha wore a leather apron spattered with blood; his arms were red from his hands to just beyond his elbows. As they entered, he was placing an organ—was it a liver?—in a shallow pot. The room stank of blood and excrement along with what might be boiled honey and burnt wax.

Unlike some of the tower masters, Sha wouldn't attract much attention outside of the fortress. Under the apron he was dressed in a plain beige shift and sandals. His black hair was cut straight at the middle of his brow and to the same level around his head, so his prominent ears jutted out. He had a square jaw and a mouth that turned down at the corners when he was resting. Smiling was an effort for him, one he did not often make. He did sing, though, often: usually sorcerous songs and mnemonics to help him remember his formulae. He was singing now, although too low for Chej to make out the words.

He didn't look over at them when they first entered, but after a moment he removed a long strip of something from the dead beast under his hands. He pointed his finger about the table and muttered the numbers from one to eight. Then he straightened.

"Chej," he said. "It is, I must say, awfully strange to see you here. Can I guess why? I confess I really can't."

"Xarim Ruesp sent me," Chej replied. "I've been helping him in the war-heart."

"Oh?" He plunged his bloody arms into a bowl of water and then wiped at them with a towel. They were still not very clean and retained a reddish-pink color. "Now you've just moved me to the previous page, as we say. What on earth compelled you to help Xarim Ruesp?"

"We are at war. I thought I might be of use."

"Or perhaps it's what you didn't want to be doing, eh?" Sha said. "Ruez, fetch us some tea, will you? And by 'us' I mean Chej and me."

Chej's throat caught. So Sha knew, too. Given what Ruesp had said, it shouldn't be a surprise, but it still hadn't fully settled on him. It made him feel unpleasantly naked.

"Yes, Master Sha," Ruez said. He hurried off and Chej heard his feet on the stairs. If things remained as they had been a few years ago, the equipment for making tea was a floor up. As fond as Sha was of taking corpses apart, he wasn't keen on blood or bile in his tea.

"So Ruesp, then," Sha said. "Yes, you were under his command, weren't you, when you were in the army? I assume he sent you for a report?" Sha dusted off a stool with his pink hands and settled on it. "I would have gotten around to sending Ruez down eventually."

"There's that," Chej said. "But there is also something else."

"How intriguing," Sha said. "What else could there be?"

"It's a delicate thing," Chej replied. "I want to approach it carefully."

"You were always far too careful, Chej. Like you thought you could live forever. Although, ironically, if you had succeeded as my pupil, you might have been immortal. Or at least, very long-lived."

"I don't believe I had the talent for sorcery," Chej replied.

"There is no such thing as talent," Sha said. "There is practice, there is determination and persistence. Talent? It is the thing that lazy people cite to excuse themselves from trying. It is how they minimize the work of those who toil tirelessly for perfection."

"I remember you saying this before," Chej said. "Many times."

Sha coughed out a laugh. "I was always amused by you, Chej. I suppose I still am. What's this you've come to tell me?"

Ruez arrived with the tea, placing the cup carefully in Sha's outstretched hand. Then he brought Chej his. It was served at room temperature, but nevertheless had a bitter heat that Chej had always found pleasing. It was Sha's favorite, from someplace in the South.

"I forgot how much I like this," Chej said. He glanced over at Ruez. "A delicate matter," he said.

"Of course." Sha signed for his assistant to leave. In moments, Ruez was no longer in sight.

"Well?" Sha said. "We're alone again."

"I won't waste your time," Chej said. "Two tower masters—Dzhesq and Hsij—have been murdered. I fear you may also be at risk."

Sha had been drinking with his eyes closed, but now they slitted open as he turned toward Chej.

"Dzhesq and Hsij, deceased? Can this be true?"

"Yes, I am afraid it is," Chej said. "And worse, both of their heads taken. It is all I know. Well—almost all I know."

"That last bit was wasted time, the thing you said you wouldn't do."

"We had a courier from Zu. He asked many, many questions about Dzhesq, Hsij, Qaxh, Xuehehs, and you. Weirdly pointed questions. As if he believed that the five of you are up to something."

"Zu," Sha muttered. His gaze flicked back to Chej, piercing this time. "Why inform me of this? Why not the Emperor? You see the pattern, I assume. All of the tower masters you've named are allies of the Emperor. This suggests a coup is planned, does it not?"

"The Emperor is aware of the situation," Chej said. "He is taking steps. This is one of them."

"You have orders from the Emperor?"

"Orders? No. That would be indelicate, and, should things go awry, the Emperor knows nothing. But were he here, there are measures he might suggest."

"I see," Sha said. "And these measures?"

"Zuah the Abalone is surely Zu's ally in this, along with Yir. But Zuah's tower is nearest yours."

Sha raised one eyebrow and took another sip of tea. "Are you suggesting I attack another tower master? Even while we are engaged in this war against the barbarians?"

"The Emperor did not choose to be betrayed, obviously," Chej said. "No more than Dzhesq did. Or Hsij."

"That's a good point," Sha said. "I wonder, did you speak with the Emperor himself?"

"No," Chej said. "Xarim Ruesp had that honor."

"That explains some things," Sha said. "As does Dzhesq's death."

"What do you mean?"

"Dzhesq was tasked with killing you," Sha said. "It was supposed to look like your bride murdered you in your sleep. But apparently someone killed him before he could do that."

For Chej, everything seemed to stop, including his heart and lungs. All he could see was Sha's cold gaze. All he could hear was the Beast breathing through the stone of the tower.

"That can't be right," Chej finally managed.

"Yes, it can," Sha said. "I was at the meeting, along with Xuehehs. Xuehehs was supposed to deliver the message to Dzhesq. I wonder if he is dead, too?" He leaned back. "To be honest, I thought you were a victim in all of this, Chej. I felt a little bit sorry for you. Like I said, you amuse me. Even with those… unnatural tendencies of yours. Disgusting. I was supposed to kill you back then, when they found out about you and that soldier. But the Emperor changed his mind. I assume he foresaw some use for you. Perhaps this very use."

"Soldier?"

"Of course I can't remember his name. I doubt that anyone else does, either."

*Ajenx?* But he was alive and well. He had been sent to Dharlet, hadn't he? He was still there, maybe married, with a few children. Still keeping the gem deep in his pocket.

He'd never heard from Ajenx again, but that was intentional, wasn't it?

It had only been a kiss. A few kisses. No more. It wasn't possible.

It was entirely possible.

His fury had been buried so long and so well that, when it came up, he didn't know what it was. It was more like he wasn't himself at all, just a meat shell filled with a demon from some other place. Still less did he recognize the scream that tore from his throat as he lunged toward Sha.

## CHAPTER NINETEEN

# THE PLACE WHERE THEY CHANGED

## DA'AN' (THE MIDDLE PAST)

### EIGHT YEARS EARLIER

YASH STUMBLED and almost fell. She closed her eyes against the blaze of the sun.

Three times the night had come and gone since her walk began. Her empty stomach hurt. Her last drink of water had been the night before.

*"I need water, Deng'jah,"* she little-voiced.

"There is none," her helper said out loud. "Not for a long while. Not if you stay on the path as you're meant to."

"Then I'm going to die," Yash murmured. "Surely Grandmother knew that when she sent me here."

"She did not mean for you to die," Deng'jah said. "She intended for you to become improved."

"That sounds like nonsense," Yash said.

"There are things that live here, in this heat, with no water for months," Deng'jah said.

"You mean like cactus and scorpions?" Yash asked.

"For instance."

"Good for them," Yash said. "And that's an excellent point you can be sure to make to a cactus or a scorpion. But I'm neither, and I don't find that helpful, Deng'jah."

Deng'jah didn't answer. Yash kept walking.

As the day was hot, the night was cold. The stars were like flecks of ice in the sky, the moon a ball of snow. But still there was no water and no food. She would have gladly eaten one of the scorpions she had spoken of the day before, but even they had more sense than to show themselves to the blistering sun and freezing stars. She had lost track of the distance she had traveled and had no sense of how far she had to go. She wasn't even sure *why* Grandmother had put her on this path, or what was at the end of it.

Eventually, her body became more like a ghost than a solid thing. Her arms and legs were made of smoke from the fire in her lungs, but even those flames soon seemed to diminish, become less a part of her. It was easier that way. She let her mind drift far away, to cool meadows and mountain streams. Her legs carried on almost without her say-so.

As her spirit slowly disengaged from her body, she entered a canyon with high, sheer walls of striated stone.

She was hopeful, at first, because canyons often meant water in some form, but here was only a dry wash that had not run with rain in months, if not years. Her vision was beginning to blur, and even the shadows cast by the stone walls radiated light almost too harsh to look at. She imagined cottonwood and willow leaves rustling in the breeze, the smell of coming rain, the rushes on the highland lakes, an on-the-surface-it-moves-swiftly dimpling a still pool with its tiny feet.

Up ahead, something moved in the shadows. Something shone there.

Closer, Yash saw it was a woman, or what looked like one. She wore a white skirt and blouse, and her hair was all white, like an old woman's, although her face looked young. She wore bracelets of coiled shells on her wrists.

"Hello, Little Mother," Yash said. It was the safest thing to call the woman since Yash did not know who she was. It hurt to talk, her throat was so dry. She wasn't even sure her words made sense.

"Granddaughter," the woman replied.

Ah. She'd had the generation wrong. She corrected herself. "Thirst is killing me, Grandmother."

"I can see that," the woman said. "But as Deng'jah has no doubt told you, there is no water here. No food, either."

"You're not here to help me, then," Yash said. "So I will continue on. Expect to find me dead a little further down the canyon. Thank you. May all go well with you."

"Don't you know this canyon?" the woman in white said. "Don't you know what it is?"

"I do not, Grandmother," Yash replied wearily.

"It is The Split Rocks Where They Touch," the woman said.

"I've never heard of it, my grandmother," Yash said.

"It is also called The Place Where They Changed."

"That—that sounds familiar."

"Think on it."

Yash swayed, and everything grew brighter, so bright she nearly passed out. But when the dizzy spell passed, she examined the walls for clues. The tilted layers of stone lay in different colors: some red, some yellow, some grey-green. And here and there other patterns showed in the stone. Shells, the bones of fish, things that looked like strange plants but also like spiders. The hard parts of living things, without flesh or breath, made into rock. And creatures of the water, as if some ancient sea had once covered this desert.

*Qeemelehk'e, The Place Where They Changed*, she thought.

"My ancestors," she managed.

"What touches here is the Silent Stagnant and the White Brilliant, the Ice Horizon and the Sky World. You recall the story of your ancestors? How they began?"

"They began as creatures like insects," Yash said. "Some stayed that way. Others didn't. They became other sorts of animals, and birds— some didn't. Some became human people as we traveled from world to world. Some didn't. Some became Rages, the Terrors That Follow."

"Of course," the woman said. "The world is change. Life is change. The Silent Stagnant is what-has-been. The White Brilliant is fast, like a hummingbird's heart, and quickly destroys us. But between those things—between these walls and the sky—there is Change. Or at least, the possibility of it."

"I'm too thirsty, Grandmother. I don't understand what you're trying to tell me."

"Is your body the same as it was when you were born?"

"It's bigger," Yash said. "And, yes, different, too. It changes all the time. *I* change."

"But you have not learned your body properly, grandchild. You have not befriended it. It is not one thing, Yash. Your body is made of many things that work as one, but they are *not* one. Not yet."

"I…" She could think of nothing to say.

"Your thirst," the woman said. "Think of that first. Of your mouth, your throat, your belly, your blood. Learn them. Befriend them."

It sounded stupid. She wanted to tell the woman to either give her something to drink or to shut up and let her die in peace. But she remembered Shede'e. She remembered the place that was no longer a place, that was creeping over outward like a disease. She remembered a dream about a monster that stood like a mountain on the horizon. She closed her eyes. She thought about her thirst and the pains in her belly, about her raw throat, and the illusion she had been painting in her mind of inviting places faltered and dissolved, drawing her spirit back into her suffering so that she was completely there, in the heat, in the pain. In her failing body.

It was awful, and part of her wanted to retreat again to the safe, easy places in her mind. But now that she was here, in her flesh, with her bones, she began to understand what the woman in white meant.

So she spoke to herself the way she had learned to speak to spirits, to the land, to all sacred things.

"*My thirst*," she sang softly.

*You are a thing alive*
*I see you now*
*I have nothing to give you but myself*
*And my gratitude*
*For without you, my thirst,*
*I would not know myself*
*All of myself.*
*Thank you, my thirst.*
*Let us be one together*
*Let us not separate*

*I will never again deny your existence*
*Even when I cannot give you ease*
*Even when it hurts*
*And I fear my death has found me*
*You are mine*
*And I am sacred*
*And I embrace you.*

And as she sang, she felt her thirst somehow grow less. Or the agony of it, anyway. And now she knew what she was doing. She sang on—to her hunger, to her hands, her arms, her legs—and as she did, each of them became real to her in a way they never had been before.

And as that happened, they changed. All of the parts of her changed. And it hurt. But she was no longer fearful of the pain, no longer ashamed of anything. She screamed in agony and in delight. And when it was over, she opened her eyes, and was new. And whole. And stronger than ever.

The woman in white was still there. She nodded and smiled.

"Deng'jah," the woman said. "Take Yash to Lightning Place so that she can master what is taught there."

Yash started walking again, feeling everything, but now certain that she could finish the journey.

## DII JIN (THE PRESENT)

AS BRIGHT'S strange creatures emerged, their eyes crackled as if their gazes contained lightning, which, perhaps, they did. But this time Yash was ready. She felt their white gazes travel across her body, burn her nerves and muscles, but she accepted the pain. She let her body face their sorcery and let it change her as she had changed in the canyon. Let herself become better.

It hurt, of course, terribly, as change often did. She gasped in agony, and she saw Bright's triumphant, gloating expression.

But Bright did not know what was happening.

The flashing in the monsters' eyes grew brighter, deadlier. Yash grasped the bag Needle's head had been in by the bottom and spun around in the Complete Whirlwind feat. She had emptied the salt Coral had given her into the bag, and now it flung out into the chamber. The air filled with the smell of lightning, hot stone, and salt. Made furious by the effulgence of the deadly gazes, the salt flared into incandescent sparks and blew through the room like a sandstorm. The little monsters shrieked as the burning particles flew into their eyes. They closed their lids against it, and the deadly light, the crackling lightning, was gone. The monsters continued to wail, their deadly eyes tightly shut.

Bright gaped. He looked from her to his monsters.

She gave him that second. Then she took the whirlwind to him.

Bright ran. He was much quicker than he looked, but that wasn't what stopped her from reaching him. Even blind and deprived of their most lethal weapons, the xualudeh were still a nuisance. They swarmed around her, beating at her with their wings, which, as it turned out, were like sharpened glass at their edges. In instants she was covered in shallow cuts. She grabbed one by the neck and slammed its head into the stone floor and kicked another so hard it flew across the room. They were hard to kill, these little monsters. They didn't have much weight, so her punches and kicks just sent them flying off, but they weren't fragile. They kept coming back. She had managed to crack another's skull on the floor when Deng'jah appeared on her shoulder.

"Jump out the window," he said. "Now."

She didn't question him. Batting her way through the bird-monsters, she ran for the nearest window. A glance back showed Bright had returned and was standing in the doorway holding a bow, pulled back to shoot.

As she tumbled through the opening into the night air, white-hot heat scorched her back and she was half-deafened by a clap like thunder. The entire roof lit up as if in a flash of lightning, like a hole had been opened into the White Brilliant. She smelled her own hair burning. She managed to hit the roof on her feet, but it was a long drop and knocked much of the wind out of her. She knew she didn't have time to recover, though, so she dashed back toward the tower, jumping through the lower window by which she had first entered. As she did so, another explosion of heat and light erupted, this one on the rooftops.

A glance back showed a big smoking hole in the roof, fire licking at its edges. Below, where she couldn't see, people screamed in agony and shock.

Bright had turned the weapon he'd been using on her people against his own.

She clambered back into the tower, back into the room with the stone pillars and bones: the door to the White Brilliant. She stopped long enough to pick up what looked like the femur of something, about as long as her own forearm. It was twice as heavy as it looked. Hefting it, getting a feel for its balance, she charged up the stairs, with Deng'jah flying ahead.

Bright was waiting for her, half-hidden behind the doorway, arrow pointed down the stairs. She hurled the bone and kept running, knowing that if he managed to shoot that arrow, there wasn't much she could do. Reaching him first was her only chance.

But luckily he'd had to wait to see her before drawing the bow. Its pull was probably too strong to simply *hold*. The bone hit Bright on his drawing hand before he could begin bending the weapon. He screeched and dropped both bow and arrow, then backed up, drawing a long knife similar to the one she'd had to leave on the roof. She saw his skin had also changed; he was covered in glistening gold scales.

She checked her charge and dodged to the side as Bright cut at her. The weapon was fast, as if it weighed no more than a willow switch. She stamped on his instep and punched him in the armpit. The scaly armor he had plated himself with absorbed most of the impact, but he nevertheless grunted in pain. He thrust at her with the knife, or tried to, but she was already inside of his reach, so she caught his arm and twisted it, disarming him and taking the weapon for herself. Before he could react, she had sliced him across the throat with the blue–white blade.

But the knife didn't cut him; it turned on the golden scales. Bright cackled and punched her in the head.

"No blade can cut this armor," he said as she staggered away from him. He ran toward the bow and arrow where it lay on the floor.

"I see that," she said. She noticed the bone she had thrown lying nearby. As he grabbed the bow, she picked it up.

"That's too bad for you," she said.

The scales couldn't be cut, but the armor was flexible, and the organs and bones underneath were no stronger than those of a normal person. It took longer to beat him to death with the bone, that was all. When she was done, and she was sure of her work, she went to investigate within the room and found all of the xualudeh were dead, burned up by Bright's flying-star arrow.

"The guards are coming up," Deng'jah told her.

"How far?"

"They've just started."

She picked up the bow and the eight arrows Bright had with him and shot one of them down the stairwell then ducked back into the room to avoid the explosion that followed. She went quickly back to the remains of Bright's xualudeh.

"Deng'jah?" she asked. "What's happening on the stairs?"

"That didn't kill any of the guards, but it sure scared them. They've stopped coming, for the moment."

"Good. Tell me if they start again."

She placed a hand on one of the strange little corpses and closed her eyes.

"*I am sorry, my foe,*" she sang.

*I am sorry.*
*But we were fated to fight*
*And me or you and yours to die*
*I am sorry, my foe*
*I am sorry I do not know your name*
*The enemy captors had a name for you*
*Xualudeh*
*Minaqe Yeł Heqani*
*Some called you*
*In the language of my People.*
*But that is also a monster name.*
*What is your real name?*
*The place that gave you life*
*And meaning.*

*Who are your kin?*
*Where is your place?*
*I want to know.*

For a moment, nothing stirred. The smell of burnt feathers and flesh stung her nose and the back of her tongue. Outside, she heard the distant wails of the injured and shouts of alarm. The sleeping fortress was now awake.

She pushed all that aside and repeated her song, more softly this time, placing all of the weight of her concern on each word, tone, phrase.

And in the space behind her eyes, something began to glow. Little yellow-green sparks drifting up from the grass, winking against the darker line of the forest beyond. A handful of stars in the deep blue sky twinkled in reflection on the quiet surface of a lake. On the horizon stood shadows of mountain peaks outlined in pale gold, and a gliding, low-throated song lifted up to fill the valley. More distantly, another song rose and fell on the faintest of breezes. She knew the shape of the mountains; she knew the valley she was looking across, the lake, the tree line. But this was not as she had seen it. This was as it had been once, before she was born. Before the hunters took its soul away.

It was where Shede'e had taken her. The first dj'ende place she ever saw.

Tears started down her face. She coughed to clear her throat.

"*I see you now,*" she sang.

*Hush'ełdiik'e', Whippoorwill Place*
*Ch'eh'mikunik'e', Firefly Place*
*Wesdzik'e', Owl Place*

*Return there*
*Be what you were*
*What you are*
*Before they unshaped you*
*Light the Dusk*
*Sing to the twilight*
*Be in Harmony*
*You are free now*
*To make your home*
*A Place once more.*

The air in the room stirred. For a moment, she felt a mountain breeze and heard the songs of whippoorwills. A handful of glowing sparks wafted out the window. Yash paused, feeling the spirits, feeling their power. She could use that power right now. Bright had awakened the fortress. Things were about to become much more difficult. Why send these naheeyiye home when she could use them to fight her enemies? She knew their names. She knew how to do it. With their power added to her own, she would be very powerful indeed. Once victorious, she could free them again.

But she felt their longing, their sorrow. Their wish to return. She would not—could not—enslave them as Bright had.

She took a deep, slow breath and let it out. And they were gone.

She realized that Deng'jah was trying to get her attention and had been for some time.

"The guards," he was saying. "They're here."

Yash jumped up, slipped one of the flying-star arrows onto the bowstring. Its head crackled and spit sparks. She pointed it at the man standing on the landing.

She found she was looking down the shaft at Deh, the xi she'd talked to downstairs. He stared at her, his face washed out by shock, a bladed mace in his hand.

"What… what did you just do?" he asked. "What went out the window?"

"Something the Empire took from my people," she said. "Something I have now returned to its proper place."

*"The other guards are behind him,"* Deng'jah said. *"They're getting ready to charge you."*

"And you killed Master Bright," Deh said.

"Yes."

His gaze picked about the room and settled back on her. "You have his bow. Was that you shooting the whole time?"

"I shot it once, the last time, to warn you not to come up the stairs. Before that it was Bright. He's the one who blasted a hole in the roof outside."

"You killed a tower master," Deh said. "And his monsters, you killed them, too. How did you do that, Tchiił? Who are you? You aren't a courier."

"Listen, Deh," Yash said. "I know the other guards are behind you. I know they're getting ready to charge. If they do, I'll kill them. All of them. If you doubt me, consider what you see here."

"I don't doubt you," Deh said. "But my duty—"

"Your duty was to protect Bright. You didn't. He's dead. How many of your men have children at home? Spouses or lovers? Fathers and mothers and siblings? I'll tell you this, Deh, and you can believe me. I am here to destroy the tower masters, including the Emperor. I thought that meant killing everyone here: every guard, every soldier, anyone who lends their arm to the Empire. And it might still. But

I know now I don't want to do it like that. It makes things more complicated for me, but that's what I have decided. And I'm taking it one situation at a time. In this situation, you and your men arrived too late. Bright is already dead. If you had died trying to protect him, that would be one thing. But if I'm forced to kill you now, who does that benefit? Not you. Not me. Not Bright. Not Needle or Yellow, who are also dead. Not the other tower masters, not the Emperor. If you live now, you may choose to fight me again, later, when you have a chance of winning. If you insist on fighting me now, I let this arrow go, and you know what will happen. All of you will die without laying a hand on me. Is that how you want it to be?"

Deh stared at her for another few heartbeats.

"You're right," he said. "But if we just let you go we will die anyway, executed for cowardice."

"Not if I was gone when you got here," she said. "Not if you never saw who murdered Bright."

She lowered the bow. "Think about it," she said. Then she ran and jumped out of the window again. She might have to kill them eventually, but right now the thought of cutting down the men she had been speaking to earlier was not appealing.

But there was more to it than that, something that was starting to itch where her mind and her soul came together.

However difficult her task had been, when she came here it had at least been simple: kill the tower masters and anyone else in the fortress who got in her way, defeat and free the captive spirits of her country. That was it.

So why was she complicating things?

"I think there's something else that needs your attention," Deng'jah said.

CHAPTER TWENTY

# GHOSTS

### DA'AN' (THE MIDDLE PAST)

### THIRTY-ONE YEARS EARLIER

"WHAT'S WRONG?" Dzhi asked.

Hsheng closed her eyes and swayed, then sat back down, fearing she would fall.

"I was dizzy," she said. "Everything looked blurry."

Dzhi's brow wrinkled. "Do you think you're sick? Maybe you've been out in the sun too long."

Hsheng considered that. The two girls sat on the high terrace that surrounded their mother's summer house in the hills outside of the city. It was a nice change from their dark rooms in the Emperor's Keep, and Hsheng looked forward to the trips precisely *because* of the sunshine, the air, the trees and flowers and wide blue sky. She and Dzhi had spent most of the day before and all morning digging little canals with spoons they had borrowed from the kitchen. The plan, once they were finished, was to have the servants fill them with water so they could sail toy boats on them.

It wasn't hot, and there was a nice breeze. The sun felt good on her skin.

"I don't think it's the sun," she said.

"Did you eat this morning?" Dzhi wondered. "You get so absent-minded."

"Yes," Hsheng said. "It's just—maybe I *am* sick."

"What?" Dzhi asked.

"It's just—the food didn't *taste* like anything."

"That's peculiar," Dzhi said. "Did you have the berries? Those were good."

"Yes," Hsheng said, "with honey. They tasted like sand." She shrugged. "I ate them anyway. And the sweet cakes. I don't think they had any salt or ash in them. And I'm still hungry."

"They had plenty of both," Dzhi said. "You *must* be sick. Maybe you should go tell Mother."

Hsheng did that, reluctantly. Her mother put her in a cool, dark room and brought her a cup of water. She took a sip.

"Could I have some honey drink instead?" she asked.

Her mother looked at her for a moment then took the cup and tasted its contents.

"This *is* honey drink," she said.

"Oh," Hsheng said.

"Lie down for a while," her mother told her.

Hsheng did as she was told. After a time she felt no better, but she also felt no worse. Bored, she rose and went to find Dzhi.

Her sister wasn't there, but the canals they had dug were now full of water. Dzhi had scooped mud from the canals and used them to form small temples, towers, and houses along the banks. It made Hsheng smile. That looked like fun. She knelt by the small ditch, reached her hand in, and brought out some mud. She looked over, across the terraces, to the distant outline of the fortress and the Earth Center Tower.

*That's what I'll make*, she thought. Her own version of the tower. It would be taller than any of Dzhi's buildings.

She started piling the mud. It didn't want to keep its shape; it kept trying to flow into a lumpy mound, but she incorporated dry dirt to stiffen it up, and finally her tower began to gain height. She was just beginning to be pleased with it when she grew dizzy again. She put her head down, smelling the damp soil. For the first time she was afraid. Maybe something *was* wrong with her. Something bad.

She started, realizing she must have fallen asleep. Then she realized Dzhi was there, talking to her. No, *yelling* at her.

"What is wrong with you?" her sister demanded.

"Nothing," she said. "I fell asleep."

"I mean *that*," Dzhi said, glaring at something.

Hsheng followed her gaze. Where Dzhi's buildings had been there was now only ruin. Someone had knocked them all down.

"I didn't do that," Hsheng protested.

"No? Then who did?"

"I was asleep!"

She stood up, but then everything spun around and around, and her knees wouldn't hold her up.

"Hsheng!" Dzhi cried as she fell to the ground.

HSHENG WOKE but could not move. She tried to cry out but was unable to find her voice. Her will moved, strove, worked to make itself felt, but her body was cut off from her. Her mind festered and filled with the rot called fear.

After what seemed a very long time, something entered the darkness, dim red snail trails that pulsed and faded away. They distracted her, lessened her fright, formed patterns that seemed familiar. Eventually she understood that they were words. Someone was talking to her. Someone was calling her name.

She asked her arm to move, and a finger twitched. She commanded her eyes to open, and there was light.

For sixty breaths she could do no more. She counted them. Then she slowly tilted her head.

She was in a room she did not know. The floors and walls were all of pale yellow stone marked here and there, as if someone had written on them, but after studying them she saw that instead the marks appeared to be various sorts of shells imbedded in the polished rock. Some looked whole, some cut in half so she could see the spirals inside. The light she saw that by came through a narrow window. She lay on a bed raised a little from the floor, and next to it a man sat on a stone bench. Talking to her. She had seen him before, although it had been a long time.

"Father?" she asked. "Emperor?"

"You hear me now, daughter? Have you come back to the world?"

"I'm scared," she said.

"It will be better from here on," he assured her. "The mind-rot will clear."

"But what happened?"

He smiled. "You are my daughter," he said. "My true daughter, my heir. I have waited so long, I had begun to think you would never arrive. If I had known it was you, I would have protected you.

But there was no way to know that. Generations have passed. Many of my children have lived and died, and none of them were *you*. But now everything will be fine."

"I don't understand."

"You were too far away from the Earth Center Tower," he said. "You could not tolerate the distance. By that I know you."

"Is that where I am? The Earth Center Tower?"

"Yes."

"But I've only been in the tower a few times."

"True. But your mother's rooms in the Keep are near enough. Her summer house—that was where you were when this happened. And it is too far away."

"But I've been to the summer house before. Many times."

"That was before you awakened. Things are different now."

"I still don't understand, Father."

"You will, in time. And you will see that what you gain from this will outweigh what you have lost."

She nodded. "I'm feeling better," she said, moving her limbs. Everything worked now, and she felt not only well, but strong. She sat up.

"Can I go back now?" she asked. "Dzhi and I were making something. And Mother is planning a party of some sort."

"You can't go back," he said.

"You mean until I'm well?"

"You can't go back, ever. From now on you will stay here, with me, in the Earth Center Tower." He spread his hands. "This is your room. If it does not please you, I will find you another."

She blinked and looked around. "This whole room is mine?"

"Yes."

"Oh. But—does this mean I shall never see Mother or Dzhi or Sueh again?"

"You can visit them when they are in their rooms in the Keep. You can stay there when you wish. And you can go out into the fortress. But if you go any further, what just happened to you will happen again. Do you understand?"

She tried to say something, but her throat was choked with sobbing. The Emperor waited patiently for a little while. Then he put his hand on her shoulder. He had never touched her before, and it shocked her so much she forgot to keep crying.

"In the tower, you will be my first," the Emperor said. "In the tower, none shall be above you but me. You are my one true child. I am so glad you are finally here."

He rose to his feet. "Rest. I'll have food and drink brought. Then we shall talk further. Later your mother and sisters will visit. All will be well, you'll see."

She watched him leave. Then she got up from the bed and walked across the stone floor. It was cool and made her bare feet tingle. She looked out the window and saw the fortress far below her, the city, the river, the distant mountains. A breeze blew in.

A little later, a small old woman arrived with a platter of fruit and sweet cakes. It was all Hsheng could do not to snatch them up and stuff them in her mouth, but she managed to wait until the woman left. She couldn't remember ever having been so hungry, and the food looked and smelled wonderful.

But it didn't taste like anything. She might as well have been eating mud. She ate it all anyway, and, although there was plenty of it, when she was done she was almost as hungry as before she'd opened her mouth.

***

## DII JIN (THE PRESENT)

HSHENG'S SERVANTS prepared the vapor bath, and when it was ready, she disrobed, entered the darkened stone chamber, and rested on a bench of jade, inhaling the fragrant steam, preparing her mind and body for what was to come. Sweat slicked her then ran down her body in hundreds of rivulets, like a mountain shedding snowmelt in the spring. When she was done, she washed with cold water then used incense wands to dress herself in dry smoke.

She mounted the steps to the top of the tower and gazed in every direction through the tall, arched windows, taking four long breaths at each of the eight points. In the northwest, lightning flickered. A storm coming their way, or moving to the north?

In the east, the moon had risen. She stared at it, feeling the slight tremble she always did, the pull of the small hairs of her arms and neck toward the dim lantern of night. She studied the marks of the ancient war, the scars of a world blasted clean of life. Images stirred in her mind of fantastic beasts, forests of gigantic flowers, plains of moss and fungi, still, silvery pools. But then—storms of lava, obsidian winds, dry lakes brimmed with shattered bones. As if she had been there, or was somehow still there, although she had not been. She had been born here, in this place, thirty-seven years ago. The visions, no doubt, were merely from dreams she did not remember having.

From the sky and the eight winds she turned her gaze downward.

The fortress below was not quiet. Things were happening. Unexpected things. Something had burned a hole in the rooftops near the Bright Cloud Tower, but it was more than that. She could sense it. She closed her eyes, focused her will, and then went to the center of the room and stood between the four mirrors there. She kindled coals in a bowl and sprinkled dried, broken flower petals on them. She stood straight and faced the north mirror, which was of obsidian. She spoke the names she knew; she sang the verses she had learned. Then she turned south, to a mirror of polished blue stone and did the same, then west to a copper mirror. To the eastern mirror—the silver mirror—she did not speak.

And they came, the *ix*, the eerie phosphorescent reflections of the dead, the parts that remained of people after their real souls were gone, the most awful bits of the people they had been. They pressed against their sides of the mirrors. They moaned and imprecated and chattered incessantly. She could feel their lust for her, their yearning to infect her with their awful substance, but they could not reach through the surface of the mirrors. But *she* could, and they knew it. She teased them, reached for them, pretending that she might touch them just a little, just slightly, if they told her what they knew.

Among them were three that were angrier, brighter than the rest. Newer. So new they did not yet understand they were dead and had not yet learned the toothless, tongueless speech of ghosts. But unlike the older spirits, who were mostly faceless, these still looked something like they had in life, so their mere presence told her a lot.

After that she sat alone, drinking tea made from a flower that no longer grew anywhere. It was sharp and bitter and the only thing she could taste, so she savored it. She burned resin of the whitegum tree to purify her from the pollution from the ix. And she thought about what she had learned.

Dzhesq, Hsij, and Zu were all dead. Three tower masters fallen in less than the span of a day. But there had been no report of it.

No alarm raised. As far as she knew, she was the only living person in the fortress aware that they were deceased. Except for the killer, of course.

She took another sip of her tea, considering. What was happening, really? According to some of the other ix—the ones who could speak—the tower masters had all been killed by the same person, but none of the spirits were able to tell her who it was or even what they looked like. That meant sorcery or at least someone protected by a spirit or spirits. Her father had just begun his war against Zełtah, which was unlikely to be a coincidence. But was the murderer an assassin sent by Zełtah, or had one or several of the tower masters decided that the war presented them with an opportunity to act?

She needed to know these things and more. The brief rest and the tea had refreshed her, but, considering the speed with which things seemed to be moving, there was no time to waste.

CHAPTER TWENTY-ONE

# THE BEAST

THE SURPRISE on Sha's face as Chej locked his fingers around his throat might have been funny if Chej wasn't so furious. As it was, he didn't want to see *any* expression on Sha's face. He wanted to squeeze until Sha simply *wasn't*. He slammed the sorcerer against the wall, vaguely aware that he was screaming incoherently, totally aware of the savage joy fueling his rage, that Sha's throat was soft. He could feel the windpipe inside it crush and crackle like a millipede's shell.

Chej was bigger than most people, but he didn't often feel that way. Now he did. He felt like a giant slaughtering a mouse.

But then Sha changed. He got bigger. Horns pushed out of his head, and Chej suddenly felt Sha pulling at his arms. He realized that the tower master's nails had become claws, digging into his flesh. The force of his fury, so strong one short breath before, was now a moth trying to batter a thunderstorm into submission. His hands were wrenched from Sha's throat; the tower master slung him by his right arm so that he flew across the room, landing briefly on a table covered in bloody body parts before tumbling on to fetch against the wall.

Only when he had crumpled to the floor did the pain really begin, a shockingly bright agony in his shoulder.

He groaned as Sha shoved a table out of the way, coming to inflict more pain. The sorcerer still had a mostly human shape, but he had grown antlers like an elk, his mouth was three times its usual size and pushed out in a muzzle, like a bear. And, like a bear, the tower master was covered in fur.

Chej tried to stand up although he didn't have any reason to. Either way, he was going to die. He *wanted* to die. The pain was intolerable. And Ajenx, poor lovely Ajenx. That was Chej's fault. He hadn't really understood, hadn't truly believed what the consequences of his actions might be. He didn't deserve to live, and he wasn't going to. He wished he could have killed Sha first, but now he saw how ridiculous that notion was.

Sha bent, grabbed him with his clawed hands, and lifted him up as if he were a child's cotton doll.

"Don't worry," Sha snarled. "I won't tear you to pieces." He thumped Chej down on a table. "When you do die, it needs to look like your tiny little wife did the deed. A slit throat, maybe. Or maybe I'll cut your testicles off for good effect. Seems like something a barbarian woman might do. But this business with Zu you've put forth complicates things. I'll have to find out if Dzhesq and Hsij are really dead, and then you and I will likely need to make a trip together to see the Emperor."

His arm hurt like a demon was chewing it, and he couldn't move it.

One of Sha's eyes suddenly stuck out toward him on some sort of tentacle or stalk. Like a crab. His thoughts all fused together, and everything in the room took on a yellow tinge. His head rang with weird music. His heart tried to batter its way out of his chest. Sha's mouth gaped open, showing bear-teeth.

Sha let go of him and spun around, and something long turned with him. Dimly, Chej understood that Sha's eye hadn't been on a stalk, but on the tip of a spear. The rest of the spear was sticking out of the back of the tower master's head. The sorcerer screeched and lurched away from Chej, and then someone different screamed. Chej jerked in reaction and then curled into a fetal position, eyes closed, wishing it would all go away.

And then it was quiet. No, not quiet. The building still shuddered faintly from the breath of the Beast. But the yelling had stopped. From where he was, he couldn't see Sha.

Slowly, Chej's thoughts began to unstick. Words began to form sentences, then sentences ideas. The first, most important idea that formed was that he had to get out of there. Now. Now! But he found it hard to move. What if Sha was still there, just waiting for him? He remembered the tower master's eye sliding out on the tip of a spear. He took four deep breaths and sat up.

And nearly screamed again when he moved his arm. He grasped it with his left hand, although it didn't help at all.

Sha was gone, although he'd left an immense amount of blood behind. There was someone there, though. Ruez, the apprentice. He was lying in a contorted position against the wall, eyes open. He looked dead. But when Chej stood up, Ruez's eyes shifted toward him.

"Help me up," Ruez said.

Chej studied him. "I think—Ruez, you may be better off resting," he said.

"I can't stand by myself," Ruez said. "We have to get out of here. We have to get to Yir. He'll protect us."

"Yir?" Chej said. "What does Yir have to do with this?"

Ruez looked somewhat puzzled. "Yir sent me here," he said. "To be Sha's apprentice. It was all arranged by Zu. Surely you know this. Zu sent you, didn't he? It's time, isn't it? That's why I had to kill him. That's right, isn't it?"

His eyes weren't quite focused anymore.

"Ah," Chej said. "Yes. That's right."

"If he had taken you to the Emperor, everything would have been ruined."

"Yes," Chej said. "You did the right thing, Ruez."

Ruez's eyes moved again, trying to look out the door. From his position and the fact that he hadn't moved anything but his eyes, Chej was starting to believe the apprentice's neck must be broken.

"Where is Sha?" Ruez asked.

"I don't know," Chej said. "He isn't here."

"You have to make sure he's dead," Ruez said. "If he's not, that spoils everything. Go after him. Finish him off."

Chej nodded. "I will," he said. "I will, Ruez."

He looked around and chose a knife from the table.

"Ruez?" he said.

The man looked at him.

"Thank you. You saved my life."

Ruez nodded. "I'm tired of living in fear. Terrified that he would find out. As soon as he finished with you, he would have started suspecting me. He probably already did. Make sure he's dead."

Chej hesitated. But he knew there wasn't anything he could do for Ruez. If he killed Sha and escaped the tower, he might be able to find a healer and send him to tend the apprentice. If Sha survived, neither of them had any chance at all. The best he could do was to follow Ruez's advice.

Thanks to the trail of blood he'd left, Sha wasn't hard to follow. Predictably, he'd gone down the ramp, toward the Beast.

He'd nearly made it. Chej found him collapsed just short of the door to the Alabaster Chamber.

The tower master had continued changing, perhaps trying to find a form in which there wasn't a spear through his head. His body was still thick and bearlike, but one of his arms had become a black-feathered wing. His other arm had a hoof at the end of it, while his feet resembled those of a dog or wolf. His head, on the other hand, was recognizably human. His remaining eye was open and staring at nothing. He looked very dead.

Chej approached slowly, holding the knife in front of him. The floor shuddered as the Beast paced on the other side of it. As if it knew. Probably it did, but Chej wasn't sure what that might mean.

Sha moved. He sat up a little, and his gaze fastened on Chej.

"Chej," he whispered. "You. Come here."

*He can't be alive*, Chej thought. It just wasn't possible. He shuffled forward. His arm was still in agony, and pain in other parts of his body was starting to register now. But his anger was also coming back.

"Ajenx," he said. "Why Ajenx?"

"I didn't kill him myself," Sha whispered. "I didn't even give the order."

"But you're the one that's here," Chej said. He was close now. He knelt and put the knife to Sha's throat.

"Goodbye, Chej," Sha said.

Chej's throat tightened, and he realized he wasn't breathing. Sha's eyes glittered like dark gems, and his lips twisted into a mocking grin. Chej slashed him with the knife, cut his throat—or tried to. But the knife didn't move. It was like it was just stuck in the air.

He tried to back up, to run, but that didn't work either. A rushing sound began in his ears, as if he were submerged in a swiftly flowing river. His vision dimmed. Sha drew himself up. He reached for the door latch. He started to turn it. Spots danced in front of Chej's eyes, and he was tired: very, very tired. Ready to sleep. If only he could take a breath, one single breath…

As it grew even darker, he saw Sha's head take flight; it just jumped up off his neck and flew. Not far, just a little way, and then it bounced on the floor and rolled until it hit the wall.

Chej started breathing again. He was still tired, still in pain, but his lungs were working. And his vision was starting to grow brighter.

"Shegan', are you well?" a voice asked.

He looked over. Yash was squatting next to him, holding a long xarim knife.

"Sha…" he muttered, trying to make her—him?—understand.

"He's dead," Yash said. "You put a spear through his head. I'm impressed."

Why did Yash think *he* had stabbed Sha? Chej wondered. But she didn't know about Ruez. It was all too much. Too many things were happening at once.

"Wait," Yash said, standing. "I can't hear it anymore. What happened?"

That, Chej understood. The Beast. It had suddenly fallen silent.

"What's in there, Chej?" Yash asked.

"We just call it the Beast," Chej said. He rubbed his brow. "It's *never* quiet."

"Deng'jah?"

"Watch out!" the bug said. "It's coming through the wall."

Yash grabbed Chej by the shirt and jerked him toward the down-sloping ramp. Then much of the wall shattered and burst outward.


FRAGMENTS OF stone stung Yash's face as she dragged her husband to the ramp.

Through the newly formed hole in the wall, she had her first glimpse of the Beast.

Most of what she could see was its head, which was huge, more than half the size of her entire body. A gigantic horn protruded from its snout and forked into two blades that curved back toward its head. It had thick, wrinkled skin and didn't look much like anything she had seen before. She couldn't make out the rest of it, but, by the angle of the head, she guessed it was currently down on all fours.

"Do you know which naheeyiye this is?" she asked Deng'jah.

"I wish I had better news for you," Deng'jah said.

The head withdrew then came back, crashing into the hole it had made. Strangely, the door itself was intact. It looked as if open it would have been big enough for the monster to fit through. She figured it had been ensorcelled in some fashion to prevent the Beast from breaking it, so it was making its own door. It wasn't quite big enough yet, but it soon would be.

She needed to find a safe place to put Chej. Her husband seemed to have taken a bit of a beating. His right arm had been pulled out-of-socket, and he looked as if he'd been mauled by a bear, although given what she had seen, it had probably been Sha the Horn, who appeared to have been a skin-changer.

"Chej," she asked. "The Beast. Is it too big to fit onto the ramp?"

"What?" Chej said. His eyes were wild, unfocused. But then he seemed to understand her question. "No. The tower was built to allow the Beast to move around. That's why there aren't any stairs. Sha would close it up in rooms sometimes, especially when he was worried about his guests. But usually he let it go where it wanted."

"Are there rooms in the tower with doors too small for it to get through?"

"A few. But it will just crash through the wall, won't it?"

"That will take it a few moments. You need to get to the nearest of those, one with a window that goes outside. Don't wait for me. Get out of the tower. Do you understand?"

"Yes," he said.

"Let's go."

Sha was a skin-changer. His monster was a horned beast. It ought to mean something to her. But like Deng'jah, she couldn't place what naheeyiye this was. Without its name she couldn't even slow it down. Probably she should just focus on killing it and sort out its identity later.

Once they got around the curve of the wall, she gave Chej a gentle push to start him down the ramp.

"Go," she said. "I'll be right behind you."

She didn't wait for an answer but instead bounded back up to the landing, taking the bow off her back and nocking one of Bright's arrows to the string.

The Beast was backing up for another run at the broken wall. The hole was now nearly big enough for it to fit through.

She aimed at one of its eyes, noticing how tiny they were relative to its overall size.

She let it go, jumped back out of sight and dove down the ramp as the flying-star arrow filled the landing with heat and light. She landed on her hands and turned the fall into a tumble. It hurt, but she didn't break any bones.

Chej was at the next landing, looking up at her with his mouth open.

She ran back up. The ramp was hot, but not too hot to tread on. The air had a sharp, charred smell.

"It's still alive," Deng'jah informed her. "Tough creature."

"What?" She peeked around the curve of the stairwell. The Beast looked back at her. It didn't have a scratch or a burn on it.

"That's not good at all," she muttered.

"We absolutely agree on that," Deng'jah said.

Then the monster pushed through what was left of the wall, and she saw the rest of it.

It had had its head lowered. Now she saw its shoulders were at almost twice her height and it was four or five times her length from head to tail. It stood on four tree-trunk-like legs that each ended in four stubby hoof-toes.

It lowered its head again, pointed its two-pronged horn at her, and charged.

She dodged and raced down the ramp. It followed. It was a tight fit for the monster, but, as Chej had pointed out, not too tight. She suspected on open ground the Beast would move four times as fast, but even between narrow walls it set an astonishing pace.

There seemed to be no point in wasting another of Bright's arrows on it, so she ran. If she could bottle it up someplace, get around behind it, maybe she could carve it up with her knife. But if the flying star arrow hadn't hurt it, would any of the weapons she had be any better?

She caught up to Chej at the next landing, which was only second from the bottom. He was standing in the opening to another room, gesturing for her to follow, which she did.

"This one is too small for him," he said. "Sha never keeps him in here." Then he yelped as the Beast reached them and crammed its head into the doorway. The floor shook with the impact.

Chej was right. The opening wasn't big enough. But it would be soon.

Yash ran to the window and looked down. The rooftops were only a level below them, touched with the pallid light of the rising moon. Across to the east, the hole Bright had blown in the fortress now glowed with a fierce orange-yellow, indicating a fire beneath. In that glow she saw people were now on the roof, milling about the opening. Some of them had torches. She couldn't make out how many of them were armed, but she was willing to guess most of them were guards. Her time was running out. But the moon, still low in the sky, cast long shadows of towers and walls in their direction. Here, on the western side, they might still go unnoticed if they jumped now.

But could Chej make the jump? And would she get another chance at the Beast?

She looked back at the monster, drew the long knife, and ran toward it. It saw her coming and tried to gore her with its split horn, but she dodged that easily enough and sliced it where the big vein in its throat ought to be. She didn't find out if it was there or not; as keen as the demon-bone blade was, the skin of the monster was too tough for its edge. The head swung back down, trying to crush her. She leapt up and stabbed it right in the eye.

She might as well have tried to pierce a gemstone.

She just managed to retreat before being impaled. The monster put its shoulder into the wall and it began to crack. Then the Beast backed up to get more momentum.

"That wall isn't going to last long," Deng'jah said.

She looked back out the window at the distant torches, at the rivers and seas of shadow below.

"Husband," she told Chej, "I think we're going to have to jump."

Chej looked out the window. "Oh," he said. "Yash. No." He was holding his dislocated arm, looking like he was only half aware of what was going on.

"It will be fine," she said. "Jump as far out as you can, so you don't go down that alley and break all of your bones. Land on your feet and let your knees bend."

"Why don't you just kill it?" he asked. "That's what you do to everything else."

"Weren't you watching?" she asked. "I tried to kill it! I'm not sure I can. Unless you know something I don't."

His eyes cleared a little. "There *is* something," he said. "I think there is."

"Well?"

He put his good hand to his forehead.

"I don't remember."

"Then we have to jump."

The doorframe had already begun to crack, and stones were dislodging from the wall.

She pushed him to the window. "Step up on the ledge," she said.

He looked back at the Beast. Then he did as she said.

"So jump out, like I told you. You have to get over the alley. You have to do it. I can't jump for you."

"I know," he said. His face set in determined lines. Then he jumped.

## CHAPTER TWENTY-TWO

# CHEJ'S COURTYARD

## TSAYE (IN ANCIENT TIMES)

THE MOON *World lay near the White Brilliant, always bathed in its light. It was a beautiful place with many rivers and streams and seas full of fish, tall forests, and lush meadows. And it was there that Tsenid'a'wi, in her (or his, or their) guise of Nelehi, The One Who Becomes Repeatedly, taught some of the people to walk on two feet and become like the human beings we know today. They built houses and villages, and for a time—a very short time—things seemed fine. But the Rages, the Sorrows, and other Terrors That Follow that had joined them on the journey multiplied, and some of them walked on two feet and could not be told apart from humans. And some humans began to like the monsters. They made pets and servants of them. They used the Rages to make war, and with them they subjugated the Moon World. They began to call themselves the masters and gods of the Moon World. And the name they called themselves was Hje.*

*But there were still people of all sorts that wanted no part of this. They did not trust the subjugation of the monsters. They did not like the Hje,*

*the self-named gods of the Moon World. Once again, Tsenid'a'wi traveled,*
*searching for a new home. But this time he had to evade the Hje and their*
*Rages. He had to find difficult, secret passages the Hje did not know and*
*that they would not find. This time, the Terrors That Follow must be left*
*behind for good.*

## DII JIN (THE PRESENT)

CHEJ LANDED on his feet, as instructed, and bent his knees. The
problem was, they kept bending, and quickly, too, so his knees thumped
the roof. He gasped and fell on his face. It hurt—he thought his nose
was bleeding now—but somehow the pain wasn't what rose to the
top of his mind. Maybe because his arm already hurt so much, or
because everything had been happening too fast for him to keep track
of. But what struck him the most—as he watched Yash land lightly
on her feet, roll, and come back to them as if she'd just tumbled like
a traveling acrobat entertaining the court—was how *funny* it all was.
He croaked out a laugh, and after that he couldn't stop. He laughed so
hard he shook and had trouble finding his breath. He finally became
so short of air he had to stop and take a lungful before continuing.

"Shegan'?" Yash said, staring at him. "Hush. There are people on
the roof."

"I… I told Ajenx I wanted to stay in the army!" he managed.
"Can you imagine, *me* in the army? How incredible would that have
been? Oh, wait, everyone! I'll hold off this charge of one thousand
men! You fellows take a break!"

Then he broke down again and couldn't talk anymore.

Yash pulled him up by the arm that wasn't killing him.

"We can't stay here," she said. "Someone will see us, if they haven't already."

"See us?" Chej said, looking back up at the tower. "Is that what we're worried about at the moment? Someone seeing us?"

"Come on," she said, yanking him. He stumbled, his laughter finally subsiding.

"Where are we going?" he asked.

"Somewhere to hide, to tend your wounds. Somewhere I can figure out what to do next."

Above them Chej heard an enormous rushing, grinding, cracking. He watched, mouth open, as the side of the tower burst and the Beast come soaring out of it, almost glowing in the moonlight. If it was possible, it looked bigger than it had before.

Yash yanked him by the hand, pulling him off-balance, forcing him to run or fall. He couldn't tear his gaze from the face of the Beast, those horrible glittering eyes welling with fury.

The Beast thundered onto the clay tiles, and everything descended into chaos. He and Yash were thrown up and separated by the buckling roof as if by an ocean wave. Dust and smoke blew up all around as he flopped back down onto the cracked tile.

When he managed to look back, he saw a huge, Beast-sized hole in the rooftop he had only narrowly been tossed clear of.

He couldn't help it. He started laughing again, even harder when he heard the Beast crashing around below and the chorus of distant shrieks of terror coming up through the gap in the fortress ceiling.

"What now?" he finally asked.

When Yash didn't answer, he looked around alarmed. The dust had cleared enough that he could see she had been thrown a little farther from the hole. And that she wasn't moving.

"Yash?" he asked. He stumbled to her and nudged her in the ribs. But she didn't respond. Her eyes were closed, and now he saw the blood on her face. Had the Beast hit her? It was all a blur.

"Yash," he said, gently tapping her cheek with the back of his hand.

He looked back at the hole. How long before guards came? Yash had said something about people being on the roof. He heard shouting, but couldn't tell what was from below and what might be up here with them. The dust cloud and the night still obscured his vision.

"We have to get away from here," someone said.

Chej's heart jumped so hard, it nearly left his skin behind.

"Bug?" he gasped.

"Deng'jah," the bug said. He saw it now, perched on Yash. "Come on. There are guards coming."

"Of course there are," he said.

He looked around, trying to get his bearings. He knew the roofs well enough. He had explored them as a child. He remembered a place, but it had been so long. It might not even still be there. And if it was…

"I don't suppose you have some magic power to help me carry her?" he said.

"No," Deng'jah said. "I don't."

Chej sighed and nodded. He'd thought as much. His right arm was still in agony, and wasn't going to be much use. But he had practiced carries when he was under Ruesp's command. He managed to get his left arm under Yash's back and shift her into a sitting position. From there, he was able to get her onto his shoulder and lift. He staggered the first few steps. She was far heavier than her small frame suggested. But then he managed to think his way beyond the pain and put one leg in front of the other.

"Hey!" someone behind him yelled. "Who's that?"

He glanced back and saw someone with a lantern. They were on the other side of the hole the Beast had made. He tried to go faster, but it seemed certain whoever-it-was would catch him before he reached his destination. He would need to have a lie ready, something to tell them…

The building shook again, and a chorus of screams rose up behind him. He looked back and saw the shadow of the Beast's head and its huge forelimbs pawing at the edge of the hole it had made, collapsing even more of the roof. He no longer saw the men who had been chasing him.

He repositioned Yash on his shoulder a little and kept going.

The old smoke vent was where he remembered it. It didn't smell like smoke, and no heat was coming from it. He still had Yash on his shoulder and was trying to figure out how to lower her down the hole when he felt her squirm. Not like she was moving, but like something under her skin was shifting around. Rearranging.

He bent over and gently flopped her onto the roof then started pulling her by the foot toward the vent, trying to remember how deep it was.

"Down there?" Deng'jah asked. "How do you think you're going to manage that?"

"I don't know," Chej said. "I didn't think ahead that far."

"Wait," the bug said. "Let me try something."

Deng'jah flew around Yash's head and then landed on her lips. He glowed, briefly.

Yash coughed and then suddenly jerked up to a sitting position.

Her eyes were wild, and for an instant Chej was afraid for his life, but then her gaze softened.

"Chej?" she asked. "Deng'jah?"

"You're hurt," he explained. "I was trying to get us someplace safe."

"He was going to drop you down that hole, I think," the insect said.

"Down that hole?"

"Yes," Chej said. "I mean, no. I wasn't going to drop you. But we ought to go down there. There are all sorts of people on the roof, and they're going to find us soon."

"Tell me about the hole."

"It's an old smoke hole," he said. "Between two walls. It goes down below the fortress, to the old fortress this one was built over."

"How far down?"

"Pretty far," he said. "I used to brace myself and go down. I don't know how I was planning to get you down."

"I think I can manage," she said. "But you, with that arm?"

"I can do it," he said.

"I'll go first," she said. "You follow. Deng'jah, keep watch. Let me know when someone gets near."

CHEJ WOKE sitting against the wall in total darkness. Someone was kneading his shoulder. It hurt, but it felt good, too.

"Yash," he said. "Is that you?"

"Yes."

"What happened?" he asked.

"You passed out coming down the shaft," she said.

He remembered then. That meant they had made it to his courtyard.

"What are you doing to my arm?"

"It's dislocated," she said. "I'm going to try to get it back in place."

"Oh," he said. "You know how to do that?"

"I know something about it," she said. "I've studied the human body. Mostly how best to destroy it, but I picked up some ideas about how to fix things as well."

"What about you?" he asked. "You were hurt."

"I was," she said. "I think my skull may have been cracked a little. But it's better now."

"How do you heal a cracked skull?" he asked.

"Bone heals naturally," she said. "Sometimes I can speed it up a little. When I change, part of me touches the White Brilliant. Everything in my body goes faster. So when I change, I sometimes heal as well."

"Change," he said. "You changed again?"

"Yes," Yash replied. "I changed again. No more penis. For now. Couldn't you tell?"

"I hadn't thought about it," Chej said. "I can't see you. I guess your voice sounds a little different."

"Deng'jah? A little light?"

"I can do that," the metal fly said. Then Deng'jah appeared on Yash's shoulder, glowing a pale blue-green. It wasn't much light, but it was enough to see Yash's face and the wall he was propped against. But the light thinned away into shadow a stride or two from the insect.

"Here's the thing, Husband," she said. "Whatever form I'm in, whatever parts I have or don't have, I'm the same person."

*Of course I know that*, Chej thought, defensively. But then he realized that he didn't. Or hadn't. Or maybe, more honestly, he didn't know *what* he thought.

"That's—you know that's strange, don't you?" he finally said. "This *changing*. Being a woman one minute and a man the next."

"I know it's strange for you," she replied. "For me, it's rather usual."

"And for your people?"

"I'm not considered odd among them, if that's what you mean."

Confusion silenced him for a few moments, so he focused on what she was doing to his shoulder. It was, he realized, the first time in a long time anyone had *touched* him. It felt wonderful, even when it hurt.

"Do I call you he or she?" he wondered aloud.

"Your language makes that distinction," she said. "Mine doesn't. We have the word *mi*, which in your tongue means he, she, they, them, it. If I have male parts, female parts, or both, I'm always mi—always Yash. You can take your pick. I don't care about that."

"I see," he said, nodding. "It's alright if I call you she?"

"Of course. As long as you understand who I really am. It's just a word."

"I understand," he said, although he wasn't sure he did. But he wanted to.

"Who is Ajenx?" she asked.

"What?"

"When you were losing your mind. Before I got hurt. You were talking about someone. I thought you said Ajenx."

"Yes," he said. He grunted as her fingers dug into a muscle. "I should tell you something."

"I'm listening."

He lowered his eyes, wishing it were fully dark again. He didn't want to talk about this, but he felt like he should. Maybe it was just more of Yash's earring pushing him, or maybe he felt like he owed her something, as crazy as that was.

"The reason they chose me to marry you," he said. "The reason they planned to murder me."

"You told me about that. So they could blame me for your killing and justify their war on my people."

"Yes," he said. "But before that, they had another justification." Chej turned his gaze to the floor, and his face flushed a little. "At first they were just going to say you refused to... ah... receive me."

"Do sex?" she said. "I mean, *have* sex."

"Yes."

"But we didn't," she said. Then she got it. "They did not *expect* you to visit me. They believed we would not have sex."

"That's right."

"Why? Did they know of our conversation in Zełtah?"

"No," he replied. "They know—they know something about me."

"What?" Yash asked.

"I'm—" He sighed and forced his eyes up. "There's a word. *Hguesyaj*. It's a man who—ah—prefers other men, for that. For love, and sex."

Yash was silent for a few heartbeats. "You're joking with me?" she asked finally.

"No," he said, starting to feel not only embarrassed but a little angry. "This is hard for me to say. Why would I joke about something like that?"

"Because it's ridiculous," she said.

"You may think me ridiculous," he snapped. "But I... by the demons, you change from male to female. Physically! I thought, maybe..." He trailed off. What had he thought, exactly? That she would understand?

"No, *you* are not ridiculous," she said. "I mean how you're *acting*. Like you did something wrong. Or like there's something wrong with you."

"I just told you," he said. "There *is* something wrong with me."

"Are you trying to tell me your people think this is a bad thing, that you prefer men?" Yash said.

His mouth hung open for a moment.

"What?" he finally managed.

"Maybe I'm not understanding you," she said. "I've studied your language, but some things about your people are very puzzling."

"Of course it's a bad thing," he said. "It's an abomination. Unnatural. I've had to hide it my whole life. Are you trying to tell me that with your people—in Zełtah—being hguesyaj is permissible?"

"Permissible?" she said. "We don't even have a word for it. We sex with who we want. We marry who we want." She tilted her head. "Well, not close relatives, I suppose. But otherwise…" She trailed off and then smiled.

"So," she said. "When I was male. When I had a penis. Did you want to sex with me then?"

"Have sex," he corrected. "No! I mean, I didn't think about it. There's too much going on. But I don't, ah, think of you that way."

"Because you think of me as a woman. You just said you weren't confused about that."

"I lied," Chej said. "I'm nothing *but* confused. Please stop."

"I don't think the confusion is coming from me," Yash said. "Even though I'm a little confused. You never told me who Ajenx was. Someone you loved? A man?"

Chej felt his breath shorten. "Yes," he said. "I think so. We were in the army together, a long time ago. We… did something. Not much. But too much, I guess. All of these years I thought he was well, living his life far away. He stayed in the army. But I just found out they killed him. Sha told me."

Now that the fury was gone, he discovered what was left was mostly emptiness. The whole life he had imagined for Ajenx, where he was alive somewhere, maybe even happy. He hadn't realized how big a part of his own dream that was, and how little remained once it was removed. He felt tears coming, but he didn't care.

"That's why you attacked Horn," Yash said, softly.

"Yes. I was so angry. I didn't know I could be that angry."

"I'm so sorry, Chej, that your friend was killed. It's an awful thing. And the reason—I won't pretend I understand the reason. It's like being killed for..." She trailed off. "I can't think of anything that my people do that's comparable."

"The problem is," Chej said, "I still want to do something. What happened, it's not enough. Sha wasn't even directly responsible. Someone else gave the order."

Yash was silent for a moment, but she kept kneading his arm.

"Once when I was very little," she said after a bit, "I thought an ember in a fire was a jewel. I picked it up, thinking I would carry it with me everywhere."

"I bet you dropped it pretty fast."

"I still have it," Yash said. "I still carry it with me. And the lesson. That the things that can really hurt you often look beautiful. And revenge—revenge seems so pretty, doesn't it? Like you want to pick it up and carry it with you. But it's not what you think it is, Chej, and it won't make you feel what you hope it will."

"It's strange for you to talk like that," he said. "Isn't your whole reason for being here revenge?"

"No," Yash said. She looked surprised. "Is that what you think?"

"I suppose I did. For us making war on you, and for stealing your... spirits, or whatever. You said we had to pay."

"I don't know your language as well as you think," Yash said. "And I was angry then, so maybe my words were corrupted by that. I meant you have to pay *back*. Give redress. Return what was stolen.

We need the spirits of our country back where they belong, Chej. And I want this war against my people ended. If I have to kill or cripple everyone here, then I will. But not because I want revenge. I just want things to be *right*."

"So if the Emperor agreed to end the war with Zeltah and return your spirits, you would just go home."

"Of course," Yash said. "But we tried that. We've sent champions in the past—not to fight, but to talk."

"And it didn't work?"

"They were never seen again," she said. "We believe they were murdered. Like your friend." She patted his shoulder. "Look into my eyes," she said.

"What? Why?"

"Just do it. Study them. What do you see?"

It was hard, looking into her eyes. He kept wanting to look away. And she was doing something else with his arm.

"What are you—"

She pushed in his arm. It popped. It still hurt, but now it felt... right.

"There," she said, breaking their locked gaze. "That should be better."

She pulled away. He lifted his arm and rotated it experimentally.

"Thanks," he said. "That *is* better. But what about you?"

"I'm fine," she said. "The Beast grazed me. Not with its horn. No cracked bones other than my head, like I said, and that seems to be better. The blood you saw came from my forehead. It was cut when we fell, and foreheads bleed a lot."

"Good, then," Chej said. "Ah—how do you say 'wife' in your language?"

"Xad," she replied. "Although you would say *shexad*, 'my wife.' Of course, you could also call me shegan', as I call you."

"I'll think about that," he said.

"Do that," Yash replied, softly. "Shegan', can you tell me more about where we are?"

He drew a slow breath. She was right. They should concentrate on their current problems. He certainly hadn't thought any further than this.

"If it were daylight, you could see better," Chej said. "Enough light comes down the shaft. It's just a big empty room, with a few half-starved plants trying to survive in the dust on the floor. I used to call it my courtyard."

"When you were little."

"Yes. I used to come here to be alone."

"Did anyone else come here?"

"Probably, but I never brought anyone here or saw anyone here."

"Are there other places you know like this? Secret places?"

"A few."

"You're full of surprises, Husband. Useful surprises. You stabbed Horn in the head!"

"Yes, that," Chej said. "I didn't do that. Ruez did. He was Sha—Horn's apprentice. Although I guess he was really serving Yir? It's confusing. Horn attacked me—well, no, I attacked him, I guess. But I lost the fight, of course. It wasn't even really much of a fight. Horn was going to take me to the Emperor and sort the whole thing out. He was there, with Xuehehs—Obsidian—when my death was ordered, so he suspected I was up to something. I'm sorry."

"For what?"

"I know you were hoping to get the tower masters to fight each other and do some of your work for you. Now that's spoiled."

She laughed. "Coral gave me the salt I needed to kill Bright. Horn's own apprentice put a spear through his head. Yes, it would have been wonderful if they had all killed each other, but how lazy do you think I am? Thanks to my plan—thanks to *you*—Bright and Horn are dead."

"And the Beast is loose."

"Yes, causing trouble as we speak," Yash said. "Distracting the guards. Perhaps they still don't even know about me. Another gift I wasn't expecting. So, return to this Ruez person. Why did he stab his master? You said something about Yir? That's Pinion, right?"

Ruez. Chej had been trying not to think about him. He had only known him a matter of minutes, but he felt sorry for anyone who had been in Sha's service. And Ruez had saved his life, even if for the wrong reasons. Was he still alive? Probably not, but if he was, that might even be worse.

"Yes," he said. "Ruez was secretly serving Pinion, and, less directly, Bright."

"I see," Yash said. "I guessed that might be the case. I hoped. Where did Ruez go, then? To Pinion?"

"Probably not," Chej said. "I think his neck was broken. I meant to go back later to see if there was anything I could do for him, but then everything with the Beast happened, and now we're here. He—he told me to make sure Horn was dead. That's what I was trying to do, but of course Horn got the better of me again. If you hadn't come along, he would have killed me." He closed his eyes. "Poor Ruez," he said. "I'm responsible for him. I should have stayed with him."

"You did what he asked," Yash said. "I think you did the right thing. I know it's difficult, but we need to turn our minds from that and consider what to do next."

"You need to kill the Beast," he said.

She shrugged. "Eventually. At the moment, it's doing my work for me."

Chej had been trying to stay away from that thought, but now it was unavoidable. The Beast had fallen through the western roof and into the administrative compounds. There were a few guards there, but most of those people weren't trained to fight at all. Not that it would matter against the Beast. How many people had it killed already? How many more would it kill?

"Yash, I know you believe everyone in the fortress deserves to die. I'm starting to feel a little like that myself. But—"

"I'm at war," Yash said, softly. "But maybe—*maybe*—you're right. Maybe I will spare who I can. But I must finish this. The tower masters must die, and the naheeyiye must be set free."

"That's what you call them? The xual? The monsters the tower masters draw their power from?"

"Yes."

"Like the Beast?"

"Yes. The naheeyiye belong in Zełtah. They are part of our land and our people. The Empire took them, ripped them from their homes. Made them into monsters. As a result, my land is sick. Parts of it are dying, and those places are getting bigger, like a disease spreading. This has gone on for too long. They must be returned."

"But Horn is dead. Why is the Beast still here?"

"Because it is still twisted into what they made it. That form must die before I can send its spirit home."

"That's why you went back to Yellow's tower," Chej said. "Even after you killed him. To return his monster to your country."

"Yes. Although after I killed it, it was no longer a monster. And that's why I must kill the Beast," she said. "Although, I admit, I'm not sure how to do that. My blade won't cut it. Even Bright's arrows will not slay it. Back at the tower, you said you thought you remembered something."

"Yes," Chej said. "I remember saying that. But I don't remember what it was. Maybe nothing. When I was training with Dzhen, Horn's old apprentice, Horn left the tower to go someplace, and the two of us got drunk."

"And?"

"Very drunk."

"Well," Yash said. "Take your time. But maybe not too much."

"Just let me think."

The silence stretched as he tried to remember the conversation with Dzhen, but in that quiet he realized that once again he could feel the structure around him shaking. He could hear the monster breathing. He hoped at first it was just his imagination, but it seemed to be getting louder.

"Yash," he said softly.

"Yes," she said. "I hear it, too. It's trying to find us."

"How?" he asked.

"I don't know," she said. "By scent, maybe? Or perhaps it heard us talking."

He lowered his voice even further. "Let's stop talking, then."

She didn't say anything. It didn't matter. The sound of the monster continued to grow louder and nearer. Dust began to fall from above.

"Do you think it's looking for us?" Yash asked Chej.

"You killed Horn," Chej said. "So, yes."

"Whatever the reason, it is coming straight for us," Deng'jah said.

## CHAPTER TWENTY-THREE

# THE SEWER

YASH EXPLORED Chej's 'courtyard' for some other way out, using Deng'jah's faint illumination to guide her. Other than the smoke hole, the only other entrance or exit seemed to be a drain in the floor partly covered by a rotting wooden grate.

"Do you know where that goes?" she asked Chej.

"It goes into an old sewer," he said. "I explored it a little bit. It still works—they connected the newer pipes and tunnels to the old ones."

"To drain rainwater?" she asked.

"Yes. And other water. You know. Wastewater."

"Sewage, you mean? Your garbage and your shit mixes with rainwater?"

"Yes."

"That's… not very clean. I imagine it drains out somewhere?"

"It drains out of the fortress under the wall. But you can't get that far; the tunnel is stopped by a stone plug. It's pierced so water can get through, but the holes are too small for a person to pass."

"But there must be shafts going up, as well? Connecting to the newer drains?"

"Yes," he said. "But I never went up into those. They're—well, you just said it yourself. Disgusting. Not the sort of place you want to crawl around."

She knelt and removed the grate. The drain was narrow. She would fit, and she had no doubt Chej had fit when he was a boy. But he was a man now, and a big one. It might be a challenge.

The entire room shuddered, and bricks cracked above. She grabbed Chej and shoved him against a wall as debris rained down through the smoke hole. The Beast bellowed, and its acrid stench rolled down to them, stinging her nose and making her eyes water. She slipped over and glanced up the shaft where faint, ruddy orange light was now spilling through. The Beast's head was pushed into the smoke-hole shaft, battered through from a room just above them. It bellowed again and angled its head down, its nose horns catching at the shaft and shattering the old brickwork and opening up yet another room on the other side of it.

"It's found us," Chej said.

"Down the shaft," Yash said. "You lead the way."

"Yes," Chej replied. He glanced up. "Do you smell smoke?"

"Yes," Yash said. "I think the fortress is on fire because of Bright's arrow."

"That's on the other side, the eastern side," Chej said.

"The Beast has doubtless overturned many lamps," Yash said. "Perhaps there is more than one fire."

"But the fortress is mostly stone and brick," Chej objected.

"There's plenty of wood, too," Yash said. "Beams in the ceilings, supports in the walls. It will burn."

"You were going to burn it down yourself, weren't you?" Chej accused.

"I considered it," Yash admitted. "I might still. Can you fit?"

"My legs are already in," Chej said. "My shoulders are a little tight—oh!"

Another shower of bricks and dust fell from overhead, and fully half the ceiling of their refuge caved in. She covered her head with her arms and bent as the fragments battered her. The Beast's head drove deeper, its mouth no more than the length of her leg away now. She still had her weapons, but using Bright's bow down here would surely kill Chej and her both and still not harm the monster. The long knife had demonstrated its uselessness. Continuing the fight right now didn't seem like the best use of her time.

She glanced over. She couldn't see Chej anymore. She found the shaft with her hands and slipped down it as the Beast dug deeper. It had been hard to see in the dim light, but now it was clear that the Beast had changed somewhat; it no longer had horns on its nose and instead of thick, hooflike toes it now had huge, curved claws well suited to digging, which it was now busily doing. One of the clawed forelimbs reached for her just as she let herself down the shaft. There, she briefly found herself standing on Chej's head, who squealed and then moved out of the way. The Beast pounded the top of the drain as Yash fell into the old sewer tunnel.

It was larger than she had imagined. The dim light revealed a vaulted ceiling over a chamber perhaps ten paces wide, with four passages running out from it. Everything was wet, and it smelled of rot and shit. In Deng'jah's dim light she saw water had collected in isolated puddles, and the floor was strewn with small bones and other trash.

"This is unpleasant," Yash said. "Which way is out?"

"That way." Chej gestured.

Before they could move, however, the ceiling of the chamber collapsed with a muted roar as the Beast tore its way through it. They scrambled back as a huge claw raked down through the ceiling. The hole wasn't yet big enough for it to get to them, but in heartbeats it would be.

"I remember!" Chej shouted, over the din. "Even Horn was afraid of the Beast. Sometimes he would put it to sleep and send in Dzhen to cut a hole through its skin. It has a spot, about the size of a fist, under its breastbone, where there isn't any hair. Dzhen thought that Sha made him do that so the Beast would have a weak spot, if it was needed. One only he and Horn knew about."

"Right," Yash said, looking up. "Crawl up the tunnel as far and fast as you can go. Do it now."

She didn't look to see if he was obeying her, and the din the Beast was making was too loud to hear him moving. She strung the bow and put an arrow on its string, then lay flat on her back, watching the monster dig toward her. The shaft they had come down was now blocked by the creature, along with the firelight that had filtered down it.

"I need more light, Deng'jah," she said.

"I can do that," Deng'jah said. "But not for long."

"Do what you can."

In the next breath Deng'jah became too bright to look at directly, casting golden rays up into the shadows. She saw the Beast's belly, fur matted like felt. She didn't see anything that looked like a hole in it.

The vaulted ceiling above her sagged, crumbled, and collapsed. She kicked herself along the mucky floor of the shaft to avoid the worst of the falling debris. One of the Beast's clawed hands slapped down an arm's breadth from her. She controlled her breathing, eyes darting through the widening holes. Deng'jah's light began to dim.

It might have been a shadow she saw as her companion's illumination failed, or just a marking on the fur. It was all she had, so she sped the arrow and then began frantically kicking away, eyes closed.

The flash came through her eyelids. The sound was deafening. Then everything above the tunnel collapsed into it, muting the rest of the explosion. She covered her head and face as falling brick and stone battered her, knowing she was about to be buried.

But a few more heartbeats passed, and the collapse subsided. Her ears continued ringing, so she couldn't hear much of anything else. She slowed, panting. All of Deng'jah's light was gone now, and it was as dark as any cave she had ever ventured into. The smell of the Beast, however, was overwhelming.

"Deng'jah?" she murmured. She couldn't hear her own voice.

But she could hear her helper as clearly as ever.

"Here," he said. And with that he began to glow again faintly.

The passage was filled with rubble. She stilled her breathing, but her ears were still useless. She placed her fingertips on the ground, feeling for vibrations.

"Deng'jah, is the Beast dead?"

"I will go see," Deng'jah said.

At the same moment, a shock traveled up her fingers. Yash threw herself back as the rubble filling the collapsed sewer began to push toward her.

"Never mind," Deng'jah said. "It's hurt, maybe fatally. But it can still kill you."

The Beast shoved its head into the passageway, digging out of the debris with the antlers of a gigantic elk. She felt more than heard its furious shriek; its antlers smashed into the walls as it pushed forward toward her. She didn't try to stand up but kept scuttling back, kicking with her feet and pushing with her hands. Its glistening black eyes were fixed on her.

Horns. Antlers. The name of the tower itself. She remembered a trip to a place where the grass was tall, a dj'ende place so awful no one dared cross into it.

*I know his name*, she realized.

"De'łgheedi!" she shouted. The name sounded to her like it came from beneath a pile of blankets, and the monster took no heed.

"De'łgheedi!" she repeated.

This time, something flickered in his eyes. He drew his head back slightly, and everything was still for a moment. Then the Beast lurched forward. He vomited blood, enough to fill up three or four grown people. His massive head shivered.

Yash stared at him for a moment. Every nerve in her body told her to get up and run, but she stayed where she was, watching the monster die. After a dozen heartbeats, she moved slowly forward. She put her hand on his muzzle, felt his hot, damp breath.

"I'm sorry," she breathed. "But it's going to be better."

The anger was gone, and only confusion remained. He took a single long, labored breath, and then even that was gone. She pulled herself closer. She stroked her hands on the sides of his head. She began to hum and then to sing.

*De'łgheedi I have heard you called*
*Horn Stabber*
*Wary One, Protector of your herds.*


As she sang, she began to see a place where mountains sloped down, flattened out, and became a prairie of tall grasses that stretched far toward mountains so distant there almost looked like smoke on the horizon. Nearer, a dark shadow crept slowly across the yellow-green expanse. She thought at first it might be cast by a cloud, but the sky was clear. Then she understood. It was a herd of bison. She had seen a few of them in her life, massive creatures with dense fur and fearsome horns, but only in scattered groups, never in numbers like this. And they weren't alone. Antelope sprang through the high grass, elk grazed near the tree line. She had never seen this place. No one living had. But she had heard the stories. Once her people had ranged here, at the very edge of their country, the place of the herds. They had come back with meat, stories, sometimes wives or husbands. But that had been long ago. For many years it had been a barrier no one dared approach closely.

"*Your home,*" she sang.


*Your home is Tłuhk'e, The Grass Place.*
*Your home is Qunghinteł, Where It Becomes Flat.*
*You have been called De'łgheedi, Horn Stabber*
*But you have other names*
*Wejetsjah, Earth Trembler, Thunderhoof*
*This is your place, the Grass Place.*
*This is your home, Where It Becomes Flat.*

*Go there. Be at home.*
*Bring it all back with you.*

She felt hot breath on her neck. She smelled crushed grass, felt sunlight on her face and the wind teasing at her short hair.

She felt relief. She felt a smile begin.

*It is good,* a voice said. *I remember now, and it is good. But you must beware, child, little one, spring peeper. He is not the same as me. He is not like Older Sister Who Watches the Spring in the Winding Canyon. He is not kin to Yeetwa, The Grey Giant, or the others you have come for. He has no place in this world. He came for us. He will come for you.*

"What do you mean?" Yash asked. "Who are you talking about?"

*The one in the center. The middle of it all. He has slept. He has waited. But now he is waking. You were not meant to kill him. It is not your purpose. You—ah, no…*

The voice shot up and rose in pitch, became a howling wind. The grassy plains blurred and blew away, a painting in sand smeared and destroyed by the gale. She felt a gaze touch her then. She didn't see any eyes, or anything at all, but she nevertheless knew she was seen. And what saw her was something awful.

Something struck her. Like a wind, it wasn't a solid thing, but it was substantial enough to stun her and send her tumbling back. Farther down the tunnel, Chej yelled and then whatever-it-was continued on crashing into things, cracking stone. She lay there, listening to the racket recede, knowing the spirit of Grass Place was beyond her reach. Tears streamed down her cheeks.

She had lost him.

## CHAPTER TWENTY-FOUR

# SIL THE EXAMINER

SIL WAS a young man with twenty-three winters at best. He wore the dark blue shirt, black skirt, and red sash of an Imperial Examiner. A thin, almost invisible mustache sat on his upper lip.

"I understand the procedure," Sil told her. "But I think it best I give my report to the Emperor directly."

Hsheng hated Examiner Sil. She hated all of the examiners, because she needed them and she shouldn't. She had tried to investigate matters herself in the past, but her status as a woman made that almost impossible. Instead, the examiners looked into things for her and reported back to her here, in a small room affixed to the outside of the tower.

"Saying you understand procedure does not make it so," Hsheng told him, trying to keep her voice steady. "My father does not allow men in the Earth Center Tower. That is very simple. I wonder why it seems you are unclear on the matter." She took a step toward him. "Or perhaps you are suggesting I go tell the Emperor that you demand an audience with him? That he must come down the stairs and meet with Sil of House Nothing because you desire it?"

Sil's mouth flattened into a line.

"No," he said. "But this is important. Too important."

"Next to my father, I am the authority in the tower," she reminded him.

"We are not in the tower, lady."

"We are, in fact," she said. "The sentry yard is not. This room, in all ways important to you, is. My father made it so. Stop wasting time and tell me what you and your men discovered."

His frown deepened, but after a few more heartbeats he sighed and nodded.

"Very well," he said, "the fortress is on fire in two different places."

"I am aware of that," she said. "I can see that from my window. I trust the flames will soon be under control. That's not what you're here to tell me about."

Sil opened his mouth. She could see him straining to close it, take a breath, and, after nodding, he began again.

"As you suspected, Master Dzhesq the Needle is dead. So are Masters Hsij, Zu, and Sha."

"Sha?"

"I sent a man to his tower. After the monster burst from it. I know it was not in my original mandate—"

"I would have included it if the incident had occurred before I sent you," she said. "I do not object to improvisation when situations change. You are, after all, an examiner."

"Yes," he said. "I am."

"We'll return to Sha later," she said. "Right now I want to know more about Zu, Dzhesq, and Hsij. Do you know which one died first?"

"Hsij or Dzhesq. I can't be certain. Both bodies were in Dzhesq's tower."

"Dzhesq was looking after the princess from Zełtah. Was she still in his tower?"

"She was not."

"And the guards? What did they have to say?"

"All of Hsij's men were slain. Three of Dzhesq's survived, but only one could talk. He believed the attacker to be a barbarian. My theory is that an assassin from Zełtah did all of this. He killed the tower masters and took the princess."

"I see," Hsheng said. "Zu's guards? Sha's? Also all slain?"

"No," Sil said. "In fact, they all survived. But none of them saw the assassin."

She clasped her hands behind her back. "Let us think about your invading barbarian," she said. "It's reasonable to suppose he went to the Blue Needle Tower first, to retrieve his princess, yes."

"Yes," Sil said.

"So he fought his way up the tower, killing Dzhesq's guards and then the tower master himself—"

"No," Sil said. "That's wrong. He killed Dzhesq first then fought his way *down* the tower."

"I see," Hsheng said. "So we are supposing he flew in through an upper window?"

"Maybe. Or he could have climbed."

"But he could not leave the same way? Could not fly or climb with the princess on his back?"

"Presumably not?"

"So, he fought his way down the tower; do the surviving guards report seeing the princess with him?"

"They don't," Sil said.

"He then went to Hsij's tower—"

"As I said, Hsij was also killed in the Blue Needle Tower."

"But his guards in the Yellow Bone Tower were slain?"

"Yes."

"But why would our assassin do that? He's slain the sorcerer who held his princess. Hsij, who was perhaps visiting Dzhesq, is also slain. And now, rather than escape to the mountains, he goes on to murder the guards in the Yellow Bone Tower, Master Zu the Bright, and Master Sha the Horn? All the while carrying the princess on his back?"

"It is puzzling," Sil admitted.

"And you can think of no other explanation?"

He spread his palms toward her. "I confess I cannot," he said.

*Idiot*, Hsheng thought. But he wasn't, not really. His reasoning was captive to his beliefs, that was all. To everything he had ever been taught.

"The monster from Sha's tower," she asked. "The Beast. Has it been killed yet?"

"No. Blades and arrows do not harm it. It is digging down into the fortress. It is causing a great deal of damage."

"I know," she said. "The Emperor assures me that he will do something soon. We must be patient. Stay here, Examiner Sil. I have something to see to, and then I will doubtless have more questions for you."

She left him standing there and walked out of her room and into the sentry yard toward the outer circle of the keep. She wasn't quite there when everything started to shake.

Her first instinct was that it was Sha's monster, the Beast. Was it attacking the Earth Center Tower?

But then the voice in her head began, muttering in a language that seemed familiar but not quite intelligible. But in those syllables, she heard triumph and malicious glee so powerful it raised the edges of her own lips. She closed her eyes, stood still to steady herself. She saw a great plain of tall grass, herds of strange beasts. It blurred and was gone. She started walking again and realized that she was now bigger, somehow. Stronger.

It was wonderful, but she was perturbed. What had just happened?

One thing at a time. She had a task to accomplish. Then she could worry about the rest of it.

## CHAPTER TWENTY-FIVE

# EARTH CENTER TOWER

"DENG'JAH?" YASH asked. "What was that? What took Grass Place?"

She was still on her back, trying to steady her breath.

"I don't know," he replied. "Something terrible. Like nothing I have ever seen before."

"Oh," someone said. Chej. She'd heard him approaching.

She turned to look at him.

"Are you hurt?" he asked.

"I'm fine," she replied. "I just need a few breaths."

"You said you would never lie to me."

"True," she said. "I'm sorry, shegan'. I am not hurt in body. That's how I justified telling you that. But I am not fine. Something bad has happened, and I… I'm not fine."

She closed her eyes as he shuffled closer. For a moment he stood still, but then, moving very slowly, he reached for her and gathered her in a gentle embrace. For a moment she didn't respond, but after a few heartbeats she returned the hug. It felt good. She hadn't been held or held anyone like this since leaving home.

But it couldn't last. There wasn't time. She patted his back and then pulled away. He didn't resist.

"Thank you," she said.

"What happened?" Chej asked. "I… I saw it. Not with my eyes, I think. But I saw it. The plain and the beasts. This is all real, isn't it? The xual. The tower demons. They really are what you said."

"I didn't know you doubted me," she said.

"I never doubted you believed it," he replied. "But people believe lots of things. But… something happened. Something went wrong. The Beast—it didn't go home, did it? I think it went past me, through the tunnels."

"It didn't go home," she confirmed. "Something else took it away."

"Something? Another tower monster?"

"I don't know," she said. "We're going to find out. Or I am. I must."

"I can see that," he said. "So, what do we do now?"

"We?" she said.

"I can't very well hide down here for the rest of my life. If I go up on my own, I'll probably be executed. Maybe I can help you find where you're going."

"That would be helpful, shegan'," she said. "But you do realize we are quite likely to die, don't you?"

Chej chuckled. "That was already the case," he said.

She shrugged.

"That's settled, then," Chej said. "What's our destination?"

"The Earth Center Tower," she replied.

"Oh," he replied. He was quiet for a moment. He lifted his shoulders and let them settle. Then he nodded.

"I think I can find it," he finally said. "Starting is easy. The Beast left us only one way to go. And I believe it's the right general direction at least." He paused. "The upper passages. I've never been there. They were too disgusting for my taste."

"How bad can they be?"

"We'll see," he said.

They started walking, and soon the passage joined another duct running horizontally. This one was too low to stand upright in; they had to go down on hands and knees. Chej was right about the upper shafts; they were rich in garbage and feces. Smaller tunnels fed into it at intervals, where the stuff piled up. None of the upward-leading shafts were big enough for Yash to get her head into, so they had no choice but to continue in the larger horizontal ones. The wind that had carried away Grass Place had disturbed the filth in the passages enough to help them choose their way when they came to a turning.

Yash wasn't sure how long they traveled, but eventually the tunnel they were following ended, or rather, it stopped going horizontally and turned straight up. Below the upward duct lay a pile of broken stone. When she got closer, it turned out to have been a perforated stone plug that seemed to have cracked and fallen from above.

"This was to stop anyone from going up there." Chej knelt nearer and examined it in Deng'jah's dim light. "It has a warning on it," he said. "I think this shaft must go up into the Emperor's Keep."

"This was just broken," Yash said, examining the stones. "Perhaps by the spirit passing. Before, the way was closed. Now it is open. And no one knows but us. Deng'jah, scout that out."

Deng'jah flew up the shaft and quickly returned.

"It's not far," he said. "It opens into a courtyard."

Yash studied the shaft. This one was easily wide enough to accommodate her body with room left over. It was big enough for Chej, too.

"You want to lead the way?" she asked him.

"I could," he said. "But if there's something up there that needs fighting, it might be best that you arrive before I do."

"Very well," Yash said.

The walls were slick and unpleasant, but Yash had little trouble bracing up it. At the top was another grate, but this one was lacquered wood and lifted easily. She pushed it up enough to look around.

She was emerging from the drain of a rectangular courtyard, probably fifteen paces to a side. It was paved in greenish stone. Four trees grew from large clay pots; Yash didn't recognize what kind they were, but they spread feathery leaves to form what would probably be shade enough for most of the courtyard during the day. Hallways led off from the middle of each brick wall.

"Do you know where we are?" she asked Chej, when he climbed out.

Chej nodded, slowly. "I think so," he said.

"Well?"

"I think we're in the Emperor's Keep."

"Deng'jah, please have a look around."

The insect vanished. Yash turned back to Chej. "Do you know this courtyard?" she asked.

"I recognize it," he said. "I've been here before, a long time ago. Or one just like it."

"Tell me more about the Emperor's Keep."

"You've seen the Earth Center Tower has a wall all the way around it," he said. "Everything between that wall and the tower is the Keep. It's the Emperor's own compound. There are four courtyards like this one. The barracks for his personal guard are here, and the dwellings of his lesser wives and their children."

"Lesser wives?"

"The Emperor… doesn't trust men. I guess. That's what they say, anyway. He surrounds himself with women. Aside from the guards, who are men, everyone in the Keep and the tower is a woman or a child, and all of the women are technically daughters or wives of the Emperor."

"That's… interesting," Yash said. "How many wives would you say the Emperor has?"

"Around sixty, I think."

"And how well does he know them?"

"I don't know." He frowned. "You're not thinking of pretending to be one, are you?"

"It might get me a little further than just charging in," she said.

"Charging in?" Chej asked. "Yes, let's please think of something better than that."

"We're already inside the Emperor's first perimeter," Deng'jah's voice suddenly added. "The Keep walls are very well watched, but the way we came in isn't, apparently. This may be your best chance to kill him."

"Exactly," Yash said. "And I don't intend to waste it."

"You don't look like an Emperor's wife," Chej said. "The Emperor's wives don't carry bows and long knives," he went on. "They also aren't covered in shit."

"I was just considering options," Yash said. "But you're right. Affecting some sort of disguise would probably take time and might not work anyway. Maybe I should make a simple plan: just run up the stairs and kill him. Do you have anything useful to tell me, Chej? Any idea what sort of monsters he has guarding him?"

"I thought you said you weren't going to charge in."

"That's not exactly what I said," Yash replied. "I'll try to sneak in. Will that make you feel better?"

"There's no way to feel good about this," Chej conceded. "He's the Emperor. He is the most powerful of all the tower masters."

"I understand that," Yash said. "But what does he actually do?"

"He keeps the moon from falling out of the sky and the sun from setting the earth aflame."

"I'm not awfully worried about either of those things," Yash said. "Is that all you know?"

"He's been Emperor since we came to this world. No one has ever challenged him."

"Bright was thinking about challenging him," Yash said. "So it must be possible."

"That's good thinking," Chej replied. "Maybe we should go question Pinion or Zuah the Abalone before you go storming up the stairs."

Yash smiled. "Stay hidden, shegan'. Or maybe try to find your way to a safe place through the sewers. If I survive, Deng'jah will find you."

"And if you don't, I'll be executed as a traitor," Chej said. "I've come this far. I might as well stick with you."

Yash regarded him for a moment.

He raised his hands helplessly. "I might be able to help," he said. "At least I can show you to the tower door."

"Oh, my sweet husband," Yash said. "You do love me after all."

"Of course. But also, I've begun to think: of all the people in the fortress, you're the least likely to kill me."

Yash regarded Chej. He wasn't a warrior, or a sorcerer, or—so far as she knew—particularly good at anything. But so far he had been a far better husband than she had ever imagined he would be. And he had pleasantly surprised her a time or two.

"I would never harm you, shegan'," she said. "You must know that."

He looked down. "I misspoke," he said. "I should have said you're the only one I trust anymore."

She thought back to their hug. "I hope you do trust me," she said. "And I shall try very hard to keep you alive."

"I do appreciate that," Chej said.

"Deng'jah," she said, "shegan' is going with us. Keep an eye on him, will you."

"It's hard enough keeping track of you," Deng'jah said.

"Nevertheless," she said.

"Whatever you say," Deng'jah replied.

"Good. Then I say we go."

Chej knew the place, at least a bit, so she let him lead. The stars above told her that midnight had come and gone. The Keep was mostly quiet, although somewhere she heard a baby fussing loudly and a woman singing, perhaps to quiet the child. She stepped past a hoop-and-stick lying on the ground, and not much later a feathered-tail-ball. Children's toys, the same kind she had played with as a child. Left outside perhaps, when they were called in for the night. What was this place like in the daytime? Probably much like a village in her own country. Villages like the ones soldiers of the Empire were destroying. Did that mean she would be justified in killing the children that lived here?

The wind smelled wetter than ever, but the sky was still clear.

The full moon had chased most of the stars nearest it from the sky, but one still shone there, defiant of the lunar radiance.

"What are you looking at?" Chej whispered. "Is there someone up there?"

"That star," Yash said. "My people call that one Menaheetsei, The One Who Walks Around and Watches Over Them. The Guardian, I think your word would be. There's a story about it. There was a person who led us through many worlds before we reached this one. They were named Tsenid'a'wi, The One Who Goes First. But when we reached this world, it is said that Tsenid'a'wi left us and became that star."

"This is an odd time for stories," Chej said.

"Perhaps," Yash replied. "But I think it means something. That star travels over the whole world, not just my country. It encircles us, as we say. But if that's the case, Tsenid'a'wi isn't just guarding my people. They are guarding everyone. Everyone in the Beautiful World."

Chej didn't say anything. He seemed to be waiting for her to finish.

"Tsenid'a'wi is what they call my mother, my clan… and me. The One Who Goes First. Menaheetsei is therefore also one of our names. Guardian. But maybe it's not just my own people I'm supposed to watch over."

"You've been watching over me," Chej pointed out.

"Yes," she said. "It may be that I must think bigger."

"After you kill the Emperor," Chej said dryly.

"There is only so big my mind can get," Yash replied. "Let's move on."

Chej took a few turns that brought them to a broader path between the houses. It led a few dozen paces to a large open area. In it stood the tower.

"That plaza around the tower," she whispered. "It goes all the way around?"

"Yes," Chej said. "The entrance is on the other side. There's a guardhouse there."

"I don't see guards on this side."

"There are a few who walk around it. The Keep is four rings. The outer ring, where the big wall separates it from the rest of the fortress, is where the barracks are for the Emperor's guard. We just came through the Wives' Quarters. The plaza ahead of us is the third ring, the tower itself the fourth. To get where we are now, we ordinarily would have had to pass the outer-gate guards and the soldiers in the barracks. We skipped all of that by coming up from underneath."

"But we still need to get into the tower." She studied it as well as she could in the dark. "Are those windows?" she asked.

"Yes," Chej replied. "The windows start at the second floor, but they have grates on them."

"Most of them do," Deng'jah said. "But the one on the east is cracked. Part of it has fallen out."

"Let's go see."

They crept across the silent courtyard to the east. There, as Deng'jah said, part of a broken jade grillwork lay on the ground.

"Grass Place must have broken this," Yash said. "As he did the plug in the sewers. And the guards haven't noticed yet?"

"I haven't seen any commotion," the insect said.

"Can you climb up the wall?" Chej asked. "I can't."

"Given time and the right equipment, yes," Yash said. "But we have neither. You're a tall man, shegan', did you know?"

"I've been told," he replied.

"So you'll throw me. You'll put your hands together with your fingers laced, like so. I'll run up, jump, land in your hand-basket, and jump again as you toss me up."

Chej cocked his head. Then he laughed. "Well," he said. "As long as I'm useful. But I fail to see how I'll follow you up."

"You won't," she said. "This time, you aren't coming. You can't, and I don't want you to. I want you to find someplace safe. Deng'jah can lead me to you when I'm done. If I don't come back, you should probably leave the fortress."

"Yash, why don't we just leave together? Now?"

"Because I'm not done," she said. "I must kill the Emperor. And I must discover what happened to Grass Place. He must be returned to where he belongs. Now, go stand by the wall. Make your hands into a basket. Bend your knees a little and straighten them as you throw me."

He nodded. "Be careful, Wife," he said.

"I'm sorry, Husband," she said. "But I do not plan to be."

She backed up as he took his position. She eyed him dubiously. He looked very uncomfortable.

*I am a grasshopper*, she thought.

*I am a frog.*

*I am the leap itself.*

She ran, she jumped, Chej heaved, and up she flew, right past the window, and too far from it to reach it. She managed to land and tumble and almost suppressed a laugh.

"I'm sorry!" Chej whispered. "I didn't do it right!"

"That was great!" she said. "Just a little more toward the window."

He grinned uncertainly but got back into position.

This time she caught the ledge and pulled herself in. She waved down to Chej. He waved back, then, after a moment's hesitation, he trotted across the plaza and vanished into the ring of the wives.

Yash turned from the window and started up the stairs.

Unlike the other towers, which had been populated only by their masters, a monster or monsters, and a few guards, the Earth Center Tower seemed *full*. Twice or more as wide as the other towers, it had many spacious rooms. It was the middle of the night, so most of the chambers were either dark or lit only by a few candles or lamps. She didn't pause to explore them, but they looked lived-in, and in some she saw women sleeping. Deng'jah, who did flit deeper into some of the rooms, reported several dozen sleeping on the first few floors. If any of them were awake, none showed any signs of noticing her.

Each story of the tower was different or at least made from a different stone. The first floor was the hard, black rock her people called *tsecheen*, sharp spires of which rose up from the softer red rock and sand of her country. But the next story was of yellow-white stone, and the next of green-grey slate. She was reminded of the canyon, The Place Where They Changed, the exposed face of the Silent Stagnant. As she went higher, the layers of stone showed small traces of ancient life: the imprint of a leaf here, a shell or bone there. Did the Earth Center Tower touch the Silent Stagnant, as the Bright Cloud Tower was in contact with the White Brilliant?

"Find the Emperor, Deng'jah," she said. "It shouldn't be hard. He's the only man in the tower."

She slowed a little as she came to the upper reaches of the building. The stone here was red and sandy, like the cliffs of her homeland, and everything smoothed as if by wind.

Deng'jah reappeared. "Someone is on the top floor, alone."

"Someone? The Emperor or his monster?"

"I'm not sure," Deng'jah said. "There is a sort of fog on everything that dulls my senses."

"Will you be able to help me in the fight?"

"Hopefully," Deng'jah said. "Did I mention I don't like this place?"

"I remember a comment like that," she said.

"I'm making it again," the insect said.

"Thanks, Deng'jah," she said. "I'll keep that in mind."

Soon she came to where the stairs ended. Whatever fog Deng'jah had been speaking of, it wasn't an actual mist. The air was clear, damp, and almost chilly. Moonlight was the only illumination, but it was bright enough, streaming in through the four high, arched windows of the room. After the darkened stairway, it seemed almost like daylight.

Someone stood in the room, gazing out one of the windows. They wore a black skirt that dropped to the knees and a dark yellow top. Yash nocked an arrow to the bow, never taking her gaze from the figure. Then she let it fly.

At the same instant, the person turned. The movement was so relaxed it didn't seem quick; it was as if they were just looking around to say hello. They tapped the flying-star arrow with the back of their hand, deflecting it so it shot out of the window, arcing into the distance, leaving a trail of sparks behind.

Yash reached for another arrow.

"Wait, won't you?" the person asked. "Can't we at least try to have a conversation first?"

Yash paused. The person, she now saw, appeared to be a woman with a few more winters behind her than Yash. Her long hair was plaited into a queue. She had a hooked nose and eyes like grey flint.

"Until your guards get here?"

"Come," the woman said. "I've known where you were since before you entered the Keep. I knew you were coming here."

"Why didn't you just have the guards let me in, then?"

"Because they wouldn't have," she replied. "As far as they are concerned, as a woman I have no authority over them."

"So you aren't the Emperor?"

"No," she said. "The Emperor is resting. I am his daughter, Hsheng. I want to talk to you."

"I've done a lot of talking today already," Yash said. "What do you want?"

"Well, to start with, I wanted to know who you are," Hsheng said, taking a few steps forward and then stopping with her hands clasped behind her back. "Now I do. I was at your wedding. I guessed it must be you, but I wanted to sure, to see with my own eyes. The tower masters, the guards: they didn't understand what you are. They are convinced to their bones that women are soft, pliant creatures. They don't question that belief any more than they question the sun rising, so of course Zeltah's little trick worked on them. But not on me. Your people either knew we weren't bargaining in good faith or didn't care. They sent you here to do murder, and you have done it spectacularly well." She took another step forward.

"I'm happy for you," Yash said.

"How so?"

"It's always nice to be right when others are wrong, isn't it? It means you must be smart and important. So I'm happy for you. But."

She knew she would never be able to fire an arrow at that range, not given how fast Hsheng had already proven herself to be, so she dropped the bow and arrow and dashed forward, drawing her long knife. Hsheng looked surprised, and just watched her come until

Yash committed to the thrust. Then Hsheng faded away from the blade, slipped inside of it, and took Yash's wrist in her hand. Yash twisted from the grip and aimed a kick at her opponent's knee, but Hsheng lifted her leg, catching the kick with her foot, and punched Yash in the face. Yash saw it coming and receded from her fist, but the blow still landed *hard*. She swept, hitting Hsheng's ankle with her foot, but Hsheng had just sunk down, widening her stance, and put her weight on her front foot, so the attack didn't budge her. Instead, Hsheng struck again, this time at Yash's throat. Yash blocked with her free hand and slashed at Hsheng with the long knife, but her foe anticipated that, too, dodging the strike, dancing out of range.

Deng'jah's vision enveloped her, so she saw the fight from all angles. Hsheng came again, trying to hide the kick coming from her back leg, but Yash saw it clearly and met it with the blade. Or tried to. The kick never came; instead Hsheng dashed by her, arcing her arm and catching Yash across the face, knocking her off her feet. Yash tucked and rolled back, but she was too slow coming up and took a punch to the ribs and another to the side of her head. She kept retreating, staying ahead of the flurry of blows that followed her. She thrust again; this time Hsheng caught her arm, rotated, threw her over her shoulder, and slammed her into the ground. The long knife went clattering off as half of the breath blew out of her body.

But Hsheng didn't press the attack. She stepped back.

*"Deng'jah?"*

*"She has something helping her,"* Deng'jah replied in the little voice. *"I can't see who it is."*

Yash rolled away and back to her feet.

"Shall we make a truce, if only for a moment?" Hsheng asked. "I wasn't done talking. I had a few more things to say."

Yash's head was ringing, and she was having a hard time drawing a breath.

*"You underestimated her,"* Deng'jah said. *"If you keep going like this, she's going to kill you or cripple you. Take the time she's giving you. Don't be rash."*

"There's something I don't understand about her," Yash said.

*"Exactly,"* Deng'jah replied. *"This is like the time in the cliffs, in The Place Where They Changed. You've got to change again, or she's going to beat you. Take this time as a gift."*

"I'm listening," Yash told Hsheng.

"We don't have to be enemies," Hsheng said. "By coming here, you have revealed a plot against my father. In doing that, you have earned some consideration. On the other hand, you have killed four tower masters and released a monster that did a great deal of damage. I assume you killed the Beast?"

*"Doesn't she know, Deng'jah? The Grass Place was drawn here. Does she know that? Do you feel him here?"*

*"I don't,"* Deng'jah said. *"But as I told you, I'm in a fog. My senses are cut off."*

Hsheng was still waiting for an answer.

"I did kill him, yes."

"I wonder why, when it was doing so much damage to us. To your enemies."

"The 'Beast' as you call him is the soul of a place in my country. Your Empire abducted him and twisted him to your purposes. Each of your xual, your tower monsters, are the same. I came here to liberate them, to send them back to where they belong."

"And did you? Send the Beast back to where it belongs?"

"I did not. I was prevented. He was abducted again. I think you know this."

Hsheng frowned slightly. She didn't answer right away.

"I don't know," she said at last. "Perhaps my father does. I will ask him when the time is appropriate. Listen, though. I will make you an offer, Princess Yash of Zełtah."

"I'm listening, older sister," Yash said.

Hsheng smiled. "Help me kill the rest of my father's enemies. You came here not just for your stolen souls but to kill them, didn't you? Let's do it together. You can do what you will with their xual."

"I came here to kill *all* of the tower masters. Including the Emperor."

"Then you must be partly disappointed," Hsheng said. "You will not kill my father. But you may have the rest of the tower masters. Eight out of nine: that's not bad at all, is it? More importantly, you can have what I suspect you really want. Peace. My father will end the war against your people."

"Bright made a similar promise," Yash said. "I didn't believe him, either. The Hje declared war on my people and my country long ago. This latest betrayal is the most recent of many, and I will not be so easily duped. And why do you need me to kill the rebellious tower masters? If you cannot do it alone, why not go to Coral and Obsidian for help?"

"What I said about the guards applies to them also," she said. "My father is content to let me protect this tower. He would not be happy were I to extend my power and authority outside of it. Neither would the other tower masters willingly cooperate with me."

Yash thought she understood then.

"You're trying to prove yourself," she said. "Prove your worth to your father, in hopes that in the future things will be different. That you will be respected by these men who hate women."

Hsheng laughed. It was surprising, and it seemed genuine. It was a beautiful sound.

"Is that what you think?" Hsheng asked. "Don't dare to think you understand me. I've explained myself to you exactly as much as I'm willing to. I've made you an offer of, if not of friendship, at least cooperation. Do you accept?"

"I'm considering it," she said. "But there is a problem. I don't trust you."

And then a thought awoke.

"You knew I was coming. How?"

"I guessed it," Hsheng answered. "When you arrived in the Keep, I knew. From then on, I observed you."

Yash blinked. It was possible. Deng'jah said Hsheng had a helper. The tower monster, probably. It seemed possible that it could have been watching them.

*Chej*, Yash thought. *Does she know about Chej?* But she must, if what she said was true.

It must have shown on her face, for Hsheng grinned.

"You wonder about Chej?" Hsheng asked. "Yes, poor old Chej. He got more than he was expecting in you, didn't he?"

"What has become of him?" Yash demanded.

"I imagine by now the guards have him. Why? Do you really care what happens to him?"

"He is my husband."

"You care about that? No matter. When he is dead, you will be released from that condition."

"Dead?" she asked. "No. If you want my cooperation, you will make certain Chej is safe."

She shrugged. "I have nothing against Chej. I don't care about his... proclivities. But as I told you, outside of this tower, I don't have any say about such things."

"But your father does."

"My father would strangle Chej with his own hands," she said. "He is not tolerant of abomination."

"Chej isn't an abomination," Yash said.

"It's too late," Hsheng said. "You think I'm not being honest with you, but, whether you believe it or not, there are things I can help you with and things I can't. I can convince my father to end the war. I'm sure of that. But I can do nothing for Chej. He was doomed the moment he agreed to marry you."

Yash nodded. "I see," she said.

Deng'jah's voice pierced her mind, as frantic as she had ever heard it.

*"She's distracting you,"* he said. *"The monster is coming. No, it's here."*

She knew by his tone there was no room for questions or hesitation. She grabbed the bow and ran back down the stairs. Behind her, she heard Hsheng's scream of frustration.

"Deng'jah," Yash commanded. "Find Chej. Do it now."

"You're about to need my help. He's all around us."

"I understand. Now, do what I said and find Chej."

The stairwell wall cracked and then exploded ahead of her, showering the stairs with stone fragments, and from the debris a skeleton leapt toward her, the bones of a monster the size of a large wolf but with a snake-like neck and tail that made it much longer than any wolf. It landed on two hind legs that bent much like a bird's; and, like a bird, each foot ended in three splayed talons with a spur in the back. Its forelimbs were short, grasping arms, also tipped with talons. The sharp-toothed jaws of its lizard-like skull opened wide as it lunged and snapped at her.

"See what I mean?" Deng'jah said.

"Go!" she shouted. "Find Chej."

She stutter-stepped, avoiding its bite, then leapt past the creature, kicking off the wall of the stairwell to change direction, thus evading the grasping foreclaws, but the tail whipped up and clubbed her mid-jump, right across her thighs. Through her shock and hurt, she realized that the monster wasn't made of bone but of stone, like the skeletons in the cliffs at the border of the Silent Stagnant. She had been right to suspect the tower was similar.

She yelped, flipping involuntarily, and crashed heavily onto the stairs. Pain from the whipping on her thighs wedded to an even brighter flash of agony as her left elbow broke her fall. Then she tumbled down the stairs to the next landing. She rolled over in time to see the stone-skeleton monster again leaping toward her, hind claws first. Heart pounding, she rolled aside, but one of the claws nevertheless sliced across her right bicep. Expecting to land on her, the monster hit the landing awkwardly and fell itself. Yash found her footing and sped on, taking three and four steps at a time, leaving a trail of the blood welling freely from her arm. The stone-bone monster clattered after her. Just as she reached the next landing, the floor hove up and shattered, releasing another stone-skeleton, this one much bigger than the first, with a head half as long as her body. This one was four-legged, and it lunged at her like a huge lizard, opening jaws with jagged rows of teeth that could easily cut her in half. She launched herself high, landed on top of the creature's skull, and bounced off as another two-legged monster similar to the first but almost twice as big wrenched free from the wall below her and darted a mouthful of stone knives toward her throat.

She stabbed her hand toward its head and caught it by the eye socket, then used that handhold to swing under the gaping mouth and strike it squarely in the breastbone with both feet, between its clawed arms. The sternum snapped, and her momentum carried her straight through into the monster's rib cage, where she caught hold of the inside of its spine as the first, smaller bird-lizard skeleton caught up and bit at her, too, only to be thwarted by the stone bars of the ribs surrounding her. The monster she was inside twisted its long neck to try and reach her through its own ribs. It couldn't quite manage that, but the attempt caused it to stumble. The smaller one struck again and this time forced its head between two ribs. Yash released her grip and grabbed its head, trapping it inside the larger monster as it fell. Then she rolled out of the ribcage, leaving the two long-dead beasts in a writhing tangle as she continued her flight down the stairs. Ahead of her, more stone-skeleton monsters broke from the walls.

CHAPTER TWENTY-SIX

# HGUESYAJ

CHEJ GOT nearly to the outer circle of the Keep before his steps slowed. He stood still for a moment, thinking. There wasn't any way he could slip out of the Keep unseen: there were guards at every gate. He figured there was a good chance that they were looking not only for Yash but for him as well. Even if they weren't, was he really going to just walk off and leave Yash to her fate?

He touched the garnet earring she'd given him.

No.

So he walked back to the edge of the Earth Center Plaza, found a narrow space between two houses to hide in, and waited, straining his eyes to try and see into the windows. All seemed quiet.

Knowing Yash, it wouldn't be for much longer.

The back of his head seemed to explode, and then he was lying face-down on the stone. Someone yanked his arms behind his back. He started to shout, but something was shoved into his mouth. Then whoever-it-was pulled something over his head.

"Walk," someone said.

He managed to come shakily to his feet. Then he tried to run.

He didn't get far. There was more than one of them, and they caught him and threw him back to the ground. Maybe it didn't matter. His head hurt so much he was sure it had been crushed. He was almost certainly dying.

"Look at that," another voice said. "He needs help walking." A moment later, someone grabbed him across the chest and lifted him back to his feet.

"Thank you," he tried to mumble through the gag.

Then something struck him in the stomach, hard. He choked and started to fall down again, but this time whoever was holding him didn't let him. As he gasped for air, the other man grabbed him, too.

"I said walk, not fall down, hguesyaj," one of them said.

Chej had been having trouble concentrating, but that word brought everything into focus. He had been caught. He shouldn't have been surprised, but he had begun to think that Yash was so competent that nothing could go wrong if he was with her, or at least nothing she couldn't get them both out of. But of course, he hadn't been with her, had be? She'd gone off to kill the Emperor and trusted that he would get to safety. Her mistake, but not her fault.

Hguesyaj. Whoever had him knew who and what he was. Almost certainly they were taking him someplace to kill him, probably Yash's room in Dzhesq's tower. That way his blood would be on the bed, wouldn't it? But why bother with that at this point? Yash had killed tower masters and monsters. They didn't need his death to justify anything. Things had gone well beyond that little scheme, hadn't they. More likely it was going to be a public execution. He had helped her, after all. And he was what he was.

Or maybe the only reason he was still alive was so that they didn't have to carry him to wherever they were going to put his corpse.

He was scared. He didn't want to die. But he found himself thinking of the things he wanted to say to them if he got the chance. What his last words would be. He wished now that he had managed to kill Sha himself, that he could at least spit that at their faces. But he could at least try to be brave, show them he wasn't afraid. Couldn't he?

What if they weren't going to kill him at all? What if something else was happening that he didn't understand? It wasn't inconceivable.

Hope, he decided, was the worst thing for courage. As long as he had the first, it was hard to summon the second.

Even through the sack on his head he heard people screaming. The Beast was dead, but it had done a lot of damage first. Was the fortress still on fire?

"Where are you going with him?"

The voice was close, maybe two arm's lengths away. And he knew it immediately. It was Xarim Ruesp's quavering speech.

"Help me!" he tried to say, but it only emerged as inarticulate noise.

"Xarim, with all respect, that is not for you to ask about."

"This man works for me," Ruesp snapped. "It is entirely appropriate for me to ask why he is being dragged through the halls like a criminal."

"He is a criminal," one of the men said. "Worse, he is a traitor. And a dirty hguesyaj. So if you really must know, we have orders to take him to the Rizua and cut his head off."

"Orders from whom?"

"He tried to assassinate the Emperor," one of the men said. "Who do you think?"

"I see," Ruesp replied. "Chej, do you dispute this? Lift your head higher if you do."

For a moment, Chej didn't answer. The guard had removed all doubt of what his fate was to be. It wasn't even going to be a public execution. The Rizua was the hole where all of the garbage from the fortress was dumped. There could be no show of dignity, no last words, noble or otherwise.

This moment was all he had. Had he planned to assassinate the Emperor? No. He would never have had the courage for that. But Yash had been planning to kill him, hadn't she? And he had been with her. He had helped her into the tower.

So rather than raising his head, he lowered it to his chest.

For a moment there was only silence. Then Ruesp spoke again.

"Understand, Chej," Ruesp said, "that you have not only betrayed your people, you have betrayed me. On with it, you two."

"Good day to you, xarim," one of the men said. Then they shoved him forward again. Chej stumbled but kept his balance. He squared his shoulders and held his head up, and, though he was still terrified, he felt oddly free. He had not thought much about The Bright Houses Beyond the Sea, where the good souls were said to go. He had, in fact, avoided thinking about them because hguesyaj were not supposed to be welcome there. Instead, they were dragged before the Rotting Lords for punishment. He supposed he would find out soon. Should he make one last chance to surprise the guards and escape? It would rob him of the little dignity he had managed to retain, but if there was a chance…

But there wasn't. He knew that now.

Not much later, they reached stairs going down. They descended, and the sounds of the fortress behind them faded.

He knew when they reached the Rizua by its stench. So vile was it that he thought he was going to throw up. He hadn't thought it possible to meet a more ignoble end than being decapitated in the trash pit, but drowning in his own vomit would probably be exactly that.

His head was hurting less. He supposed he wasn't dying after all. Yet.

"Take the sack off him?" one of the men asked.

"Why bother?" the other replied.

"We could let him beg. I'd enjoy that."

One of them poked him in the back with something sharp. "Hear that, hguesyaj? You want a chance to beg? To save your disgusting, abominable life?"

Chej concentrated on his breath, his heartbeat, all of the things he was about to lose. If there was remembering after death, he wanted to remember what it had been like to live. And Ajenx. And Yash, although she had gotten him killed. At least she had shaken him awake first, so he didn't die in the decades-long sleep he'd been in. He wished he could thank her for that.

"Yes," one of the men said. "I think this is too easy for him. Get that hood off his head. And strip those clothes off him. No point in leaving anything for *him* to take to the Rotting Lords."

The sack came off, and now he could see the Rizua, a broad hole forty paces wide half-filled with water and garbage, much of it bones and rotting meat. It was enclosed by a chamber carved into the rock the fortress crouched on, at about the level of the sewers he and Yash had been in. He tried to turn and see his captors, but one of them slapped him.

"Don't look at us," the man snapped. "You won't go from this world thinking of me."

The thought was so ludicrous, Chej almost laughed. Was that what these men thought? That all men inspired desire in him, to the point that he would die lusting after his torturers? Was that what they thought it was to be like him?

They took his clothes off and beat him a little more. Finally they removed his gag.

"Well?" one of them said. "If you want to beg, we're ready to listen now."

Chej took a breath, then another. He was shaking.

"Would you hurry up?" he finally said. "I'm so bored of the two of you."

Something hit him in the side of the head, hard, and for a moment it was like he could see far into the distance, to a dark horizon, and stars, more than he had ever seen...

## CHAPTER TWENTY-SEVEN

# FATHER AND DAUGHTER

HSHENG DODGED her way down through the tower, trying to give chase to Yash, but the tower guardians were making such a mess of things she lost sight of the other woman almost immediately. And even though the creatures of stone weren't attacking *her*, they were still in the way. After the first landing, she saw it was hopeless The guardians would either catch Yash and probably rend her into a hundred pieces, or—more likely in her estimation—the woman from Zełtah would escape to wreak further havoc in the fortress.

Either way, it wasn't her immediate responsibility anymore. The fact that the stone-bone guardians had been released meant that her father was awake.

With a sigh she started toward his chamber.

She found him fully dressed in a robe of pale-grey and black feathers draped over a bone-colored shift.

"Daughter," he said. "I was about to send for you. The tower guardians have awakened. Did you see them?"

"I saw them."

"Do you know why they are so agitated?"

"I met with Yash of Zełtah. The woman who has been assassinating the tower masters."

"The woman?" he asked.

"Yes. The woman."

He smiled. "Does that give you ideas, daughter? Does it lend credence to your ambitions as a woman?"

"This woman killed Dzhesq, Hsij, Zu, and Sha. Along with them she slew their xual. She came here for you. I stopped her."

"She's dead, then? Then who are the guardians chasing?"

She didn't pause. Lying to him would be a bad idea. He was fully awake, and so was Nalzhu. He might know everything; he might be testing her. She had to be straightforward and own her actions. After all, she was his second here. He had given her authority.

"I didn't kill her," she admitted. "I tried to bargain with her. She has removed four tower masters. It occurred to me she could have been useful in eliminating the rest. Then I would have killed her."

He shrugged. "That was good thinking," he said. "If you had been right, if she had accepted your bargain, that would have been fine. It doesn't matter, though."

"The stone-bone guardians have killed her, then?"

"They haven't. They might yet. If they don't, the guards probably will. No matter what, her time has run out. But she's already done most of our work for us. We can finish it ourselves."

"Finish killing the tower masters?"

He cocked his head and regarded her from the verge of his eye.

"Do you know why? Why we want the other tower masters dead?"

"Because they covet your throne."

He shook his head. "No," he replied. "My throne does not matter. I see that clearly now, as I did not when I was younger. Nalzhu has shown me." He smiled. "You will see. It's nice to have you here, at the end."

"The end?"

"Not yours," he said. "But mine."

She had a river of words waiting, but that dammed them up. For a moment all she could do was stare at him. But she found her tongue.

"What do you mean? You've lived for centuries. You will live for many more."

He shook his head. "Walk with me, daughter. To the top of the tower."

CHAPTER TWENTY-EIGHT

# RUZUYER

TSAYE (IN ANCIENT TIMES)

IN HER *travels Tsenid'a'wi found another world, Nyen'łchuuni, The Beautiful World. The Beautiful World had forests and grassy plains, mountains, deserts, and oceans. The Beautiful World had its own spirit-people-animals, and they are the ones we know today. The trees and bushes and plants were also those familiar to us, because Nyen'łchuuni is the world we now inhabit.*

*Tsenid'a'wi went back to the Moon World and gathered the people. He sang a powerful song and became a huge bird, a raven so large that his wings blocked the light from the White Brilliant, casting the Moon World into utter darkness, and under cover of that darkness his people slipped away to the Beautiful World. They left the Hje and their monsters behind. They left parents and grandparents and cousins behind, and they wept at doing so, but they could not live in that place, and that way, any longer.*

*But the Beautiful World was not hospitable at first, either. They first came to a land on the seaside, with abundant fish, seals, and whales in the ocean, game and nuts and fruit on the hillsides. But those spirit-people-animals did not welcome them. They did not want the strangers in their country. They went next to a vast, tall forest, but received no welcome there, or in the great river valley, where all kinds of food grew in abundance. But then, guided by Tsenid'a'wi and her dog, they found a country between the mountains. It was tough and dry: hot in summer and cold in winter. But there were springs and small rivers. There were forests and game in the mountains, and lakes with fish. The minute they saw it, they knew it was sacred, but they did not know why.*

## DII JIN (THE PRESENT)

YASH SLASHED with the long knife at another monster as it emerged from the tower wall, slicing neatly between two of the vertebrae that supported its head. The head fell off, but the rest of the thing kept chasing her, trying to disembowel her with its talons. They were coming at her from everywhere now, and without Deng'jah's extra eyes she was having a difficult time keeping track of them. She dove down the stairs and tumbled, breaking out ahead of the pack trying to hem her in, and had almost made it to the next landing. Unlike those earlier, this one had a window, but she had lost track of how high she was now.

She was no longer in the upper stories of red stone; the tower here was a green-grey color. She thought that was more than halfway up, but she couldn't be sure, and she couldn't slow down to look outside.

The inside wall of the tower burst apart, and another stone-skeleton leapt at her, the largest yet. While balanced on two legs like some of the others, this one had a much shorter neck and a head that was at least half as long as she was tall. It had a horn on its nose and two smaller ones over each eye socket. The skull was narrow, like that of a huge crow, but instead of a beak, it had a mouth full of serrated teeth as long as her fingers. It reached for her with four-clawed hands and opened its mouth very wide. She tucked and rolled under it, but it was quick and blocked the staircase down. Beyond it, she could see the walls crumbling, and the monsters from above reached the landing.

She hurled herself out of the window.

She was even higher than she thought. For a moment, everything seemed still, as if she were suspended in the wind. The moon was high and bright; she could see most of the fortress: the smoke rising in black columns from the fire the Beast had started, the towers, the lightning-filled clouds in the middle distance. The rooftops and courtyards inside of the Keep stretched below her, and the wall around it loomed high enough to block her sight of what was immediately beyond. In the sky above, stars vanished and reappeared as a shadow moved across them: the bird Chej called Ruzuyer, still patrolling above the fortress.

In her mind, she was again in the canyon at Qeemelehk'e, The Place Where They Changed. With one hand she touched the Silent Stagnant to give her time. With the other, she felt the quick of the White Brilliant.

*I am a butterfly*, she thought as she fell. *I am a cottonwood seed*.

Her bones went light; the tips of her fingers, her eyelids, her nostrils burned. Her lungs filled with heat, and her vision burned white.

For a moment she didn't know where she was, but memory returned quickly. She lay on stone shingles, atop the Wives' Quarters of the Emperor's Keep. She scrambled up in time to see the big stone-skeleton with the horn on its nose falling toward her. She rolled aside as it banged into the roof then bounded to her feet and began running again, this time toward the wall surrounding the Keep. There were guards everywhere, some with bows. At first they just yelled at her, but then some of them had the presence of mind to start shooting. Her left ankle hurt badly, as did the knee on her opposite leg, forcing her to run with a limp. An arrow grazed her side, and she broke stride a little. Then she felt as though she were kicked in the ribs as another arrow struck dead-on. She stumbled again, but she was almost to the wall. She didn't need to look back to know the stone-bone monster was right behind her. Another arrow hissed by her and clattered against the stone. Earlier, she had reckoned the perimeter wall of the Keep rose to the height of four warriors or more from the rooftops of the outer fortress, but the Wives' Quarters were built higher, so from where she was now the wall only rose twice her own length. She leapt, caught the edge, and slung herself over.

She twisted as she fell. The drop wasn't as far as from the window, but it was still substantial, and she landed badly. Her ankle felt shattered, but she didn't have the option of stopping. Her bones ground painfully together as she started off across the roof as quickly as she could manage.

More arrows flew by, although these weren't so close. She became aware that the arrow that had hit her ribs was in deep and needed attention, but a quick glance back showed the stone-skeleton monster leaping up from behind the wall, landing on it with both feet and springing on toward her.

She tried to get her bearings as she ran. She was back on the xarim side of the fortress: the Bright Cloud Tower was just ahead, the Red Coral Tower off to her right. She settled on Bright's tower. She could imagine making a stand there. But as she got closer, she saw guards there, too, and ducked down behind a higher jut of roof to avoid them.

She lay there panting. She heard the snap of wings quite near. Ruzuyer was right above her, although it didn't seem to notice her.

Instead it flew down toward the horned stone-skeleton and struck it with its claws. The monster fought back, snapping at the colossal bird, but Ruzuyer was already turning back up.

Tch'etsagh. That was the spirit's real name. Her song to him earlier was still working; to Tch'etsagh, she didn't exist. Maybe it was time to change that.

"*Tch'etsagh*," she sang, feeling a whistling in her throat.

*Tch'etsagh, do you see me?*
*I was hidden before*
*I sang you another song*
*But see me now*
*I am here,*
*Helpless,*
*Dying,*
*Dead.*

Then she lay still, listening to the guards shouting as they approached, watching the stone-bone monster regain its sense of direction and start back toward her.

Huge wings flapped, growing closer. Wind beat down on her.

Then Tch'etsagh snatched her as a hawk might a squirrel, wrapped his claws around her belly and she was in the air, watching the fortress diminish. The bird's grip was so strong she couldn't move, and it had snapped the shaft of the arrow in her back. She thought she was inured to pain, but this agony was like a sliver of ice buried in her, and she forgot to breathe. But she didn't struggle. She remained as still as a dead mouse in the talons of the huge raptor. As she watched, it circled toward the Standing Pinion Tower. In the west and north, huge thunderheads loomed, pulsing red as lightning snaked within their depths. Blue-white bolts jagged to the ground in the distance. Powerful gusts of wind buffeted them, but the bird seemed unperturbed as it approached the flat top of the tower.

Heartbeats later, Tch'etsagh dumped her there. Yash had a fleeting glimpse: the flat roof of the tower, an opening with very steep stairs going down, a scattering of bones.

The bird settled next to her. It nudged her with its beak.

Yash lay as still as possible.

*Dead*, she thought.

*Drum slowly, shejeey'e, my heart*
*Rest, shediq', my pulse*
*Sheyets, my breath, be still*
*Like a windless day*
*Be motionless, shets'ihyi, my body*
*Like a tranquil lake*
*Like a standing mountain.*

Ruzuyer's breath moved across her. She smelled blood and meat. The xual's claws scratched into the stone of the roof.

Its wings snapped forward, and wind pushed down on her. The gigantic pinions beat again as the bird took back to the air.

It had worked. Ruzuyer thought she was carrion.

Yash rolled over, unlimbered the bow from her shoulder. The bird saw her move, realized its mistake, and turned, one wing up and one wing down, coming back for her.

She jumped to her feet and put an arrow to the string as she limped toward the opening in the roof. She released and leapt.

The 'stairs' were steep, more like a ladder carved of stone than those in the other towers. She hit them once, bounced. She closed her eyes, but the flash was still so bright it hurt her eyes. Heat pressed her down, singeing her hair before she rolled away.

The tower trembled as the bird hit the roof. The reek of burning feathers filled her head. Blazing chunks of flesh and feathers fell down the hole after her.

Everything went still. She reached her hand around to where the arrow had hit her in the back. The remnants of the shaft and the head were still in but not terribly deep. She thought that it had missed her kidneys and not made it as far as her lungs, but it still hurt a lot. She couldn't get a grip on the broken shaft, and the head was probably barbed anyway. Even if she could pull it out, that probably wasn't the best idea at the moment; as long as the hole the arrow had made was still filled with arrow, it wouldn't bleed that much. Having it in there made most movements agonizing, but right now it was the best she could do.

"Deng'jah," she murmured. "Are you here? Did you find Chej?"

The insect didn't answer, and she couldn't wait. She slung the bow across her back and armed herself with the long knife, noting that she only had two of Bright's flying-star arrows left. There had been two more besides the one she killed the bird with; she must have lost them on the way, in all of the jumping and falling.

The room was windowless, but the light from the burning bird above illuminated it well enough to see that it was mostly empty. A dozen niches had been cut into the wall, each with a small shelf just about the level where a person would sit. In fact, she guessed that's what they'd been made for, for they were just about the size for a sitting person. Was it some sort of council chamber?

Three of the niches, however, had been closed, plastered over, and each of these was covered with many colorful symbols she didn't understand.

The smell of burning feathers reminded her she had something to do.

Tch'etsagh.

She ran back up the stairs, toward the dead bird. She felt his spirit there, hovering, waiting for her to tell him who he was and where to go.

She had just reached the doorway to the roof when a wind hit the building, a wind so strong that only by gripping the doorframe with both hands could she hold on. It smelled of wet ash, and it snuffed the flames in an instant. And in the same instant, Tch'etsagh was gone. Not his corpse, but his spirit lifted away by what looked almost like a hand of grey smoke before it dissolved into the dark sky. No, it wasn't quite gone. The stars blurred as it moved across them, toward the Earth Center Tower. She brought the bow back out, but by that time there was no target at all but the tower itself. She stared down the shaft for a moment anyway, but after a few heartbeats she took the arrow from the string.

Tch'etsagh had been stolen, just as Grass Place had. She took a deep breath and then another, feeling the pain of her wound, the loss of the spirits she was meant to set free. She thought of Chej, maybe dead already, the fortress now fully alert to her presence.

She inhaled once more, very slowly, focusing her awareness on the air filling her lungs, on the life still burning in her.

She had always known it would be hard. And it would likely get harder from here on, especially if she stopped to rest any longer.

She rose and descended the stairs, limping on her injured ankle.

A small, glowing thing sped toward her from deeper in the tower. Deng'jah, casting a pale light like a dust of glowing pollen.

"Did you find Chej?" she asked.

"I did. He's in considerable trouble."

"Can you lead me to him?"

"Yes, but… I think he will be dead before you can reach him."

"No," she said. "I won't believe that. Lead. Keep me informed of trouble."

"What about Yir the Pinion?"

"Later. If he doesn't get in my way, I'm not going after him right now."

But of course, Pinion got in their way, emerging from the shadowed stairwell.

Master Yir the Pinion looked old, older than any of the tower masters Yash had seen thus far. He had long, grey hair but it was thin; his scalp was clearly visible. The wrinkled skin of his face wrapped tightly on the bone underneath. But his eyes were golden yellow and sharp, studying her as she descended into a large chamber, this one also windowless but lit by a pale amber mist floating near the ceiling.

"You killed my bird," he said.

"He wasn't yours," she replied.

He shrugged his bony shoulders. "It doesn't matter now, does it? I can forgive you. I think you know you and I can help each other."

"I'm in a hurry," Yash said. "Move, please."

"Hear me out," Pinion said. "The Emperor—"

Yash lunged forward. Pinion suddenly wasn't where her blade was cutting. It was like he were as thin as a blade of grass—thinner—and had suddenly turned sideways. She overbalanced and stumbled with her wounded foot, and the arrowhead lodged in her back cut her inside. Waves of pain and weakness surged through her muscles. Her lungs wouldn't fill.

But Pinion wasn't between her and the stairs anymore, so she gritted her teeth against the pain and charged forward, intent on rescuing Chej.

A bitter cold wind blew up from the stairwell, strong enough to knock her off her feet. It kept blowing, but she saw Pinion from the rim of her vision, behind her and to her left. She whirled and attacked him, this time slashing instead of jabbing so that if he turned sideways again she would hit him anyway. Or so she thought. But Pinion turned aside and kept turning, and her blade found only empty air.

"Let me go," she shouted.

"You haven't listened to my offer," Pinion said from behind her. "I can offer you anything you might want."

She faced him.

"You can't offer me anything I can't take," she said. "And right now, I have no time for bargaining. In fact, even if I had plenty of time, I'm tired of talking to tower masters."

She lunged. He slapped his hands and once again turned aside.

The wind was gone, she noticed. Her skin felt weird, as if it were being pricked all over.

She realized there wasn't any air.

She dropped the knife and took her bow in hand, drawing one of the last two arrows. She put it to the string. She saw the arrow fall and bounce on the floor soundlessly. She bent to retrieve it and kept bending.

CHAPTER TWENTY-NINE

# THE RIZUA

THE AFTERLIFE, Chej realized, looked pretty much exactly like the garbage pit he'd been killed in. It smelled the same, too. That sort of made sense. If there was no place for his kind in the Bright Houses, maybe his good soul would just remain here, haunting the spot of his death along with his ix.

Or maybe for him, there *was* no *xhues*, no good soul. Maybe he was all ix. That was probably the tidiest explanation.

Certainly he was being tortured. He hurt almost everywhere.

"Chej?" The voice was familiar. He'd heard it just a little while ago, when he was still alive.

"Xarim Ruesp?" he mumbled, rolling over.

"Can you walk?" Ruesp asked.

Was the old man dead, too? He took a deep breath. No. And neither was he, was he? He remembered the guard hitting him. He must have lost his senses for a moment. And then—where were the guards?

He saw them lying still on the ground behind Ruesp. One, the bigger of the two, he thought he had seen before. The smaller he didn't recognize at all. He wondered which one had hit him.

"What... what happened?" he asked, feeling foolish the instant the words were out of his mouth. It was very clear what had happened. Ruesp had followed them down here and rendered the guards unconscious. The question he meant to ask was *why*.

"Take your time," Ruesp said. He turned, bent over, and dragged the smaller man to the pit, then tipped him over into it. He landed with a muted splash.

"What are you doing?" Chej asked. "He'll drown."

Ruesp barked out a humorless laugh. "No, he won't," he said. "He's not breathing."

A tingle of shock went up Chej's spine followed by... confusion. "You killed them?"

"Would you rather I let them kill you? That's what they were about to do, you know." He went to the other guard—the big one—but instead of putting him in the pit, too, he began to undress him.

Ruesp must have seen the look on his face.

"They threw your clothes down in the hole," the xarim said. "This one's ought to fit you well enough. When you feel up to it, you should get dressed."

Ruesp finished stripping the corpse and then dragged it into the pit with the other.

Chej pulled on the dead man's clothes, acutely aware that that was what they were. The touch of them made his skin feel weird.

"Thank you," he told Ruesp as he fastened the shirt.

"It's fine," Ruesp replied.

"It's just that I don't understand," Chej said. "What you said in the hall—"

"I couldn't kill them in the hall, could I?" he asked. "Others would have seen. More guards would come. They told me where they were taking you. I knew that here, there would be no one to see. Are you ready?"

"For what?"

"To go," Ruesp replied. "I take it it's true that the Emperor gave the order for your execution?"

"Yes," Chej said.

"So, obviously you can't stay in the fortress. Or the city, or the Empire, for that matter. Fortunately for you, this is an ideal time to leave. The fortress is in chaos. We are at war, so there is already a lot of coming and going from here. No one yet knows I helped you, so I still have some authority. I can say that I'm sending you to the battle, get you some supplies and a few pack animals, start you on your way."

Chej stared at the old man. Was he kidding? Was this all some sort of elaborate punishment? He wanted to believe it. He *desperately* wanted to believe it. But it seemed too easy, too... hopeful. Ruesp was Hje, like him. No, not like him: pureborn. He had served the Empire with distinction his entire life.

"Wait," Chej said. "If I escape, what about you? Won't they figure out you helped me?"

"They might," Ruesp said. "They might not. I'm not going to tell them. You aren't, I assume."

"But if they do?"

Ruesp shrugged. "How much longer do I have to live? Me, they'll give a clean execution. Or maybe I'll die fighting when they

312

come for me. Either of those would be a more satisfying way to leave this world than just waiting for my life to leak out of me."

"They will say you were a traitor. They will deny you the Bright Houses."

"You think they can do that?" Ruesp asked. "Do you believe the Emperor or anyone can determine what happens to my soul after I die? I don't. If they could—if only those the righteous elect get to go to the Bright Houses—I wouldn't want to go there anyway. Let me return to an old battlefield. Let me reunite with my old comrades and my valiant foes. Or let me haunt the fortress and give the tower masters boils. Or fade like smoke in an afternoon breeze. Chej, it just doesn't matter to me. It hasn't mattered in a long time."

"But I do?" Chej said. "Why?"

Ruesp held up his hands. "I'm giving you this," he said. "Just take it."

The more Ruesp talked, the less Chej believed he was carrying out some elaborate deception. The xarim was direct, sometimes to the point of being hurtful. Chej had never known him to play games. Reluctantly, he began to let relief into his damaged thoughts. And hope.

"Thank you," he said, softly. "I don't understand why. Why me. But thank you."

"You already said that," Ruesp said. "So if you've decided to trust me, let's go. Because we might not have that much time."

"Right," Chej said, nodding. "I'm ready. I'll do whatever you say."

Ruesp nodded and started walking, beckoning for him to follow.

Chej followed. But he didn't get far.

"Wait," he said. "I can't."

"Can't what?" Ruesp asked.

"Leave," Chej replied. "Not while—I think Yash needs me."

"Yash? Your wife? What do you care about her?"

"It's very complicated," Chej said.

Ruesp rolled his eyes. "Is she still in Dzhesq's tower?"

"Oh no, she's—oh, you don't know, do you?"

"Explain," Ruesp said.

"Yash—she's the one *doing* all of this. Killing the tower masters and their monsters. Letting the Beast go."

Ruesp listened as he briefly explained the events of the afternoon and night.

"I mean no offense to you, Chej," Ruesp said when he was done. "But if this woman is all you say she is, how do you expect to help her?"

"I know I'm not a warrior," Chej replied. "I'm not a sorcerer. But I think she needs my help."

"In what way?"

"For one thing, I remembered something about the Beast," he said. "Something that helped her kill it. For another, I'm compelled to help her."

"How so?"

Chej pointed to his earring. "This. I thought we were just performing some charming barbarian custom, but it seems I'm bound to serve her. I can't take it out."

Ruesp reached up, and before Chej could react, tugged at his ear. He dangled the earring and its red gem in front of Chej's face.

"This is what compels you?"

Chej blinked. He didn't feel any different.

He sighed. "Maybe not. Maybe there was never any sorcery in that at all. Maybe I always knew I had to help her."

"How, then?" Ruesp said.

"I've got to find her first," Chej replied. "This is good, though. It means you don't have to be implicated in all of this. You can just go back to the war-heart, and—"

"The Beast destroyed the war-heart," Ruesp said. "And even if it hadn't, I would not be of a mind to return to that pointless task. I may have a few years left in this life. Or days. Or heartbeats. But whatever remains of it, I will spend it how I see fit. And right now, that apparently means looking after you."

"I think I understand you," Chej said, after a moment. "I won't say I can't use the help. But the last time I saw my wife she was going up the Earth Center Tower to kill the Emperor."

"She ought to be easy enough to find, then," Ruesp said. "At the very least we know where to start."

CHAPTER THIRTY

# YIR THE PINION

WHEN LIGHT and knowing came back to Yash, she was standing upright. Master Pinion was sitting in a stone chair not far away, studying something on a table by the light of a large lantern. She tried to start toward him, but found her limbs wouldn't move. Her feet seemed a part of the floor, and in the same breath she understood that her body wasn't holding itself up but rather was gripped by some unseen force, as if a powerful wind had somehow become motionless but retained its strength. As consciousness returned, so did pain and profound weakness.

Pinion didn't seem to have noticed she was awake. She was able to move her eyes, and so she wandered them around what she could see of the room without turning, which she could not do.

To her right four slim pillars of blue stone connected floor and ceiling, arranged so their bases formed a square with sides the length of her arm. On her left stood another four pillars, these made of black stone. The pillars in front of her were white, flecked with silver. All of this was visible in the light of Pinion's lantern, but it wasn't enough to illuminate the rest of the room, which remained shadowed to her eyes.

"Master Pinion," she said.

He frowned at what he was studying—she now saw it was a sheaf of papers with writing on it—then looked up at her.

"Hello," he said. "I wasn't sure you would wake up again, considering your wounds. I'm impressed. And also hopeful, because I'm having trouble deciding what to do with you next and you might be able to help me. But we have no time to waste. You could die at any moment."

"You could tend my wounds," she said.

"I have already done what I am able," he replied. "I removed the arrow, and I bound your ankle. But you are bleeding inside. I've slowed it as much as I can, but there is no stopping it. Anyway, you won't need that body for long."

"What do you mean?"

"You'll have a new one soon," he said. "It's only—there is so little time, and the match has to be right."

"I don't understand what you're talking about," Yash said.

"You killed my bird, Ruzuyer," Pinion replied. "You must replace him."

"No, I don't think I must," Yash said. "Tch'etsagh was not a thing you owned. Neither am I."

"Saying that doesn't make it true," Pinion said. He narrowed his eyes. "Anyway, it isn't about that, is it? It's not about my vanity, my pride in my power. Don't you know? Don't you see what you've done?"

"I'm tired," Yash said. "And as you point out, dying. Can't you just explain? Imagine I have no idea what you're talking about."

"The tower monsters. Don't you know what their purpose is?"

"What did I just say?" Yash replied.

Pinion sighed. "Just so. I'm wasting time. This caution, this—trying to guess who knows what and who doesn't. It is an old habit, born from years of dealing with the other zuen"

He folded his hands together.

"Your people, my people. Both came here from the Moon World. This you know."

"Yes," Yash said. "Mine came many years before yours. Fleeing yours. The Hje had gotten too friendly with the monsters."

He shrugged and held up his hands. "Perhaps so. But your people left, and some few generations passed. There was a war, a terrible one. Those who survived fled the destruction of the Moon World; we came here, to this place, and found all of the things we needed to endure. But we also made enemies, of course. Barbarians, savages. We had to fight to keep this place, to preserve civilization. Fight we did, and we became good at it. We extended our domain. But what we wanted most was peace, the peace we could never have in our ancient home.

"Then the Emperor tamed Nalzhu, the first xual. We don't know where he got it, although most of us believe it came from your country, Zełtah, because it is filled with them. Nalzhu's power was great. In time, it was too great. We began to fear the Emperor and his monster. And so we—the tower masters—found xual of our own. Using the sorcery we derived from them, we were able to tame the Emperor's dread beast, to keep it in check. To render it quiescent, asleep even. This curbed the Emperor as well and made him receptive to our advice and guidance. This balance existed for centuries.

"And now, in less than a day, you have slain five of the xual and four tower masters. The balance is gone. The Emperor's monster is waking, and it is angry. It knows its restraints have loosened. You saw what happened to Ruzuyer, yes? Or what did you call him? Che something?"

"Tch'etsagh," Yash said. "Yes, something took him. The same thing happened to the Wejetsjah, the one you called the Beast."

Pinion's brow wrinkled impressively. "I didn't know about that," he said. "I knew he was slain, but not that Nalzhu took him. Even worse. He has two xual, then; their power joined with his own. And the others you slew?"

"They are gone," Yash said. "Safe, back where they belong."

Pinion nodded. "Qaxh still has his Thing, Xuehehs his Nasch, and Zuah his Taxual. Unless you know better."

"I did not slay them."

"So three remain. But the three of them are not enough. Not alone. Nalzhu will devour them, just as he did the Beast and Ruzuyer. But I will remedy that."

"And this involves me, I take it?"

"Yes. You will be my new xual." He smiled. "You, who have worked so hard to destroy us, now will be our salvation."

Yash tilted her head. Was he joking?

"Are you joking?" she asked.

"Not at all."

"But I'm not a spirit," she pointed out.

"You are much more than bone and sinew," Pinion said. "That is evident. You are linked to your country, much like the tower monsters. You derive strength from it, as they do. And you have this."

He lifted something from behind his lantern. She saw it was a glass jar, sealed at the top. Through the distorted glass, she saw a blue-green insect, a big-one-who-carries-things-in-his-basket. Deng'jah.

"I'm not a naheeyiye," she said. "Neither is he. This will not work."

"It will work," Pinion replied. "I was one of the first tower masters. I know the process. How I made Ruzuyer, for instance. Our hunters found him, long ago. The spirit of a place, its stone and earth, its plants and animals, its weather, its *essence*. A spirit as old as existence with no form and many forms, a spirit that has changed many times as the world itself changed. But in all of those shapes, all of those incarnations, there are one or two incarnations that represent the bleakest, angriest, most destructive form it has taken or might take. Once we discovered that, we shaped it to our needs and it became Ruzuyer. And that is what I shall do with you. But what is your nature? What are you in the Dream of the World? Qaxh would be able to see that easily, as I cannot. Unfortunately, Qaxh cannot be trusted. He is rather mad. But I can work in my own way, through the worlds that surround this world, of which everything is some admixture. The White Brilliant. The Silent Stagnant. The Sky World. The Ice Horizon. Ruzuyer was all of these in part, but he was mostly a creature of the Sky World. You see? Around you are gates to those four worlds. Once I guess your dominant nature and open that corresponding gate, I will be able to create a xual version of you."

He leaned forward and poked a bony finger toward her. "But understand this," he said. "If I shine the light of the wrong world upon you in this state, it might kill you outright. I spent a year in research before incarnating Ruzuyer. In your case, I have only a fraction of this night to make the right decision. So, please, help me."

He was right, she realized. He could indeed make a monster of her. She felt that promise from each of the gates. But he was also wrong: whichever gate he opened, she would be bent to its power. She would be lost.

All but one of them, perhaps.

"This is all nonsense," Yash said. "I am human, born of human parents." But now she understood what he was about to do. And what she had to do, if she could manage it.

"Your insect friend is not human. Or an insect. And you are bonded to him. Which is it? Where should I search for your true nature? The White Brilliant? The Ice Horizon? The Sky World? The Silent Stagnant?"

"No," Yash whispered.

"I heard that," Pinion said. He sat still for a moment then smiled slightly. "You meant for me to hear you. You want me to think your connection is to the Silent Stagnant. You would rather die, I see, than serve me. But you haven't tricked me. I surmise from your pretension that the Silent Stagnant is the wrong choice."

"I meant 'no' to all of them," Yash said.

"No, you didn't," he said, waving the back of his hand at her.

"Believe what you want," Yash said.

"I already knew," Pinion said. "All the signs pointed to it. But in trying to deceive me, you have helped me be certain."

Yash closed her eyes. She took a deep, slow breath.

"You are dying," Pinion said. "I am out of time. Answer me and you will live, albeit not in this form."

"I have done what I could," Yash said. "I do not fear death."

"The opposite of the Silent Stagnant," Pinion said. "The White Brilliant. That's the answer."

Yash didn't open her eyes. But in the next instant every inch of her body burst into flames, inside and outside. She tried to hold back a scream, but one tore from her lips anyway.

She took a very long, deep breath, although it brought nothing but greater agony. She held it.

*My legs*
*My arms*
*My torso*
*My head*
*My organs*
*My breath*
*My bone*
*I have listened to you before*
*Now listen to me*
*It is time to change again.*

She opened her eyes and found herself surrounded by blindingly bright sheets of rainbow that curved away in all directions. The still wind that held her was gone, and her dying body crumpled to the ground. Her heart beat with the speed of a bee's wings; she felt the blood pooling within her. Her thoughts came sluggishly, seeming to take days to form as her body rushed toward its end.

But then, slowly, her mind sped up, going faster until her heartbeat seemed normal, until the blood moved into her veins and her body responded to what she was asking of it.

*We are a tree, filling our wounds with sap*
*We are a burned forest, sprouting green again*
*We are skin making scars*
*We are bones knitting*
*We are a lizard, growing a new tail*
*We are a sea-star, spreading new hands.*

Her pain began to fade. The strength in her center began to move out into her limbs. Her body changed, male, female, both, neither, over and over again.

The rainbow faded, and now she stood on a plain of salt. Mountains drew blue lines in every distance under a white sky. Her heartbeats merged until they were no longer distinct, just a humming in her bones.

A figure stood watching her. It was bone-colored, only slightly darker than the salt. It didn't cast a shadow. It was inconstant, changing shape and size constantly, so her gaze could not easily fix on it.

It moved toward her.

She didn't see the point in waiting. Her fingers became curved knives as her skin hardened into chitin. The thing coming for her changed as well, became a huge bear with sun-bright fur. It flung its arms to gather her in a deadly embrace, but she leapt high, tumbling over its head, stabbing her claws into its rock-hard skull. When she landed, it had become a scorpion, its venomed tail striking down. She slashed that half off, but her claws stuck, and she realized the creature was made of pitch. It began to melt, forming a pool, sucking her arms farther in. She was already up to her elbows. She snarled, set her feet, and pulled harder, but the pool was oozing toward them, too.

Together, the creature said. Together we will be stronger.

She knew that was true, but it would also be the fulfillment of Pinion's plan. She would become his new tower monster.

I'm strong enough, she returned. She was remembering the time she had traveled to the western ocean, what was left of the Ocean World, before dry land came from the Ice Horizon. At one of their camps, her cousin had shown her a tree oozing pitch and the insects that lived there. They hadn't been in a hurry, and she had studied them for hours. Pitch wasps, someone had called them.

Remembering, she changed, fluttering her wings, pulling her thin, slick limbs from the sticky pool, and taking to the air. Below her, the creature was changing again, but she saw a thin sliver of shadow now, the doorway out of the White Brilliant. She entered it, regained her human form, slowed her heart, quieted the air rushing in and out of her lungs with the speed of a hurricane.

It might not be enough, she thought. When she passed through the shadow she might burst into flames and fall into a pile of burnt bones. But better that than to have the thing Pinion had called catch her, swallow her, become the skin of her xual.

She went through the opening. She smelled lightning and burnt air. Her eyes were open, but she saw only blackness like a night without moon or stars.

She could hear, though. The rasping of her breath in her ears. The rapid hammering of her heart. She was cold, freezing, shivering so hard she couldn't stand.

"Master Pinion?" she gasped. "Pinion?"

He didn't answer.

And she began to wonder where she was. Had she somehow ventured into the Silent Stagnant? Was she a skeleton encased in stone? Or was she frozen inside a glacier in the Ice Horizon?

## CHAPTER THIRTY-ONE

# THE EMPEROR'S MONSTER

THE STAIRS were littered with parts of the stone-skeleton guardians. They were no longer articulated, but they yet possessed a semblance of life, shifting about like winter-torpid lizards, vibrating, burrowing back into the stone floors and walls. The tower itself continued to quake, which concerned Hsheng a great deal, although it didn't appear to alarm her father in the slightest. His step was strong as they climbed the stairs, navigating the unnatural debris with ease. He seemed, in fact, more robust than she had ever seen him, which was at odds with the peculiar and uncharacteristic fatalism of his recent comments. During the ascent, however, he didn't speak at all. When they reached the top floor he went directly to the steep set of steps— almost a ladder, really—that led to the roof. Hsheng followed him up.

The wind had risen, and the stars were more than half-blotted by an approaching storm. Thunder shuddered the air, and the stone beneath her feet quivered in response. Far below, the huge hole made by the Beast had become the draw hole of a furnace; fire licked skyward from it, and the roof tiles surrounding it glowed dull red. The moon, huge and yellow-orange, was only moments from passing behind the storm. In the east, the rim of the world was faintly visible, the herald of approaching dawn.

"I was young when we fought the war," her father said, staring up at the moon. "More terrible sorcery you have never seen. Forests flashed into flame and burned to charcoal in instants. Seas boiled and climbed the heavens as storms of living steam. Mountains fell from the sky.

"We won. But the cost. The elders died, all of them, consumed by the very conjurings that destroyed the enemy." He smiled and glanced at her.

"Did they know, I wonder? What the price of the war would be? That their children would have to leave the world of their birth for another? They said nothing of it. They made no plans. I was an apprentice then. I fought alongside my master. I saw him die. I saw my world die. And only when it was over did we, the survivors, realize what we had to do."

He shook his head. "We were children. We knew nothing. But we did it. We gathered in this tower and in it we came here. We settled in this place, and we built a fortress, then a city, then an empire."

"Yes, you did," Hsheng said.

"But it wasn't easy," he said. "In the early days, we almost perished. Until."

"Until what?"

He put his hand on her shoulder. "I thought at first I was going mad," he said. "That the voice in my ear was my own. When I realized the truth, it was almost too late, but I did have a choice. I made my decision, and all that has happened in the centuries since has been built on that choice."

"What choice, Father?"

"He was feeble, at first. Feeble enough that if we had all combined our might, we could have destroyed him. But then we, too, would have died, overrun by barbarians. The last of our world, the Moon World, would have perished. The end of our people and our sacred ways. So I accepted him. Nourished him until he was strong enough to nourish me. Our people grew mighty."

"Are you talking about the xual of the Earth Center Tower?" she asked. "Are you talking about Nalzhu?"

His head shifted in the slightest of nods. "I'm talking about Nalzhu," he said. "But he is no xual."

"I don't understand," she said. "I thought he was the first of the tower guardians. That you fought and tamed the spirit of this place, this valley, and made it serve us, as the river and the soil serve us."

"That is the story," he said. "But it is not true. I could never tell the truth. Not until now. Now, when all is done, and my time is finally at its end. When yours, daughter, is beginning."

"Mine? What do you mean? Father, if Nalzhu is not a xual, then what is he?"

"He came with us," her father whispered. She heard the tremble in his voice. For a moment she could not find her own.

"With us?" she finally asked. "From the Moon World? You mean, he's—"

The tower shook so violently she almost lost her footing. Her father put his other hand on her other shoulder and then drew her in close. It was shocking; as far back as she could remember, he had never hugged her.

It terrified her.

"Emperor?" she asked. "Father?"

"I made a bargain with Nalzhu," he said. "At the very start of it. A bargain that included us all. Which made the Empire possible. In my youth and arrogance I thought I would never have to pay my end of it, that I could defer it forever. But that was long ago, and I am no longer young. All debts come due. And I am finally happy to pay them." He squeezed her tighter. "Farwell," he said. "My daughter. My old friend."

Then the stone of the tower gave way beneath their feet, and she was falling, still in the circle of her father's arms.

## CHAPTER THIRTY-TWO

# THE TOWER OF THE BIRDS

CHEJ AND Ruesp emerged in the western half of the fortress, in the administrative domain. It was like being in an anthill kicked open by a giant. People were scurrying about seemingly at random. All sorts of people. It wasn't just the physical walls that had been broken by the Beast and Zu's arrows, but the unseen barriers that kept people in their accustomed compounds, doing their usual work, following their routine paths through the day. Men and women from every xarim domain and ministry mingled in the halls, united by their panic. Many of these were guards and soldiers; Chej expected to be recognized and arrested at any moment, but he quickly realized not one of them was looking for him or even *at* him. He also began to see patterns in the apparent chaos. Great clumps of people huddled in chambers and doorways. Others moved cautiously, stopping to examine every junction before crossing. Most of these were moving toward the outer terrace and the gates. They were evacuating the fortress. Chej saw one of the exits; it looked so crowded as to be impassable. The din was incredible: hundreds talking, screaming, praying to the gods.

Ruesp grabbed hold of a fellow in the red and silver of the reserve guard. Chej looked around nervously while they shouted in each other's ears. After a moment, Ruesp took Chej's arm and began guiding him north and east from the administrative domain. This was near where the Beast had come through the roof, and much of it was rubble, with huge gaps open to the sky through which flames were sucked into vortexes whirling heavenward. There were a few squads of house minders fighting the fire with buckets of water and sand, but everyone else had cleared out. Ruesp directed him to winding routes around the damage until they were in mostly quiet, abandoned corridors with the fires behind them, although even those were full of smoke.

"Ruzuyer took your wife," Ruesp said, when they could hear each other's words without screaming.

Chej didn't look at him. They continued in silence for a few steps. "What?"

"She was seen fleeing the Earth Center Tower. Reports are that she was wounded. Yir's bird picked her up and took her off to his tower."

"Is she dead?" he finally asked.

"If it were anyone else, I would imagine so," the xarim replied. "But after the bird got her to Yir's tower, some sort of flash was seen. Like lightning."

"Zu's arrows," Chej muttered. "It must be. Is that where we're going? Yir's tower?"

"Against any sort of sense, yes," Ruesp replied.

"Good," Chej said.

As they neared the tower, it started getting crowded again, but, as before, no one was paying much attention to anyone else. That changed when they came to the entrance of the tower, where Yir's black-and-brown-clad guard met them with spears in hand. The fortress shuddered, whether from the rolling thunder outside or some other cause Chej did not know.

For a moment, no one said anything. Then Ruesp nodded at the xi.

"You know me, Hsaj," he said. "You served with me for a time. What is happening here?"

Hsaj was a lean, tall man with a scar above one eye.

"I wish I knew, xarim," he said. "Something. All sorts of strange sounds. But we've been told to remain here and prevent anyone from coming up."

"You won't prevent me," Ruesp said. "I've got business with Yir. The Emperor's business."

"Do you have orders you can show me, xarim?"

"Have you had a look around lately, Xi Hsaj? No, I don't have orders to show you. But you will let me in to see Yir or you will personally go up to fetch him and bring him down here." He cocked his head. "Do you remember me as a man who talks or brooks nonsense?"

"No, xarim. It's just that Yir said—"

"Yir is not the Emperor," Ruesp snapped. "And this is no time to delay me. I have given you options. Turning me away is not one of them. Choose one of the others."

The xi took a few breaths, brows knitted.

"You can go up, xarim," he finally said. "But I would beware if I were you. I do not think it is safe up there."

"Where do you think it is safe, Xi Hsaj?"

"You may have a point there, xarim," the guard said.

Ruesp motioned as if to push the guards aside.

"Lend us a lantern," he said.

The xi obliged, taking one from a hook and handing it to Ruesp. Then the men cleared a path and, in a few moments, they were mounting the winding stair of the Standing Pinion Tower.

Chej had only been in Yir's tower once, many years before, on an errand for Sha, but he remembered the trip well. Yir had not only Ruzuyer; he was a collector of birds of all sorts. Each room of his tower was closed with a double door of woven cane mesh; you would enter one, close it behind you, then proceed through the next, so that the winged inhabitants of the room could not escape. The rooms themselves were fancifully decorated with artificial trees and plants of wood and stone to provide his many pets perches and shelter. On his visit, Yir had been in good spirits and given him a tour of the hundreds of birds in the tower. There were birds of every color of the rainbow, and some were rainbows in and of themselves. There were birds bigger than a man, who could not fly but that stalked about on thick limbs. Yir had owls and hawks, jays and pelicans, ravens and hummingbirds, stranger birds from very far away.

And to feed and water them he had servants, quite a few of them. They lived in tiny rooms, much smaller than those of the birds. On the second florr he saw one he recognized standing between the two doorways holding a lantern. Behind her, a lamp in the room revealed birds with bright emerald plumage flitting about.

"Xol," Chej said.

"Yes," the small, hunched woman said. "That is me."

"I met you years ago."

She shrugged. "I don't remember you."

"That's understandable. Do you know what's going on upstairs?"

"Someone killed Ruzuyer," she said. "Burned him with the lightning. Yir has the killer. He told us to stay down here and watch the birds, keep them calm. He's going to do something."

"Do what?"

"Some sort of sorcery," she said. "Something bad, I can feel it. Everything is bad now, isn't it?"

"Maybe," Chej said.

She glanced behind Chej and her face softened. "You are Xarim Ruesp, yes?"

"I am."

"The birds," she said. "What should I do?"

"Maybe you should let them go," Ruesp suggested.

"Some of them wouldn't live," she replied. "They won't find the right food. The weather outside is wrong for them."

"None of them will live if this place burns down," Ruesp said. "Think about it. You may be in charge soon."

"How can that be?" she whispered. "Yir is master here."

"Just keep it in mind," he said. "If you cut open the window mesh, they can leave. It's what they want to do, isn't it?"

"Most of them," she said.

"We have to go," Ruesp said. "Do as you see fit."

They continued up the stairs.

"I smell something burning," Chej said as they neared the top. "Something other than the fortress, I mean. Like flesh."

"Yes," Ruesp replied.

"Perhaps it is Ruzuyer?"

"No," Ruesp said. "I've smelled this before. It isn't burnt bird."

They reached the next landing. Chej remembered that Yir's workshop was windowless but usually illuminated by lamplight. Now it was completely dark, at least until the light of their lantern entered it. The burnt smell was strong here. A little smoke curled in the lamplight, drifting up from tables and stools that looked like they were made of charcoal.

In the center of the room four sets of four columns stood floor-to-ceiling. A stone chair faced them. When they drew closer, Chej saw there was someone—no, what was left of someone—in the chair. His clothes had been burned off and his flesh charred black. His eyes and hair were gone.

Chej backed against the wall and closed his eyes. He understood the smell now. It was suffocating him. The back of his throat burned.

Too much. He'd seen too much. Too many dead people. Too much blood and ash and horror.

"Master Pinion?" someone asked. "Pinion?"

He knew the voice. He forced his eyes open and darted his gaze around the room. Then he saw her, crouched against the wall. It looked like she had a film of ashes on her, but other than that she was naked.

"Yash!" he said. "You're alive."

"Ch-Chej?" she managed. He realized her teeth were chattering. She was shivering. And her eyes: they were looking in his direction, but not *at* him.

"It's me," he said, taking a few steps toward her. Her gaze shifted toward his feet. "Are you—you don't seem well."

"I…" she said. "I don't know. Pinion! Chej, watch out for Pinion."

"I… I can see him," Chej stammered. "What's left of him, anyway." A sob escaped his lips. He was crying. Of course. What else was there to do?

"Chej?" she said. "What's wrong? Are you hurt? I can't see you."

Of course. That's why her eyes seemed so strange. They weren't looking at anything.

"Yir is all burned up," Chej said. "He's—" He couldn't finish.

Ruesp put a hand on his shoulder and squeezed. "Chej isn't hurt," he said. "He'll be better in a moment. Because he has to be."

Chej drew in a deep, quavering breath. He remembered his father's hand on his shoulder like this, just after his mother died. How he'd felt better not because it fixed anything or lessened his grief, but because it reminded him that he wasn't alone. But when his father also traveled off beyond the sunset, there hadn't been anyone. There hadn't been anyone since.

"Chej?" Yash asked. "Who is with you?"

He drew himself straight and wiped his eyes. "It's Xarim Ruesp," he said. "My friend. I'm fine." He walked past the burnt corpse to where Yash was trying to stand.

"Why are you blind?" Chej asked. "I'm coming to you. Don't kill me."

He knelt before her and tentatively put a hand on her shoulder. She didn't feel cold—in fact, she felt feverish—but she was nevertheless shivering. She grabbed him by the wrist.

"Chej," she said. "I thought you might be dead. I shouldn't have left you."

"What happened to you?" he asked. "You're cold?"

"Freezing."

"A moment," he said. He gently pulled her fingers from his wrist and then pulled his shirt over his head. Then he helped her put it on. On her, it was a gown, and he still had his skirt to cover him. Then, carefully, he wrapped his arms around her and helped her stand up.

"Is that better?"

"Yes," she said. "Thank you, shegan'."

He tried to let her go, but now she was holding him. It was a dozen heartbeats before she let him go.

She took a deep breath and nodded. "I think my sight is improving," she said. "Ruesp has a lantern? I think I can see it. But I still can't see you."

"Let us hope it continues to improve," Chej said. "But... what happened to you? What happened to Yir?"

"He was trying to change me," she said. "To make me into a monster."

"You're already a monster," Chej said.

She chuckled. "Into a tower monster," she said. "A xual, as you call them. To replace his bird. But I tricked him. Sort of. Into casting me into the White Brilliant. I knew I would either die there or come back stronger and still myself. If he had thrown me into one of the other worlds, he might have gotten what he wanted. But change is my nature. I guess when I returned from the White Brilliant I was... hot."

"Very hot, I should say," Ruesp said.

"We cannot stay here, I think," Yash said. "If Pinion was right, we cannot stay here."

"Your eyes—"

"My sight is returning. It's like I looked into the sun too long. It will clear."

"If Yir was right about what?" Ruesp asked.

"I'll tell you as we go, xarim," she replied.

"Ruesp will do. Can you see well enough to walk?"

"Not yet, but the two of you could guide me," she said.

"Yes, we can do that," Chej said.

"I missed you, Husband," she said. "I am glad you're not dead."

"He isn't safe yet," the old man said. "The Emperor has ordered his execution. He cannot stay in the fortress. He shouldn't remain in the Empire. I tried to convince him to leave when it was possible, but he insisted on finding you first." He sighed. "Things are in great disarray. But with all of this confusion, I think I can still get you out of the city."

"Get Chej out of the city, by all means," Yash said, taking a few tentative steps. "But I have more to do here." She stopped. "Wait. Deng'jah."

"What of him?" Chej asked.

"Pinion had him captive. In a glass jar on the table near his chair."

"Wait," Chej said. He took the lantern and searched around the corpse. He found the jar on the floor. Zu's bow and arrows lay near it unscathed, although the quiver had been incinerated. The long demon-bone knife Yash has been so handy with earlier was there also, now lacking the leather wrapping its grip.

"It's shattered," he told her. "I don't see the bug. But I have your weapons."

Her eyebrows lifted, and Yash held out her hands. He handed them to her and watched as she examined them by touch. She felt the weight of them then nodded and reached the bow and arrows toward Chej.

"You should take these until I can see again," she said. "You know how to shoot a bow, I imagine?"

"Yes," Chej said, taking them. Yash kept the knife. "I'm sorry about your bug."

"Deng'jah?" she asked. "I doubt he's dead. I don't know if he *can* die. He can take care of himself. But I feel…" She frowned and turned slowly in a circle. "I feel as if I missed something." Her eyebrows lifted. "Oh, wait. Do you feel that?"

At first, Chej didn't know what she was talking about. But then the stone of the tower trembled beneath his feet. It stopped. Then, after a short pause, it happened again, stronger this time.

"Yes," he said. "What is that?"

"Run," Yash said. "We must run."

They made it to the stairwell and then to the next landing before the tower quaked so violently that Chej lost his footing and tumbled painfully. He let go of Yash's hand to protect his head.

When he looked back up he saw Yash and Ruesp above him. They had fallen, too. He had dropped the lantern, and it was broken, spreading a puddle of fire on the stone that was dripping in blazing cataracts down the stairs. The fire struggled, though, as water spattered onto it from above. In the same moment Chej realized he was wet and getting wetter. And cold. Somehow, rain was pounding down on him.

Then he understood. The top of the tower—including the room they had just been in—was gone. Lightning lit the clouds above from within and, against that, a shadow moved, coming toward them. It was huge, like the sky falling.

But then lightning flashed, and a face appeared, filling most of what he could see of the sky: an inhuman visage of stone covered in flower-shaped jewels, its eyes lightless depths, its mouth yawned open to reveal bristling teeth of sharpened agate, quartz, obsidian, jade, coral, garnet. It loomed above the tower, and now a hand reached into the broken tower, the smallest finger as long as he was tall.

"Run, I said," Yash yelled, taking his hand and grabbing Ruesp's with the other.

CHAPTER THIRTY-THREE

# AMONG THE FLOWERS

IN THE instant the tower collapsed, Hsheng knew her future; the brutal impact of stone on bone and flesh, the breath crushed out of her, blood and brains filling her mouth and nose, impossible pain, but gone quickly, and then the deepest silence imaginable. She knew all of this before the stone even enveloped her, while she was still staring at her father's bemused face. She felt it so vividly she knew it was real.

And then—something else happened instead. It was like sliding down into warm water that enveloped her on all sides. She felt at peace, protected. Her mouth and lungs opened and let the water into her, and she understood that it wasn't water at all: it was light made somehow liquid. Life, existence. She wasn't falling. She wasn't being crushed. Then what was happening?

Whatever it was, it felt glorious. Maybe it was death, but not as she had ever imagined it.

*Not death. Rebirth.*

It wasn't her thought. But it was where her thoughts dwelled, in the center of her.

She sat in a darkened hall. She remembered it from the banquet of rotting food, but none of the other guests were there. The moonflower vines had grown to cover almost everything and were in glorious bloom not just with moonflowers but with blossoms of every size, description, and color. A haze of pollen hung in the air and dusted the table yellow. Above the courtyard, the heavens blazed with stars so bright they left marks on her vision.

"Are you ready?" someone asked.

She'd thought she was alone, but now she saw a person sitting at the head of the table in her father's seat. And it looked like her father a little. His face, at least, seemed familiar. But she now saw that the flowering vines all originated from him. They sprouted from his head like hair; his fingers tapered and elongated to become vines;, thick runners pushed out of his chest and torso.

"No," she said. She didn't know who he was or what he meant, and she didn't care.

"You are," he said. "You have been. But the time wasn't right. Now it is. Three of the xual are gone, and I have feasted on two. *We* have feasted. And we are ready."

"You and I are not *we*," she said.

"Look again."

She didn't want to. She stretched the moment, staring into the face that resembled her father's but wasn't. Reluctantly, she finally turned her gaze down.

The vines were also growing from her. She tried to stand, to shake them loose, but it was no good. They were rooted to her very bones. Her blood, her nerves were in them. They were extensions of her body. She felt *him*, and the thousands of strands that connected them.

She tried to stand up again, but her legs weren't there, or at least she couldn't feel them. Her arms weren't, either—or her body or her head. Just the vines, spreading everywhere.

The man stood, and the walls of the courtyard sagged and then slowly collapsed, entombing her in flowers and creepers. She tried to push through them, to tear them, but they were *her*, and there was no escape. But she was growing. And as she grew, her arms and legs came back. Her sense of body returned. Different than she remembered. Better. Bigger, more massive with each passing moment.

Who was she, anyway? She'd thought she was Hsheng, the daughter of the Emperor. But she was more than that, wasn't she? Much more. She remembered things now. Places, people, worlds, rage—and above all, hunger.

*No,* she thought. *That's not me.*

*But it is. Your father made you for this. I helped him do it. All of your life, you have been waiting for this, to become this. To be me. To be Nalzhu. To walk once more, and do what we do.*

Now she could see. She was looking down at the fortress, as if from a height. She realized that she was still at the summit of the Earth Center Tower. The top had collapsed, but the rest of the tower still retained a semblance of its structure. That was changing, however. Stone-bone guardians swarmed from it, joining together, gathering the broken parts to themselves, re-forming the building into something else. Vines sprang from the stone, guiding it toward a new shape.

*But I will not be Hsheng,* she protested.

*Nor were you ever meant to be.*

The sky was pouring rain now, and the clouds were fat and hot with lightning. They hummed with life and spirit, and beyond them a world of plains, mountains, oceans, life to learn and destroy. The fortress below her seemed tiny. Not worth her time.

*But it is. We must finish here first. We must be free.*

*Very well.*

She felt them, the xual striving against her. The coiled power that Qaxh called his Thing. Nasch. Taxual. They were all that remained of the troublesome bonds that had kept her quiet, smoothed over her malice, prevented her becoming. They were still strong, even though now there were only three. But there was something helping her, too, something working in the remains of the Earth Center Tower, a shape-giving force flowing from the Dream of the World, directing the bones and vines, informing them with might. She—Nalzhu—had an ally. Who or what was it? Not her father. He was gone.

Besides the surviving xual, there was another that must be dealt with. Yash. Nalzhu felt her there, the enemy. She passed her gaze through stone until she saw the barbarian. Then she pulled her feet from the rock that had moored her for so many ages. She was distantly aware of the remaining walls collapsing, of the rooms of the tower crushing together to form her corpus, of a hundred souls torn from their bodies in the instant of her first step. To the delusion that had been Hsheng, that would have mattered. To Nalzhu it mattered not at all.

It was good, in fact. It was like pulling splinters from her flesh; the pain brought release, and there was no reason to care for what became of the splinter. So she took another step toward the Standing Pinion Tower. Where Yash was.

## CHAPTER THIRTY-FOUR

# THE GIANT OF STONE AND FLOWERS

YASH STRAINED her recovering eyes at the darkness. Without the lantern and with the moon drowned in clouds, the only light was from the lightning in the sky, and they were leaving that behind as quickly as possible. Which was not as quickly as she would have liked. It also was too dark for Chej and Ruesp to see, so they all had to make their way by feel as whatever was at their backs dug into the tower, tearing huge hunks of it out.

"What is it, Chej?" she asked.

"A monster," he said. "Bigger than the Beast. Much bigger. The size of a tower. It's trying to get to us."

"Nalzhu," she said.

"The Emperor's xual?" Chej said.

"It must be," she replied. "Give me the bow and arrows."

"But—"

"Give them to me and keep running," she said. "It's after me. Eventually it's going to realize it should shatter this tower at the base."

"Can you see?"

"I'm not sure. It's dark, right. Can you see?"

"It's dark," Chej confirmed.

"Then I'll take a chance. If it's as big as you say, I won't have to see very well to hit it," she replied.

Chej sighed, but she felt the bow against her hand and took it, followed by the arrows. She handed him the knife.

"Keep the knife," she said. "I only have two hands."

"I'm not certain of that," Chej said. "Be careful, Wife. Don't die."

"I can only avoid death for so long," she said. "But I'll do my best to see we don't meet up tonight. You do the same." She paused. "Go to one of the remaining tower masters. Coral, maybe. If any of them can help, it's Coral."

"He's the Emperor's ally."

"He was. But if Nalzhu is free, destroying the fortress, he might have a change of heart."

"Maybe," Ruesp said. "We can try."

"Yes," Yash said. Then she began running back up the stairs, putting an arrow to the string.

Twenty steps took her to what was now the top of the tower and a gale of wind-whipped rain. For a moment she saw nothing, but then lightning brightened the clouds and a giant shadow appeared between her and the sky. She shot at it.

The arrow flared and then flashed, and in its light Nalzhu was revealed. A thing of stone and jewels, he stood as tall as the Earth Center Tower. The arrow had struck him in the chest and continued to flare for a moment before sputtering out, leaving a red blotch of molten rock.

"Who are you, my enemy?" she shouted into the wind. "What name did we call you by?"

In response, Nalzhu slammed the back of his fist into the tower. She leapt as high as she could. Stone shattered beneath her as she came down on top of the gigantic arm, to which she was, in comparison, no bigger than an insect. But she was an insect with a sting. She ran a few steps up the arm and released another arrow. This one struck him in the face, showering sparks and lava into the storm. In the burst of light, she suddenly knew she had seen him before. Or something like him. But where?

She jumped from his arm, dropping toward the roof of the fortress, singing of being a leaf, a butterfly, cotton tufts in the wind, but the landing was still hard. She barely recovered in time to dodge the palm that slapped down after her.

The fiery wound in Nalzhu's chest was already congealed; part of his head glowed red, but that was quickly fading to black as well. But a light was building in the hollows of his eyes.

*I need to know its name! If only Deng'jah were here.*

"I am here," a voice said, right in her ear. "But I don't know its name."

"Deng'jah!"

"Yes," he said. "The little prank you played on Pinion was nearly the death of me, too. But here I am."

"Good," she said as she dashed across the roof. If she could stay near the giant's feet, it might make it harder for him to reach her. "Feel free to offer advice."

"I just told you all I know."

"But if he's not naheeyiye, what…" She paused. "I remember now," she said. "I remember why he looks familiar."

"Does that mean you have a plan?"

"Yes," she said, glancing across the roof toward the Red Coral Tower. It was too far away. She would never make it. But the Obsidian Spear was just a run of a few dozen steps.

"Watch out for me, Deng'jah," she said. Then she turned her back to Nalzhu and sped toward the tall black spire. At the same time her gaze was fixed on it, she saw, through the insect's eyes, Nalzhu coming after. She heard the crash of his stone feet, even through the thunder. She dodged north as the monster bent to smash her then hugged close to the remaining base of Pinion's tower. She leapt up onto the wall at the edge of the roof and skittered to where the inner wall of the fortress almost connected the two towers. What was left of Pinion's tower shattered as she jumped across the gap; she managed to take shelter behind the curve of the Obsidian Spear as stones flew as thick as the rain. Then she leapt up, gripped a windowsill, and heaved, fingers fighting for purchase on the wet stone.

She rolled into the tower. Behind her, Nalzhu paused for a moment, trying to figure out where she was. Then he strode toward the tower, his feet crushing through the roof of the fortress with each step.

Yash found the stairs and ran down. She had not reached the bottom when the Obsidian Spear jolted from impact. She drew a breath and smelled a sharp, carnivore musk.

She knew it was the xual the Hje called Nasch. She didn't know what its real name was and now she might never.

She saw Nasch through Deng'jah's eyes, emerging from the broken Obsidian Spear, a sooty cloud of smoke that quickly condensed into a form nearly as large as Nalzhu. She saw the tiny figure behind it that must be Xuehehs the Obsidian, gesturing and shouting words she could not hear. Nasch now had a long, sinuous body and a head that was something like an otter and something like a bear. Nasch crashed into Nalzhu, savaging the bigger monster with powerful, heavily muscled forelegs.

"I'm sorry, cousin," she said with a sigh. "But you will help me, I hope. Delay him for a moment. And when this is over, I will do my best to find you, name you, send you home. Deng'jah, back to me."

The vision vanished.

An ear-splitting shriek carried down the stairwell as she burst into the guard chamber. The men were already staring fearfully at the stairwell, and the door to the fortress was open. She shouted, as loudly and shrilly as she could. The men, taken by surprise and obviously confused, scrambled out of her way as she charged through the door and into the ruined, burning fortress.

The few people who remained in the place were trying their best to get out. Almost no one seemed to notice her, and certainly no one got in her way.

"Deng'jah," she called.

"Here," the insect said from her shoulder.

"I've made a mistake. I need you to find me the quickest path through all of... this."

"To where?" Deng'jah asked.

## CHAPTER THIRTY-FIVE

# THE PAINTING

CHEJ AND Ruesp met Yir's guards coming up the stairs as the two of them descended.

"Don't go that way," Ruesp said. "The whole top of the tower is gone, and the rest of it will not be far behind." He didn't stop as he said this but continued his progress down the stairs. The guards hesitated.

When Chej glanced back, he didn't see any following.

"We should—"

"They were warned," Ruesp replied. "They'll figure it out."

They passed from the tower and back into the halls, pushing toward the ring of barracks around the Earth Center Tower. They found them crushed and open to the sky. To his relief, Chej didn't see any corpses, although he knew there must be many buried in the rubble.

Ruesp stopped to stare through the rain into the darkness above them.

"Xarim?" Chej asked.

"It's gone," Ruesp murmured. For the first time since Chej had known the older man, he seemed almost stunned.

"What?" Chej asked. "What's gone?"

But then lightning blazed inside of a cloud, and Chej realized that it was a cloud he shouldn't be able to see.

"The Earth Center Tower?" he ventured.

Ruesp nodded.

Now Chej was staring. Where was it? What could happen to something so big? Had the monster knocked it down? Even now he could hear it crushing stone and masonry back toward the Standing Pinion Tower. Was Yash fighting Nalzhu? Or was she already dead?

"We had best go," Ruesp said. "Chej. Let's go."

"Right," he said. "The Red Coral Tower."

"No," Ruesp said. "The gate. Out. Before the entire fortress is completely destroyed."

"I can't!" Chej said. "I told Yash—"

"What does it matter what you told her? Don't you understand? That giant that destroyed Yir's tower—it *is* the Earth Center Tower."

"That's insane," Chej said. But it had been made of stone, hadn't it? He remembered his father saying that the Hje had brought the tower with them from the Moon World. He'd never said anything about it being a monster.

"I agree," Ruesp said. "With all my heart and mind. It *is* insane. Which is why we should go as quickly as we can to a place where sanity is still the same as reality. Qaxh won't help, even if he could. He's likely already gone, along with his xual."

Chej shook his head and oriented himself. "The Red Coral Tower is this way," he said. "I'm going."

"Again, why? This is your moment, Chej. You can escape and no one will follow you. Anyone who survives this mess will reasonably assume you are dead. It's perfect."

"It's not perfect," Chej said. "The Earth Center Tower is a monster? That's what you said. It's destroying the fortress. I don't know what it is. I don't know anything about it."

"It's after your wife. We know that."

"And if it kills her, what then? Will it just walk back here and become a tower again? Or will it continue destroying the fortress, and then maybe the city? I don't know. Maybe Qaxh does. And maybe he can help."

"Why do you care, Chej? What happens to this place? These people?"

"I don't care what happens to the Emperor. Or the tower masters. But what about everyone else? There are thousands of people in the city. They don't all deserve to die. Most of them don't, I have to believe that. Ruesp, I've spent this whole night watching as Yash fought and bled for her people. I'm not her. I'm not even a warrior. But I have to fight for my people, as well. I can't just run. How can you? You've given your life to the Empire."

"Exactly," Ruesp said. "And I hate it. Maybe I've always hated it."

"Maybe the Empire and the people aren't the same thing," Chej said. "Not exactly, anyway."

Ruesp quirked his mouth. He looked at Chej from the rims of his eyes.

"Very well. I've been prepared to die for most of the night. If you're not worried for yourself, I can't waste any more energy on doing so for you."

The old man sighed and began walking toward the Red Coral Tower.

They had no trouble entering: the guardroom was empty. They found Qaxh the Coral in his workshop, hard at work with his paints. So busy was he, in fact, that he didn't seem to notice them enter.

Chej had been here a few times. He had always been fascinated by Qaxh and his weird, unsettling paintings, how he only made them in shades of grey and black. All painting was sorcery of course: that lines and colors and shading on flat paper could cause the mind to see a person, a thing, a place, to conjure most or all of its qualities was an astonishing and obviously supernatural feat. But that abstract shade and shape applied with a brush could evoke joy, pain, longing, fear, clarity, confusion? That was wholly more mysterious.

The other thing that had always struck him about Qaxh was his sense of order, the meticulous neatness with which his things were arranged. His brushes were always lined up in a particular way, the furniture in the room spare and symmetrically placed.

But that's not how things were now. The desks, cabinets, and stools had all been dragged to the edges of the room. Jars of pigment and oil, mixing pallets, and brushes were strewn about everywhere. Nor was Qaxh painting on parchment or paper. Instead, the master of the Red Coral Tower was adorning the floor and walls. With his *hands*. What he was painting wasn't immediately evident, but Chej could not take his eyes from it. It didn't seem to figure any one thing or person or place, but there was nothing random about it. Every stroke, swirl, and choice of paint was clearly intentional. Patterned. And the patterns seemed to move. They suggested vines and strange flowers, mountains and seas, clouds blowing through a black sky. It crawled through his eyes and into his head, a language of structure, light and shadow that had no words, that skipped past words and straight to meaning and emotion.

It was wonderful, dreadful, convincing. And though there was no body, no face in the painting, he knew without question what he was looking at. It had just looked down at him from above the broken top of Yir's tower.

The stone giant. The Earth Center Tower come to life. Ruesp had it right.

In an instant, Chej was completely certain. And in the same moment, he did something completely outside of what he believed his character to be.

He acted.

"It's him," Chej yelled, gripping Yash's knife and sprinting toward Qaxh, his heart pounding. "Qaxh did this."

"Stop him, Thing," Qaxh said without looking up.

Chej collided with something unseen. He slashed at it with the long knife. The weapon struck whatever-it-was but turned rather than biting. Chej ran to the right, trying to get around it, but the Thing wrapped around him.

It became visible.

He was bound up like a rat in the coils of a snake. Two heads, two sets of bulging yellow eyes with black slivers for pupils stared down at him. Unlike any snake he had ever seen, Thing was covered in soft, fine hair, like a mink, and each head had a mane that resembled porcupine quills. He pushed against the coils, but the earth might as well have swallowed him. He could scarcely breathe. One of the heads stretched over and bit the knife, pulling it from his hand and tossing it aside.

"Don't kill him," Ruesp said. "Qaxh, tell your xual not to kill Chej."

Qaxh shrugged, but he still had not turned his head toward them. "He meant to kill me. Chej has become more interesting than I ever thought possible. You, too, Ruesp. I wonder what brought the two of you here." He laughed. "Thing, release Chej, but keep watch. If he comes after me again, kill him."

The Thing unwound from him, and Chej's breath came back. The hairy snake-monster coiled up again, just in front of him—between him and Qaxh. Both heads continued to stare at him.

Chej looked away from the horrible yellow eyes so that his gaze fell on one of the four windows in Qaxh's workroom. It faced northwest, across the city. It was still night outside, but he could see the stone giant; it was glowing, shedding a silvery light through the darkness and pounding rain. Its feet had gone through the roof of the fortress, hiding its ankles and the lowest part of its shins, but there was still plenty to see. Like its face, the whole creature seemed to be pieced together from chunks of stone, but not randomly. Its rocky flesh was patterned like Qaxh's painting, and, like the painting, those designs seemed to slowly shift. Flowers sprouted all over it—violet, vermillion, ivory, viridian—blooming and closing, the flowers shining even more brightly than its skin.

The stone giant wasn't alone; it was grappling with what looked something like an elongated bear nearly as large as it was. As Chej watched, the stone monster bludgeoned the bear-beast in the back of the head. It faltered, then clamped its mouth on the arm that had struck it. Their struggle was quickly destroying what remained of the fortress. Yir's tower was gone, and the Obsidian Spear ended halfway up. The inner wall of the fortress was broken, and, even as he watched, the two gargantuan combatants crashed into the farther wall of the Outer Terrace, knocking a hole large enough for a small army to come through.

"The stone monster," Chej managed. "It really *is* the Earth Center Tower."

"Yes," Qaxh said. "It is Nalzhu."

"The Emperor's xual?"

"No," Qaxh said. "Nalzhu is not a xual, and the Emperor is dead." He laughed. "Can you imagine, trying to keep a thing like that quiet? Trying to tame it? We did it for centuries. Other than the Emperor, the other tower masters never even knew what Nalzhu really was. But my eyes told me long ago. I knew this day would come, and I dreamed I would be a part of it. But something was always missing. And then one little barbarian comes along, and— well here we are."

"Yash?"

Qaxh did look up then. He turned his strange eyes toward Chej. Then he smiled and stood up. He regarded his painting.

"He told me his name was Tchiił," he said. "But he—and she—is also Yash, I suppose. I did a painting of him. One of my best. And in painting… her? I realized what I had to do. That it was time. Your bride had already killed two of the tower masters and their xual. Without them, there was no way to keep Nalzhu in check. Nalzhu would have figured it out. Was figuring it out. He devoured the Beast and Ruzuyer, after all. He would have become, but not this beautiful, not this powerful. Not without me. I have been planning on this, preparing for this day. I have seen all of this in the Dream of the World, and now I'm doing what I was born to do. No more painting little things, changing sweet water to salt, daubing tiny changes into the world. No more small thoughts, tiny ambitions.

These eyes of mine, there is much they have been denied. I have lived a very patient life, waiting for them to reveal their true worth. And now I am rewarded."

"Nalzhu is destroying the fortress," Chej said. "He'll destroy the whole city. Thousands of people will die. Thousands of *our* people."

"The field must be cleared before it can be planted," Qaxh said. "The ruins must be razed before something new can be built."

"I thought you better than the rest," a voice said. "But you're the worst of them all."

Yash stood in the doorway.

"You look at a thing, a person, a place, and all you can think is how you would change it. What you would replace it with."

"Ah," Qaxh said. "We were just talking about you."

Yash seemed to be only half listening. Most of her attention was focused on the painting that covered the floor and walls.

"You made it bigger," she said.

"Better," Qaxh replied. "You were helpful in that. When I painted you, I discovered some things I hadn't seen before. To do with the push of change and the pull of stability. I finally understand what Nalzhu needed to break free and take on his true form."

"Nalzhu and his kind destroyed the Moon World."

"Our war with his kind destroyed the Moon World. I do not intend to go to war with Nalzhu."

"It will end the same," she said. "Our ancestors fought and fled from the monsters for many generations across a dozen worlds. They cannot be bargained with. They cannot be controlled."

Suddenly she was in motion, running faster than anyone Chej had ever seen run. He felt a lift inside, a savage pride. No one could stop Yash.

*She's going to kill Qaxh. She's going to kill Nalzhu. And it will be over.*

The two-headed snake was even faster than Yash. Both sets of fangs darted for her. She leapt high to avoid them, but then the monster's tail came whipping around and slapped her out of the air. Yash smacked into the wall with a meaty thud and collapsed. The snake went after her.

Chej yelped and flung himself forward, wrapping his arms around one of the monster's necks. It jerked back hard, trying to spin around and get him. The second head twisted, attempting to strike at him, but the angle wasn't quite right. As long as he held on, the Thing couldn't get to him.

But his arms were already aching with the strain. He tried to get a grip with his legs, too, but the central body of the snake-monster was too broad, and it was shaking hard, like a dog after a bath. His grip loosened further, and then Chej was in the air. He landed quite ungracefully on the floor. He tried to get up, but the snake was so fast, he would never make it—

"Stop it," Ruesp said.

At first Chej thought the old man was talking to him, but then he managed to roll over and take in the situation. Ruesp was standing behind Qaxh. He gripped the sorcerer's hair with one hand, and the other held the demon-bone knife pressed just below the base of his skull.

"Thing," Qaxh said calmly. "Xualtrexx, be still." He sighed.

Chej came shakily to his feet, eying the twin serpent suspiciously. From the verge of his vision, he saw Yash was now standing.

She pointed at the twin-snake with her lips. "I know you now," she said.

And she began to sing in her own language.

## CHAPTER THIRTY-SIX

# IN THE SKULL

*He names you Trexx*
*I have heard you called Dl'ehheja*
*In old stories*
*But you are Dednii'k'e,*
*Thunder Place*
*Where He Bent the Sky.*
*I am not your enemy.*
*Dednii'k'e,*
*I am not your foe*
*We have been family*
*For many a winter.*

THE DOUBLE-headed snake paused.

*Yes*, it said.

*Yes, I know that. For a moment only. You know what you must do.*

It bowed its heads. She watched it, took a long breath, let it out. She centered around how her body had changed in the White Brilliant. How it had adapted.

> *My hand*
> *sped by the White Brilliant*
> *unyielding like the Silent Stagnant*
> *cold, like the Ice Horizon*
> *hard, like the Sky World.*

She punched through the scales of the snake's breast, through its heart, out the bones of its spine. She withdrew her arm, bloody to the shoulder, as the xual fell. Then she turned toward Coral, where Ruesp still threatened him with a knife.

"*I'm here,*" Deng'jah said, next to her ear. "*Dednii'k'e kept me out until you killed his xual-form.*"

"*Good,*" she replied. "*I have a feeling I'll need you for this.*"

"*Be careful,*" her helper cautioned. "*This is all wrong.*"

"Your protector is gone," Yash told Coral. "Undo what you have done."

Coral cocked his head. "Ruesp will release me."

"Will I?" Ruesp said.

"If I am to do as she says," Coral replied.

Ruesp frowned, but he let go of the sorcerer's hair and took the knife from his spine.

Coral smoothed his hair and then looked over his painting. "It is a pity," he said. "It is beautiful, you agree?"

"In its way," Yash conceded.

Nodding, Coral reached for a broom that stood against the wall.

He paused and looked at the painting one last time.

"Must I?" he asked.

"Yes," Yash said. "And quickly."

Coral sighed and then began to sweep, smearing the patterns.

Yash glanced out the window. Nalzhu had dispensed with Xuehehs's xual. Nasch lay in a motionless mound. But something else was coming toward the giant now. It looked like a black whale that had grown arms and legs. That had to be Taxual, Zuah the Abalone's monster. It was big, too—bigger than Nalzhu.

"Nalzhu is still there," Yash said. "I said to undo whatever it was you did."

"And I am doing my best," Coral said. "Undoing what it is possible to undo. But there are things I cannot reverse, you know. I cannot unkill Xualtrexx, for example. In fact, I couldn't have killed him, either. That you did yourself. And thank you."

"You wanted me to kill him?"

"I was fond of him," Coral said. "But in the end, he was like the other xual: created as a check on the Emperor's moon-monster. It was not within my power to kill him, any more than the other tower masters could kill their xual. It was something we did together, you see. And I needed Xualtrexx to give my painting life. It took a great deal of will to keep him here for that purpose. If you hadn't killed him, I would have soon lost control, and he would have attacked Nalzhu. He would have killed me first. Now I have his spirit to offer the moon-monster."

"No you don't," Yash said. "If you don't stop this in your next eleven breaths, you won't draw a twelfth."

"It's all done," Coral said. "The painting has served its purpose. I have served my purpose. There is no longer any chance of stopping him."

*"He's telling the truth,"* Deng'jah said. *"He started the avalanche, but now it's out of his control."*

Yash looked back outside at Nalzhu then returned her gaze to Coral. "Then I will have to be satisfied with killing you," she told him.

*"Yash,"* Deng'jah said. *"Nalzhu."*

She didn't have to turn. She saw through Deng'jah's eyes as Nalzhu's titanic fist hit the window. The impact shattered the coral wall and the arm burst through. She leapt to the side, just enough to avoid the grasping fingers. As in the White Brilliant, her heartbeat accelerated to a whir in her chest. Fragments of coral drifted by her. Chej's mouth was open; Ruesp's face didn't register emotion. Coral appeared… smug.

Her feet touched stone, and she leapt again as her heart slowed and everything else picked up speed. She landed on the monster's wrist, dug her fingers into the cracks between the fragments he was made up of, and hung on.

An instant later, she was back in the sheeting rain, the Red Coral Tower a receding shadow in the night as Nalzhu pulled her higher and higher, until she was facing the caverns of his eyes. They flickered yellow, as if there were a fire in his skull. One of the eyes had a pupil, standing long and narrow like that of a viper. The other did not. But then she realized it wasn't a pupil at all. It was a person. It was Hsheng, whom she had battled in the Earth Center Tower.

Something was coming up behind Nalzhu fast, something bigger than he was. Taxual, Zuah the Abalone's whale-monster.

Yash released her grip on the stone giant's wrist and, with a shout, dashed up his forearm. For ten running steps nothing happened, then Nalzhu flung his up arm, trying to toss her into the air, but she had been waiting for that and leapt with all the

strength in her, spreading her limbs to try and catch the wind like
*sits'miłnut'chagh*, the flying-with-its-skin squirrel. She landed on the
monster's head, missed her grip, and tumbled, fetching up against
the bulge across his forehead pretending to be eyebrows. The huge
dome tilted back and she jumped again. Her feet hit the rim of
his cavernous right eye. She curled forward and fell into his skull,
just as the other monster coming up behind Nalzhu collided with
him. She was slung against a wall, then the floor, then another wall
before she finally crashed to a stop. Outside, through the vast hole
in the monster's skull, she saw the whale-monster grappling with
Nalzhu. She got her feet under her, but, before she could fully
stand, a hand reached around from behind and caught her. She hit
it with her elbow and twisted out; talons dug at her flesh. Another
arm came around and grabbed her.

"Ah," she said as she saw what held her. "My old friends."

The inside of the skull was a mosaic of the stone-bones, and,
even as she struggled, more of them reached for her—clawed hands
and feet, snake-like tails, toothy jaws, beaks—and all clamped upon
her, until she was held all but motionless. But they did not draw her
blood.

The woman, Hsheng, watched all of this happen. Outside, Nalzhu
hit Taxual; it sounded like a gigantic wave slamming against cliffs.

*"Deng'jah?"*

*"I'm here. But there's nothing I can do. Not yet. Stay alive."*

Yash found she still had wind to speak.

"Qaxh the Coral did this," she said to Hsheng. "*Is* doing this."

"Qaxh?" Hsheng said. Her voice was the same, but the cadence
of it was different, the articulation. "Oh. The painter. Yes, he did his
part. So did you. But mostly it is time. After so long, it is finally time."

"You're him," Yash said. "You're Nalzhu. What have you done with Hsheng?"

The woman stepped closer. A huge tentacle flashed across Yash's field of vision. Taxual seemed to be changing into something else, something much less whale-like.

"Hsheng is here," the woman said. "Hsheng is me."

"You need her," Yash guessed. The longer they were talking, the longer she would live. And the more she might learn.

"She was made for me," Nalzhu said. "Her father made her for me. I had no bones when I came here to this world. Nothing to hang myself on. I had to leave them behind in the ruins of the Moon World. And even when the Emperor found me, understood what I was, used me to make himself strong, he gave me playthings, but nothing to wrap myself around, nothing to incarnate upon. Until now. It was the bargain we made. And now I collect."

"Why?" Yash asked. "What will you do?"

"What will I do? I've been starved for centuries. I'm going to eat. Bear witness."

The stone-bones gripping her moved her forward, toward one of the eyes, expanding her field of vision. Taxual now looked like some strange mixture of sea creatures. Nalzhu tore a huge tentacle from it, and then a long crab-like pincer. Whatever head Taxual had manifested was now a hole oozing blue-green blood. Nalzhu plunged his hands into the squirming mass and tore it in half. As it shuddered, a wet breeze kissed Yash with salt and seaweed. She remembered an ashen sky and foam-topped waves crashing into a black cliff, a horizon all of water.

*"That is Tehłenyk'e,"* Deng'jah said.

"You're right," Yash said. "I see it now. When we traveled to the West, to see the ocean. The Old One From the Water World."

*"Nalzhu is about to swallow her."*

"Yes," Yash said. "I see that, too."

*"You can eat her first."*

"No," she replied. "I can't."

*"You mean, you won't."*

"It's the same thing," she shot back.

"Who are you talking to?" Nalzhu-Hsheng asked. She was behind her, so Yash could not see her face.

She didn't say anything, but the woman answered her own question.

"Oh," she said. "I see. You have a helper. And you—oh, let me look."

The stone-bones turned her around, and Nalzhu's gaze fell on her. Yash closed her eyes, but she felt it anyway, felt it strip through her skin and flesh and down to the center of her.

Nalzhu-Hsheng laughed. "Look at that," they said.

*"Deng'jah,"* Yash said. *"Fly. Fly as far and as fast as you can. Do it now. Tell Grandmother I'm sorry. Warn my people of what is coming."*

*"You're not going to lose,"* Deng'jah said. *"You can't."*

*"I might. Zeltah must be warned. Go. You can't help me anymore."*

*"That's why I'm here. To help you."*

*"Nalzhu will take you, too. It will only make him more powerful. Go."*

Deng'jah hummed, a peculiar little sound she had never heard him make before.

*"You know what to do,"* he said.

*"I won't,"* she replied.

*"Then get free,"* he said. *"Whatever you have to do. Don't let Nalzhu take you. If he does, the Beautiful World will end."*

Then he was gone, whirring out through the eye-opening.

The bones holding her tightened and writhed like snakes. She looked down and saw they had become green tendrils, vines growing fast enough to see. They exploded from the inside of the stone cranium and shot out of the eyeholes, blossoming as they went, festooned in flowers of every color. Deng'jah dodging them as they reached for him. Then he turned sideways and vanished.

She was alone.

The flowering vines kept reaching, invading the ruined corpse of Tehłenyk'e, where they fastened on his spirit and began to eat it.

Yash strained to free herself, but the vines held her tight. Worse, she began to feel her own strength ebbing, as if she, too, were being devoured.

She didn't have much time, but there was one thing she could still do, even immobilized.

"*Tehłenyk'e*," she shouted.

*Child of the Ocean World*
*The Place that made us all*
*Before our wanderings*
*Firstborn of this World*
*Tehłenyk'e is your name*
*You don't belong here*
*Go back to your Ocean*
*Return to your fish and whales and shell-life.*

Her senses extended. Tehłenyk'e was in pain, confused, full of longing. The distant waters pulled at her, but so did Nalzhu. It was a battle of spirit, not substance. The body the Hje had forced on the ocean spirit was gone.

"I see what you're doing," Nalzhu said. "It is of no use. She may know who she is and where she belongs now, but she is not strong enough to escape me."

"Let her go," Yash said. "Let her go to her rightful place. You had a home once. You had a place once. You must know how it feels to be torn from it."

"I wasn't torn from anywhere," Nalzhu said. "I have no home, no place to be from. I followed. The Moon World was not my first home. I followed your people there. From world to world I stalked you."

Nalzhu was not one of the naheeyiye, no spirit of her country. No xúal. He was a Rage. A Terror That Follows.

"Why?"

"To end you. To eat you. There is nothing else for me."

"And when we are all gone?"

"I do not know. I do not care."

Tehłenyk'e was still struggling, but, as Nalzhu had predicted, the sea-spirit's strength was waning.

I thank you, Tehłenyk'e told Yash. For what you tried to do.

It was nearly over. She would die and Nalzhu would destroy the Empire. Then he would annihilate Zełtah: every person, every spirit, every animal. Every place. And she didn't have the strength to stop him. She had been sent to kill the tower masters and cripple the fortress. But not even Grandmother had known what Nalzhu really was.

I tried, Grandmother, she thought.

She knew what Deng'jah wanted her to do, but she couldn't. She could not become like the tower masters. If she did, all of her struggles would be for nothing, and she would become what she fought against. And Nalzhu would probably win anyway.

But maybe there was another way.

"*Tehłenyk'e*," Yash sang.

*It is not done yet*
*We are not beaten*
*Give me your strength*
*As you lived in the skin of Taxual, live in mine*
*I am asking*
*You don't have to*
*But I have room in here*
*In the house of my bones*
*I have fists to fight with*
*This battle is not over*
*As long as a single one of us remains*
*And two of us are stronger than one.*

Her song died away. The Whale Place spirit continued to struggle against Nalzhu as if she had not heard Yash at all, desperate to escape.

*I understand*, Yash said. *You will have a moment to try and escape. I can give you that. Be ready.*

She closed her eyes, and summoned The Place Where They Changed in the darkness there. She pulled on the White Brilliant through the doorway in Bright's tower. Nalzhu's hold on her loosened. She surged against the vines, broke free, and leapt toward the body of Hsheng. All of Nalzhu's strength turned to her, and, in that heartbeat, Whale Place broke free.

The vines festooned Yash once more and slammed her into the stone. She tasted blood on her tongue.

The mouth and throat of Hsheng howled in frustration. Her eyes narrowed, and the vines tightened around Yash's neck, closing off her breath. But she grinned fiercely at Nalzhu's doll. Tehłenyk'e was free. The moon-monster wouldn't have her. He wouldn't have the others she had sent home. What she had told Whale Place was true. As long as any spirit or person of Zełtah was still alive, there was hope. Even if she wasn't one of them.

Black spots danced before her eyes. Her heart, beating furiously in her chest, began to slow.

But then Yash was bigger. Stronger. Like the tide and waves and deep waters.

*Tehłenyk'e?*

*I'm with you.*

The vines snapped away. Air rushed back into her lungs. She lunged toward Nalzhu.

Nalzhu lashed at her with talons of stone, but they glanced off the abalone shell that was now Yash's skin. She dodged and tore at the vines trying to ensnare her again, striking at Nalzhu's throat. The monster-woman deflected her blow and knocked her back. Yash returned like a wave, punching Nalzhu below the chest-splint bone. She felt something crack, and Hsheng-that-was-Nalzhu staggered. Vines sprouted from her head, her fingers, her mouth and eyes. Yash struggled to hit her again, but, once more, the woman was gone, enveloped in vines. At the same time something gripped Yash like a fist—no, two fists, pulling her apart. Words invaded her skull, syllables formed of grievance, of bitterness, of disease.

*The whale-monster is mine*
*You are mine*

*Everything is Mine*
*I will be everything until there is nothing at all.*

Tehłenyk'e's strength was not enough. Nalzhu had already devoured three other xual. He was still winning. In moments, he would have her and Tehłenyk'e as well, and then it would be over. Nalzhu would spread, a hungry pestilence, until nothing was left, until her world was as dead as the Moon World, the bones of a world. Less. Unless she did something.

Unless she denied him his prize.

*Get free*, Deng'jah had said.

One way or another, she would, and she would take Tehłenyk'e with her.

She turned and charged toward the hollow of the eye nearest her, burning all of her strength and all of the might borrowed from Tehłenyk'e. The vines gripped her, but they found no purchase as she leapt from the stone giant's skull and into the pouring rain.

And fell.

She tried to ease her fall as she had before, to change so that the drop might not kill her, so she could run, rejoin her people, fight again. Her abalone armor was gone, but she felt heavier than she ever had. She was not a cotton boll, not a winged seed fluttering to the ground, not a butterfly. She wouldn't get away. Death would have to do.

Everything turned white as she struck the roof of the fortress. It didn't hurt as much as she thought it would.

CHAPTER THIRTY-SEVEN

# A MOTHER'S GIFT

YASH HAD avoided the stone giant's grasp, of that Chej was certain. But when the huge hand withdrew through the broken wall, she was gone. He stared at the irregular hole where the window had been, trying to see where she was, but in the darkness and the rain he couldn't make out much: the glowing shapes of the monster and the other monster—Taxual?—revealed in flashes of lightning. Xuehehs's xual, Nasch, was no longer moving. Yash, if she was there at all, was too small and dark to see.

And the fortress—the fortress was in shambles. More than half the roof was destroyed. Fires burned everywhere, even in the driving rain.

"How many do you think made it outside?" he wondered aloud. Then he turned to Qaxh. "How many remain to be trampled by this horror you have made?"

"I won't pretend to care," Qaxh said absently. He had moved

closer to the hole in the tower. "You can't see, can you?"

"Not much," Chej admitted.

"I loved my mother," Qaxh said. "But there were days when I hated her. Years, even. She gave me these eyes when I was far too young to understand what was happening, much less consent. I can barely remember seeing through the eyes I was born with. I often believed I would have been happier had she allowed me to be like everyone else." He gestured at the darkness beyond. "But this… is so beautiful. I have no choice but to forgive her now."

"And what is beautiful?" Ruesp asked.

"What I was born to witness," Qaxh said. "You will never understand."

Chej noticed a wisp of smoke coming from each of Qaxh's eyes.

"Qaxh," he said. "Your eyes—"

"It was to be expected," Qaxh replied. "Never fear, Chej, I have never been more at peace." He cocked his head slightly to the side. "Your friend—your wife—she is also beautiful."

"I don't need you to tell me that," Chej replied. "I've always thought so. She looks exactly—"

"—like herself," Qaxh finished. "At first, I couldn't see it entirely. She's an abomination, you know, quite unacceptable to Hje sensibilities. And yet, now, I find her exquisite. It's wonderful after all these years to see something new, Chej. To change my mind about something. It's quite remarkable."

"Then help her," Chej said. "Please."

"She's putting up quite a fight," Qaxh said. "You should be proud of her. But she's going to lose. He's too strong."

"Then take his strength! You gave it to him."

"I didn't," Qaxh said. "What I did was more like opening a door—no, no. Like building a bridge. And he has already crossed it. Even destroying the bridge would be useless."

Now dark streams of smoke were pouring from Qaxh's eyes.

"There," he said. "She's fallen. Yash. It's over. No…" He paused. "I never imagined!" he gasped. "Wonderful. Far better than what I planned."

Sparks began to spit from his eye sockets, bright flecks of light in every color of the rainbow. Still smiling, Qaxh's slumped until his knees were on the floor. His chin rested on his chest as the sparks turned into twin jets of golden flame.

Outside, a flash of lightning brighter than any Chej had ever seen lit everything for an eyeblink, and then all was dark again.

"Did you see?" Ruesp asked.

"I… I think so," Chej answered.

The fires in Qaxh's eyes sputtered out.

## CHAPTER THIRTY-EIGHT

# ZEŁTAH

### DA'AN', DII JIN (THE MIDDLE PAST AND THE PRESENT)

T'ADE SAT on a rock at the edge of the wash beneath the shade of the willows, her feet planted in gently flowing water not quite deep enough to cover them. An on-the-water-surface-it-moves-swiftly darted almost in reach of her, its hair-thin legs dimpling the creek but never breaking through it. She did not try to catch it. They were hard to catch, but her cousin had managed it once, in this very place. In capturing it, though, he had broken its fragile limbs, and it had died. So T'ade never tried to catch them anymore. Anyway, what would she even do with one if she did manage to catch it?

She wiggled her toes and watched the bug skitter away from the tiny waves. She looked farther up the stream where her mother was wading in the wash. She looked small with distance. Beyond her was Zełwai Mountain, all grey with a touch of white on its highest peaks. And behind that…

She thought it was a cloud at first, looming up behind the mountains. But then she saw it was moving, and that it had a shape: something like a human being from the chest up. Its legs must be hidden by the mountains, which meant it was very, very big. But also very far away.

"What is it?" she asked.

She wasn't expecting an answer, but after a few heartbeats someone spoke, right next to her ear. It should have scared her, but it didn't.

"It's something that isn't here yet," the voice said. She looked over and saw an insect perched on her shoulder. It had a long blue-green body and delicate-looking wings that stuck out the sides.

"Hello, big-one-that-carries-things-in-his-basket," she said. "Did you say something?"

"That giant monster you see. It isn't here yet. That's years from now. So am I, for that matter."

"That's a funny thing to say," she replied.

"It's not so funny," the big-one-who-carries-things-in-his-basket said. "That monster is going to destroy everything."

"What, even the Zełwai Mountain?"

"Yes."

"And this creek?"

"Yes."

"And my friend there, the on-the-water-surface-it-moves-swiftly?"

"I'm afraid so."

"Well," she said, looking back at the monster peering over the mountain. "I guess I'll have to stop him, then." She picked up a dry piece of juniper the wash had brought from someplace and hefted it.

"That's very brave," the insect said. "Are you going to fight it all by yourself?"

"You said it's not really there yet."

"I did."

"And you—you aren't here yet either?"

"It's complicated," the big-one-who-carries-things-in-his-basket said.

"Then I'll start getting ready now," she said. "That way when he comes, I'll be ready."

"Are you sure about that?"

She looked around at the willows, the stream, the sky, the mountains. Her mother.

"Yes," she replied.

"I'll tell your grandmother, then," the bug said. "One day, she may send me back to you." A little wind touched her ear, and then he was gone.

Her mother was coming back. T'ade watched her slosh through the shallow water. She thought how, to the insects running across the top of the stream, her mother was a frightening giant.

Her mother sat by her on the flat rock.

"Did I hear you talking to someone?" she asked.

"Yes," T'ade said.

"Did you learn anything?"

"Yes," she told her mother. "I have to learn to fight monsters."

Her mother looked at her then looked away. She placed her palm on T'ade's hair, smoothing it back.

"I see," she said.

"When can I start?"

"You've only been here for three winters, sweet child. There is time."

"I know," T'ade replied. "But it might not be enough."

"Well, all you can do is your best," her mother said. "And you will have help. From all of us."

"Promise?"

"Of course," she said. "Come along. It's time to go."

Everything grew whiter, washing everything away. Her mother grew pale, became a shadow, vanished. The trees thinned until they weren't there. The mountains and the sky merged, and only brightness remained.

"Come along, it's time to go."

"Deng'jah?"

"Yes," Deng'jah said.

"I was—did that really happen? I remember that day. Being by the wash, anyway, and mother. Or was it a dream? I've never known."

"Memory and dream are not very different at all, are they?"

"No," she said. "I'm glad you're back."

"And I've brought help."

The light dimmed and vanished, and Yash realized she was lying on a stone floor in the fortress. Had she broken through the roof when she fell, or had it already been broken? It was raining harder than ever, but she hardly felt it. Steam rose around her. No, *from* her. Above, through the shattered ceiling, Nalzhu's two yellow eyes glared down at her. Lightning flashed, as he reached for her again.

Then lightning hit her. It burned through her body, wrenched her heart to a stop, caught her breath in her lungs and held it there. Her limbs were senseless, her ears rang. She saw only darkness and rain and the eyes of the monster.

And then a voice spoke, like Deng'jah's little voice, in her head.

*I'm here, Nelehi*, someone said. She smelled wildflowers through the rain. *T'chehswatah is here.*

*And I*, another voice said. *Older Sister Who Watches the Spring in the Winding Canyon is here.*

The voices blended together now.

*Whippoorwill Place, Firefly Place, Owl Place*
*Tehłenyk'e, Whale Place*
*We know your name*
*You are*
*Tchiił*
*T'ade*
*Yash*
*Yeqeeqani*
*Daughter*
*Son*
*Brother*
*Sister*
*Mother's side cousin*
*Father's side cousin*
*You are Nelehi, The One Who Becomes Repeatedly*
*And we are with you.*

Yash stood up. Something rattled inside of her as the dark and the rain stripped away. Her gaze became lightning, and Nalzhu stood fully revealed. The vines and thousands of flowers covered him now. They trailed into the fortress and rooted there; they crawled over the walls into the city beyond. But inside, he was still stone and bone, fish and lizards, strange plants, dead seas, and dust of ancient mountains.

Looking beyond him, to the fires burning in the thunderheads, she saw Zełtah. Yellow's storm, sent back to its origin after she killed him. Sent back by the land she fought for, carrying those she had saved.

You came for us. Now we come for you.

She wept, but they were fierce tears of pride, sobs of exultation and joy. Lightning struck again, and this time she went with it, climbing up the bolt like a spider up a strand of web. She arrowed through the dark clouds, gathering vigor, burning brighter than the White Brilliant. The stars appeared in absolute glory, and, far to the east, coral light marked the edge of the world. Morning was near.

The wind beat against her; the air grew thin and cold, the stars even brighter. Her ascent slowed, and for a moment she was still in the high, thin air. Then she turned and stooped down like Tch'etsayashi, the falcon that stoops like a lightning bolt, like a flying star. She shot down toward the clouds, faster than she had risen. In the west, in the north, she saw the mountains, her mountains, the boundaries of Zeltah.

The world flattened out. She hit Nalzhu with the force of a hundred thunderbolts. She sliced through his head, split it open, and it grew red with heat. Parts of it melted and lava flowed like blood. Hsheng was inside. Yash started toward her, but the vines gripped her, tried to still the life coursing through her. She twisted and tore them, broke free, shot above the clouds again and returned, striking the monster at the shoulder, crushing it, melting it. The stone arm sagged, remaining attached to the shoulder by a smoldering thread. Yash didn't wait; she shattered Nalzhu's knee and then returned to the sky, diving once more to strike him in the back, in the center of his spine. Stone splintered and liquefied. The bones of monsters from ages past crawled away from the wound, melting as they did so.

She rode Nalzhu's back down as the immense giant fell, crushing most of what was left of the fortress.

She waited there for a moment, as lava pooled from his back. The Giant of Stone and Flowers did not move again.

Rain hissed from Yash's flesh. She turned her face to it, feeling everything inside of her, the spirits of her homeland. Felt her skin tighten and her bones quiver.

Thank you, she said.

*Thank you, T'chehswatah*
*Thank you, Older Sister Who Watches the Spring in the Winding Canyon*
*Thank you, Whippoorwill Place, Firefly Place, Owl Place*
*Thank you, Tehłenyk'e, Whale Place*
*You have done what you came for*
*Now it is time, at last, for you to return home.*
*Leave this poor body before it breaks*
*Take my gratitude and keep it in your hearts.*

She took a deep breath, let it out, and took another. With each exhalation, one of the naheeyiye left. After four such breaths, they were all gone.

Yash rested then, breathing, listening to the uneven beating of her heart. The rain broke and the clouds above began to thin. And as the roar of the rain faded, she heard the wails, the moans, the screams of those who had also survived the night.

Something fluttered on her shoulder.

"Are you there, Deng'jah?" she asked.

"I am," the creature replied. "I thought you might want a moment to rest."

"I appreciate that," she said.

"But that moment is over, I fear."

"I know," she said, standing.

A figure emerged from the ruined head. The vines all lay slack now, their flowers shriveled.

Hsheng stopped a dozen paces away.

"Did you think you had killed me?" the woman asked.

"You, or Nalzhu?" Yash asked.

"We are the same," Hsheng said.

"You think so, I know. But, no. I have killed enough xual to know when I have finished. And I have not finished with you yet."

"Your helpers are gone," Hsheng said. "You are alone now."

"I was never alone," Yash replied. "I have never been alone. I am part of something, Hsheng. Part of a world. Part of a history. I know what I'm fighting for. Do you? Do you really know?"

"The end of all things," Hsheng said. "The end of me, even."

"But why?"

"There is no answer to that," Hsheng said. "I... he... we—have no answer. But we know what we want. What we have wanted for ages."

"And you know I won't let you do it."

"Then you must slay one more monster. Or I will slay you."

Yash took a step forward. "Do you know your name, Nalzhu?" she asked. "Your real name? Your true name?"

"I have no real name."

"Every spirit has a real name."

"I am not like the xual," Hsheng said. "I am not of this world."

Light from the east touched her face. Overhead, the clouds were breaking. Hsheng lowered her head. Her eyes narrowed.

She took another step, hesitated. Her head dropped, her shoulders relaxed. And then she came.

Four quick steps; her fist darted for Yash's face. Yash ducked, blocked the kick that followed with her forearm, then punched Hsheng in the ear. Hsheng answered; her fist flew out; Yash sidestepped slightly so the blow missed her throat and passed over her shoulder. She brought her knee up into Hsheng's belly. She caught the other hand clawing toward her eyes then slammed Hsheng in the side, just above her highest rib. Hsheng staggered and dropped to her knees. She put a hand on the ground and started trying to stand back up.

"Listen to me," Yash said. "Nalzhu. Hsheng. Listen. You came from somewhere. Where?"

"I just follow," Hsheng gasped. "You left me behind. I came after. You left again. One world to the next. The others died. I kept coming. Now I will die, too, and it will be over."

"Nalzhu," Yash said softly. "I kill monsters. That is what I do."

"Then do it."

"If you tell me your name, I can do more."

"I told you. I have no name. I have no place."

Yash took a deep breath, preparing. "Very well," she said.

*I am sorry, my foe…*

But Nalzhu's words tickled at something. A memory. A story told in winter, only on the coldest days.

"Deng'jah?" she asked. "Is it?"

"Yes," he said. "I believe… yes."

Hsheng-that-was-Nalzhu turned her eyes up.

"What are you waiting for?" she asked. "Why do you hesitate?"

"Nalzhu," Yash said, "don't you know where you are? What place this is? Hsheng, don't you?"

"No place," Nalzhu said. "Just another miserable world of many."

"No," Yash said. "You are wrong about that."

## CHAPTER THIRTY-NINE

# MINAD'HA'WI

## TSAYE (IN ANCIENT TIMES)

THE HEEYETS *gathered in their new country. That evening, the spirit-people-animals native to that place came. This place we live now. They came down from the mountains and up from the plains, across the waters. The spirits of the trees and plants came as well, to represent the sacred mountains and forests, springs, and other places. Tsenid'a'wi met with them, and in her heart she feared that they would turn her away, too. But instead, they asked her a question.*

*Do you know this place? What is this land to you?*

*And as she drew in the mountain air, she knew the answer. She smiled. She laughed.*

*This is Nyen' Tu, The Ocean World, Tsenid'a'wi said. This is where we set out from, so long ago. As we have changed, it has changed, too. Dry Land has grown. In this place where there was once deep ocean, now there are mountains and plains. But this is where we are from. And you, the inhabitants of the place, you are the cousins who chose to stay here, the cousins we left behind us. You are Heeyets, like us.*

*All of this is true, they told him. We are also Heeyets, The Ones Having Breath, born when this world was Nyen' Tu, The Ocean World. And since it is true, and since we are all kin, you will be welcome here. But you must learn how to behave here. You must learn the ways of the land, of Zełtah, The Land Among the Mountains. How to keep it good, and beautiful, and sacred. How to protect it, so it can protect you.*

*There are many tales of this time, of how the Heeyets became the people, how they became friends with the animals, the plants, and the spirit places on the land. And for many generations, all was well.*

*Until the Hje crossed over from the Moon World. Until the Empire came, and our cousins from long ago and far away returned.*

### DII JIN (THE PRESENT)

"NALZHU," YASH said. "You are home. This is where you were born, where you came from. Like me. Like the naheeyiye. Like the Hje, even though they are also ignorant of that truth."

"You're wrong," Nalzhu said. "I remember the first world. It has been so long… But I remember. It wasn't like this."

"It has changed," Yash said. "Just as my people have changed. When we left this world we were not human yet. We were Heeyets, with many different forms. This world changed. We were frightened, we feared what it would become, and we fled it. But each world we fled to, each year that passed, we changed, too.

"We called your kind the Rages. Because you were angry we left you. Because you blamed us for your fury. You believed you could not change, should not change, and so you didn't. You remained whatever you were in the Ocean World. And although this is the same world, that place is long gone. It is captured in the Silent Stagnant. As you are. No wonder you are angry. No wonder you are miserable. Our people have survived because we are able to become continually. You survive only on your resentment and your anger. We call you Nelch'en'i, The Rages, but that name can also mean 'the Sorrows,' 'the Miserable Ones.' The place that made you—the place that gave you your name— it is long gone. Stone and bones, like the monsters you sent after me."

"Then you have lied. I truly have no place to return to."

"Not unless you become again. Not unless you change."

Nalzhu held her gaze for a moment then looked past her to the sunrise.

"I don't know how to do that."

"Release Hsheng," Yash said. "She has her own life, her own purpose. She has no place in a vendetta a thousand generations gone."

"Then I will have nothing, as when I came from the Moon World."

"I will kill her if I must," Yash said, "and you will have nothing anyway. Play this game with me, Older Sister, Older Brother. Let her go."

Nalzhu stared at her through Hsheng's eyes. Her face drew back in a scowl. Yash saw her muscles stiffen. She saw the fury on her features, but also the defeat. The resignation.

"You belong here," Yash said softly. "Just as Hsheng does. Just as I do. Let me show you."

Nalzhu closed his eyes against the rising sun. Then the body of Hsheng toppled face-first onto the stony back of the slain giant.

But Nalzhu remained before her, a space, invisible. Undeniable. Waiting.

"*My Foe*," Yash sang.

*It is bad to have no name*
*No home*
*No place*
*To be always angry*
*Continually miserable*
*But maybe*
*Maybe*
*I can give you a name.*
*You were defeated not by one*
*You were defeated by many*
*And they all watch you now*
*You have been far from home*
*In alien places*
*The home you remember is gone*
*But it still is your world*
*A holy world*
*Life and death,*
*Joy and pain.*
*You can belong here*
*Or you can fade into the eternal*
*This is a living world*
*Different with each breath and heartbeat*
*Breathe with it*
*Beat with it*
*Become again*
*Learn the Changing Lesson*
*Be different from year to year*
*Shake off your long travels*
*Leave your misery*

*Come home*
*Come home.*

Yash waited then. She waited as the sun rose, the storm went away, and the fortress burned.

Finally, Nalzhu, The Terror That Follows spoke.

*I want to come home*, it said. *I want to try.*

"It is good," Yash said. "And we will all help you. And I will give you a name. Your name is Minad'ha'wi, He Returns Home."

The sunlight brightened, and the ruined fortress faded into mist. The mist thinned, and Yash saw a vast bowl-shaped valley of black rock. Patches of green clung in places. A lake lay quietly in the center.

A new place, she realized, recently come up from beneath the ground, a piece of the Silent Stagnant returning to the living world, to weather and erode, to form soil, to become the home of plants and animals. A place that now had a spirit.

"Q'anittah, I also name you. Among the New."

"Thank you," she heard as the vision faded.

"You are welcome," she replied. "I look forward to visiting you."

Yash took a long breath. She was exhausted. Her body trembled with reaction and fatigue. The cries of the injured and dying drifted on the breeze. She gazed around at the ruin of the fortress, at the broken bodies in the rubble. She was numb, but not too numb to cry. For another few heartbeats, she wept and watched her own long shadow cast by the rising sun.

She heard the flutter of wings. She raised her head and saw a bird with a red belly and bright green feathers on its back and wings. It had landed on a broken wall and seemed to be watching her. She felt the stirrings of wonder, for she had never seen such a bird.

After a moment, it took flight, and as she tracked its progress into the sky she saw more birds, all colorful, all strange to her, all different from one another. A flock of different kinds. They dwindled with distance and were soon beyond her sight.

She nodded to herself and then walked toward the nearest cries for help.

"Help me, Deng'jah," she said. "Help me find the ones who might survive."

"You're certain of the that?" Deng'jah asked.

"Yes. They are not my enemies. These are also my people."

"Then I will help."

CHEJ FOUND Yash digging through the debris. Near her lay the bodies of a woman and a man. They were bloody, covered in ash and dust, but when he got near enough he saw they were breathing.

Yash looked up as he approached. Deng'jah rested on her shoulder. Tear runnels streaked the dust on her face.

When she saw him, Yash rose, took him by the shoulders, and embraced him.

"Hello, shegan'," she said. "I'm glad you are alive."

"And I'm glad you are, shihad," he replied.

Yash smiled. "Shexad," she corrected. "But that's very close."

He glanced at the pile of rubble. An arm was sticking out of it, moving feebly.

"Maybe I could help you with this," he said.

She squeezed him harder. "I can always do with help, shegan'. Where is Ruesp? Did he survive?"

"Yes," Chej said. "He said he had something to attend to."

She nodded. Then together they began excavating the buried person.

It was hard work, but he was grateful for it. He could not forget all of the dead and dying he had seen. He never would. But it helped to have something to do. Something *right*.

As the sun climbed the sky, they pulled seven living people from the ruins of the fortress.

Around noon, Yash paused in her digging.

"Hsheng," she said.

Chej turned. The daughter of the Emperor was there, watching them. She opened her mouth as if to say something, but nothing came out.

"How can I help?" Hsheng finally said.

"There's someone under here," Yash said. "Help me lift this slab."

Chej kept digging, but he shifted so he could see Hsheng. But after a while, he realized nothing was going to happen. She was really helping. Not that it made a huge difference to have one more. Deng'jah said there were dozens buried and that most of them wouldn't survive until sundown. There was only so much three people could do. But he knew they had to do it.

"Soldiers," Deng'jah warned. Chej started. It was still weird to hear the insect talk. He looked around and a group of about thirty men were approaching.

"Yash," he said. "You should leave now."

"No," she said. "I don't think I will."

She glanced at him from the corner of her eyes and inclined her head ever so slightly. She knew that he was also in danger. His death had been ordered. But she was leaving it up to him.

And so it was.

He nodded. "I understand." Then he rose and walked to meet the men. He probably knew some of them. Maybe they would listen to reason.

He was preparing what to say when he noticed that Ruesp was with them.

"Xarim!" he said.

"I told you," the old man said. "I'm done with that nonsense." He looked past Chej to Yash and Hsheng.

"I see you've made a start," he said. "I've brought more help."

## CHAPTER FORTY

TEQEQANDE (THE DAWNS TO COME—THE FUTURE)

HSHENG WALKED the grounds of her mother's summer house, tracing her gaze along the faint scar in the earth where she and Dzhi had dug their canals so long ago. She had hoped being here would bring back fond memories, but she could only think how she had destroyed all of her sister's buildings. Nalzhu had been in her for that long. His grievance had shaped her that much. She was glad he was gone, but without him she felt like half a person. But that half-a-person, it seemed, could go where she wanted. She could leave the fortress. She could come here, where she had not been since the day she had fainted.

It seemed a poor prize, but, given what she had done, it was still more than she deserved.

She did smile a little when she looked up and saw her nieces and nephews playing in the distance, batting a trailing-feathers-ball into the air between them. Yash's strange insect hadn't found her sisters in the wreckage of the tower: they were alive, having evacuated when the Keep was in danger of catching fire. For her, it was the only blessing of that awful night.

The worst of it was, she still remembered how it felt as Nalzhu had killed almost everyone in the Earth Center Tower. No compassion, no sorrow. Only bitter, terrible joy.

She noticed someone coming up the path to the house. An old man. Ruesp.

"Xarim Ruesp," she said, as he arrived. "I hope you're well."

"I'm well enough to die at any moment," he replied. "But I am still here, so. And you? How are you?"

"Must you ask?" she replied.

The old man looked off toward the mountains in the east then back at her.

"You aren't to blame," he said. "At least, not solely to blame. This was our fault. Your father, the other tower masters, old men like me: we all share the blame. We built this place on blood and suffering, on complaint and hubris. Those are the materials for a poor foundation. We robbed Yash's people, lied to them. We were prepared to exterminate them. It's hard to fault *her* motives. And without her Nalzhu would have destroyed the city—and, well, everything. You know that, don't you?"

"Yes," she said. "I do. And she let me live, so I should be grateful."

"But you aren't."

"What use am I, xarim? What am I to do?"

"The tower masters are all dead," he said. "The fortress is destroyed. The Empire remains, but without an emperor, without the leadership of the fortress, it is precarious. There are challenges before us. We need to meet them."

"Why are you telling me this?"

"I thought I was done with this life," Ruesp said. "Done with the Empire. But I think we have a chance to change things. You are the Emperor's daughter."

"A woman. No one will follow me."

"They already have," he replied. "In the ruins, when we were saving the trapped and injured."

"That was Yash. And you."

"That's not how the soldiers are telling it," he said. "They're talking about how the Emperor's daughter saved sixty lives. How you took charge after his death, worked with your own hands, like one of them."

"But that's nonsense," she replied.

"Is it? If it is, it is useful nonsense," he said. "It's nonsense we can build on, something with stronger foundations."

She looked at him, trying to see whether he was kidding with her. It didn't look like it.

"I was a monster," she said.

"Only four people know that," he said. "Two of them are already on their way out of the Empire. The other two are sitting here."

"How sure are you of this?" she asked. "That they will follow us? Me?"

"Not very," he replied. "But I have hope. And it gives us something to do. Something that might be *worth* doing."

She gazed out over the city in the distance, the ruins of the fortress, the mountains beyond.

"Why not?" she replied.

★ ★ ★

"ARE YOU sure about this, shegan'?" Yash asked. They were on a height, the valley stretched out before them. From here, things hardly looked different than they had a few days before; the city itself was so large, you had to know where to look to notice the dark patch that had been the fortress.

Chej nodded, winded from ascending the steep trail. "Yes," he said. "That's not the place for me, at least not right now. Maybe someday…" He shrugged. "Who knows. But for now I'm content to go along with my dutiful wife."

"I'll ask again in a month or so. By then you may be finding our way of life… primitive."

"I can adapt," Chej said. "Can you?"

"To what?" Yash wondered. "I'm going home."

"You've trained your whole life to fight, to steal back the naheyige—"

"You said that *very* well," she interrupted. "Naheeyiye. But very, very close."

"Thank you," he said, looking pleased. "My question is, what will you do now?"

"You mean after I've helped drive the Empire out of Zełtah?"

"Well, Ruesp seems confident that the army will now withdraw and return to the city. But yes, after the war is over, how will you spend your time?"

"That's a silly question," she said. "And you've answered it yourself."

"How so?"

"The world is a wide, wonderful, beautiful place, and life is far too short. I spent my youth training, preparing for a battle now fought. Now I plan to do everything I missed when I was younger—and everything else. There are mountains in the north that always have snow on them. There is an ocean I've only seen once, and another in the east no one I know has ever been to. There are lakes so salty you can lie on the surface of the water and not sink. There are places where the trees are so tall and so many that the sun never reaches the ground. I must visit Q'anittah, the place Nalzhu has become! There are games to be played, stories to be told. Chej, I might as well be three years old, so far as this life in concerned."

"That sounds like a lot," Chej said.

"It is a lot," she said. "But never fear. You can take it easy. My family will feed you and take care of you while I'm busy. And I'm sure you'll find something—or perhaps someone—to spend your time on. Safely, with no risk or great hardship involved."

"Well, *some* of what you plan sounds interesting," Chej said. "I might be persuaded to go along now and then."

"Of course," Yash said. "If you want. And, you know, eventually I must slay the Yaniyeet'jah. Compared to them, this last battle will seem easy. But that is probably years from now. Why don't we make camp, shegan'? You look tired."

"What?" Chej said. "Slay what?"

# ACKNOWLEDGEMENTS

ONCE AGAIN, I thank Steve Saffel for acquiring this book and seeing it through its early stages. Thanks to Fenton Coulthurst for editing and Louise Pearce for doing the often unappreciated but very necessary (and in this case excellent) task of copyediting. Thank you to Chris Chambers for laying out the book and Tiffani Angus for a very thorough proofread. The beautiful cover design is by Natasha McKenzie. Thanks also to the publicist, Olivia Cooke, and editorial assistant, Claire Schultz.

Many thanks to my early readers: My youngest child, Rosemary, who loved my tentative stab at a first chapter and exhorted me to write more. Adam Gross, Laura Gross, Tracey Abla, and, as usual, Lanelle Webb Keyes.

# ABOUT THE AUTHOR

BORN IN Meridian, Mississippi, Greg Keyes has published more than thirty books, including *The Basilisk Throne*, The Age of Unreason series, and The Kingdoms of Thorn and Bone series, also writing books for *Babylon 5*, Star Wars, Planet of the Apes, The Avengers, and *Pacific Rim*, and novelizing *Interstellar* and *Godzilla: King of the Monsters*. He lives, writes, fences, and cooks in Savannah, Georgia. He is found on Facebook at https://www.facebook.com/greg.keyes1 and on Instagram as Gregkeyes1.

For more fantastic fiction, author events,
exclusive excerpts, competitions, limited editions and more

VISIT OUR WEBSITE
**titanbooks.com**

LIKE US ON FACEBOOK
**facebook.com/titanbooks**

FOLLOW US ON TWITTER AND INSTAGRAM
**@TitanBooks**

EMAIL US
**readerfeedback@titanemail.com**